Kitty Ray graduated from St Martin's School of Art in 1968 and has worked as a designer, window-dresser, illustrator and even a stewardess aboard World War II DC3s for a regional airline. She lives in Suffolk, with her husband and two sons. She won the RNA Netta Musket best newcomer's award for her first novel, *Stoats and Weasels*, published by Warner in 1996.

A Fine Restoration

KITTY RAY

WARNER BOOKS

A *Warner* Book

First published in Great Britain in 1997
by Little, Brown and Company and Warner Books

Copyright © Kitty Ray 1997

A CIP catalogue record for this book
is available from the British Library.

ISBN 0 7515 1927 8

Typeset in Palatino by M Rules
Printed and bound in Great Britain by
Clays Ltd, St Ives plc

Warner Books
A Division of
Little, Brown and Company (UK)
Brettenham House
Lancaster Place
London WC2E 7EN

I am grateful to Tony Cox, of Claude Cox, Antiquarian Booksellers, Silent Street, Ipswich, for his expert help – any inaccuracies are entirely my own. My thanks to Richard Temple, for patiently answering my silly questions, to Sarah Molloy, my agent, and to Imogen Taylor for her sensitive editing.

To the B's, with love

Chapter One

Clementine Lee stretched herself out experimentally on one of the beds in her hotel room. The hotel was in the middle of Amsterdam, facing out over the Singel-Gracht towards the Leidseplein, and the sound of an organ-grinder playing creaky hurdy-gurdy music drifted through the slightly open window, along with the tinkle of bicycle bells, the warning *ding-ding* of a passing tram and the metallic voice of a tour guide with a microphone, pointing out the sights from one of the tourist boats on the canal.

Clementine was not paying any attention to the noise, or the view. She was worried about her champagne satin nightgown, an uncharacteristic piece of frivolity bought at Jean's insistence in Harrods' sale. She was staring at her reflection in the mirror on the other side of the room, examining with critical attention the generous curve of her hips, the heavy swell of her ample bosom and the thick sweep of glossy brown hair spreading across her broad shoulders. She looked, she thought despairingly, like a cross between an operatic Valkyrie and the model for a particularly over-ripe Rubens.

She looked like a complete idiot, but it was too late to do anything about it.

Clementine Lee was over the hill, past her sell-by

date, on the shelf. At thirty-two she was still, as her friend Jean never tired of reminding her, unattached, childless, and therefore missing out on two of life's greatest achievements, a man and a family of her own. Jean Hawe possessed both, and though she never said so in as many words Clementine knew perfectly well what she thought; any woman who hadn't managed to catch a husband by the time she reached her thirtieth birthday was by definition a failure. The fact that these days the rest of Clementine's life was a great deal more interesting than Jean's didn't count because to Jean any occupation, however worthwhile, was of use only to fill in time whilst waiting for Mr Right to come along. Jean would be thrilled if she could see her now.

Clementine pulled a face at herself in the mirror, then propped herself higher on her elbow and rearranged her bosom in an effort to make her cleavage less conspicuous. Jean would think waiting in a sexy nightie in a hotel for a man to come and make love to you was the ultimate romantic fantasy. And Jonathan Harris was the nearest Clementine had come to sticking her neck out. This time she had allowed herself to dream.

Jonathan was the senior partner with the interior design company she worked for. Eight months previously, whilst attending a dinner party at a bachelor flat she had decorated for a colleague, he had persuaded his host to give him Clementine's telephone number and on the strength of what he had seen he had approached her with the offer of a junior partnership.

His company was in need of new blood, he had explained over lunch, and Clementine was just the woman he was looking for. Clem, bogged down in designs for corporate boardrooms and open-plan typing pools, was flattered to be headhunted, excited by the prospect of being allowed a free hand to expand her own ideas, and intrigued by the set-up Jonathan showed her. His company was small, just Jonathan and his team of three young designers, but riding on the back of the property boom, only now beginning to show the first signs of slowing down, it was also immensely successful. His business was almost entirely in the private sector, anything from one-room flats to Belgravia mansions. He was clearly enormously talented, if somewhat avant-garde, and she liked the air of eccentric enthusiasm he exuded. He gave his staff complete autonomy, he assured her, their own clients to do with as they pleased, and the challenge was irresistible.

She had had to buy her partnership of course, borrowing from her trust fund to do so, and since the amount required was comparatively large, it had been necessary to seek permission from Uncle Harry to use some of her capital.

Uncle Harry was very careful with Clementine's money. 'My dear, if poor Ambrose had thought you capable of managing your own finances,' he had pointed out as she perched stiffly on the edge of a chair in his study, five months after the accident that had killed her parents, 'he would have left everything to you outright. But since he left it in trust, and me in charge of that trust, I must consider it my duty as your guardian to take a personal interest, make sure you don't fritter it all away.' He leaned across his big mahogany desk and wagged a fat finger at her. 'Make no mistake, my girl,' he threatened, 'we are talking here about a very substantial sum of money and I shall not hesitate to interfere if I think it necessary. Your business will be my business; I shall look after your interests as if they were my own. Of course . . .' He rose from his desk, a huge man, as tall as Daddy, and even broader, blocking out the light from the window as he moved across it. 'Of course, that is not to say that any reasonable request for funds will not be looked upon sympathetically.' Clementine frowned at his back, confused by the double negative and irritated by his pomposity. 'Once we have finished sorting out the details, the money from the Ashington business alone should be enough to provide an adequate income for the foreseeable future, and I have no wish after all to stint my own brother's child.' He jingled the change in his pockets with loud enthusiasm. 'Just so long as you are *sensible*. And as I'm sure you are aware, your father's will stipulates that when . . .' he turned to run his eyes over his niece's ample frame and corrected himself, '. . . *if* you marry, everything reverts to you outright, to do with as you please. All right? That understood?'

Clementine, still pale and weak from five months in hospital and the sudden, violent loss of both her parents, nodded obediently, then wandered out through the french windows into the garden to wait for the tears. As they had from the beginning, they refused to come.

It wasn't just her parents. All the things she had grown up with were taken away from her too. When she came out of hospital it was to Uncle Harry's house in Letchworth, light years away from the world she was familiar with. Marshmeadow, the only home she had ever known, was gone by then, put up for sale without reference to her, and all the familiar things, furniture, books, paintings, were gone too, auctioned off piecemeal on Uncle Harry's instructions. He had taken advice, he explained, on how to 'squeeze the maximum' from her assets, and the outcome, he was happy to assure her, had entirely justified his actions. Some of the finest pieces had gone at auction for prices well above their reserves; it had all been very satisfactory.

Satisfactory?

'A fresh start,' he exhorted her, patting her briskly on

the back as she stared around the tiny bedroom that would be hers from now on. 'That's what you need my girl, a fresh start. You're only sixteen, got your whole life ahead of you. You just have to pick yourself up and carry on.'

'We thought it would be too upsetting for you,' said Aunt April when Clementine asked where her eiderdown had gone, what they had done with her childhood books, what had happened to the teddy she had slept with all her life. 'And besides, frankly, we're already dreadfully cramped, what with having to find room for one extra . . .'

They had their own children to think about, she pointed out. Admittedly, Geraldine was almost off their hands, away at university, but Martin was still living at home and he was just at that age, seventeen, when a boy needed his space. Ironically, Martin was the only one who actually seemed pleased to have Clem there, at least to begin with.

'Now don't you worry about a thing,' Uncle Harry boomed at her when she asked how she could finish her education when she was living so far away from her school in Norfolk. 'There're plenty of good schools round here, we'll organise something, and we'll be keeping an eye on you, we'll make sure you're all right, you'll see.' He had been interfering ever since, even though she had left the house in Letchworth with abrupt finality just days after sitting her A levels and without even waiting for her results.

It had been entirely her own fault, allowing Martin to oh-so-casually seduce her the night she finished her exams. She was looking desperately for love, but Martin was winning himself a tenner – a wager with a friend, he taunted her afterwards, payable if he managed to go 'all the way'.

He was too impatient, too inexperienced, to manage the subtleties of foreplay. It was wham-bam-thank-you-Ma'am, and not until afterwards did he notice the ugly puckered tramlines that scored Clementine from hip to groin, a visible legacy of the accident two years previously. Had he noticed her scars earlier, he wouldn't have touched her even for money, he informed her – he didn't go for *damaged goods*.

It was obvious she couldn't stay after that. She couldn't face sitting opposite him at breakfast, knowing he despised her, or watch him sniggering with his friends over her shameful secret. She didn't tell her aunt and uncle why she was leaving; the sun shone out of Martin's eyes as far as they were concerned, and she didn't think they would believe her anyway. Thank God, he hadn't got her pregnant. 'Good riddance to bad rubbish!' he shouted from his bedroom window as she staggered down the drive with her suitcase to wait for the taxi in the road. '*Gross*, that's what you are!'

She rented digs in London. Her private income saw her through college, tided her over until she found a job and the top-floor flat in a North London terrace where she had lived ever since. She saw her aunt and her cousins not at all, her uncle only when she had to, in connection with the trust. She put Martin out of her mind and learned to tolerate living by herself. If she was lonely sometimes, then so what? Most people were lonely sometimes, weren't they?

Uncle Harry had been particularly tiresome over releasing the capital to buy her partnership, demanding to see Jonathan's projected sales figures, current profit margins, last year's balance sheets. When they were not immediately forthcoming he insisted on meeting Sebastian Brown, Jonathan's reclusive partner who, although he had nothing to do with the day-to-day running of the company, was the man who held the purse strings, and he had finally agreed to put up the funds only on condition that the capital would eventually be repaid to the trust out of Clem's earnings. He was not prepared, he said pompously, to allow her to curtail her financial options unnecessarily.

After years of frustration working for second-rate companies it had been the best career move Clementine had ever made, worth all the aggravation. When the professional respect she already felt for Jonathan began gradually to turn to affection, an affection which seemed, astoundingly, to be more than reciprocated, she found it hard to believe the direction in which her life was moving.

Jonathan should have been with her in Amsterdam last night, but for a problem that had unexpectedly cropped up as they were leaving the office. He had stayed behind to sort things out and was catching the mid-morning flight instead. Clementine hadn't wanted to go without him but he insisted.

'Find us a good restaurant, sweetie,' he suggested as he saw her off at Heathrow, 'and take the opportunity to explore.' He chuckled, then pecked her cheek and added teasingly, 'After all, you'll be too busy once I get there.' She laughed with him, then hurried off to check in for her flight, embarrassed by the implication. They were going to consummate their relationship, at last.

It was Clementine's fault it had taken them so long. She had prevaricated as she always did, putting off the final step in case it ruined everything. Being *damaged goods* makes you wary.

It had taken Jonathan four months to convince her his pursuit was serious. She might be lonely but she was not lonely enough to be desperate, not prepared to take up his offer to begin with just because it was better than nothing. He seemed to understand her reluctance to get involved. He didn't appear to mind either that, at five foot ten and a half, he was over an inch shorter than she and rather slighter in build. He was very good-looking, in a round-faced, boyish sort of way, with an artistic mop of curly brown hair, an interestingly crooked nose and nice ears, and he made up for his lack of height by being very, very charming. He *adored* big women, he said, always had. He wooed her with flowers and chocolates, put no pressure on her at all to go to bed with him.

He told her one night as they sat in their favourite restaurant, eating pasta with just their forks so he could hold her hand across the candlelit table, that he wanted to marry her, and he squeezed her fingers while Clementine swallowed her wine the wrong way and choked.

'I want children,' he explained imperturbably. 'I'm nearly thirty-five and time is passing me by.' He squeezed again, harder this time. 'We'll buy a little place in the country and make beautiful babies. We'll have six, and I hope they all take after you.' He put his fork down and reached across to pat her solicitously on the back as she spluttered into her glass. 'Generous, that's what you are. A generous woman in every sense of the word.' He raised her hand to his lips and kissed it, then released her, poured her a glass of water and leaned back in his chair, waiting for her to recover. 'If you'll marry me, Clem, I'll make you happy, I swear.'

Clementine wiped her mouth on her table napkin and stared at him with watering eyes. She had known him for only eight months, been close to him for only four. 'Jonathan,' she began, 'you don't know me, you don't—'

'I've seen enough of you to be sure you're the girl for me.'

'But we haven't even . . .' Clementine lowered her head, ashamed of the colour that was flooding her cheeks.

'Ah.' Jonathan leaned across and took her hand again. 'I've had an idea about that, angel. How about a naughty weekend, just the two of us, in a romantic setting, good food, lots of wine in case we're in need of Dutch courage . . .?'

That was how they fixed upon Amsterdam; Clementine promised to think about his proposal, then reached across the table to touch his beaming face and tell him how grateful she was for his patience. All good things, he replied gallantly, were worth waiting for, and she felt so lucky to have found him that her eyes filled with tears for the second time.

She shifted uneasily on the bed and ran her hand over her left hip. Feeling the striations beneath her fingers she wished she had worn cotton, or winceyette instead of satin, and was seized by apprehension again. She longed for Jonathan to arrive so she could get it over and done with. When his knock came she jumped nervously, then rose from the bed and smoothed herself down with unsteady hands.

'Here goes nothing,' she said to her reflection as she passed, bending her knees so she could see to tweak her hair out of her eyes. This time it was going to be all right; really, it was going to be fine. She was so looking forward to seeing him. She took a deep breath, adjusted her gaze slightly downwards so she could meet him squarely in the eye, then fixed a welcoming smile to her face and flung open the door to confront not Jonathan's familiar figure but the tall, angular person of Sebastian Brown.

'Ah, Miss Lee.'

'Yes?' Clementine peered over his shoulder, looking for Jonathan.

'Sebastian Brown, Jonathan's partner.'

Clementine readjusted her gaze. 'Yes, I know.' She had met Sebastian Brown only half a dozen times. Something must have happened to Jonathan! Her heart began to thump uncomfortably in her chest.

'What's the matter?' Her imagination ran riot. He'd had an accident, he was lying under a London bus . . .

'May I come in?' Brown's voice was high-pitched, plummy and rather effete. He continued to stand on the threshold, stony-faced, and Clementine's panic increased.

'Please,' she repeated, 'won't you tell me what's the matter? Where's Jonathan?'

'May I come in?'

She stood back reluctantly, and he walked past her into the middle of the room. It was a typical hotel bedroom, two beds, two easy chairs and a coffee table, a television, a dressing table and a wardrobe built in along one wall. Sebastian Brown looked out of place in such mundane surroundings.

He was as tall as she, with thick, improbably red hair brushed back from his temples and pale, almost colourless eyes. His bony elbows made sharp points in the sleeves of his crumpled linen jacket and underneath it he wore a dove-grey shirt with a brightly coloured scarf knotted at the neck. In his hands he held a soft straw panama, which he rolled constantly between his fingers as if he was nervous, or irritable.

'Jonathan will not be joining you,' he said. He cut each word off sharply before he started on the next, like an elocution master teaching pronunciation.

'Why not? What's happened to him? Is he hurt? Is he ill?'

'I am Jonathan's partner.' Sebastian Brown twirled his panama and averted his eyes from her cleavage.

Why did he keep going on about it? She knew perfectly well who he was. 'Yes, I know. Is there some crisis at the office? Is that what the matter is? I thought it was just a minor problem that was delaying him—'

'Minor? I hardly think so.' Brown took a large handkerchief from his top pocket and mopped his face. He was sweating, despite the cool breeze stirring the net curtain at the window. 'This is very difficult for me, Miss Lee.' He allowed his gaze to slide briefly over her satin nightgown then looked away again, clearly finding her state of undress an unwelcome distraction. 'When I say I am Jonathan's partner . . .' he paused to mop his brow again, '. . . what I mean is . . . I am Jonathan's *sleeping* partner. As in sleeping. As in bed.'

'I beg your pardon?'

'Jonathan is my boyfriend.'

'What?'

'We have been lovers for years. Why do you suppose I set him up in business?'

Clementine's panic increased, metamorphosed into a different kind of shock. She stood by the door, staring blankly at the man's perspiring face, and waited for him to explain what he was talking about. This must, she thought, be Jonathan's warped idea of a joke.

It wasn't, as it turned out, funny at all. After a while she sat down, slumping heavily on the end of the nearest bed as Sebastian Brown told her about Jonathan and sweated into his handkerchief.

The poor boy was a hopeless romantic, he explained, a *Walter Mitty*, a *Don Quixote* constantly tilting at windmills. It was his flights of fancy that made him the creative genius he was, but they got him into *dreadful* trouble, and he, Sebastian, had had to bail him out time after time.

He bent his long back to peer into Clementine's pale face. She did agree, didn't she, that Jonathan was a creative genius? Oh yes, Clem stammered, yes she did, he was brilliant. That was why she had wanted so badly to work for him. She stared up at Brown's cadaverous features and nodded obediently. She was finding his physical presence completely mesmerising, and wondered through the shock whether he mesmerised Jonathan too. She supposed he must.

This was not the first time the boy had succumbed to one of his mad whims, Brown continued, it was not even the first time there had been a *woman* involved (he said 'woman' as he might have said 'Martian' or 'hippopotamus'), but he was prepared to tolerate the odd sexual adventure. It was just that Jonathan had an unfortunate tendency to go too far. Last year it had been a Spanish girl half Jonathan's age who couldn't even speak English – he had wanted to put *her* through college. But *marriage* . . . Coming from Brown's refined mouth the suggestion was of necrophilia, or bestiality. It simply was not *on*, he said, it would not *do*, not after all the time and effort he had invested in the relationship.

He apologised towards the end of his dissertation, said he realised it was his fault for allowing the relationship to go so far, but he had not expected it to get so serious. And after that he explained why Clementine could not possibly go on working for the company. He had put a great deal of *effort* into Jonathan, he said, and she must see that he had to look after his own interests. Jonathan was quite simply too weak, too easily led, to risk leaving temptation in his path. He would, he promised, make sure she did not suffer financially over this 'embarrassing little affair' and he was really quite polite, considering she had unwittingly tried to steal his boyfriend. But Clementine could tell he was finding it difficult to see what had attracted Jonathan to her in the first place and after a while, as he began to sound like Uncle Harry, quoting facts and figures, refunds and compensation, she grew weary, stopped listening. When he reached into his pocket and offered to write her a cheque there and then, she came to with a start.

'What?' she asked, struggling to collect her scattered wits. 'I'm sorry, I wasn't . . . er, what?'

Now that the difficult part was done and it was clear Clementine wasn't going to make a fuss, Brown became urbane and relaxed, stopped sweating quite so much. 'I shall of course settle your hotel bill in full immediately. And if you need some money for your airfare home . . .?'

Clementine's shaky self-control slipped. 'No!' she said, and stood abruptly just as Brown, brandishing his chequebook, turned towards her. She took the full force of his spiky elbow in her left eye.

'Ow!' she yelped, grabbing at his sleeve to keep her balance, and as he swung towards her, her jaw connected hard with his beaky nose.

She bit her cheek and tasted blood but Sebastian Brown bled better; he bled like a stuck pig all over the front of her satin nightie. Clementine, clutching at her eye with one hand and her cheek with the other, staggered up again and made for the bathroom. She could hear him moaning in the bedroom and she could imagine how he felt, but she was a practical woman and the first priority was to stop the blood. She grabbed a box of tissues and rushed back to her visitor.

'Here!' she commanded, stuffing Kleenex in the general direction of his nose. 'No, hold it there!' She clamped her hand over his, pressed hard.

'Urr,' he mumbled thickly. 'Can't greathe!'

'Sorry,' she said.

Her second priority was to get rid of him.

'Ice! That's what you need, lots of ice!' She grabbed more tissues, shoved handfuls of them into his pockets, then heaved him upwards, jammed his panama firmly on his head and propelled him towards the door, linking her arm through his to stop him toppling over. 'Ask at reception, they'll have some!' She fumbled for the door handle, flung the door wide, pushed him out into the corridor and slammed it hard behind him. Then she leaned against it, closed her eyes and began to shake all over.

She explored the inside of her mouth gingerly with her tongue as she splashed her left eye with cold water, and she found a distinctly wobbly tooth. When she had finished sloshing she took off her bloodied nightgown and dropped it in the wastebin, then stepped into the bath to stand under a shower so fierce it felt like red-hot needles against her skin, allowing the crescendo of noise and steam to blank off the thoughts beginning to swirl around her head, prolonging the excruciating physical sensation for almost ten minutes in an effort to delay the other pain she could feel, waiting in the wings to creep up on her. When she could bear the stinging heat no longer she stepped out onto the bathmat, wrapped herself in a towel and strode back to the bedroom to turn the television on full volume, filling her head with more noise while she dressed and packed.

She was slow, and even clumsier than usual, sat for forty minutes distracted by an incomprehensible Dutch game show, then stood at the window for another half an hour watching the world go by in the street below and hoping pathetically that Jonathan would prove his partner wrong and turn up. Despite all her efforts, by the time she left the room her thoughts were beginning to overwhelm her.

The corridor was long and it seemed to take forever to

reach the lift. As she walked she went over the past few months looking for clues, and because she was looking she found plenty. The mutual acquaintance through whom Jonathan had contacted her was openly homo-sexual, yet it hadn't once occurred to her to wonder about Jonathan – should it have? She had been slightly puzzled that such an attractive man was still unmarried at the age of thirty-four, but only slightly, and as for his whimsical ideas, his 'flights of fancy' as Sebastian Brown called them, she had found them endearing, childlike; it had never crossed her mind that his determined pursuit of her might be just another fantasy, that marriage and a family might be, for Jonathan at least, merely part of a quixotic dream and not reality at all. She hadn't even thought it odd that he kept a signed photograph of his partner on his desk, as other men keep snapshots of their wives.

He had been completely uninterested in the financial side of the negotiations when she joined the company. 'We'll let the money men sort it out between them, shall we?' he had suggested airily. 'Now, what do you think of this jacquard? *Wonderful* colour, isn't it, *fabulous* tex-ture . . .?' Such sweet-natured exuberance, such airy dismissal of the practicalities of life – had he really, as Sebastian Brown claimed, thought he could sire six chil-dren whilst running a male lover on the side? Maybe it was not surprising, in the light of what she had just been told, that he had shown so little impatience to climb into bed with her. As she walked she prayed, please God, let the lift be empty, please, please, if it's full I shall *die*.

Her outfit, specially purchased for the trip, was soft russet-coloured crêpe lined with silk, and it rustled as she walked, mocking her with every step. She had thought it so sexy when she bought it, subtle but seduc-tive. 'Perfect,' she'd said to the assistant, 'it's absolutely perfect,' and she had twirled in front of the mirror, enjoying the feel of the fabric against her legs, the way it draped over the cream silk top that matched the jacket lining. It had made her feel . . . *voluptuous* instead of merely big. Now it seemed to emphasise her height, her size, her generous bosom . . . and her stupidity.

Her left eye continued to swell, throbbing in time with the loud thudding in her chest. When the lift doors parted she let go a sigh of relief. Thank you God, she blessed the empty interior, I owe you one.

Schipol airport was crowded. Clementine's left eye was completely closed by the time the hotel bus deposited her and her bags outside the terminal and walking across the concourse she was painfully aware of the curious heads turning, the whispered asides at the passing of a six-foot tall, one-eyed Amazon. She addressed her maker again, in blasphemous terms this time.

There were no flights leaving for Heathrow; as if even the weather had deliberately turned against her, the whole of southern England was fogged in, blanked out beneath an impenetrable layer of wet, white cotton wool, everything south of Luton at a standstill.

'But I have to get back!' she protested, gripping the desk hard to hold herself together. 'There must be somewhere in England that's not closed!'

The Dutch ground girl shrugged phlegmatically. 'I am sorry, Madam,' she said, 'but I do not know what to suggest. I think perhaps Dan Air are making it into Manchester, but I cannot say for sure . . .'

Clementine's eyes filled painfully with tears. She felt as she had when she was a child, picked on at school, ridiculed for her size, her clumsiness. She wanted to go home, hide behind her mother's skirts, be comforted. She swung her bags up again, turned abruptly away from the desk and strode off into the crowd to look for an information desk.

She found what she was looking for above the main shopping area, row upon row of flickering screens, and she stared at each one with her good eye until her neck began to ache as well as her jaw, running down the lists, Nairobi, Istanbul, Johannesburg, Los Angeles, New York and Boston, then the European destinations, Paris, Antwerp, Frankfurt, Bilbao, until she found England at last, London Heathrow, delayed, Gatwick, cancelled, Southampton, delayed . . . delayed, cancelled, delayed, delayed.

She was about to give up when halfway down the last screen she saw it. Norwich. Boarding in thirty minutes.

'Oh!' she said out loud, and sat down with a thump on the nearest seat . . . home.

Chapter Two

Rufus Palliser paused by the flower stall, bending to examine the prices and calculating in his head, converting guilders into pounds. He bought two big bunches of roses, not because he had anyone to give them to, just because it was a way of wasting time and their summer colour lightened his mood a little.

It happened to him often, this reluctance to go home. He was frequently overcome by the conviction that during his trips away he was merely out on licence, that the train or plane he was waiting to catch was taking him back to resume a life sentence from which there was no parole. So he wasted time buying trinkets or cheap paperbacks – the sort of books he despised – boxes of chocolates or cheeses, then, losing interest, left them behind on aircraft seats, in taxis or in trains.

He was not a stupid man; he was aware that the prison to which he returned was of his own making, that by a single act of self-will he could free himself any time he chose. He had been thinking lately that he must do something about it, make a decision, sell up and start again, but somehow he couldn't seem to take the final step. The feeling persisted that he hadn't finished yet, and until he had he couldn't walk away.

This trip had been a waste of time; he had come to

Amsterdam on the promise of a first edition of Robert Louis Stevenson's *Strange Case of Dr Jekyll and Mr Hyde*, in its original printed paper wrappers, but had found only a much later edition, worth comparatively little. Still, pleasingly, its pages, only slightly foxed, were uncut and the cover, of green-sprinkled morocco, was almost unmarked. He held it, carefully wrapped in brown paper and string, in his left hand, protecting it from the damp stalks of the flowers as he wandered slowly in the direction of his flight.

Rufus Palliser was a crumpled giant, with broad shoulders, a stubborn jaw and a mane of thick, wayward grey hair that hadn't seen a pair of scissors for far too long, another decision he never seemed to get round to. His eyes were grey too, beneath heavy black brows and when he wasn't smiling, which was most of the time, his mouth was grim. His shirt, which he had forgotten to unpack the previous night, was creased, his tie askew at the neck, and his ancient tweed jacket and corduroy trousers proclaimed his lack of interest in matters sartorial. He progressed carelessly, apologising frequently for his inability to look where he was going and trying not to think about anything, especially about home.

At least, he encouraged himself as he fumbled in his pocket for his boarding pass, this particular flight carried a pleasure of its own, that of flying to an airport no one had ever heard of, in an aeroplane only a tinpot rural airline would insult its passengers by using and only a war veteran or an aircraft enthusiast would recognise. As he swung his bag on to the KLM bus he raised his face to the hazy September sky and felt slightly better.

He noticed her almost immediately; he had always been drawn to oddities. She was sitting right at the back of the bus, gazing fixedly out of the window and shielding, rather unsuccessfully, a badly swollen black eye. She had a red patch on her jaw too, the sort of mark a fist leaves, and Rufus, strap-hanging by the folding doors, stared hard, fascinated.

Her skin was peaches-and-cream, flawless from a distance, and her wide mouth curved up at either end, imbuing her with an air of amiability she couldn't possibly be feeling, given the battering she had just sustained. Her hair was thick chestnut brown, twisted into a careless and unfashionable knot at the back of her head. Rufus couldn't decide whether she was plain or handsome but she was different, if somewhat big-boned, singular. Rufus was attuned to rarities, books or people.

As if she was aware of his scrutiny, she looked up as the bus stopped to disgorge its passengers, straight at him, and he saw that her good eye was brown, the bright, soft orb of an anxious Jersey cow, oddly vulnerable set in such a strikingly unconventional face. She turned away when she saw him staring, covering her bruises self-consciously, then rose too fast to leave the bus and knocked her reddened cheek against the nearest hanging strap. She grimaced, then lowered her head hurriedly to fumble with her luggage. She was tall and wide-shouldered, her height and stately bearing in keeping with her figure; Rufus stood unmoving as the other passengers disembarked around him, wondering who it was she reminded him of.

Clementine left the bus with her eyes fixed on the ground, embarrassed. When she looked up and saw the aircraft she couldn't believe it was real. It was a joke, out of a *Boys' Own* comic. It was tiny, old-fashioned, scruffy. It sloped, its nose sitting high up in the air and its tail resting on a tiny wheel at the back, almost touching the ground. It looked like a begging dog. It was out of the ark. She had to bend her head to pass through the door, and once inside she still could not straighten up because the ceiling was too low. It didn't look as if there were more than thirty seats in the cabin altogether.

She found a vacant place halfway up the aisle, literally up, since the floor sloped like a steep hill, next to the emergency exit where there seemed to be more leg room, and arranged her bags on the seat next to her, hoping to be left alone. She felt a violent surge of illogical anger when the man who had stared so hard on the bus appeared beside her and made it clear he was going to sit down, forcing her to move everything. He sighed as he lowered his large frame to the seat.

'I'm sorry . . .' His voice was deep and slow and he examined her face with open curiosity. Her irritation increased and Clementine clamped her jaws together, wincing as her jolted tooth complained, '. . . but I have to sit next to the emergency exit because of my legs.'

He stretched his lower limbs luxuriously, demonstrating their considerable length, and waited for her to speak. She merely nodded curtly then turned to look out of the window, wishing he would go away.

There was a loud bang from the engine as the propeller began to turn, and a cloud of thick black smoke belched from beneath the wing. Clementine recoiled in alarm and swung round to see if anyone else had noticed. Meeting her neighbour's insistent gaze she exclaimed, 'Did you see that?'

'It's all right.' Interesting voice, thought Rufus, soft like that single brown eye, and slightly husky. 'They always do that, it's quite normal.'

'But—'

'Really. Look at the wing.' He pointed past her at the wide expanse of grey metal outside the window. Clementine stared obediently.

'What about it?'

'See all those rivets?'

'Yes . . .?' They marched in rows, along the wing and across it, single rows, double rows, hundreds, thousands of them. What did a thousand rivets have to do with exploding engines?

'What about them?' She turned back to face him, indignantly demanding an explanation, and he smiled, revealing strong, rather endearingly crooked teeth. Clementine was taken by surprise; it was such a nice smile, considering the grimness of his face in repose. He expanded upon his theme.

'They don't make aircraft like these any more. She's an old lady, a veteran of the Second World War, so she complains when she's woken up and her bones creak when she moves.'

As if on cue, they began to roll ponderously forward and the brakes squealed loudly in protest.

'There you are,' said Rufus triumphantly. 'There are hundreds of Dakotas still flying around the world and they all groan and cough, but they all keep on flying. Just wait and see.' He was a sucker for anything old, anything eccentric.

Clementine stared out again at the wing, flexing gently as they taxied. It didn't look as if it was going to fall off, and all airlines had basic safety standards, didn't they? Anyway, she thought with macabre pleasure, it would serve Sebastian Brown right if she went to the bottom of the North Sea trapped in this ramshackle museum piece, *and* Jonathan, it would be poetic justice. She leaned back in her seat, imagining Jonathan sobbing at her rain-sodden funeral, and Jean, all in black, haranguing him while Robert looked embarrassed and little Eddie created his usual havoc amongst the mourners . . . mourners? How many people could she muster, she wondered, half a dozen, a dozen? Overcome by bone-deep weariness, she leaned back and closed her eye. The blood pulsed heavily beneath the other, already shuttered, one.

'Would you care for a drink, Madam?'

'No,' said Clementine, wincing as she turned her head. 'Oh, maybe, er . . .' The girl waited, swaying with the movement of the aircraft, her pencil poised. Clementine made up her mind. 'Yes, I'll have a mineral water, please.'

Rufus ordered beer, and a bottle of duty-free Scotch.

'Oh, and a bottle of gin.' She could drown her sorrows when she got home, maybe it would help.

'Drowning your sorrows?' asked Rufus.

'Hope you thumped him back,' said the stewardess, laughing at her own wit.

'I walked into a door, actually,' said Clementine with dignity, and turned to stare out of the window again.

The view made her feel better. As they approached the Dutch coast they passed over flat, evenly divided fields, a tidy patchwork quilt of brown and green. She leaned forward, resting her head on the glass so she could see better.

'Tulip fields,' said her neighbour's deep voice in her ear. 'It's a spectacular sight when they're in bloom.'

Clementine nodded, but she couldn't summon the energy needed to reply. The engine noise was beginning to throb unevenly in her head and the ground disappeared as they climbed into cloud. The aircraft bucked and vibrated, but the sun came out comfortingly, warming her left shoulder through her jacket. She watched the wing outside and tried not to think about her destination.

Rufus offered to pay for her drink when it came, he thought the gesture might encourage her to talk and he wanted to hear her voice again. But she shook her head and proffered her own money to the stewardess. He followed the movement of her hand as she reached across him to take her glass and was intrigued again. Close to, her complexion was almost as perfect as it had looked from a distance, her face, completely bare of make-up, had the pink-and-white bloom of an Estée Lauder advertisement. Her hand belonged to an Irish navvy.

It should have been elegant; it was long-fingered with wide, spatulate nails, but the nails were cracked, jagged and discoloured in places, and the joints were rough. When she turned her palm up to take her change there were thick calluses all along the cushion of skin below the knuckles. How very odd, thought Rufus, but since she obviously had no intention of talking, he leaned back in his seat and sipped his beer in silence.

The long stretch of sandy beach was clearly visible as they flew over Great Yarmouth. Now that it was too late Clementine began to wish she could change her mind. She should have gone to Aberdeen, the Orkneys, Outer Mongolia, anywhere but home. As they descended towards the airport she peered hard, looking for familiar landmarks, recognised nothing at all and felt relief rather than disappointment.

By the time they landed, taxiing in to squeak to a halt outside the terminal, the clouds were burning off in the late summer sun, thinning out and drifting away. Clementine sat immobile in her sloping seat, staring at the flat expanse of grass and sky outside her window as the other passengers stood and queued to disembark. She could see the car park on the other side, and the chain-link fence dividing it from the wide open space where the aircraft had stopped, its propellers winding lazily down to a standstill. Daddy had taken her to an air show once. He had thought she would be interested in the planes, but the only memory she had retained was of his big hand lying warm and heavy on her shoulder and the sensation of complete safety, the childish conviction that whatever happened, he would always be there to protect her.

Her intrusive neighbour made one last attempt, leaning over the seat to examine her closely. 'Are you all right? You're looking a bit seedy.'

When Clementine rose briskly, anxious to prove she didn't need any help, and hit her head on the coat rack, he reached out unexpectedly and ruffled her hair, soothing the hurt, making it better. Daddy used to do that, she thought, swamped by nostalgia.

'Don't!' she said, brushing his hand, and the reminder, angrily away.

As she emerged from the aircraft she heard a lark, high up in the sky above the runway, singing its heart out, and she stopped to listen, holding up the line behind her. How had she survived all these years, she wondered, without that joyous sound? She began to feel better.

It annoyed Rufus all the way across the tarmac, through Baggage Reclaim and on into the Customs hall. Who *was* it she reminded him of? He had seen her in a photograph: the hair, so Edwardian the way it swept out and up, then twisted into that thick chignon; the curvy shape, generous hips, deep bosom . . . she swayed as she walked, and those soft, clingy clothes, long and fluid, making no concession to fashion . . .

'Lillie Langtry!' he exclaimed, remembering.

'Beg your pardon?' said the Customs officer.

'The Jersey Lily.' Rufus nodded his head in the direction of her departing figure. 'Lillie Langtry, that's who she reminds me of.'

'Ah . . .' said the man noncommittally, following Rufus's eyes and wondering who Lillie Langtry was. '. . . bit big for me, frankly.' He was on the short side. 'Successful trip?' Rufus Palliser was a regular.

Rufus shook his head. 'No, waste of time.'

'Any more jaunts planned?'

Rufus shrugged. 'Only if something unexpected comes up.'

'Off for a nice quiet rest then, taking the missus some flowers?'

Rufus glanced down at his roses and wondered why he had bought them. 'No, I'll go to the shop for a while, get some paperwork done.' He was aware as he said it that it was merely another way of filling a few hours, putting off going home. The second-hand bookshop he owned, in a narrow cobbled street near Norwich cathedral, was only part of his antiquarian book-dealing business, a sideline, and his assistant Sal ran it perfectly competently without any help from him, but he enjoyed going there, filling his lungs with the comforting smell of old leather, glue and yellowing paper, a unique combination of must and history.

Excuses, he thought, excuses, excuses. When was he going to *do* something about his life?

The Customs officer examined his receipt, then waved him on. 'Glutton for punishment, you are,' he said. 'Now, if it was me I'd be off home like a shot, see the wife and kids. Can't wait to get out of here of a night, me. Work to live, that's my motto, not live to work. See you again.' He turned away, leaving Rufus to go in search of his van.

The woman was standing in the entrance hall when he emerged, looking hesitantly around, lost.

'Can I give you a lift?' he asked. 'I'm going into the city, I could drop you somewhere.'

She jumped, then turned slowly to look at him. He had the feeling her mind was miles away. 'No,' she said, 'I'm . . .' He waited, coughed, and she jumped again. 'I'm going to hire a car.' Her eyes filled suddenly with tears and she brushed the back of her hand across her battered face. '. . . I think I'm going home.'

'Here,' said Rufus and thrust his flowers at her.

Startled, she took the bouquet without protest, staring down at it as if she did not quite know what it was. Then, without looking at him at all, she straightened up, raised her chin as if defying some invisible enemy, and walked away.

Rufus Palliser stood quite still, watching her back. How very odd. He should have persevered, made her talk to him; she might have been interesting. He tightened his hold on his book, hanging on to certainties, and made his way out into the pale sunshine.

He hadn't even thought to ask her name.

Chapter Three

Clementine chose a big Ford, although it was frighteningly expensive, because it looked solid and reassuring. She didn't even try to analyse why now was the right moment to go back, she just knew suddenly that it was. She was in need of something to hang on to and she had to find the key to her existence again, renew acquaintance with her roots if she was to survive.

For a year after the accident she had dreaded travelling in cars, had had to force herself to sit beside Uncle Harry, clutching the upholstery and sweating with terror while he drove her round Letchworth. If another driver performed an unexpected manoeuvre she yelped with fright, and every time they passed an oncoming car on a bend she braced herself, expecting a collision. On days when the roads were damp she waited for the skid, anticipating the waltz of death she had danced when she was sixteen, then climbed out of the car as white as chalk and took an hour to recover. Surprisingly, Uncle Harry had understood, had praised her dogged determination to overcome her fears and been uncharacteristically patient with her. His encouragement had spurred her on when all she wanted to do was run away.

She remained an indifferent driver though. She had had to take her test three times before she passed, and she drove purely out of necessity. She was slow, nervous, hesitant; she dithered, changed her mind, forgot to signal, even on occasions forgot which was her left hand and which her right. She handled the powerful hire car like an old lady in a Morris Minor, gripping the steering wheel hard with both hands and leaning forward as if being nearer the windscreen would somehow make the car more obedient.

As the confined space heated up it filled with the sweet scent of a soft summer's day. Clementine breathed deep of her unexpected gift and fixed her attention on the road, ignoring the clamour of the future she was going to have to face when she returned to London, concentrating on the past.

She had never been back. To begin with it was simply too painful, and then as the years went by she had become aware of a reluctance to confront the finality of what had happened. But she had taken the familiar road often in her mind, cresting the last hill of her imagination to begin the winding descent into the village, passing into the flickering shade beneath the ancient stand of beeches that lined the last stretch to emerge in the sunlight where the old houses huddled cosily round the green with the Post Office, the pub, the school and the church. She remembered the route with the clarity of long association.

She turned left at the T-junction, leaving Marshmeadow until last, and drove along the edge of the tussocky patch of open ground that constituted the green, peering at the familiar places.

The pub sign was gone. The Old Ship had closed a few years back, been bought by a retired accountant and turned into a private house. He had put up cast-iron street lamps in the garden, planted thick *Cupressus* hedging across what had once been the pub car park and installed plastic chains looped between white-painted posts along the path to the door. Jean had described it to her over the phone, with withering sarcasm. 'Home Counties kitsch, you know the sort of thing Clem – *ghastly.*' But moving on, Clementine was comforted to see that the Post Office looked much the same as it always had, with its red phone box, its off-white rendering, the hole-in-the-wall postbox and the old-fashioned bay window, lined with shiny yellow cellophane to protect the goods inside from the bleaching power of the sun.

Madge was still running the shop, still spreading her poison, according to Jean. She had lived in the village now for nearly twenty years but soon after her arrival she had called Jean's boyfriend Robert, now her husband, a 'bucolic hayseed' and Jean had never forgiven her, never ceased to treat her like the outsider she considered her to be.

Jean, born and brought up in the damp, draughty vicarage next to the flint-faced church, was dismissive of all incomers, but she reserved her special wrath for those who looked down their noses at Robert Hawe and the other 'real' villagers as she called them, the farmworkers, council house tenants and tied cottage dwellers of Lower Dinningham, linked to Upper Dinningham by a hump-backed bridge but separated from it by the narrow river that cut the village in two.

Jean's father, the Reverend Hilary Smith, was retired now, thanking God daily for his deliverance and living in a centrally heated bungalow in Walton-on-the-Naze. His church had been absorbed into a combined parish and where the vicarage had stood were two new houses, both occupied by incomers. '*Luxuriously appointed executive-style family homes*', Jean had quoted contemptuously from the sales brochure when she phoned Clem to tell her of the desecration. The only one of the vicar's children still living locally, Jean had taken upon herself her father's role as defender of the status quo; it was she, not he, who had resisted the bulldozers.

Clementine drove a little further and parked, then sat back to examine her childhood landmarks as best she could with her one eye. She flexed her fingers, stiff from gripping the steering wheel too hard, rubbed her painful cheek and let the memories come: birthday parties, minor accidents, secret hiding places, plots hatched and games played. It was easier than facing the future, soothing, even comforting.

A pigeon cooed with fat self-satisfaction in the beech trees behind her and a man came out of one of the new houses and started up a mower. They were built of hard yellow brick and they had not been standing long enough to mellow yet. The right-hand garden was dominated by an ornamental Japanese cherry, its purple leaves and columnar shape out of place in the rural setting, and the house on the left was disfigured by plastic window boxes and blue-painted shutters. Their borders were neat, suburban, still bright with bedding plants, fading orange marigolds and clumps of purple petunias. Clementine restarted the car and moved slowly on past the church.

The garden of Manor Hall, what she could see of it hidden behind its thick barrier of overgrown shrubs, looked much the same as it always had, exuding the same air of shabbiness and neglect it had worn all through her childhood. The house was handsome, with stone mullions and tall chimneys patterned in black and red brick, and its position was good, set well back from the road behind iron gates at the end of a gravel drive, but for as long as Clem could remember it had been quietly falling to pieces, disintegrating from lack of care.

It had changed hands a few years ago, the spinster

sisters, Miss Judith and Miss Emily Walker who had lived there all their lives, having died within six weeks of each other. The sale had gone through with almost furtive haste, so Jean said; their only surviving relative and sole beneficiary, a great-nephew with, it was rumoured, expensive tastes and debts to match, was suspected of having found a buyer even before probate was settled. Jean had been able to supply very little information about the new owner (although no doubt, she said waspishly, Madge would know what he ate for breakfast and what colour socks he wore) and she couldn't imagine why he'd bought the place. He'd had a wife living with him to begin with, and he had got going enthusiastically enough, carrying out major repairs to the roof and damp-proofing the place, but then the wife had disappeared and either he had lost interest or run out of money. The rumours had started flying of course. According to Madge there had been a succession of other women since his wife left, but he played no more part in village life now than he had at the beginning.

Manor Hall had always fascinated Clementine. As children, bribed with liquorice sticks to deliver the parish magazine, she and Jean had crept through the tall gates, shuddering with delicious terror as they clanged shut behind them, then run as if the devil was after them through the darkly enclosed shrubbery to stand side by side on the stone steps panting with excitement. They had yanked hard on the cast-iron bell-pull and peered through the coloured glass panels of the front door to listen to the bell jangling hollowly in some distant pantry, then waited for the tapping of Miss Emily's stick along the echoing corridor. They had even been inside a few times, collecting for the church jumble sale, invited to follow Miss Emily across the dark hall to the small front parlour the old ladies used as their sitting room. They had sat, fidgeting nervously on worn button-backed velvet chairs, eating stale arrowroot biscuits and imbibing the smell of unwashed clothes, dusty carpets and the four cats that snoozed contentedly on the furniture, while Miss Emily, shielding her movements furtively from their sight, fumbled in an old roll-top desk, making mysterious clicking noises as she searched for hoarded pennies.

'There you are, girls,' she would say, holding out the coins in a hand curled by arthritis into a prehistoric-looking yellow-nailed claw. 'You may buy yourselves a sherbet dab each.' They could hear Miss Judith rummaging somewhere above their heads for crocheted doilies grey with age and musty, fusty shawls riddled with moth holes. 'Oh dear,' said Jean's mum when they bore them back in triumph. 'So kind, but we can't possibly use them.'

They had longed to see the rest of the house but been too paralysed by shyness to ask, so they never got to explore down the long corridors or peek behind the closed doors that beckoned so tantalisingly from the shadows. In the absence of solid facts they had made up stories to explain the sad state of decay in which the old ladies lived: tales of ghosts, lost inheritances, murder and mystery, far more interesting than the mundane reality of age, lethargy and an obsessive desire for privacy that had trapped the sisters in their mouldering time warp for so long. It was Manor Hall that had started Clementine's lifelong passion for old houses, and set her on the path she had chosen to follow in adulthood.

The only difference she could see now was the tall iron gates, standing carelessly wide open to the road. Miss Emily would not have approved.

She moved on again, past the war memorial with its neatly clipped box hedge, past the bridge leading to Lower Dinningham, then the flint-faced village school with its tall arched windows, closed down a couple of months ago and all boarded up with a For Sale sign at the gate, until she came at last to the heavy wooden farm gates that guarded the entrance to her old home.

'Never go back,' Uncle Harry had told her once. 'Everything is always smaller and meaner than you remember.' But the lilac Daddy had planted near the front wall when she was twelve had more than trebled in size. It hung over on to the road, its branches heavy with brown seed-pods, and the big lime tree stood guard over the drive as it had always done. Every summer it had dropped black sooty deposits all over Daddy's car, and every summer he had threatened to cut it down. How ironic, thought Clem, that it should have outlived him in the end. Marshmeadow nestled behind it, a long low farmhouse built of soft red brick and swathed in Virginia creeper, just beginning to change colour with the approach of autumn. She climbed stiffly out of the car, her left eye throbbing heavily in time with the beating of her heart, and her mouth dry with anticipation.

For the past sixteen years the place had been owned by a diplomat and his wife, but it was occupied only for the couple of months a year when they were not abroad. They held parties, Jean said, *posh* parties, not like the one Clementine's parents had thrown for the whole village when she and Clem were children. Charles and Caroline Davis were, said Jean, relishing her own disapproval, *obscenely* rich.

Clementine had imagined herself approaching these gates a hundred times, had pictured a stranger straightening up from the herbaceous border and asking, in the cut-glass accent of Jean's sarcastic impersonation, who she was and what she thought she was doing, peering over her gate. She could explain, she apologised, she didn't mean any harm, it was just that she had lived here as a child . . . Sometimes the new owner invited her in, sometimes she sent her packing; either way the interlude had always been a painful reminder that the place was no longer hers.

The gate was padlocked – the Davises were long gone from their summer visit – and the shutters were closed to protect the furnishings. The smell of newly cut grass hung in the air and in the lime tree a hooligan gathering of sparrows quarrelled noisily. The sound conjured memories of other Septembers, of dawn choruses and fresh air, sharp autumn smells in the morning and the promise of Hallowe'en, bonfire night, Christmas, still to come. She should have returned sooner, she thought, if only to remind herself of how things ought to be.

Jean had been trying for years to persuade her. 'You could attack the village from the other end,' she had encouraged, 'come and see Robert and me first, that way if it all gets too much for you, you can just turn round and leave . . .'

Time after time Clementine had stubbornly declined. 'It wouldn't make any difference,' she said, 'I'd know it was all still there, just the other side of the bridge.' It didn't matter that Jean and Robert lived in Lower Dinningham, down a long track on the far side of the river; you could see Marshmeadow from their kitchen window and it was too close, or so it had seemed until today.

She was surprised how much she had forgotten; the starlings, burbling and chirruping to each other under the eaves above her bedroom window like gossipy housewives, the lowing of Robert's Friesian cows as they made their way in single file across the meadow beyond the river for milking, another skylark, gloriously celebrating the joy of living, high above her in the blue, sounds she never heard from her London flat, which provided only the incessant hum of traffic and the noise of other people living their lives in close proximity to her own. It dawned upon her for the first time that it didn't matter who lived here now, because she owned her memories and nobody could take them away. She leaned against the top bar of the gate, resting her sore chin gingerly on her arms and letting the sun warm her. Why had she left it so long?

She walked slowly back to the car and climbed in, breathing in the perfume of her unexpected present. As she pulled away she was smiling. She would be able to survive now, she thought, now she had remembered where she came from.

Remembering where you come from is not much help when everything is disintegrating around you, and neither is a bunch of roses, however generously given. It was nearly seven by the time Clementine dropped her bags in the hall of her London flat and wandered through to the kitchen with her flowers and the bottle of gin. Her eye was beginning to subside and she could see, just, through the slit, but her jaw still ached and her tooth wobbled when she touched it; she would have to see the dentist on Monday.

She would have to see Jonathan too, face him with Sebastian Brown's accusations and make up her mind what she was going to do. She had already, during the long train journey from Norwich, rejected the idea of confronting him straightaway; she needed time to recover first.

She leaned against the sink, contemplating the future. She had had too little experience of men to be sure that Jonathan was the one true love of her life, but over the past four months she had allowed herself to become terribly fond of him, had begun to look forward to seeing him and to miss him when she did not. For the first time she had dared to imagine a future of sharing, of companionship instead of solitary independence, had allowed herself to dream of a real home with a partner, children, even a place in the country, a garden. And now suddenly she was back where she had started, with the added pain of humiliation and betrayal to come to terms with. She felt as if she was standing on the brink of an abyss from the depths of which, if she once fell, she would never be able to climb out. And on top of that there was Sebastian's threat to oust her from the company.

She searched in the cupboard for a vase. The roses' scarlet heads drooped over the edge of the draining board; wilting from lack of love, she thought in a moment of sour self-pity, just like her. She filled an earthenware jug full of water and cut the stems, then plonked them carelessly, carried them into the sitting room and placed them on the table by the window, jiggling them half-heartedly to spread them out. She recalled the peculiar man who had given them to her, his size, his unkempt appearance and the abrupt way he had thrust them at her. Did he make a habit of buying flowers to give away to complete strangers, she wondered, or had he bought them for his wife, then had an argument with her and decided to off-load them on the first woman he saw? She was reminded that marriage was not the be-all and end-all of existence, that being alone was less painful than losing someone you loved. Feeling chilly, she turned on the gas fire, kicked off her shoes and took the phone off the hook, just in case. Then she wandered back to the kitchen in her stockinged feet and poured herself an extremely large gin and tonic, drowning her sorrows.

Chapter Four

Rufus greeted Sal with a peck on the cheek.

'Good trip?' she asked.

'No.' He'd had this conversation once already today. 'Waste of time.'

'So what are you doing here?' Sal regarded him critically. 'Why aren't you on your way home?'

Rufus shrugged his arms out of his jacket, avoiding her eye. 'Thought I'd get some paperwork done.'

'No you didn't, you thought you'd waste some time so you didn't have to go home.' Sal rose from behind her rickety table in the alcove by the door, challenging him to deny it. 'Coffee?'

'Mm.' Rufus followed her meekly past the densely packed rows of floor-to-ceiling bookshelves to the tiny office at the back, breathing in the familiar musty smell of leather and cloth. Sal rarely used the office, she liked to be out front at the heart of things, but Rufus preferred it. He enjoyed its Dickensian squalor, the sagging shelves laden with files, reference books and directories, the ancient desk with its peeling green leather top and ill-fitting drawers, the old-fashioned safe sitting squatly in the corner. He was fond of his ramshackle chair too, although half the spindles were missing from its arms and it deposited bits of kapok and horsehair on to his trousers. He dropped his jacket over it, put his parcel down carefully on the desk and flopped.

'So what did you find?' asked Sal from the cubbyhole where the kettle lived.

'Late edition, nothing exciting. How's business?'

'Okay.' She put his coffee down beside him and perched on the edge of the desk, appraising him. 'Darling . . .' Sal called everybody darling, it wasn't personal. 'You are a complete shambles.'

'Thanks,' said Rufus. 'You're fired.'

Sal laughed. 'Oh, yeah? You and whose army?'

Rufus picked up his coffee and pulled a face at her. It had crossed his mind more than once that he and Sal were made for each other. They shared so many interests: a love of old books, a fascination with the unusual and eccentric, a warped sense of humour. Sal was a highly intelligent woman, a qualified accountant who had swapped one sort of dry, dusty book-keeping for another. 'No ambition,' she had said simply, when he asked her during her interview why she was throwing up a lucrative career for a dead-end job. 'And I fancy a change.' That was nearly six years ago, and he couldn't imagine now how he had ever managed without her.

He sipped from his mug and smiled at her through the steam. They even liked their coffee the same – strong, stewed and black. Sal grinned back at him, displaying perfect, dazzling white teeth. It could have been a match made in heaven, if only they'd fancied one another. She was a lovely girl, slim, dark, elegant. She drew to the shop more male customers than he would have believed possible, fluttered her eyelashes at them, then sent them away with books they'd had no intention of buying and soppy smiles on their faces. Her private life was hectic and promiscuous and Rufus was aware that he seemed to be in a minority of one, not finding her irresistible. He was jealous of the uninhibited enjoyment her good looks brought her, but not of her frenetic lifestyle. He felt about her as he might have felt about a bawdy and much younger sister and in return Sal treated him like a favourite, if rather ridiculous, great-uncle.

'Just because you're a boring old fogey,' she told him when he teased her about her boyfriends, 'doesn't mean I have to live like a nun.'

Sal sized him up shrewdly. 'When are you going to get your act together, Palliser?' she asked. 'When are you going to *do* something about yourself?'

Rufus stretched his long legs and crossed them at the ankle, examining his scuffed suede shoes with studious interest. 'Funny you should ask that.' He took another slurp at his coffee then put his mug down and began to unwrap his parcel. 'That was just what I was thinking on the way here.' He smoothed the brown paper, picked up the book and handed it to her to examine. 'Nice, isn't it? I bought you some flowers in Amsterdam, but I gave them away to this woman . . .'

Sal turned the pages, running her fingers over the paper. 'Mm, but not worth enough to justify the trip.' She glanced at him curiously from behind her shiny curtain of hair. 'Do I smell romance?'

'Fool. She was just some woman, she reminded me of Lillie Langtry, the way she carried herself.'

'Yes, and?'

'And she started me thinking . . .' Rufus ran his fingers absent-mindedly through his hair, leaving it sticking out untidily, '. . . about what I was doing with my life.'

Sal snorted derisively. '*Not* doing with your life, you mean.'

'All right, *not* doing with my life. Stop interrupting, impertinent child, *not* doing with my life. So on the way here from the airport I made up my mind—'

'Yes? All right, go on then, astound me.'

'I'm trying to, if you'll just let me get a word in edge-ways. I'm going to sell the Trollopes.'

'What?' Sal put the book down and stared at him in disbelief. 'But you've spent the past God-knows-how-many years getting them together. It was the Palliser novels that started you off on all this.' She waved an indignant hand at the ranks of books visible through the open door of the office. '*And* saddled you with that dis-integrating pile you so quaintly refer to as home. What the hell's the point of selling them now?'

'If you will just let me finish I will tell you.' Sal sub-sided. She had learned the hard way over the years when not to push her luck. 'I need the capital. The mort-gage drains all the spare cash I generate, but if I put the place on the market in its present state I probably won't even recoup my outlay—'

'If you hadn't sold all your dear old granddaddy's shares to pay that greedy little tyke way over the odds in the first place—'

Rufus straightened up in his chair and frowned irrita-bly. 'All that's water under the bridge. You know perfectly well why I did it, and anyway if I ever finish sorting through it all it may yet turn out to have been worth every penny. Why don't you listen before you shoot your mouth off?'

'Sorry, darling.' Sal bowed her head and picked up the book again, turning it over and over between her hands. 'Go on then.'

'Howard Carrick's been begging me to sell for years. He'll give me a good price for them.' He paused, expect-ing the usual sarcastic rejoinder, then carried on. 'It'll give me a breathing space so I can make up my mind where I go from here.'

'So how much have you still got to do?'

Rufus shrugged. 'How long is a piece of string?' He leaned forward in his chair, clasping his big hands between his knees, trying to explain. 'Look, Sal . . .' Sal was a good kid. She'd lived through it all with him, supporting him when Helen was against the whole thing, never telling him what a fool he was, to think renovating a crumbling museum piece could heal the ills from which he was suffering. He began again, stubbornly determined to finish what he was trying to say. '. . . Look, Sal, I know it's stupid, but I don't think I can move on until it's sorted out. I still have this feeling that if I can make the house better, maybe somehow I'll make myself better too.'

Sal shifted her bottom on the desk, then put the book down in front of him and patted his shoulder. 'Rufus,' she said, 'it'll take more than a house to cure you. What you need is an expert in restoring broken hearts. Unless you let yourself take risks again whatever you do will be just another exercise in wasting time. Get yourself together, you damn fool, before it's too late.' She rose, leaned across unexpectedly to kiss his cheek, then picked up her coffee and marched back to the front of the shop, raising her voice to add briskly as a parting shot, 'And in the meantime, why don't you bugger off home? You know how I hate you hanging around interfering.'

'Nag, nag, nag,' growled Rufus from his sanctuary. 'I'm glad I gave your flowers away, you don't deserve them.'

Sal giggled. 'So what did she say when you gave her my flowers, this female of yours?'

'Nothing.' Rufus remembered the tears in the woman's eyes, the way she had straightened her back as if she was squaring up to march into battle. 'I don't think she even noticed I was there.' He drew his legs in beneath his chair and turned back to his desk. 'Now shut up and let me do some work.'

He reached for a scrap of paper and a pencil, fumbled in his jacket pocket for his spectacles and began to write. It was six months since he had given up reading newspapers and even with his glasses on he was having trouble with his business letters unless the light was good. It must be years since he had last had his eyes tested; it was time for a visit to the optician. He sighed. Not only was his life going to the dogs, only forty-two years old and his eyesight was falling to pieces.

But the germ of an idea was beginning to form in his head, an answer to the question: what was he going to do with his life?

Rufus Palliser was an only child. His father David was an eminent QC, a high-profile lawyer who attracted a constant stream of celebrity clients. He was in demand on the international lecture circuit and when the BBC needed a pundit to pronounce upon the out-of-court settlements of the rich and famous, it was David Palliser they called. He had even turned his hand to fiction, writing best-sellers with the same ease as he did everything else. He was handsome, charming, urbane and extremely telegenic. Rufus's mother Celia, lay magistrate, prison visitor, tireless charity worker, was a powerful woman in her own right, and Rufus was an enormous disappointment to them both.

It was unfortunate, Celia complained, frequently and aloud, that the child had to take after his paternal grandfather, a mining engineer who worked for Rio Tinto Zinc, travelled the world while his wife stayed at home in England bringing up his family, and took no interest in his offspring at all. It was from Christopher Palliser that Rufus had inherited his unruly shock of black hair, his unusual height and his complete inability to conform to the rules, but the likeness had skipped a generation; Christopher and David Palliser had only one thing in common, a hearty and implacable dislike of each other.

On the day Rufus was born, his father was with Montgomery, watching the German High Command surrender at Luneburg Heath; within forty-eight hours the child had been handed over to a nurse and Celia was back running her WVS soup kitchen. By the age of five Rufus had already begun to display the same eccentricities as his grandfather; a predilection for his own company, a voracious appetite for the printed word and a seemingly instinctive antipathy towards the Establishment, the very people he was expected to admire; by the time he was sent away to prep school at eight he had grown into an awkward, gangling, precocious boy who appeared to have no idea how to behave and no inclination to excel at anything.

Brought up almost entirely by a bewildering succession of housekeepers, his relationship with his parents was already practically non-existent; Rufus quickly came to look upon his school boarding house as home, his housemistress as the mother he had always lacked. He enjoyed himself, began to achieve, was reluctant to go home and looked forward to the end of the holidays when he could go back. Almost all his *exeats* were spent at school because his parents were too busy to visit. At thirteen, as the sap began to rise and his height topped five foot eleven, he was sent to public school and his grandfather came into his life.

They met only once, at one of Celia's parties. Rufus was home for the Easter holidays when Christopher, displaying a talent for mischief that age had done nothing to dim, turned up on the doorstep as the guests were arriving for his son's forty-first birthday celebrations.

Had his unexpected appearance not coincided with that of the evening's celebrity, a BBC Radio producer with whom David was hoping to close a deal for a serial based on his second book, Celia would have shut the door in her father-in-law's face.

Rufus, crouched behind the landing bannisters with his bony knees drawn up to his chin, watched as his mother reluctantly ushered the tall heavily-built old man into the hall. Christopher stood, legs planted wide apart, hands stuffed into the pockets of a shabby overcoat, and laughed at Celia's discomfiture. That was peculiar in itself – nobody *ever* laughed at Rufus's mother. Celia pursed her lips, pointed the BBC producer in the direction of the drawing room and her husband, then turned back to her unwanted visitor, apologised brusquely for not inviting him to join the party and suggested that if he wished to speak to David he should come back the following day. Christopher laughed again, a deep rasping chuckle that sounded from Rufus's vantage point like stones rattling in the bottom of a bucket, then announced jovially that he had no desire at all to see his poxy son, he had merely stopped by because he had read about the party in the paper and thought it would be amusing to annoy them both. Then, aware that he was being watched, he raised his face to the balcony and winked at the skinny boy squatting almost directly above his head. Rufus sat back on his haunches, disconcerted by the sudden unexpected attention. None of his parents' friends ever noticed him at all, let alone winked at him.

Christopher Palliser, in England for the first time in nearly ten years, was between assignments, at a loose end and fairly drunk. Until he spotted Rufus lurking above him on the landing he had had no intention of staying to be bored by his son's pretentious friends – he had planned merely to disrupt the proceedings, then leave. But the scrawny boy at the top of the stairs looked rather promising. When Celia suggested he see himself out and left him alone in the hall, he took his hands from his pockets and leapt up the stairs two at a time, intent upon investigating his grandson.

In later years the memories Rufus retained, like snap-shots in his mind, were of his grandfather's eyes, the way the leathery brown skin folded round them when he laughed, his thick hair and heavy moustache, both pure white, and his huge gnarled hands. He waved them extravagantly in the air as he lounged on the end of Rufus's bed, conjuring up pictures to illustrate his stories of exotic places, strange people and dangerous adven-tures, and he chain-smoked, flicking his ash in Rufus's wastepaper bin when he remembered, on the carpet when he did not. He smelled strongly of whisky and when he leaned close to answer Rufus's naïve questions the fumes swirled around the boy's head, a potent mix of alcohol and tobacco that left him feeling lightheaded and vaguely nauseous.

Christopher Palliser, despite his decadent way of life, was a well-educated, cultured man and their talk was far ranging. Rufus, a passionately devoted fan of Henry Rider Haggard and Robert Louis Stevenson, listened enthralled as his grandfather regaled him with tales that could have come straight out of either, but as the whisky began to wear off the old man grew restless, then bored. He scribbled on a piece of paper. 'Write to me,' he said, growing maudlin and, because he felt no responsibility towards the gangling youth who looked so like him, sen-timental. 'They'll forward it to me via the company mail.'

'Where are you going?' asked Rufus, trying to spin the magic out, make it last.

'Tanganyika.' Christopher lit a last cigarette and flicked the spent match into the bin with a brown finger. 'Prospecting for gold.' He chuckled at Rufus's awed expression, went on to describe the Arab quarter in Dar-es-Salaam, the aromatic smell that permeated every corner of Zanzibar, the world's largest producer of cloves, basking in his grandson's admiration. Then he rose and stretched, filling the room (or so it seemed to Rufus) with his huge frame and scattering ash from his clothes. Was that what he would be like when he was old, Rufus wondered? His grandfather's departure left him exhausted, as if a whirlwind had passed through his room.

Christopher wrote, occasionally. He even sent presents, not for birthdays or Christmas but irregularly as the mood took him, wooden artifacts from Nyasaland, woven wall hangings from Bolivia, leatherwork from the Kingdom of Libya. Rufus wrote back, reams and reams in big, childish handwriting, pouring out his heart because his grandfather was remote enough not to mock or disapprove; it was almost like writing a private diary.

As he grew older Christopher's letters petered out, but the occasional present still arrived, sent mostly to school rather than home. When Rufus opted for the newly founded University of East Anglia (purely to annoy his father, an Oxford man) to read English, they followed him. He continued to write, recounting every insignificant detail of his academic progress, describing novels he was reading, lectures he was attending, and although his grandfather no longer replied, he began to send him books.

Not just any books. During a lifetime spent constantly on the move Christopher Palliser had amassed few material possessions, but for over fifty years he had been a passionate collector of the printed word. As he grew older he felt no inclination to go home. All his adult life he had roamed the world, his wife was dead and he had no place he felt was his. It was pure chance that he ended his working days in Rhodesia, and he stayed only because he couldn't be bothered to move on. When his eyesight started to fail, determined that his library should not fall into the wrong hands, he began, month by month then, as he felt his mortality approaching, week by week, to bombard his grandson with the only possessions that mattered to him. Rufus, struggling to adapt to the disciplines of university life, was overwhelmed by the old man's generosity, took to lying in wait for the postman, and looked upon his growing collection of ancient, leatherbound volumes as proof that his grandfather, unlike his parents, loved him.

He had tested his parents, unintentionally to begin with then, as the books began to pile up, on purpose. When he first arrived in Norwich, travelling all the way from Hampstead by tube and train with his possessions packed into two large suitcases because his father could not find the time to take him, he phoned home to tell his mother he had arrived safely. She was out. He left a message, asked the current housekeeper to pass on the number of the payphone on the landing outside his room so she could ring him back and waited in, missing his evening meal because he needed to hear the reassurance of a familiar voice. She didn't call.

He tried again towards the end of the week.

'Rufus, darling,' cooed Celia down the line, 'lovely to hear from you, must rush, Daddy and I are just off to the Mansion House for dinner. Terribly good cause, all those poor starving children in Africa. I'll call you.'

He waited ten days before he gave up and phoned again. His mother sounded pleased to hear from him, apologised for being so remiss, 'but you know how it is darling, what with the WVS, and Daddy's new TV series starts filming in a couple of weeks . . . actually, you've only just caught me, can't chat for long, committee meeting in half an hour . . .'

After that he left it, to see how long it would take her to get in touch. She didn't phone at all. When he returned home for Christmas his parents were in America, on a coast-to-coast tour to promote his father's latest book. They hadn't thought to let him know they were going. As his grandfather's volumes continued to mount up, spreading out to take over his cramped accommodation, spilling off shelf and table on to floor and chair, piling up beside his bed, the proof mounted with them. It was perfectly clear to Rufus who cared the more.

His mother sent a letter from America, posted on New Year's Day, containing the compliments of the season. She was sorry she hadn't had time to write before, she said, but what with the pressure of work, she was sure he would understand . . .

It was too late by then; Rufus was past caring.

By the time he had presented Sal with his bottle of whisky (making up for the flowers), then left her to lock up the shop and set off reluctantly for home, he had worked out what he was going to do. All that remained now was to find someone to help him do it.

Chapter Five

Monday brought Clementine more misery, the pain of a complaining tooth and the exhaustion of a sleepless night spent tossing pointlessly over what the following day might bring. It descended rapidly into farce.

Jonathan was waiting for her when she arrived at the office, all solicitous attention, horrified by her black eye and desperately apologetic that he had been, albeit indirectly, responsible for her injuries. But he was unable to deny the truth of what his partner had told her. Hard though she tried not to, Clementine found herself seeing him in a different light, wondering as she never had before about the way he moved, the way he used his hands, even the way he spoke. She became aware that he wasn't quite able to look her in the eye, that when he greeted her, although he called her 'sweetie' and his smile was as charming as ever, he was nervous, sheepish. The kiss he planted on her cheek was snatched, perfunctory, as if he half expected her to smack his face.

After a while, when she failed to react to his awkward overtures he began to waffle, to justify himself. He was just a child when he met Sebastian, he explained, and terribly naïve. Sebastian had recognised his talent when no one else was prepared to give him a chance and he was so persuasive, so charismatic . . . he had been *susceptible*. Clementine, remembering the hypnotic effect Sebastian Brown had had upon her in that Amsterdam hotel room, believed him. He had meant every word, he said, when he proposed, he *did* long for marriage and children, but he had underestimated how strongly Sebastian resented Clementine, and now he was threatening to pull the plug on the company . . .

'It's not as if I've ever lived with him,' he protested plaintively, 'at least, not in this country, and he's had other lovers while we've been together. It's just that he seems to have this *hold* over me . . . and he's put so much into the business over the years. We can work something out, can't we darling—?'

Clementine shook her head. However much affection she felt for Jonathan, it was not enough, she was beginning to realise, to surmount the insurmountable.

'Clem,' he stammered, 'you must understand, I truly want . . . I mean I thought we could . . . oh darling, this is awful!' He loosened his tie and tried again. 'You know my work is the most important thing in the world to me . . . you do understand that, don't you, Clem?'

'Jonathan . . .' It was becoming embarrassing. Clementine tried desperately to shut him up. 'I really don't think we—'

'We could go on seeing each other!' He grabbed eagerly at her hand and missed when she hastily snatched it away. 'As long as we postpone the marriage bit, he'll come round eventually . . .'

'Jonathan, for God's sake, wake up!' Clementine's voice rose, her temper fraying at his refusal to face reality. 'He doesn't even want me working here!'

'*Rowenstall!*' hissed Jonathan.

'What?'

'Mrs Rowenstall . . .!' Jonathan rolled his eyes in a comic pantomime of dismay.

She was standing in the doorway. She was one of their best clients, she had an appointment with Clementine and she was early. Clementine groaned.

'Good morning, my dear.'

Mrs Rowenstall was a tiny, well-preserved widow in her late fifties with a habit of speaking her mind. She trotted past Jonathan, pointedly not noticing his outstretched hand and the shaky smile he had fixed to his face, then reached up to pull Clementine down so she could place a motherly peck on her cheek.

'My dear, what a *frightful* black eye. Are you all right?'

'Me?' Clementine made a tremendous effort, and smiled. 'I'm fine, thank you, Mrs Rowenstall, I walked into a door. But I . . . look, would you mind awfully waiting while I just . . .' She waved vaguely at Jonathan, wondering how much of their conversation had been overheard.

'Yes, dear, of course, carry on,' said Mrs Rowenstall, moving determinedly not back towards reception, but across the room to Clementine's desk, where she sat down and crossed her legs. The silence lengthened.

'Mrs Rowenstall—' stammered Jonathan.

Mrs Rowenstall ignored him. 'I'm sorry, dear—' she began to tidy Clem's desk, moving blotters and papers around, straightening pencils, '—but I couldn't help overhearing. I must say you do seem to have got yourself into a bit of a pickle—'

Jonathan tried again. 'Mrs Rowenstall, I really am sorry to keep you, but if you wouldn't mind waiting in reception we'll be with you—'

'Be quiet, young Jonathan,' said Mrs Rowenstall sharply. 'I'm not talking to you!' She rose and returned to pat Clementine's hand. Mrs Rowenstall knew all about men. Having devoted the best years of her life to her beloved Harold, only to discover after his death that for the past thirty years he had been keeping a mistress, she was using some of her newly inherited (and in the light of her late husband's unsuspected and persistent infidelity, thoroughly well deserved) wealth to redecorate every trace of his memory out of her life. She had come to the inescapable conclusion that all men were cheats and liars, and over the past three months she had grown rather fond of Clementine Lee.

'Take my advice, dear, cut your losses right now.' She pursed her lips and glared at Jonathan. 'He's too short for you for one thing. Find someone your own size, and always look at the feet.' She glanced meaningfully down at Jonathan's elegant Italian brogues. 'Small feet, you see, first thing I noticed about young Jonathan. I always look at the feet, my Harold had small feet and you know what they say . . .' She glanced around, making sure there was no one else near enough to overhear, then laid her hand conspiratorially on Clementine's sleeve and continued in a loudly penetrating whisper, '. . . small feet, small willy. Now, my Harold's willy—'

'Mrs *Rowenstall*!' Jonathan blushed scarlet with embarrassment and Clementine choked, unable to stifle the laughter that was bubbling unexpectedly from the pit of her stomach. Jonathan opened his mouth to protest then changed his mind and shut it again.

'Place is bound to be riddled with Nancy Boys, of course.' Mrs Rowenstall glanced suspiciously around her, as if expecting a dozen Nancy Boys to leap out of a cupboard, then straightened her jacket and smoothed her skirt. 'It's that kind of business, isn't it? Stick together, you know, that sort.' She squinted up her sharp nose at Jonathan. 'As for you, my boy,' pursing her lips disapprovingly, 'you want to make up your mind which side your bread's buttered.' She patted Clem again, as if she was a favourite dog, ignoring Jonathan's incoherent bleats of protest. 'That's the trouble with men, dear, think we girls are so desperate we'll put up with anything just so long as we can get a ring on our fingers. It's all pure ego, of course. Don't you let him flannel you, dear, you put your foot down and stick up for yourself. Now, my Harold . . .'

Afterwards Clementine couldn't remember exactly how she managed to get the little woman out of her office. She was practically hysterical by the time Mrs Rowenstall left, teetering on the edge between laughing and crying, her jaw aching and tears of inappropriate mirth oozing from beneath her blue and purple eyelid. It was not, she thought, as she collapsed behind her desk, the ideal way to finish a relationship. Jonathan had already fled in terror, and if it hadn't been so funny it would have been unbearable.

She thought about fighting for her job, but her pride would not allow it. It seemed to Clem that she would invite more humiliation by staying than by cutting her losses and starting again. So she spent an hour packing all her things into a cardboard box, then left Jonathan a note.

She would talk to him later, she wrote, when they had both calmed down, and in the meantime he could reassure Sebastian Brown that she had cleared her desk. She would need, she added, being practical, to discuss with him the return of her investment – as the innocent party she was sure there would be no argument about her entitlements – then she squared her shoulders, signed it, '*Yours, Clem*', and added a postscript to the effect that she would be grateful if the money could be returned directly to her in the form of a cheque rather than sent to her uncle. That would at least spare her the ghastliness of trying to explain to Uncle Harry what had gone so dramatically wrong. She wished, as she scribbled

Jonathan's name on the envelope, that she could force herself to be angry with him, it might have helped if she had been able to scream and shout, it might have made her feel better. But all she could manage was sorrow, for Jonathan as well as for herself. She picked up her possessions and took one last look around. Where, apart from the dentist, did she go from here?

There was a pile of mail on the hall mat when she got home. The house had been empty, except for her top-floor flat, for over three months now, the last tenant having moved out in June, and most of the letters were for her ex-neighbours. They would have to be forwarded to her landlord to be passed on.

She riffled through the envelopes as she walked up the stairs. There wasn't much for her: an electricity bill, a circular and a handwritten envelope postmarked three days ago in her landlord Terry's round schoolboy hand-writing. She dropped the pile on the table next to the flowers and went to make a cup of tea, finding solace as she always did in the domestic routine, placing cup, saucer, teapot, caddy, letting the simple tasks soothe her as her journey back in time had done. She had designed and laid out the kitchen herself and its well-organised efficiency never palled; the cup she used was white bone china; she liked to drink from a thin-lipped vessel. When it was ready she took it through to the sitting room and settled down wearily in her favourite armchair, curling her feet up under her and leaning back against the cushions.

She had lived at her present address for nearly ten years, had turned it, with some help from Jean (curtains, cushion covers, blinds), from a seedy, dingy dump into a warm, comfortable home. She had replastered walls, tiled kitchen worktops. She had fitted new cupboards, painted, papered, learning new skills with every task; she had even taken out the leaky, rattling window frames and reputtied the glass before installing home-made double-glazing to stop the howling gales that billowed the curtains and froze her in the winter. She was proud of what she had achieved, thought of herself as a skilled craftswoman who could turn her work-roughened hands to anything, and despite its drawbacks she was rather fond of the place.

He was very sorry, Terry wrote, but he really had no choice. His elderly mum had tried to set herself on fire last week, smoking in bed again, and they simply couldn't go on lurching from crisis to crisis any longer. All the homes they had investigated were so expensive, something was going to have to go, and what had to go was Clementine. He realised, he continued, that her lease still had two months to run, and he wouldn't dream of turning her out before then, not after all the time she had been there and the improvements she had made, but the only way they could manage the nursing home fees without bankrupting themselves was to sell the house with vacant possession as soon as possible. He was sorry, he wrote, repeating himself, Clem had been the perfect tenant and he quite realised that she had put a great deal of her own money into the place, but needs must and he knew she would understand. Of course, if he heard of anything going he would let her know immediately, and two months should give her ample time to find some-where nice . . . and so on, and on and on.

Clementine rested her head on the back of the chair and laughed out loud. 'Out of love,' she complained to her flowers, finally holding their pretty heads high after their long journey from Norfolk, 'out of work, and out on the street. Oh, *bloody hell.*'

*

'Hello, it's me . . .'

Not now God, pleaded Clementine silently, it's not fair, I'm not strong enough just now.

'. . . Jean Hawe, remember me? I'm the congenital idiot who thought you were a friend of mine.'

'Oh, Jean . . .' Clementine resigned herself, lifted the telephone from the table and took it across to the comfort of her chair. 'I was going to phone you . . .'

She settled herself down for a long, one-sided conversation. Her mouth was still sore from its mauling by the dentist, her eyes still red from the laughter that had turned quickly to weeping.

'How are you, Jean?' asked Jean sarcastically. 'Oh, I'm fine, thank you very much, considering. Nice of you to ask.'

'Considering what?'

'Considering little Eddie went into hospital on Friday to have his tonsils removed. Considering my best friend didn't even bother to phone on Saturday to see whether he'd died on the operating table—'

Oh Lord, how could she have forgotten? 'Jean, I'm so sorry – I was going to ring you tonight, I swear, I – how is he?'

Jean snorted disapprovingly. 'Where were you on Saturday anyway? I phoned and phoned. Eddie's fine. Little bastard screamed the place down for two hours, then decided he was better and wrecked the ward playroom. After he'd spent an hour ricocheting off the walls they asked me to take him home because he was disturbing the other children, then when we got back Robert was in Suffolk overnight looking at a prize bull, so I put him in our bed where he promptly threw up. I could,' she sounded hurt, huffy, 'have done with some moral support.'

'I'm sorry,' said Clem, then, excusing herself, 'I've lost my job.'

'What?'

'I've lost my job.'

'Why?'

'Because . . .' Because my boyfriend's lover caught me lolling on a double bed in my nightie and told me to keep my hands off his property. '. . . Because my boss couldn't afford to keep me on any longer.' She had given up telling Jean about her love life, or lack of it, years ago; it was too embarrassing, having to explain every time yet another infant relationship came to an end.

'So what are you going to do then?'

'I don't know.' Clementine sighed. 'Just at the moment I can't even think about it. I've spent most of the afternoon at the dentist.'

As an emergency she had had to wait two hours for the dentist to get through all his other appointments. After she had read everything in his waiting room, including a couple of romantic short stories notable only for their complete lack of resemblance to real life, and a magazine called *The Lady* which opened up a privileged world requiring nannies, cooks, butlers, and live-in couples for villas in the south of France, she had explained, to her dentist's sceptical laughter, that she had walked into a door. Then he had peered into her mouth, waggled her tooth, to the accompaniment of howls of anguish (not entirely physical), taken an X-ray and told her to come back in a week. She was tired, demoralised and no longer capable of making any decisions about anything.

'Poor old you.' Jean was briskly dismissive. 'But look on the bright side, something better's sure to turn up. Why don't you ask Uncle Harry for some more of your capital and set up on your own? You've got the experience, after all.'

'Ah,' said Clem bitterly. 'Of course, why didn't I think

of that? A brilliant suggestion.' The idea of Uncle Harry trusting her with her own business was ludicrous.

'There's no need to be sarky. Eddie, will you stop that!'

Clementine pounced on the distraction. 'What's he doing?'

'Picking his nose.' Jean snorted disgustedly. 'I keep telling the little sod his face'll cave in, but he doesn't seem to care.' There was the sound of hand sharply meeting hand, then a loud wail.

'You shouldn't smack children,' suggested Clem mildly. 'It stunts their emotional growth.'

'Bugger his emotional growth, it's where he wipes the snot I worry about. Look, I'll come up and see you. I need the break and it'll cheer you up—'

'No!'

'Why not?'

'I—' Clem racked her brains for an excuse. She didn't want to be braced and bullied into feeling better. She wanted to be left alone to wallow in her misery. 'I'm decorating. You know how you hate the smell of paint.'

'You're always decorating. That flat must be three inches smaller than it was when you moved in, all the layers of paint it's had over the years.' Clem could hear from Jean's tone of voice that she wouldn't come. She raised her face and grimaced at her roses. Thank you, God.

She promised to ring as soon as she had anything to report, then dropped the receiver on its rest and rose to put the phone back on the table. She still had to break the news to Jean about the flat, start looking for somewhere else to live. She leaned over the flowers, reminded again of the peculiar man who had given them to her. The blooms had opened in the warmth of her sunny room and the smell was wonderful. They made her feel better.

Jean was right, something was bound to turn up. She stroked a red velvet shell with her finger, then wandered out to the kitchen to pour herself a gin and tonic.

The bottle was nearly a third empty already. 'Oh well,' she said out loud. 'What the hell? Cheers.' And she raised her glass in a self-mocking salute.

Chapter Six

Clementine's appointment with the dentist was for two o'clock.

During the preceding week she had bought and read all the trade papers, perused the Situations Vacant columns in the *News* and the *Standard*, and rung every contact she could think of, looking for an opening. She had begun a collection of cardboard boxes which sat in a corner of the sitting room waiting to be filled with all her worldly goods and she had looked at a dozen poky flats in a dozen noisy streets. Every time she entered the room the boxes smirked at her, rubbing it in, and she was beginning to hate them. Her injured eye had faded to shades of blue, green and yellow and her tooth had settled down at last. It didn't look as if she was going to lose it, but that was small comfort since it appeared she was going to lose pretty well everything else.

She picked up the post on her way out, a couple of circulars from the property letting agents advertising more grotty flats, and a letter from Jonathan which she read on the bus, rambling, heartbreaking, redolent of remorse and regret and accompanied by a cheque for considerably more than she was either owed or had expected.

He had pointed out to Sebastian, Jonathan wrote, that if he didn't do right by her, Clementine would be perfectly entitled to make a fuss about her peremptory dismissal, with all the attendant bad publicity that would bring, and Sebastian had agreed; accordingly the cheque included compensation for the ghastly time she'd had. Of course, he went on, she had only to ask and he would give her the most glowing of references; he had thought of nothing but her all week, he missed her desperately . . . He signed it *'With deepest love always, your Jonathan'*, then added in a postscript, *'I shall think of you forever as my own* sweet *Clementine, the most wonderful woman I have ever known.'*

Clem knew she should be cheered, not so much by the money as by the realisation that she had narrowly escaped marriage to a man who was prepared, quite seriously, to address her as *sweet* Clementine, but she wasn't. When the receptionist asked her how she was she said, 'Fine,' but she didn't mean it. It wasn't really Jonathan, she told herself, for whom she had felt such tenderness, it was the idea of having someone (anyone?) to love that had led her to make such a monumental fool of herself, but the thought gave her no comfort at all.

The dentist was running late; an emergency, the receptionist said. Clementine resigned herself and sat down to renew acquaintance with the magazines she had read so thoroughly the week before. *The Lady* was lying on the top of the pile. Perhaps she should apply for a job as a butler, she thought, she might end up in the south of France . . .

'How's it feel now?' asked the dentist, prodding at her tooth with an implement that looked as if it should be removing stones from horses' hooves.

'Aargh,' said Clementine.

'Good, good. Black eye's clearing up nicely too. Who'd you say did it?'

'Aargh . . . rgh.' Why do dentists insist on talking to you, like sadistic over-qualified hairdressers' assistants, when they must know you can't answer?

'Riotous life you career girls lead, never a dull moment eh? Going anywhere nice for your holidays? Spit please.'

Clementine spat obediently and wiped her mouth. 'South of France,' she said briskly and climbed out of the chair before he could polish her. She had just had a preposterous idea.

She stole *The Lady* on the way out.

She didn't even glance at the pages of flats and houses. She found a red biro and went through every single advertisement in the Situations and Appointments section.

She was not looking for a permanent retreat from life, all she needed was a breathing space, an opportunity to get away from London, recharge her batteries and recover. Just a few months would be enough to sort herself out, make up her mind where she wanted to go from here. She would put her possessions in store and step off the treadmill for a while. The more she thought about it, the more the idea appealed to her. It was the answer to all her problems.

She discounted the ads involving children; she felt no inclination to play surrogate mother to other people's babies and anyway she had no experience, unless you counted occasional confrontations with Eddie, who was unique. That left housekeepers, maids, butlers, couples. Couples? Ha ha. But there was the occasional 'husband to follow own occupation' or 'possible part-time work for spouse' and the 'handyman' ones sounded interesting. She grew so excited by the idea of living in other people's houses, being able to nose around elegant, beautiful, gracious homes, in whatever capacity, that it was twenty minutes before she remembered the magazine was out of date. The realisation slowed her down, but only briefly.

She listed telephone numbers, agencies specialising in housekeepers and odd-job men, general helps, and when she had a dozen or so she started phoning. She was so wound up by then that her hand was shaking. She imagined somewhere in Wiltshire, or the Cotswolds, soft yellow stone, latticed windows, immaculate gardens, was enthused by the idea of Hepplewhite and Sheraton, lovingly polished mahogany tables, elegant chaises longues, valuable paintings . . .

How wrong can you get?

'How are you?' asked Jean.

'Better. Employed.'

'Great! Tell me all.'

'You won't believe it, I—'

'I'm ever so glad. You sounded miserable last time we talked, I was feeling really sorry for you. So when do you start?'

'Five days. I've got to get everything packed up and put into store—'

'I rang you on Thursday, but you weren't in. Where were you?'

'Thursday? I was at this agency. It was the sixth one I'd tried and I was getting really down about the prospects. It was so weird, Jean, I had to persuade the woman I'd be up to it, he wanted a couple, she said, then when she told me where it was I thought I'd misheard—'

'I wish I'd known, we came up to London on

Thursday, to the Natural History Museum. We were going to drop in and see you but by the time we'd finished messing about . . .'

Clementine opened her mouth to speak, then gave up trying to compete, leaned back against the cushions, and let Jean wash over her. She knew from long experience there was no point in fighting the flow once Jean got going.

'. . . We thought we'd go by train, give Eddie a bit of a treat, but they were doing repairs to the track between Colchester and Witham, so we had to get off, make a forty-minute journey by coach, and then get back on again. I *ask* you!' Jean huffed indignantly down the phone. 'With a *five*-year old! Anyway, to cut a long story short, Eddie whinged all the way there, Robert fretted about his bloody cows all day and apart from the dinosaurs Mummy's Little Darling was bored rigid . . . Now, tell me all about this job!'

Clementine smiled at the phone and decided to keep her news to herself for a little longer. It would be so much more fun to surprise her. 'I start next week, I'll tell you about it then.'

'Righto. Let me know when I can come and visit, and we'll have a good old chinwag. I haven't been up to stay for months and I'm *dying* to see you.'

'Um . . .' Clementine twisted the phone cable round and round her finger, tempted to tell, after all. 'Leave it till next week, and I'll see what I can arrange. I might even—'

'What? You might even what? Eddie, put them down! No! Eddie, just give them to me . . . *Eddie* – sorry Clem, I'll have to go, he's got the kitchen scissors and he's just about to scalp the cat. Talk to you next week, bye!' and she was gone.

Clementine began to giggle. 'I might even,' she had

been about to say, 'come and visit you.' She hadn't recovered yet from the shock; it was such an extraordinary coincidence she was finding it hard to believe it had really happened.

The interview started unpromisingly. Mrs Green was a plump, motherly soul, which seemed like a good omen, and she listened attentively enough while Clem explained, as she had to all the other agencies, what she was looking for. But when she had leafed through her books she shook her head, just as the others had. 'We really haven't anything, I'm afraid, dear. You've no experience, you see, of this sort of work. I mean, most of our clients want someone to cook and clean, not wallpaper their hall.'

'But I'm a perfectly competent cook,' pleaded Clementine. 'And I can turn my hand to anything. Some of the ads ask for odd-job men, or general handymen?'

'But you're not a man!'

'It may have escaped your attention,' said Clementine drily, 'but I'm more powerfully built than most men.' She leaned forward, laying her hands on the table and turning them palm up to prove her point. 'See? You don't get hands like this by practising needlepoint all day. I can change fuses, mix concrete, plaster walls . . . really, I can do anything.'

She was all dressed up in her Amsterdam suit. Mrs Green examined her dubiously. 'Well, I suppose I could put you on the books and we'll see what turns up . . .' The phone rang, and she reached across to pick it up, '. . . but I can't promise you anything dear, you do understand, don't you?'

Clementine nodded, then sat back in her chair, disappointment washing over her.

Mrs Green listened for a while to her caller, said, 'yes',

then 'no', then listened again. 'You do? You have? Well, frankly, no, I haven't yet, the ad doesn't go in until next week, we were too late for last month's issue . . .' She raised her eyes from the paperwork on her desk, regarded Clementine with her head on one side, frowning. 'Look, just hold on will you, I've got someone here now . . .' She placed her hand carefully over the mouthpiece. 'This chap,' she nodded at the phone, 'lives way out in the sticks, his ad's supposed to be going in the next issue of *The Lady* and he's looking for a couple, housekeeper and general handyman for a short-term contract, six months . . . He's got a cleaning lady comes in two days a week and she does his ironing, but she's reluctant to do any more than that and he's looking for someone live-in to help him tidy the place up to sell.' She sighed. 'Frightful nuisance, he seems to be in a tearing hurry, and I really haven't anyone on my books that'd suit him. He's been driving me barmy, changes his mind every five minutes about what he needs, male, female, live-in, live-out – I've never come across anyone so vague. Anyway, having finally made up his mind, of course he wants them yesterday! You see what I have to put up with? But there you are, client's always right, isn't he? Now, where was I? If, I only say *if*, mind you, he would be prepared to take you on to do both jobs . . . I'd need references of course, to prove you really are as competent as you say you are—?'

Clementine nodded vigorously. 'No problem.'

'Right.' Mrs Green took her hand away from the mouthpiece. 'I tell you what I'll do . . .'

Her client was clearly not keen on the idea of a woman on her own but Mrs Green handled him with the ease of long experience. 'She's got *wonderful* references,' she lied, pulling hopeful faces at Clementine. 'And she's not afraid of hard work. She's also rather, er . . . *well built*, if you know what I mean,' mouthing a silent apology at Clementine, who grinned. 'So you wouldn't need to worry about her not being up to the physical side of things, and she's an ex-interior designer so she could be really useful . . . what? Oh, yes . . . yes. Um, hang on, I'll ask her. He says you must be able to drive because it's rather isolated. Would that bother you at all, living out in the wilds?'

Clementine hesitated, imagining Bodmin Moor, the wilds of Scotland. 'Where is it exactly?'

'Norfolk.' Mrs Green riffled through her papers again. 'Tiny village in north Norfolk, er . . . Dinningham. Place called Manor Hall . . .'

Chapter Seven

Clementine took a taxi from Thorpe station, accompanied by two suitcases and a soft bag, containing her clothes, books and a few treasured possessions, her portable radio and her precious toolbag, which accompanied her wherever she was working. Everything else had gone into store, and now that theory was about to be put into practice she was terrified of what she had done.

The journey, out of Norwich and on along the Cromer road, soothed her as it had two weeks ago. The countryside was little changed, the pubs and villages looked much the same, the same fields even seemed to hold the same cows. But by the time the taxi turned off the main road on to the narrow winding lane to Dinningham the nerves had begun again and she was having trouble with her breathing. She was going to be early too, not the way to make a good first impression. As the taxi emerged from beneath the beeches she turned her face resolutely away from Marshmeadow. She must have been crazy to think she could do this. It must have been the black eye, or concussion, or misery, and now it was too late to change her mind.

It felt odd, driving through the iron gates of Manor Hall, and the distance to the front door was shorter than she remembered. She paid off the taxi at the foot of the stone steps, carried her bags up one by one and dropped them at the top, then watched the driver reverse and disappear back into the overgrown shrubbery before turning to face the house with growing trepidation. No escape, she taunted herself, you're committed now, you fool. She swallowed hard and squared her shoulders. It's only for six months, she reminded herself, and you don't have to stay if you hate it.

The stained-glass panels in the front door were just as she remembered them, cream lilies with golden stamens on long twining green stems set against an azure blue background, the glass thick and uneven. Peering through them she was transported back twenty years, a giggling schoolgirl sneaking a look into the witches' lair, and she began to feel a little braver. She was stupid, she should have rung Jean, told her what she'd done and asked her to come with her for moral support. She had been so busy planning the surprise she was going to give her, she hadn't stopped to think that she might need her best friend to give her courage.

She cupped her hands round her eyes and squinted. The hall wavered and shimmered, the patterned floor tiles shifting and undulating through the glass. It was smaller than she remembered, when she was a child it had seemed as big as a football pitch but now it was just a larger than average hall with lots of rooms leading off it. When she rested her forehead against the door, trying to make out the shapes in the dim light, it swung slowly open, creaking on its hinges and she stepped backwards, disconcerted.

Come on, cowardy custard, ring the bell. Ring the bell and face the dragon. She reached across to the bell-pull, then hesitated. Tantalisingly, the door swung wider. She spread her hand, splaying her fingers against the glass, and pushed. It felt warm beneath her palm where the sun had been on it, reassuringly solid.

'Hello?' she called. Silence. 'Hello, is there anybody home?' She pushed again, until the door stood wide, then stepped gingerly across the threshold, holding her breath.

She had forgotten the detail of the floor tiles. Typically Victorian, black, brick-red and cream, they formed a symmetrical pattern, squared and quartered, with an intricate border running along the outer edge. They were in good condition, what she could see of them in the gloom, but the woodwork, doors, lintels and deep, elegantly turned skirting boards, were lacquered in dark, drab tobacco brown. The walls, hung with hunting scenes and stylised flower prints spotted with age, and drearily papered above dados running round at waist height, were almost exactly as she remembered.

She took another hesitant step, then turned to look back through the open door at the sunlit shrubbery. She was tempted to take flight, it all looked so sad and gloomy, but curiosity drew her in. She craned her neck to see round the slightly open door of the parlour into which Miss Emily had ushered her and Jean when they were children, but all she could see was a strip of bright light. The door across the hall to her left was firmly shut, as were those further in.

Her soft leather boots were flat and composite soled, her footsteps squeaked and she began to walk on tiptoe, feeling like an intruder. She was wearing her Amsterdam suit again, aiming to impress, and her skirt rustled in the silence.

She came to a halt at the foot of the stairs, opposite a pretty, cast-iron fireplace with a carved motto faintly visible on the grey stone surround, *Omnia-something-something*, she couldn't make out what because the light was too dim. She didn't remember either stairs or fire-place – she had never been this far into the house before.

The staircase was beautiful, wide polished oak treads, partially covered by worn red-and-blue Axminster car-peting held in place by brass stair rods, and turned oak bannisters running up to a long galleried landing with carved wooden arches along its entire length. From the bend of the stair, six steps up, rising almost to the ceiling of the first floor, the wall was obscured by a length of plywood three feet wide and over eight feet high, held in place with battens nailed across it. The cheap material and the hasty way it had been tacked up added to the general air of decay, increased the atmosphere of neglect that pervaded everything. This was not what she had envisaged at all when she started on this lunatic scheme.

'Hello?' she called again. Her voice sounded small and tremulous in the silence and the sunlight beyond the front door beckoned enticingly. She could call a taxi from the phone box next to the Post Office. She could go straight round to Jean's, stay there until she felt strong enough to move on, forget this idiotic idea altogether. She had made up her mind, even taken the first couple of steps towards the front door and escape, when there was a distant crash and she heard the sound of a human voice .

It was too indistinct to make out the words, but it seemed to come from the shadowy corridor at the back of the hall. Clementine hesitated, stopped. She ought at least to face the man, explain that she had made a mis-take thinking she could do the job, apologise for changing her mind. She took a deep breath and moved reluctantly towards the noise, the soles of her boots squeaking loudly on the tiles.

The door at the end led to a kitchen. The big room was bright after the hall, with a wide window looking out across a badly neglected walled garden, and it was warm, heated by the old-fashioned blackleaded range which filled the huge fireplace. The floor was laid with dark red pamments, worn by the passage of many feet into dips and hollows, and a heavy pine table stood in the centre of the room, stained and gouged by careless use and bleached by years of scrubbing. An ancient marmalade cat with one ear, as shabby and moth-eaten as anything she had seen so far, was sitting on it, the tip of its tail flicking rhythmically, watching something.

On the far side of the room, surrounded by shards of crockery, a man lay stretched on the floor, long legs in faded denim spread across the flagstones, head, one arm and most of his right shoulder invisible beneath the big oak dresser that stood against the wall. Every time he moved the remaining plates above him rattled a loud refrain.

'Excuse me . . .'

'Ouch!' came the snarled reply, muffled by the confined space. '*Bitch!*'

A large hand shot out into the light, was shaken hard, then disappeared again. The cat yawned, showing a cavernous pink mouth, then raised a back leg and began to wash its genitals.

'Excuse me . . .?' repeated Clementine.

'Hang *on*, Doris!' growled the disembodied voice from beneath the dresser. 'Damn thing's got itself stuck.' The body on the floor writhed again and incoherent chirruping noises began to emanate from the hole.

'Can I help?' Clementine was beginning to feel extremely foolish, talking to his rear end.

There was a violent upheaval, an 'Ow! Bloody hell!' and the man shot backwards across the floor, twisted, jerked his head up, catching his temple on the edge of the dresser, and swore again. Then he sat up with his back to her. He was covered in dust and cobwebs and he looked like an enormous, shaggy scarecrow.

'Damn thing's making my life a misery,' he complained angrily over his shoulder. 'If I ever manage to get it out of there you'd better take it away before I throttle it!'

Clementine began to back away. She was thinking longingly of the open front door and the sunshine. She was wondering if she had time to escape before he turned and saw her.

Chapter Eight

Rufus Palliser swung sharply round. He was expecting Doris Medler, employed to clean, to do his ironing and (not something he had either asked for or wanted when he took her on) to fuss around him like a plump, irritating mother hen, telling him how to run his life. He was spoiling for a fight.

He was not expecting Lillie Langtry to step out of his dreams, looking almost exactly as he remembered her, tall, stately, an uncertain half-smile curving her generous mouth, but this time with two big brown eyes, both wide open in alarm. He froze, sitting on the floor with his long legs scrunched up to his unshaven chin. He had imagined Clementine Lee would be another Doris, fat, dowdy, uninteresting, and he was having difficulty taking in what he was seeing.

'Oh!' exclaimed Clementine. The flower man!

Rufus lumbered hastily to his feet, attempting to pull himself together. 'Sorry.' He dusted himself off as best he could, wiped his hands on his jeans, then straightened up and held out a huge, grubby paw. 'I thought you were Doris. Rufus Palliser. You're not . . .?'

Clementine placed her hand reluctantly in his. 'Clementine Lee,' she said, and smiled tentatively, completely thrown by this latest coincidence.

Rufus, watching his new housekeeper's already amiable mouth curve further upwards at the ends, was unexpectedly attacked by a sensation of great warmth. It began somewhere beneath his ribs and radiated outwards, filling him with a glow of extreme wellbeing; when she tried to remove her hand he tightened his grip, not wanting it to stop.

'Clementine Lee,' he repeated, quoting from the agency details. 'Clementine – Ambrosia – Thomasina – Lee.' It was the wonderful ridiculousness, the sheer *silliness* of her name that had made him decide to employ her; if he had known who he was getting, the thought occurred now it was too late, he would have made sure he was clean when she arrived.

She laughed at the mention of her full name, a low-pitched, husky chuckle with an irresistible sort of hiccup at the end. The heat beneath his ribs increased and Rufus tightened his grip again.

'My father wasn't expecting me.' Clementine, trying unsuccessfully to extract herself from the vice within which her hand was so firmly clamped, and unnerved by her putative employer's unblinking stare, began to waffle. 'He was convinced I was going to be a boy, you see, so he fixed on Clement, then Ambrose, which was his name and Thomas, after his father. I was to be Clement AT-Lee. He was a great admirer—'

'Ah,' said Rufus, not really paying attention because he was watching the way her mouth moved when she talked, then irrelevantly, because he was so unused to women who reached higher than his chest, 'you stand up very straight.'

'What?'

'For a woman, I mean. That is, you stand up very straight for such a tall woman.' Shut up, he cursed himself, you sound like a complete idiot, but she smiled again and his tongue carried on regardless. 'What I mean is, so many tall women are inclined to stoop . . .'

'My father taught me to be proud of my height. He was six foot five.' With a quick flick of her wrist Clementine extricated herself from his grasp and whisked her arm behind her back, flexing her fingers surreptitiously to help bring the circulation back. Rufus, feeling the loss keenly, noticed as she slid away from him how rough her skin felt and remembered her nails, the calluses. It occurred to him he could ask her now how her hands had got into such a state.

'Should we do something about the dresser?'

'Sorry?' Rufus was uncomfortably aware that he was being even more vague than usual, but he couldn't seem to pull himself together sufficiently to do anything about it. 'Ah, oh yes, right, the dresser.' He ran his fingers through his untidy hair, depositing a large lump of fluff just above his left eye. Unable to help herself, Clementine chuckled again, then reached up and brushed at his dishevelment.

'You've scraped yourself,' she said, touching his temple lightly. 'You're bleeding.'

Rufus, assailed again by that spreading warmth, was rendered speechless, and helpless, by a wild desire to grab Clementine Ambrosia Thomasina Lee by her waist and kiss her inviting mouth. He turned his face hurriedly away, appalled. Kissing the housekeeper? Sal would have a field day. He felt around gingerly until he found the scrape, distracting himself, then winced as he touched it, reminded of what he was supposed to be doing.

'I can't get the damn thing out,' he explained. 'I've tried bribing it, coaxing it, threatening it, but every time I get near it, it goes for me. It's got teeth like razor blades.'

Clementine's imagination was running amok. 'What has? What is it under there?'

'Eh?' Rufus was still examining his wounds, transferring the blood from his temple to his jeans while sucking his other, bitten, hand. 'Oh, it's a dog . . . well, a puppy. Doris gave it to me, silly woman said I needed the company.' Not quite accurate – Doris, watching him grow increasingly uncomfortable at the thought of sharing his home for six months with a strange woman, had suggested it would break the ice, provide something to talk about if needed. He moved back towards the dresser, still wiping his hands on his jeans. 'Do you know anything about dogs?'

'A little.' They had always kept dogs, until the accident. Uncle Harry had taken the elderly family spaniel to the RSPCA while Clementine was in hospital. There was nobody to look after it, he said, and Aunt April was allergic; they couldn't possibly keep it . . .

'What sort is it?'

'Haven't a clue.' Rufus frowned heavily at the dresser. 'It's black and hairy, it's a bitch and it bites.'

'What's her name?'

Rufus, who for the past five days had been calling his unwanted present 'Stop-It-You-Bloody-Mutt', thought about it. 'Mary,' he said at last.

'Mary?'

'As in quite contrary . . . no, as in extremely contrary.' Rufus went over the top. 'As in abso-bloody-lutely contrary. What the hell am I going to do with it?'

Clementine moved hesitantly towards the table. The cat gazed at her with impassive yellow eyes and yawned again. 'Well, why did she go under there in the first place?'

'What?'

Rufus, watching her hand as she reached out to stroke

the cat's mangy coat, was distracted again. Clementine repeated the question patiently.

'Ah, er, the cat frightened it.'

'Her, you said her name was Mary, didn't you?'

Rufus had to force himself to take umbrage at the kind condescension he could hear in her voice. 'Yes,' he said briskly, taking charge, 'I did, but I've got better things to do with my time than spend it crawling around on the floor after a scruffy mongrel. She'll just have to stay where she is for now. Shall we get on?'

The change in his demeanour was startling. Clementine took her hand from the cat and straightened her shoulders. 'Yes of course,' she said meekly. 'Whatever you like.'

Rufus, having asserted his authority, didn't know what to do with it now he'd got it, and he didn't like the alarm he had caused in those brown eyes, the way she bit her lip in consternation. He shifted his weight from one leg to the other and stared at her, waiting for her to say something.

'Er . . . has the cat got a name?' Clementine was searching for the courage to tell him she wasn't staying, becoming more convinced every moment that she had made a dreadful mistake coming here at all. The man was quite clearly deranged.

'Um . . .' Rufus struggled to remember. 'Ginger, Doris calls him. He lives in the cart lodge and I don't even feed him. I inherited him.'

'Inherited him?'

Rufus plunged his punctured hands into his pockets and glared at the cat as if it might help him pull himself together. 'The two old ladies who lived here . . .' Ginger stared coolly back and he lost his thread again.

'. . . Miss Judith and Miss Emily?'

Rufus jumped, and snapped. 'I was about to tell

you, if you would just let me finish my sentence!'

'Oh, I'm sorry,' Clementine apologised stiffly, disconcerted by the childish display of petulance. 'Please, go on.'

'The two old ladies kept cats—'

'Yes, four—'

'How would I know what for? Because they liked them, I would imagine.'

Watching his black eyebrows descend into an irritable frown, Clementine clapped her hand over her mouth, pleaded, 'Sorry!' again and then, because she was so nervous, began to giggle.

Bloody hell, thought Rufus, melting in the heat, I can't handle this.

A bedraggled, long-haired mongrel appeared unexpectedly from beneath the dresser. It skirted the table, avoiding the cat, then sidled up to Rufus and squatted to piddle on his left shoe. Clementine's giggles turned to helpless peals of laughter.

'Oh, *bugger*!' said Rufus.

Chapter Nine

'Lord knows why he needs me there.' Doris Medler fumbled her way into her cardigan sleeves. 'Said he was nervous, poor lamb, said he wouldn't know what to say to her.' She chortled richly. 'Reckon he's likely right at that. Took him nigh on a week to pluck up the courage to talk to me when I first started.'

Frank regarded her quizzically over the top of his glasses. 'Couldn't get a word in for all your rabbit more like,' he said drily, then chuckled with his wife as she shook with laughter at the accuracy of his joke.

'Anyway, shan't be long.' Dorrie straightened her flowered pinafore and arranged her cardigan over the plump frontage Frank affectionately referred to as her superstructure. 'You be here when I get back?'

Frank folded his newspaper and eased himself out of his sagging armchair. 'Nah, feed man's coming this afternoon and Robert's away up top field, muck spreading. Promised I'd hang about till the bloke come and then it'll be time for milking.'

Dorrie chortled again. 'That'll please our Jean. Not right keen on her darling Robert smelling like a midden.' She stepped over the shaggy mongrel stretched snoring on the hearthrug, mother of Rufus Palliser's recalcitrant puppy, and fumbled on the floor beside the armchair for her brown oilcloth shopping bag. 'Surprised she didn't ask you to do it.'

'She did.' Frank's ruddy face creased with amusement and his watery blue eyes disappeared in a hundred lines. 'Robert said he'd rather do it hisself, thank you. He hates that delivery man, always trying to sell him twice as much as what he wants. If I'm there I just say no-can-do, boss is away, and that's the end of it. Go on, four o'clock you said, you'll be late.'

'Righto. See you later.' Dorrie carefully lowered the stew in its sealed Tupperware box, right way up into her bag, planted a kiss on her husband's bald pate and went on her way, smiling.

Frank had been making her smile since they were kids, that was why she'd married him. Dorrie had had offers from better lookers, and better earners than Frank. She'd been a looker herself when she was young, shapely, pretty, all the boys'd been after her, but none of them could make her laugh like Frank so she'd married him. They had brought up six children in their small tied cottage, along with assorted cats, dogs, bantams and a permanent live-in population of voracious mice, all tolerated with the same placid equanimity by Dorrie, who shooed hens from under her feet as she fed the latest baby, spooned mouse droppings out of the sugar bowl before her offspring sprinkled it on their breakfast cereal, and greeted unexpected puppies and kittens with the same imperturbable calm as she accepted the arrival of each new human mouth to feed. The only mystery to the rest of the village was how underweight, overworked Frank had managed to put her in the pudding club so regularly without dropping dead of a coronary.

She often thought they must look like one of those postcards nowadays, the Donald McGill ones you used to be able to buy on Cromer pier; she'd put some weight on, what with the kids and the cooking, while Frank had stayed stubbornly skinny; wiry he called it, but truth be told he was downright scrawny, always had been. It was trying to feed him up, put a bit of meat on his bones, that'd done for her, that and the kids. Fattypuff and Thinnifer they were now, but Frank could still make her laugh when she was down in the dumps.

She bustled out of the back door and along the worn path to the lane, then turned left, making for the bridge and Manor Hall. Funny old business, she thought, examining the sky to see what the weather was doing, all this malarky about a housekeeper.

Dorrie had worked all her married life, helping to eke out Frank's meagre income as cowman up at Hawe's farm. She'd polished and swept and hoovered, first at the vicarage for the Reverend Smith, then later at the village school, progressing as the kids grew to dinner lady, a comfortable, reassuring presence in the playground who knew not only every child in the school, but their grandparents, parents, brothers, sisters, cousins. She'd taken an interest when Rufus Palliser moved in, like everyone else in the village, and she'd seen him occasionally in that clapped-out old van of his, but he never joined in with village things, never went to church or the Bring and Buy. Then a couple of years back he'd put a card in the Post Office window, looking for a cleaner.

Even before the school had closed, killed off by dwindling numbers and government cutbacks, she had been looking for something part-time; Palliser was offering good money, and Manor Hall would suit her down to the ground. His wife had left him, Madge Dixon warned when she asked about him, that was why he was in need of help, but she hadn't expected him to be in almost as bad a state as the house.

Two years on nothing much had changed; Rufus was still a difficult man to work for, unpredictable, moody, but at least the constantly changing stream of unmemorable females passing through Manor Hall when Dorrie first arrived had petered out over the past few months. He didn't interfere, or criticise her work. She gave him two days, the maximum she was prepared to do at her age, cleaning the few rooms he lived in, doing his washing and ironing, cooking the occasional meal, and they had learned to rub along together. She knew little more about her employer now than she had the day she started.

She stopped on the bridge and leaned over to watch the water eddying round the stone arches. It had always been a favourite spot with the village kids. It was here they had congregated on long summer evenings to lark about on the slippery banks, dangling their legs from the gnarled sloe that trailed its branches out across the water, lying in the long grass with jam jars submerged in freezing water, catching sticklebacks, or sitting patiently with home-made rods at the foot of the precarious path running down from the lane to catch the elusive brown trout that lived in the dark beneath the crumbling brick pillars. The bridge was the centre of the village then, the umbilical cord connecting the two halves of its population, but the children were few now, their freedom curtailed by the dangers of modern living. Crying shame, thought Dorrie, remembering her own large brood and their carefree youth.

She turned right past the war memorial and plodded through the gates to scrunch up the overgrown drive to Manor Hall. Rufus seemed to know almost nothing about this handyman-housekeeper he'd engaged. He'd had to make do with what he could get, he'd explained grudgingly when she asked, but the agency had promised the woman was built like a tank and could turn her hand to anything. He was dubious as to how much use she would be, but he wanted to get on with it so he could put the place on the market the following spring. It was the first inkling Dorrie had had that she might soon be out of a job and he had offered no explanation for his sudden decision to move on. It was absolutely typical of the man, she told Frank ruefully.

The front door was wide open so she didn't bother to ring the bell. She saw the cases on the step, guessed she was late and crossed the hall at a trot, making for the long corridor and the kitchen; in Dorrie's experience people always started in the kitchen.

Rufus was standing awkwardly by the dresser, legs set wide apart, holding the puppy she had given him while it dripped forlornly on to the floor between his feet. Facing him, with her back to Dorrie, was a very tall, broad-beamed woman. She was dressed in soft, expensive-looking clothes and she was shaking with gales of laughter. As Dorrie walked through the door she turned her head, stopped laughing and said, 'Good Lord! Mrs Medler!'

Dorrie squinted, moved nearer, peered. 'Well I never! Clementine Lee? It *can't* be!'

'Where the hell have you been?' demanded Rufus belligerently, as if it was all Dorrie's fault.

He carried Mary to the back door and dumped her unceremoniously on the grass outside, ignoring her whines of complaint. Then he made coffee, padding around in his socks, avoiding the shards of crockery and eyeing the two women with suspicion. Having made a resolution to pull himself together and change his life, he was beginning to wonder whether he had taken on more than he could manage.

'Right,' he said, slapping two chipped brown mugs of strong black coffee on the table and attempting for the second time to assert his authority, before it was too late, 'as soon as you've finished we'll get on.'

'Sugar?' Dorrie prompted, used to Manor Hall coffee. Rufus gritted his teeth and stepped carefully across to the dresser to pick up the sugar bowl. 'Got a sweet tooth,' Dorrie explained to Clementine. 'As you can see.' She patted her ample stomach and winked.

'Do you have any milk, please?' Clementine, who took her coffee weak, white, and only when forced, was not yet aware that Rufus was all bark and no bite. When she raised her eyes to his they were wary and Rufus was swept by remorse.

'Sorry,' he said, shrugging apologetically, 'I don't drink milk.'

'Oh . . . right.' Clem gazed dubiously at the thick black stew in its ugly brown mug, then back at Rufus. 'Thank you,' she added politely.

They stared awkwardly at each other, maintained eye contact for a second too long, then both looked hastily away, each as embarrassed as the other. Clementine was thinking how daunting Rufus Palliser's black eyebrows and grim expression were, pining wistfully after sunshine and taxis, and considering, even at this late stage, bolting down the road to Jean's, then escaping back to London and booking into a hotel. Rufus was wondering how he could make her smile again.

'So why now?' asked Dorrie spooning sugar into her coffee.

'Why now?'

'Why did you wait all these years to come home?'

'Oh, I . . .' Clementine, painfully aware of Rufus Palliser's grey eyes fixed on her face again, became tongue-tied and awkward. 'I . . . er . . .' She should have thought it through. She should have realised this would happen, there must be a dozen people in the village who would remember her. Everywhere she went she was going to be stared at, asked difficult questions; this was merely a foretaste of what was to come. 'I just sort of—'

'Come home?' Rufus began to pay attention to the conversation. 'What do you mean, *come home*?'

'Isn't it time we got on?' Clementine rose abruptly, leaving her coffee untouched. Not now, she prayed silently, don't make me explain now, I'm not ready.

'I think I'm going home,' she'd said, standing in the entrance hall at Norwich Airport with her eyes full of tears. Had she meant here? Rufus set his jaw stubbornly, demanding an answer, Clementine compressed her lips, determined not to provide one, and for the second time they stared defiantly at each other across the table.

Oh dear, thought Dorrie, *not* a good start. 'Now then Rufus,' she said briskly, 'why don't I clear up this mess while you show Clementine round?' She waved at the broken plate and the puddle soaking into the pamments. 'Then you can explain to Clementine what you're wanting her to do.'

Rufus gave in. 'Right . . .' Get your act together man, *concentrate*. 'If you've finished your coffee then?'

Filled with gratitude for the timely intervention, Clementine put everything she had into the smile she gave Dorrie. Rufus, that unaccustomed warmth spreading beneath his ribs again, was seized by a fit of pure, infantile jealousy.

He led the way back along the corridor, hands in pockets, big feet padding silently in his socks. They collected the bags from the front step, then tramped up the wide staircase in single file, Rufus first, carrying the two suitcases and the toolbag, Clementine following with the rest, her stomach churning with apprehension.

'I've put you in here, but you can move if you don't like it.'

The room was spacious, high-ceilinged, with a bay window looking north across the walled garden to the river and Hawe's farm, and a second, smaller window facing east towards the school, both curtained with faded velvet. It had the same deep skirting boards Clem had seen downstairs, covered in the same dark brown lacquer, and a blanked-off fireplace. The walls were papered in an old Liberty print, 'Peacock Feathers', and the floor was of unpolished pine boards, partially covered by a threadbare oriental rug. The furniture was sparse but good quality, an easy chair with prettily turned legs and stuffing leaking from its fat arms, a double wardrobe with a mirrored door, a chest of drawers and a pair of small square tables, one either side of the double bed, which had carved curlicues on its mahogany head and footboards. The bed was neatly made up, by Dorrie, Clementine guessed, with clean sheets, blankets and a flowery eiderdown. It was clean, uncluttered, impersonal, a strange bed in a strange room. Don't panic, she told herself, you can manage this. You have lived in your warm cocoon for far too long; this will do you good. *This will do you good*, she repeated, as if repetition could make the words come true.

'Will you be all right in here?'

Clementine moved across the room to the window. The apprehension in the pit of her stomach had eased a little and the room was neutral, it had no atmosphere, either good or bad, but it had the potential to be lovely. Rufus watched her shoulders rise and fall. 'Yes,' she said. 'This will be fine, thank you.' What was she doing? He had just given her the opportunity to escape and she had let it slip. The panic rose again. Why couldn't she make up her stupid mind?

She followed him back to the landing to go through more bedrooms, some piled high with the jumble of elderly furniture Rufus had bought with the house, one full of trunks and ancient battered suitcases, one littered with curtains, linen and rolled up rugs, another echoingly empty of anything but dead bluebottles and dust, all dingy, depressing. He had chosen the best room for her.

They paced the corridors, examining the faded, peeling wallpaper, the stains on the ceilings where the roof had leaked before Rufus had it fixed. They peered into boxrooms, opened wardrobes reeking of mothballs, cupboards empty but for ancient, yellowing newspapers and scuttling spiders. They stood in the doorway of a small square room containing nothing but dozens of pictures with their faces turned to the wall, and Rufus suggested Clementine choose whatever she liked to adorn her walls. He pointed out the areas of new plaster, the replaced sections of copper and brass, carefully matched to the original pipework which served the fat Victorian radiators, while Clementine ran her fingers along windowsills and mantelpieces, touching, examining. He showed her the old-fashioned bathroom that would be hers, explained, 'I have my own bathroom off my bedroom,' so she would know they were not likely to meet embarrassingly on the landing in their nightclothes, then found himself wondering what sort of nightclothes Clementine Ambrosia Thomasina Lee wore, whether she went in for sexy negligées or favoured shapeless striped pyjamas. He didn't show her his spartan bedroom at the front of the house, and she didn't ask to see.

They made their way down the stairs again, Rufus explaining on the way about the blocked-off wall, not a wall at all, but a window which was finally, after three

years of vacillation on his part, away being repaired by a
stained-glass specialist. Then he led the way across the
hall to show Clementine the handsome panelled dining
room, waving a hand in passing at the servants' quarters,
a rabbit warren of tiny rooms and passages leading off at
right angles through a door beneath the stairs. He took
her back through the kitchen, where Dorrie was dealing
with his damp shoe, to show her the big pantry, all lined
in slate with marble shelves to keep the food cool, and the
wash house where an incongruously shiny washing
machine, a tumble dryer, a fat central heating boiler connected to a spaghetti junction of new pipes and a
capacious freezer sat smug and pristine alongside an
ancient copper and a mangle with perished rubber
rollers. The floor still sloped to the drain in the middle of
the room where the washday suds had been poured
when the house was first built, the past thumbing its nose
at the upstart children of twentieth-century technology.

When they passed through the kitchen again, Ginger
had disappeared, Dorrie was washing up the coffee
mugs and Mary was noisily chasing a blue china bowl
with 'DOG' written on its side around the floor, searching for the last scrap of food. She attached herself,
wagging, to Clementine.

The parlour in which Clementine had sat with Jean,
fidgeting and sniggering amongst the cats, was now
Rufus's office, with reference books and files filling the
alcoves either side of the fireplace, a cracked leather armchair, a big desk in the window covered by a confusion
of papers, and bare floorboards. It was spartan, aggres-
sively male, unwelcoming.

'This is where I spend most of my time,' said Rufus.
He looked around the room and because he was showing it off, saw it for the first time as a stranger might see
it. Its bleak air of impersonality appalled him. Glancing

across at Clementine Lee's face he could see her thoughts mirroring his own and when she turned he caught the sympathy in her brown eyes. You poor man, they seemed to say, what an empty life you must lead if this is the best you can do. 'It's quite cosy when the fire's lit,' he defended himself, and she smiled politely.

'I'm sure it is.'

'I'll show you the library.' He turned abruptly, humiliated, and marched on ahead, leaving her to follow.

Clementine, trailing obediently in his wake and trying to avoid Mary, who somehow contrived constantly to be under whichever one of her feet was descending to the floor, was waiting for another opportunity to tell him she was not staying.

There was just too much to put right. It was not, she thought as she danced a jig across the hall with Mary bouncing energetically in and out between her legs, the amount of work required to make the place sound, the major repairs had already been done, and perfectly competently judging by the patches of fresh pink plaster, the replaced floorboards, the new plumbing and wiring. It was the indefinable air of defeat that hung over everything, the sense of a task abandoned in despair. She was finding the atmosphere profoundly depressing, and she didn't need any more depression just now.

'The library.'

It faced east, towards more overgrown garden and the gable end of a dilapidated open-fronted cart lodge, under the shelter of which an ancient white van was parked. Clementine laughed out loud when Rufus stepped back and ushered her in.

The light from the uncurtained window illuminated the chaos. Leather and cloth, paper and board, the room seemed to be drowning in books, sinking beneath a sea of words. There was no order to it, old was mixed with new, tall columns of cheap paperbacks piled askew on dusty gold-tooled leatherbound tomes. The oak shelves lining the walls were stacked with more random volumes, large and small, thick and thin, cheap and expensive, the few pieces of furniture were almost obliterated beneath tons of literature.

'I use it as a storeroom,' Rufus excused the shambles, annoyed by her laughter. 'I bought the house partly because of this lot.' He waved a big hand in front of her and Clementine, feeling the wind of its passing, flinched. Rufus folded his arms across his chest out of harm's way, then continued, trying to explain what he did for a living. 'You have to take what you can, you see, you might only be after one book but sometimes you have to buy a dozen or a hundred to get it. That's partly why I started the bookshop, as an outlet for all the surplus stuff. Some are auction lots, or junk dealers' bargains, some are from house clearances. I get asked by people to look at Granddad's books, or Auntie Vi's collection of priceless first editions. Most of them turn out to be worthless, but you spend hours on your hands and knees in other people's attics, or crawling around in boxrooms, wading through trunks and cupboards on the off chance.' He was aware that he was talking too much, making up for his previous inability to think of anything witty or charming to say, but once again his tongue rambled on without him. 'Actually, most of these books were already here. I bought them with the house because I thought there might be something worth having . . .'

'And was there?'

Rufus shrugged. 'I don't know, I haven't started investigating yet. Get off, Mutt!'

Mary was mountaineering across the piles of books, tail waving, tongue hanging out, panting with enthusiasm.

Clementine clapped her hands. 'Here,' she called encouragingly. 'Come on, Mary,' and Mary sidled back to her, her rear end gyrating with pleasure. 'How long have you been here?'

Rufus, unaccountably annoyed by her success with his dog, and interpreting the question as a criticism, answered tersely, 'Three years,' then led the way back to the hall without another word. Clementine bent to caress Mary's shaggy ears and stuck her tongue out at his back. The man was as prickly as a porcupine, and it was time to tell him she was not staying.

'That's about it,' he said, waiting for her at the door. 'You can see roughly what there is to do.'

Clementine straightened up and took one last look around. It was a shame. If it hadn't been so depressing she might have stayed; the possibilities were endless . . . 'I don't see how you can hope to do it justice in six months—' she prevaricated.

'I'm not after a complete restoration job, I just want it cleaned up, a bit of paint slapped on so I can get my money back.'

He sounded so defensive, so angry, that Clementine's stomach churned with alarm again and she moved past him towards the sunshine she could see through the open front door, anxious to get away.

'Look, Mr Palliser—'

'Rufus.'

'Look, Rufus, I think I should tell you before we go any further, I—'

'I know, you're an interior designer. The woman at the agency told me. And I told her I was looking for a housekeeper and a handyman. I took you on because she said you could turn your hand to anything and you needed a job, and whilst I realise you must be looking at this as one of your projects that's not what I want . . .' He followed Clementine's lead, staring out at the afternoon sun slanting low across the weed-infested drive. I just want to walk away, he thought, stop pretending that putting all this right will put me right. He felt terribly, bone-achingly tired. This tall woman, with her mobile face and voluptuous figure, aroused feelings in him he had never experienced before, but his mood had changed, as it always did when he was brought face to face with his own shortcomings, and he didn't want those feelings. He wasn't fit, he reminded himself, to form any sort of relationship with a woman, and while this house continued to confront him with his own mistakes he wasn't going to be.

'We haven't seen in there yet, have we?' It was the only door in the house that was not covered in dark brown lacquer. The heavy panels had a sheen to them that glowed in the dim light.

It took a great effort for Rufus to drag his mind back to the matter in hand. 'It's just the drawing room,' he said dismissively. It was weeks since he had been in there at all, almost three months since he had spent an evening sitting staring morosely into the fire. Doris kept it dusted and he avoided it. Of all the rooms in the house, the drawing room provided the most potent reminder of what he might have done if he had just been able to find the will. He led the way reluctantly back across the hall and flung the door wide. 'This,' he said bitterly, 'is what I started out to achieve.'

Clementine stood in the doorway and stared. The room was breathtakingly lovely, light, elegant, generously proportioned. The mullioned bay windows overlooking the front garden had deep cushioned window seats, stained-glass panels at the top, cream and golden lilies set in azure blue like those in the front door, and folding shutters. The woodwork had been carefully stripped and waxed, the floorboards were polished and scattered with rugs, the furniture was mahogany and rosewood. The fireplace, with its embossed cast-iron grate and handpainted blue, green and gold tiles, was a collector's item, as was the flamboyant rococo mirror above the mantelpiece. The walls were cream, hung with vibrant primitive paintings and rich hangings evocative of faraway places. The deep alcoves either side of the chimney breast, with the exception of one glaringly empty shelf, were lined with books, not like the ones in the library, shoved in any which way, but meticulously arranged, as if their owner cared deeply about them, and on a pretty inlaid table between the windows carved African figures shared space with jade dishes, a lump of glowing amber and a fat miniature buddha fashioned from soapstone. Against the wall opposite the window stood an open roll-top desk with a dozen drawers at the back of the writing surface. Clementine was reminded of Miss Emily, of clicks and fumbles, pennies and sherbet dabs, and she wondered if it was the same one. A pair of big plain sofas faced each other across the fireplace, their plump squabs upholstered in a subtle blue hopsack that picked up the colour in the windowpanes, and a low table made of some sort of oriental hardwood, with delicate open fretwork along its sides, stood between them.

The mix of styles, traditional and modern blending harmoniously with exotic artifacts from all over the world, was perfect, the atmosphere of the room quite different from the rest of the house. Clementine, guessing from its unnatural tidiness that it was rarely used, wondered why Rufus should prefer his coldly impersonal study to this warm, peaceful oasis of civilisation. Rufus, watching the shades of surprise and admiration cross her face, felt that pleasurable heat rise beneath his ribs again and his bad temper subsided. It occurred to him that he had not even provided a television to entertain his housekeeper. Helen had taken theirs with her when she left and he had never bothered to replace it.

Clementine Lee didn't seem to notice. 'Oh,' she said. 'Oh, it's *beautiful* . . .' and she smiled properly at him for the first time, as she had smiled at Doris earlier. Caught by surprise, Rufus gave in, allowed the warmth to flood his bones and smiled back because he couldn't help himself.

It was his turn to catch Clementine off guard – she had forgotten his disarmingly crooked teeth, not noticed the cleft that formed in his cheek when his mouth lifted. It occurred to her that he was younger than she had thought, despite his grey hair and heavily lined face. Rufus Palliser's smile imbued him unexpectedly with the air of a large, rather engaging schoolboy.

'So what do you think? Would you be prepared to help me fix it up?' He could not decide whether he wanted her to say yes or no.

There was a long pause. 'Yes,' said Clementine at last. 'Yes, all right, I'll give it a try.' What am I saying? I must be stark, staring mad! 'On one condition.' Give yourself a get-out clause, don't commit yourself to anything. 'If it doesn't look as if it's working I can go immediately without any hard feelings on either side.'

Rufus felt a rush of exhilaration, decided she had given him the right answer. 'Fair enough,' he said, holding out his hand. 'It's a deal then.'

Clementine, remembering his last crushing handshake, was reluctant, but he held her for only a second, aware in his heightened emotional state how easy it would be to frighten her off.

'More coffee?' he suggested, just for something to say. Mary sat suddenly in the doorway, her tail brushing rhythmically on the floor and began to bark shrilly. 'Now what?'

'Maybe she needs to go out.' Clementine stooped and did what she had been wanting to do for the past hour. She swept the puppy into her arms and made for the hall and the front door, enjoying the feel of the warm wriggling body against her and relishing the long-forgotten smell of ripe dog paws. Mary squirmed and yelped, high-pitched squeaks of enthusiasm, then attacked her ear with needle-sharp teeth. 'Ow,' complained Clem, laughing as she gently detached her. 'That hurts, my love.'

She released her on the steps and watched her lollop down on to the drive. When Mary began to run purposefully in circles, then squatted, clearly just in time, she praised her, 'Oh, good girl, clever girl!' and glanced over her shoulder to see whether Rufus was paying attention. 'There,' she said triumphantly. 'She knows just what to do. She must have been upset before.'

Rufus nodded. He wasn't sure whether to be amused or irritated by the woman's easy usurping of his responsibilities. They stood side by side on the top step and watched Mary nosing at the unfamiliar territory. Rufus, who had been terrified ever since Doris gave her to him that the dog would escape, to be squashed by a car or drowned in the river, shot for sheep worrying or poisoned by a farmer, became alarmed when she trotted off purposefully down the drive.

'Hey!' he called urgently, 'You stupid mutt, *no!*' Mary laid her ears back and continued determinedly on her way. 'Oh, Christ! She'll get run over—'

'Mary, here, darling . . .'

It was an irresistible invitation, a delicious enticement spoken in a soft, husky murmur. Rufus was not in the least surprised when Mary pricked her ears and bounced enthusiastically back towards them, tail wagging furiously.

She skittered up the steps to Clementine's feet, dropped, then rolled on to her back, spreading her legs to expose a tender pink underbelly and begging to be praised. Clementine obliged, squatting on her haunches with her skirt spread around her to scratch the puppy's stomach with expert fingers. Mary's expression became positively beatific. Rufus didn't blame her. If Clementine Ambrosia Thomasina Lee were ever to address him in such tones, he thought, he would probably roll over on his back and beg to be scratched too.

'Right,' he said, dragging himself back with difficulty to the business in hand, 'about that coffee . . .'

'Er, no, thank you.' Clementine swept Mary into her arms and straightened up. 'If you don't mind, I think I'll go and do some unpacking, have a wash.' She smiled, that half-smile again, which promised so much but did not deliver, then reluctantly gave Mary a last caress and held her out for Rufus to take.

'You'd better hang on to her,' said Rufus. 'She seems to have taken a liking to you.' Which makes two of us, I think. He reached out awkwardly and ruffled Mary's untidy head, resisting the temptation to do the same to Clementine Lee. He had not forgotten the feel of her thick hair, or the angry way she had brushed him aside when she had hit her head, the first time they met. Her brown eyes slid away from his. She had clearly not forgotten either. 'Look, I . . .' he began.

'Yes?'

'. . . nothing.'

'Right.'

'Right.'

Rufus watched her cross the hall, hips swaying. Somewhere or other, it occurred to him, he seemed to have mislaid the art of conversation.

*

'So tell me about her.'

'I don't know . . .' Dorrie was dubious. The poor girl might not want everyone knowing her business.

'Look.' Rufus leaned across the table, intent upon information. 'If you don't tell me I'm going to keep putting my foot in it, aren't I? It's perfectly obvious she's been here before, but it's also clear she finds it difficult to talk about it. I don't want to inadvertently say something that'll upset her, do I?'

'Well . . .'

'Did she live here?'

'Oh, no. She lived at Marshmeadow, you know, the other side of the school.'

'So why did she leave, how long ago, do her family still live there?'

Dorrie blew loudly on her coffee and demurred. 'I don't know as I should tell you anything without her say-so . . .' Anyway, where to start, what to tell, without intruding into Clementine's private business?

'Perhaps I should ask her then . . .?'

The threat had the desired effect. Dorrie stirred her coffee, sucked her spoon, then laid it down and nodded. 'All right,' she said reluctantly. 'But you make sure you keep it to yourself. I don't want her thinking I've been talking behind her back.'

'I swear,' Rufus promised. 'Cross my heart and hope to die.'

Dorrie frowned at him, suspecting him of taking the mickey. 'Ambrose Lee, Clementine's dad, was a gent, everybody said so, but they were a very . . .' she paused, trying to think of a way of putting it, '. . . a very *self-contained* family, if you know what I mean, private. He owned the Auction Rooms on the Cromer Road, Thomas Lee and Son, although it's run by someone else now, his brother sold it after . . .' Rufus knew the place she meant.

He had attended auctions at Thomas Lee a dozen times, had even bought Manor Hall because of it, indirectly. 'Ambrose was "and Son", see, took over the business from his father, being the eldest. There'd been Lees in the village as far back as anyone could remember, and Clementine was born at Marshmeadow. Her mum was a nice woman too, a bit reserved, but she didn't look down her nose, not like some. Adored each other, they did. It was a tragedy all round, specially for poor Clementine.' She and Frank had wanted to go to the funeral, like everyone else in the village, but Mr Lee's brother had taken over the arrangements and they'd been spirited away to be buried somewhere down south. It wasn't right, Frank'd said at the time, folks ought to lie amongst their friends when they went.

'What was a tragedy all round?'

'The accident. Road accident. They'd been on holiday, somewhere foreign, Spain I think it was, Clementine's first time abroad, and they were coming home up the A11 – dreadful road that is, awful – when they skidded on a patch of oil. Clementine was the only one who survived. Mind you, it was touch and go to start with, she was in intensive care for nearly a month . . .' No, Jean'd said when she returned from a fruitless mission to the hospital, they hadn't let her see Clementine, she had head and hip injuries and they weren't allowing visitors. Jean was really shaken up by it all, Dorrie had never seen her so upset. '. . . And then as soon as she was well enough to be moved she was sent to a hospital in Hertfordshire, to be near her uncle's family, so they said—'

'They?'

'Eh? Oh, Jean and her dad. Jean Hawe, Robert's wife from the farm, you know, him my Frank works for, she was Jean Smith then, the vicar's daughter, and her dad was called in early on – he was the only one allowed to see Clementine when they thought she was going to die. Jean and Clementine were best friends, see . . .' She was going to be all right, Jean had assured Dorrie when she asked her in church one Sunday, but she wasn't ever coming back. 'And after she came out of hospital she went to live with her uncle—'

'How old was she then?' Rufus imagined a child.

'Sixteen – she had her sixteenth birthday in hospital. After she moved, Jean was the only one that kept in touch.' Dorrie had often wondered whether it was deliberate, young Jean keeping Clementine so fiercely to herself. It was a small community they lived in, everyone knew everyone else's business and maybe, she guessed, Jean needed a bit of a life outside the village, something to escape to. Robert Hawe was a nice enough chap, but a typical dour Norfolk farmer, took after his father Geoffrey, who had never been known for his jollity. When Clementine didn't even come home for Jean and Robert's wedding the rest of the village gradually lost interest. '. . . And she's never been back since, till now.'

Oh yes she has, thought Rufus. I think I'm going home, she'd said and her eyes had filled with tears. 'Brave,' he said, talking to himself, 'to go back to the place where you lost everything.' He couldn't do it, couldn't go within a bloody mile.

'I don't know.' Dorrie tested her coffee, then helped herself to more sugar. 'This was a good place to grow up in, she must have some happy memories of the village. And it's not as if it actually happened here, is it?'

Rufus moved across to the range to refill his mug. It makes no difference where tragedies happen, he thought, you take the consequences with you wherever you go.

'So why has she come back? Why isn't she decorating houses in London? That's what she does for a living, you know, she's an interior designer. Why isn't she married with two-point-four kids?'

This was going too far for Dorrie. 'I don't know why,' she said disapprovingly, 'and I won't ask. If you want the answer to that one you'll have to ask her yourself.' She drained her mug and folded her cardigan over her bosom with stubborn finality. 'Now, if you don't need me any more, I'll be off. Frank'll be wanting his tea.'

Rufus apologised awkwardly. 'I wasn't prying, I just didn't want to . . .'

'You said. I'll see you Tuesday.'

He had made her regret she'd told him as much as she had, Rufus could tell. 'I'm sorry,' he repeated as she retrieved her bag from the table and moved stolidly towards the door. 'Thanks, Doris.'

'You're welcome.' She sounded slightly mollified. 'Now I've left you a stew in the fridge. Don't forget to pop it in the oven, she won't want to cook tonight, she'll be tired.'

'Yes Doris.' I will endeavour to behave like a civilised human being, if I can remember how.

Dorrie paused on the bridge to look across at the village school. The asphalt in the playground was sprouting weeds, the swings were already turning red with rust and the brickwork beneath the sagging gutters was growing a fine covering of green algae. All six of Dorrie's kids had been educated there, as had Clementine until she was nine. She moved on, shaking her head. That party had been a great ordeal for the famously private Ambrose Lee.

Clementine stood out from the others right from the start. Large, plain, too sensitive for her own good, she moved up through the school in the same class as Jean Smith and Sandra Medler until some of the boys started making jokes about her height, calling her Giant Wimbleweather after the kind but stupid giant in the C.S. Lewis book they'd been reading in class. Poor Clementine was an easy target, head and shoulders above the rest of them – not surprising with both her parents being so tall – and clumsy too. It hadn't mattered to begin with but it grew worse as she got older, as she began to develop and the boys became more competitive. They didn't like being looked down on and she disturbed them with her precociously budding bosom and her rounded hips. It wasn't really malicious, just a bit of teasing that got out of hand, but Ambrose Lee was very protective of his only child.

Everyone knew the Lees had tried for years to start a family before she came along – Mrs Lee had even been to London to see a specialist according to their live-in help, who'd told her friend at the pub who'd told her mum, who happened to be in the Post Office when Geoffrey Hawe's wife came in. The word was all round the village in no time; Dorrie would have hated everyone to know if it'd been her, but she'd had the opposite problem, seemed to fall for another baby every time Frank so much as winked at her.

When they tired of the giant joke, the boys started on poor Clementine's name, belting out the old song every breaktime, '*Oh my darlin', oh my darlin', oh my daarlin' Clementine.*' The line they liked best was, '*and her shoes were number nine*', which was unfair, as her feet were quite small for her height, and the upshot was that Ambrose Lee took his daughter away from the village school and sent her to the girls' convent five miles the other side of Ashington. That made things worse, at least for a while. What with the fancy uniform, and the fact that the Lees had to buy a second car so Clementine's mum could drive her to school, the village kids labelled Clementine snobby and even her best friends wouldn't play with her. Jean was one of the worst, despite her dad being the vicar.

Ambrose Lee solved the problem when his daughter's birthday came round by throwing a party for all the children in the village, with clowns and a huge cake, and games and bunting. They roped Dorrie in to help with the food, and she'd not seen such a spread since Coronation Day. Jean and Clementine were inseparable from that day on, despite their different schools.

Dorrie pottered slowly up the path and round the side to the kitchen door. So now she's ended up right back where she started, she thought. What will she make of it after all these years?

Frank was sitting at the table and the cloth was laid. 'You're late,' he said. 'Tea's mashing.'

'Lovely.' Dorrie dropped her bag in the corner by the door and shed her cardigan, then settled down to enjoy herself, greeting the dog as she passed. 'You'll *never* guess who I've just seen . . .'

Chapter Ten

Clementine declined to eat with her employer, emerging only briefly from her room, accompanied by the dog, to seek him out in the kitchen. 'I'll take it upstairs if you don't mind, I haven't finished unpacking yet and I think I'll have an early night.'

'Whatever you like,' said Rufus, trying to hide his disappointment as he set ungracefully about transferring knife, fork and plate from the table to a tray. He had imagined them sitting cosily together in the warm kitchen while he outlined his plans for the house, had surprised himself by looking forward to her company and hoping he would be able to correct the negative impression he had undoubtedly made upon her. She was probably right though, he acknowledged ruefully, it was much more likely they would have sat in embarrassing silence wondering what to say to each other, or he would have put his great hoof in it by making some stupid remark about her past. When she left the room Mary followed her, tripping over her own feet in her enthusiasm, and he discovered that the two of them had taken his appetite with them.

How had she got over it? How had she come to terms with the sudden, violent death of the people she loved most in the world? Perhaps she could teach him some lessons, if he could only work out a way to ask the question without offending her. He threw the remains of his half-eaten meal into the bin, washed up his plate and poured himself a last coffee. Then he banked up the range, closed the damper to keep it in overnight and took his mug along the corridor to his study to do some work.

For the second time that day he was hit by its bleak lack of comfort. Where had Clementine Lee come from to take this job? What had she given up, and why?

He worked until after eleven, doing his monthly accounts, straining his eyes to pay bills and answer business letters, then dropped his glasses wearily on the desk, put his papers on one side and rose to go to bed. As he made his way across the shadowy hall, he met Clementine Lee coming down the stairs with Mary at her heel. She had changed into a pair of baggy denim dungarees and a thick woollen sweater. She looked big, plain, and Rufus mocked himself for a fool – during the hours since his solitary supper he had been finding it hard to get his new housekeeper out of his mind.

She came to a halt when she saw him and when he greeted her she failed to meet his eye. She looked uncomfortable, embarrassed. If he had not known from her agency details that she was thirty-two years old and long past that sort of thing, Rufus would have thought she was shy.

'What time would you like your breakfast?'

It had not crossed his mind that she might expect to provide him with breakfast. 'Oh, don't worry about me,' he began. 'I've been fending for myself for long enough . . .' Stupid bugger. Let her cook you breakfast, that's what you're paying her for, isn't it?

'Oh, well, if you're sure . . .' She gave in much too

easily, clearly relieved she would not have to face him over the breakfast table. 'What time would you like me to report for work then, eight o'clock, nine?'

As she talked she moved, as steadily as she could with Mary tumbling in and out between her legs, towards the front door. Rufus, drawn to her feet by the antics of the dog, smiled when he saw what she was wearing. Beneath the dungarees she had on a pair of black school-girl plimsolls, and as Mary curvetted around them she made little dives at the laces, tugging and growling. For such a big woman her feet were surprisingly small, almost dainty, and he wondered why he hadn't noticed them before. Impeded with every step, Clementine forgot her embarrassment and began to laugh. Rufus, seduced for the second time by that husky chuckle, wondered how he could possibly have thought she was plain and felt his spirits soar.

'Eight,' he said firmly. 'We'll have breakfast together and we'll decide where to start while we're eating.'

'Oh . . . right.'

He felt her reluctance like a slap in the face, and wondered why he should cause her such unease. Don't be stupid, he told himself, it's bound to be awkward until we get used to each other.

She opened the front door and ejected Mary into the dark with an encouraging pat on her rump.

'Won't she run away?'

'No, she'll come back as soon as she's had a pee. She likes the company.'

'She doesn't like *my* company.'

'Of course she does, you just have to treat her gently, that's all.' Clementine moved out on to the stone step, breathing the sharp night air. She could smell damp grass and, faintly, Robert's muck heap; as she raised her face to the sky a bat swooped low, catching insects. The sharp, pungent smell was delicious, the void above her huge and full of stars, just as she remembered the Norfolk skies of her childhood. Tomorrow, she decided, lifted by a wave of enthusiasm, she would go and see Jean, surprise her. And she would explore the house on her own. Maybe she would be able to persuade her peculiar employer to let her mend its ills properly instead of just patching them up.

When Mary bounced back to her, begging for approval, she was lavish with her praise, picked her up and held her close. Mary yawned hugely, then licked her chin.

'Where does she sleep?'

Rufus moved past her to shoot the bolts on the front door. 'Wherever you like,' he said. 'Take her to bed with you if you want.'

He watched her make her way back across the hall, the dog still cradled cosily in her arms. 'I should be so lucky,' he murmured, visited unexpectedly by a wave of primitive lust. He followed slowly in her wake. Fancying the housekeeper? He had better watch himself.

Chapter Eleven

Clementine was down early the next morning, hoping to beat her employer to it; if she was already at work when he walked in it would be easier, she thought, not so unsettling. But when she pushed open the kitchen door he was already there, dressed in corduroy trousers and a brushed cotton shirt open at the neck, the sleeves rolled up over powerful forearms covered with soft black down. He was clean, freshly shaven and making coffee. He looked quite respectable, except for his thick grey hair, as unkempt as the first time she had seen him. The windows were wide open and the room was full of the smell of cold, early-morning air and strong coffee.

'Oh!' she said, disconcerted. 'Er, good morning.'

'Morning.' She looked bleary-eyed, as if she hadn't slept too well and Rufus was relieved. He hadn't slept well either, had lain awake for nearly two hours feeling ridiculously randy, wondering what Clementine Ambrosia Thomasina Lee was doing in her room at the other end of the landing and what she looked like with no clothes on, which complication was not at all what he had envisaged when he had agreed to take her on.

When Mary bounced up to him, whining with enthusiasm, he bent to pet her, avoiding Clementine's gaze in case his thoughts might be read in his face.

'There . . .' Clementine put her supper tray down next to the sink and made for the back door, swinging it wide to let Mary out. 'Look how pleased she is to see you.' Thank God for small scruffy mongrels, who provide a topic of conversation when you are tongue-tied with shyness and suffering from a wakeful night.

'Did you sleep well?'

'Not really.' It slipped out accidentally, and she bit her lip. Rude, to admit to sleeping badly in someone else's house.

'Why not? Is the bed uncomfortable? I wasn't sure about it when I put it in there, I'll change it—'

'No, the bed is fine, really. It was the clock that kept me awake.'

Rufus paused for a moment, holding the coffee pot in mid-air, then put it down very slowly and said in quite a different voice, thick with strain, unfriendly, 'You mean the cuckoo clock.'

'Mm, the one on the landing.' Clementine couldn't think why she hadn't noticed it when he showed her round the house, a frivolous, chocolate-brown Swiss chalet hanging from the wall along the corridor from her room. It had a steeply pitched roof, jolly, brightly painted carved shutters and window boxes, and it looked completely incongruous amidst all the nineteenth-century gloom. 'It's just that I'm not used to it.'

'I'll stop it.'

Rufus poured two coffees, wrapped his hands round the mugs and brought them to the table. His face was tense, as strained as his voice, and Clementine was left in no doubt that she had struck a tender spot, said something tactless, even offensive.

'No, no,' she assured him hastily, trying to put things right. 'There's no need, really, I'll get used to it in a couple of days. What would you like for your breakfast?'

'Or I can move it if you want me to. Are you sure?' He sounded grateful, relieved.

'Positive,' said Clementine, smoothing prickles. 'We had a grandfather clock when I was a child, and after the – after I left home I used to wake up in the middle of the night, listening for it.' She smiled, remembering the sound. 'I'm sure it was not hearing it that woke me up.'

After I left home. Did she mean after the accident? How could she smile at her loss when he couldn't even bear to think about his?

'After the accident?' he asked nastily, lashing out in a sudden violent spasm of temper.

The smile faded and she withdrew, instantly on the defensive. Stupid great oaf, Rufus cursed himself. What's she ever done to you?

'Sorry,' he began, stumbling over his words, appalled by his own capacity for cruelty. 'Look—'

Clementine turned her back and called to Mary through the open door, buying time while she regained her composure. Dorrie Medler must have told him. She should be grateful, she supposed, it saved her explaining if he knew.

Rufus moved across to the fridge on the other side of the room and bent to stare blindly into the interior, cursing his recalcitrant tongue. She had put her foot in it by accident, he had retaliated deliberately, struck out like a spiteful child. Stupid great oaf. 'Bacon and eggs?' he asked, trying to mend fences.

'Yes. Yes, whatever you like.' Clementine took a deep breath of cold morning air and turned back to face him. If she was going to make this work she would have to be less sensitive. 'But I'll do it, otherwise you've no proof I can even cook.'

Rufus straightened up, eggs in one hand, foil-wrapped bacon in the other, and grinned, still apologising. 'I'll have to show you how to use the range, it's temperamental.'

Clementine grinned back. 'Like you?' she asked bravely and discovered that Rufus Palliser had a sense of humour after all.

He also had the most infectious laugh she had ever heard in her entire life.

Chapter Twelve

Attempting to read his housekeeper's face so he could anticipate her reactions, Rufus discovered during the first few days after her arrival that she could look, depending upon her mood and the light, both exceedingly plain and rather beautiful. Every shade of expression that crossed her features changed them, like clouds racing across a wide Norfolk sky. She had two smiles, a polite, distant one, which curved her lips sweetly enough but did not quite touch her eyes, and a spontaneous one, which seemed to light her entire face from within and stretched her mouth wide, inducing in him, on the rare occasions when it happened, the same sense of wellbeing which had warmed him the first day. So he tired himself out trying to make her laugh, succeeded most of the time only in alarming her. He could tell she thought him extremely odd, almost mad, and on the whole he was inclined to agree with her, wondered if he was indeed going slowly barmy.

In the process of trying to read her face, he discovered other, equally fascinating traits. She would not use his chipped brown mugs, she had her own delicate china, and her own tea, which she produced with a certain amount of diffidence at breakfast on the first morning to make a pale straw-coloured liquid which looked to

Rufus like a urine sample, and which she drank from then on, although she was quite happy to make his thick black brew for him once he had shown her how.

On the same evening, having spent most of the day striding purposefully around the house with a notepad before preparing a more than edible chicken casserole from ingredients she found in the fridge, she left him, despite his grovelling invitation to stay, to dine upon it alone. If he didn't mind, she said, she was going to take the dog for a walk. His offer to wait his meal for her return was politely refused; she had already eaten, she told him, and he was left with no choice but to take the leather lead Doris had given him from the hook on the back of the kitchen door and watch her disappear down the corridor with her faithful companion bouncing at her heels. For the second night running he discovered he was not very hungry.

It was after ten when she returned, he knew because he had spent the entire evening in his study listening for her footsteps on the gravel. She had mysteriously acquired a torch, but she did not vouchsafe any information as to where she had been and merely said 'Yes, thank you,' when asked if she had enjoyed her walk. She must know people locally still, he supposed – who was it Doris had said, her best friend, the farmer's wife? As she passed him in the hall, he smelled the wine on her breath, basked in the genuine, if slightly tipsy smile she bestowed upon him, then turned back to his study as she went on her way, feeling even more dissatisfied than usual with his barren existence.

During that first week she repeated the performance every night, preparing his meal then decamping with the dog to return hours later smelling of wine, or gin, once or twice of garlic and herbs, as if she had been fed as well as watered. It was none of his business, he told himself when the resentment threatened to spill over into snappy sarcasm, but she could have left the dog behind to keep him company. He was in the same position, he thought irritably, as a powerless parent waiting up for a worrisome teenager.

She was quite different with Doris, relaxed, animated, even chatty, and it dawned upon Rufus as he eavesdropped on their conversations that her reserve was quite specific – it was he whom she wished to keep at arm's length. When he entered the kitchen her tea-break reminiscences with Doris came to an abrupt end and she would vacate the room, taking Mary with her. Rufus began to wonder, was she escaping from an unhappy love affair? Had some man turned her against the entire species? Someone had beaten her up the first time he saw her. Was she running away from that someone? Having felt no inclination lately to seek out female companionship, he began to look forward to every fleeting encounter with his large but oddly insubstantial housekeeper, found himself frequently filled with unrequited lust by her mere presence, and occupied most of his spare moments devising schemes to spend more time with her. She neatly sidestepped his every ploy.

He had no cause for complaint regarding her work. Toiling to a constant burble of voices from the radio, *Today, Woman's Hour, The Archers,* even the shipping forecast, she set about performing the tasks he gave her with easy competence and Rufus, who had grown used since Helen's departure to silence and echoing emptiness, found the noise uplifting, was convinced the house approved of the new life Clementine Lee had brought to it.

She talked to Mary while she worked, murmured words of affection and encouragement, strengthening the bond she had already formed with the dog, and only when Rufus hung around did she become flustered. She grew clumsy then, knocked things over, spilled things. Asked to clear the bedroom across the landing from hers so it could be swept and a decision made about its future, she performed the task with swift efficiency, hauling heavy furniture along the corridor without assistance while he was out, then banishing Mary to the walled garden before proceeding with a broom, and a scarf tied over her face like a Wild West outlaw, to throw open the windows and whip up a dust storm of major proportions. It was when they came to decide what to do with the room, a task which involved sitting down together and talking instead of doing, that she began to display signs of unease; Rufus found himself speaking more slowly than usual, folding his arms across his chest instead of waving them around as he normally did to make his points, asking her opinion instead of imposing his own. He discovered in passing that once he had got her on to the subject of the house she became animated and decisive, leaning across the kitchen table to draw finger pictures on the warped wood and glowing incandescent with enthusiasm. When she looked like that he became so distracted, watching her mobile mouth and trying to control the thoughts that flooded unbidden into his head, of kisses and explorations . . . he almost forgot what they were supposed to be talking about.

'Just let me have a go at this one room,' she urged, fixing him directly (a rare occurrence) with those brown Jersey-cow eyes, 'and if you don't like it when I've finished, then we'll think again. I promise I won't go over the top. I'll just make it look a bit more cheerful . . . Well?'

'All right.' Rufus capitulated because he was busy wondering what she tasted like, how her skin smelled close to. 'Do as you please. But nothing fancy, I can't afford it.'

'I promise I won't go mad,' she repeated.

No, thought Rufus, gulping coffee to calm himself down, but I probably shall.

She rose from the table, aiming for the door and an evening at Jean's. 'Thank you,' she said, and smiled hugely, as if he had just given her a gift. Rufus, feeling as if it was he who had received the present, beamed back, causing her visibly to withdraw. He had, he thought, left alone in the kitchen once more, definitely lost his touch.

Rufus Palliser had been rather successful with women when he was younger. At university his tall athletic figure, his long-lashed grey eyes and his thick black hair had turned heads in the refectory, led to scrums in the lecture hall as girls vied to sit next to him. He had, he discovered to his initial delight, become an object of desire and he made the most of it.

But by the time he dropped out at the end of his second year, giving up his degree to concentrate on the book collecting which was rapidly taking over his life, Rufus was convinced there was something seriously wrong with him. He was getting as much sex as he could handle, sometimes more, but as his contemporaries began to pair off and settle down, the conviction grew that he was somehow missing the point of the mating game – so far he had found no one with whom he could remotely imagine wanting to share the rest of his life.

Brought up in a house where parental affection was notable only for its absence, he found it difficult to be demonstrative, failed completely to grasp the etiquette of love. The self-confident young women with whom he conducted his liaisons puzzled and intimidated him; when females little more than half his size tried to change his haphazard way of life, took it upon themselves to organise him into conformity, or attempted to browbeat and bully him into declarations of intent he was not ready to make, he felt immediately trapped, would panic, dump them and move on. The word quickly spread around the circles in which he moved that Rufus Palliser was a cold, calculating heartbreaker. The inevitable scenes with which his affairs ended, with accusations of selfishness and arrogance, frequently outweighed the pleasure he had gained during them, but confusingly the more his reputation as a Casanova spread, the more the women flocked, each one convinced that she alone possessed the secret of taming the untameable.

And then Helen stumbled into his life. Helen was completely different, there was the boy, with all the problems, the delights, associated with him and somehow things just seemed to fall into place . . .

They met on Liverpool Street station, at the ticket barrier. Rufus, in London on business, was impatient to get back to Norwich and Helen was holding up the queue, blocking the gate with a bursting suitcase and a carrycot, struggling to find her ticket while clutching a wailing baby and trying to rescue the bag full of paraphernalia which had upended itself at her feet. She was crying, big shiny tears rolling unheeded down her cheeks, and when Rufus offered to hold the baby she thrust the child at him without a word. She looked completely desperate.

Rufus had never held a baby before. He was fascinated by the milky smell, the tiny fists the child waved in the air as he settled him within his arms, the way the button nose puckered as his temporary charge filled his lungs in preparation for more deafening yells. When Helen finally located her ticket and took her son back, he relinquished him reluctantly, then carried Helen's belongings along the platform for her, stowed them in a corridor compartment and sat down beside her to listen as she off-loaded her misery. She told him later it was because he was a stranger that she found it so easy to talk to him.

She was going home, she said. Her boyfriend had walked out on her and she couldn't manage on her own. The boy cried all the time and she had been evicted from her flat because the other tenants had complained about the noise. Her mother, who had never liked her boyfriend and had disapproved of her moving in with him, was preparing to make her life a misery when she got home, and had wasted no time in pointing out that she had known all along he was no good. As Helen talked the tears continued to roll down her face and she blew her nose, loudly and frequently, on Rufus's increasingly sodden handkerchief.

She was reading Modern Languages at London University, the child had been an accident and the boyfriend had tried to persuade her to have an abortion, had never really forgiven her when she'd refused. Rufus was shocked, had always been careful himself, and couldn't understand how anyone could contemplate killing a helpless unborn baby.

Helen was tiny, coming up barely to his chest; she had lustrous blue eyes and soft brown hair and she made him feel strong, in control. When, a spur-of-the-moment gesture as the train pulled into Norwich's Thorpe station, he offered her the spare room in the small terraced house he was renting off the Unthank Road, for as long as she needed to stay, she accepted with alacrity; anything, she said, was better than going home.

She brought out a protective instinct in Rufus he had not known he possessed. She was only twenty-one, young for her age, and unlike all the other clever, efficient, liberated young women he had been involved with until then, she did not remind him even remotely of his mother.

He took her home, stopping on the way to pick up tins of powdered SMA milk, zinc cream and talcum powder. Helen mixed a feed, filling Rufus's tiny kitchen with the sickly smell of baby formula, then changed the boy's nappy and slumped in tears on the sofa beside her son, exhausted. When Rufus offered to feed the child, by now purple with rage and hunger, she handed him over without a word and promptly fell asleep. She was suffering from postnatal depression and she simply couldn't cope.

The moment Rufus took the boy in his arms he was hooked. He had never been in close contact with such a vulnerable human being before, stared, mesmerised at the small face as the child, quiet at last, suckled greedily on his bottle and examined him with indeterminately grey/brown eyes. He was only seven weeks old and soon they would turn a definite blue, like his mother's.

Right from the beginning, even though the boy was not his, Rufus seemed to have the knack of soothing him, but Helen spent her time either crying or sleeping and he had to learn the hard way what to do. He went to Mothercare, his huge frame and palpable ignorance causing tittering enjoyment amongst the teenage assistants who served him, and bought a baby sling so he could carry the boy about with him, then set off for the city library to consult Dr Spock and any other childcare experts he could find, discovering on the way that once the boy was strapped, bouncing gently, to his chest, he was as quiet as a dormouse.

He sat awkwardly in the reading room, sideways on to the table, trying to decipher the diagrams, boning up on nappy rash, infant thrush and cradlecap, while his charge watched him wide-eyed from below. When he smiled at him, the boy beamed back gummily and he was completely smitten, fell in love not with Helen but with her son, in Norwich City Library on a dull Thursday afternoon.

It was then he decided; his orphan family, as he thought of them, were going to need him around. He would put his book dealing on hold, be there all the time until they could manage without him. Helen, struggling with her disobedient hormones and the aftermath of a disastrous relationship, was overwhelmed by his dedication, clung to him as the only fixed, reliable point in a terrifyingly unreliable universe.

It was during those first months that Rufus, his finances becoming stretched to the limit, began to look for suitable premises. A second-hand bookshop seemed the perfect solution; it would provide a steady income without the necessity for all the travelling he had been doing over the past few years. He was responsible, for the first time in his life, for someone apart from himself and he found the sensation exhilarating, exciting.

It was over eighteen months before he and Helen slept together, and the boy was already walking. When Rufus asked her to marry him, because the step seemed to be a natural progression, Helen said yes because she couldn't imagine managing without him.

They would move, Rufus decreed, now they were a proper family. Children needed space to grow and his tiny terraced house, already stacked to the rafters with books, was too small for three people. She would house-hunt, Helen volunteered, while he was working, and Rufus, encouraged by her enthusiasm, agreed without hesitation when she appeared one day in the shop with the boy sleeping in his pushchair, and told him she had just signed a lease on the 'perfect' house. It was time she made some decisions for herself, after all.

The boy was nearly two by the time they moved, and into everything. Rufus had thought, without really discussing it with her, that Helen would want what he wanted for him – a place in the country with a garden and space to breathe. Her 'perfect' house turned out to be a suburban box off the Earlham Road, a few hundred yards from the university. It had sliding patio doors and nylon carpets, violently patterned wallpaper, a tiny garden and close neighbours on three sides; Rufus hated it on sight. The boy, terrifyingly mobile, had to be watched every second, the garden was unfenced at the front and the road outside dangerous. Helen seemed unperturbed. She liked it, she said stubbornly, if she decided to go back to college it was within walking distance and there were plenty of other children around for the boy to play with. Finally beginning to emerge from the depression that had held her captive for so long, she was eager to take charge of her life again and her first action, the day they moved in, was to enrol at the university for evening classes. Rufus channelled his frustration into a flurry of buying, then stored the resulting piles of books at home because there was no room for them at the shop, until they seemed to have less space than they had had before they moved.

The resulting chaos, as Rufus tried to juggle work with child rearing, infuriated Helen. How could she concentrate, she demanded, in the midst of all this mess? They must move again, she announced, asserting herself again, and they must buy – it was time they had a place of their own. They must look for somewhere more practical, less cramped. As if, thought Rufus sourly, the house had been his choice in the first place.

That was when things first began to go wrong between them, but it wasn't until later that the situation became insupportable. Rufus blamed himself for making a spur-of-the-moment decision about Manor Hall without consulting her, but losing the boy, before they could even move in, made things infinitely worse.

It wasn't until nearly a year later, a year during which they were forced to re-examine their relationship, that they both realised there was nothing left, that maybe there had never been anything there in the first place.

It was over two years now since Rufus had parted company with his wife. Since her departure he had reverted to the pattern of his student days, picking up, then dropping, a succession of more or less forgettable women, unable to handle anything more emotional than a brisk, uncomplicated fuck.

Over the past couple of months he had given up even these shallow pleasures, and by the time Clementine Lee arrived at Manor Hall he had just about settled for the life of a recluse.

Chapter Thirteen

Clementine sat in Jean's cramped kitchen, sipping from a glass of red wine and half-listening to the television mumbling in the corner. Eddie sat next to her, his plump legs tucked under his bottom to make himself taller, leaning heavily against her arm. He was having trouble staying awake.

'So tell me what he's like, this boss of yours,' demanded Jean, peering into the pot in which her stew was bubbling.

'Peculiar.' Clem put her glass down and shifted on her chair to accommodate Eddie's weight. He jerked upright and she smiled at him. 'All right?' she asked.

'Peacoolier,' repeated Eddie. 'Who's peacoolier?'

'No one!' said Jean sharply. 'Time you got your pyjamas on young man, it's way past your bedtime.'

Eddie struggled awake, limbered up for an argument. 'But Mummeee . . .!'

'If you get ready for bed right now, I'll read you a story,' offered Clem. 'How would that be?'

'Yeah!' Eddie unfolded his legs and beamed at her. 'Postman Pat, Auntie Clemmie, the snowy one.'

'All right, but only when you're in your pyjamas.'

'I's gone.' Eddie fell eagerly off his chair, disturbing Mary who was lying, dreaming hard and twitching, at

Clementine's feet. Mary yelped with alarm and dived for cover between Clementine's knees, eyeing Eddie with suspicion.

'Well, go on then.' Jean was growing impatient.

'What?'

'What's so peculiar about him? – Eddie, go to bed! – Is he merely the mad professor type, or something more alarming? – *Eddie*, I said go to bed! – Is he going to bite your neck in the middle of the night *à la* Dracula? – Thank you, about time too, and shut the door behind you – Should you be stockpiling cloves of garlic and crucifixes? Or have you discovered the grisly remains of his six previous wives in a locked room in the attic?'

Clementine laughed. 'Nothing so sinister. He's just . . .' How to describe Rufus Palliser? 'He's just so *odd*. One minute he's all smiles and the next he's descended into some private hell, all black scowls and silence.' She thought for a moment, then added decidedly, 'and he's too big.'

'I should have thought you of all people would be able to cope with a big man.'

Clementine shook her head. 'Not any more, I'm not used to them any more – it's intimidating.' She finished her wine in one gulp then leaned across the table to pour herself some more.

'All right, so what else is eating you?' Jean added salt, then replaced the lid on her stew, moved it across the hob to simmer and joined Clem at the table. 'You've got your knickers in a right old twist about something. Tell your Auntie Jean all about it.'

Clementine fiddled with her glass, running her finger round the rim, fishing an imaginary speck of cork out of the wine. 'I've got to go into Ashington with him tomorrow. He says I ought to learn to drive his van.' When she looked up Jean was waiting for her to expand.

'So?'

'So . . .' She couldn't explain it. There was the usual apprehension about driving a strange vehicle, but there was too the added complication of sitting in a confined space with Rufus Palliser, who made her feel awkward and uncomfortable even at a distance, while she was doing it. Just the thought of it was making her nervous. She shrugged her shoulders, dismissing the problem. 'It's only me and driving, you know what I'm like. How long till supper? Have I got time to read Eddie's story?'

'Ages, Robert's still bedding down the calves, and don't change the subject.' Jean examined her friend with renewed interest. 'You fancy him or something?'

'Don't be daft!' Clementine was indignant. 'He's years older than me!' She took another swig at her wine. Of course she didn't fancy Rufus Palliser. He was much too weird for her. The trouble was she still missed London, and Jonathan. She had left in such a hurry. Maybe she should phone him, just to make sure he was all right . . . She sighed.

'Auntie Clemmie . . .' Eddie's piping voice drifted down the stairwell.

'Coming.' Clementine rose smartly from the table. 'Trouble with you, Jean Hawe,' she said, making for the door with Mary, nervously eyeing the tabby cat asleep on the top of the television, trotting close at her heel, 'is you've got a vivid imagination.'

Jean made a face at her departing back. 'Oh yeah? Well, we'll see, won't we, whether I'm right or not. We'll see.'

Time to pay a visit to Manor Hall, she thought, gauge for herself what the set-up was. Ever since the previous week, when Clem had turned up so unexpectedly on her doorstep towing that scruffy mongrel behind her and beaming like the Cheshire Cat, she had been even more evasive than usual. Jean still hadn't got over the fact that she had plucked up the courage to come home at last, and there was something her friend wasn't telling her. She felt a niggling resentment, told herself not to be silly. Clem would put her in the picture in her own good time.

She wondered in passing how much washing Eddie had done.

Chapter Fourteen

'Here,' said Rufus, handing Clementine the keys, 'you drive.'

His van was sitting, no, *lurking*, thought Clementine resentfully, at the foot of the stone steps, but he had done the difficult bit, backing it out of the cart lodge and bringing it round to the front door where she was waiting. It was a mess, inside and out, white with brown patches of rust along the door sills and round the headlamps, tatty bucket seats fraying at the edges, plastic trim peeling along the doors and windows. There was a large, clean blanket neatly folded in the back, 'for wrapping books'.

He took up, or so it seemed to Clementine, every square inch of available space. Sitting side by side they touched shoulders, and every time she moved her arm she brushed against his sleeve. His knees occupied more space than any pair of knees had a right to, and his head touched the roof. She stalled the engine twice before they were halfway down the drive, and again as she turned on to the road. She took the winding lane out of the village at funereal pace, and Rufus, who had expected the same quiet competence from her driving as she displayed when cooking or clearing bedrooms, folded his arms across his chest and stared fixedly out of the window, trying hard not to laugh.

Clementine was aware of his silent amusement; it made her worse. 'Sorry,' she attempted to justify herself. 'I haven't driven for ages . . . the gears are a bit difficult . . .' Then, as the wipers began to sweep ponderously back and forth across the dry windscreen, squealing loudly, 'Oh! . . . No, oh, I was looking for the indicator!' When she managed, whilst attempting to turn the wipers off, to activate the indicator, the screenwash and the horn all at the same time, then took both hands off the steering wheel and yelped in alarm, Rufus choked.

'Oh!' she wailed. 'Look, wouldn't you like to drive? I could watch you for a while, couldn't I, just to see where everything is . . .?'

She turned her head briefly, begging him to let her off the hook, and Rufus, making a desperate effort, managed to straighten his features sufficiently to meet her panic-stricken gaze and say soothingly, 'You're right, should have thought of it myself.' He reached across and tweaked the steering wheel just in time to prevent them running up the bank, then suggested mildly, 'There's a passing place coming up, pull in there and we'll swap.' He wondered, watching her tumble out of the driver's seat as if the devil was after her, about the accident. Does she remember it? Is that why she's so nervous? Then irrelevantly, what are her legs like inside those shapeless dungarees?

Once safely ensconced in the passenger seat, Clementine began to recover. 'I'm sorry,' she apologised again. 'I'm not usually that bad, it's just that it's a strange car . . .' She met his eyes, registered the sympathy and looked hurriedly away. 'It's nothing to do with the accident,' she said defiantly. 'I don't get much practice, that's all.'

Rufus put the van into gear and pulled away. 'I'm surprised you had the nerve to learn to drive at all,' he said, thinking aloud. 'Takes guts after something like that.'

There was a heavy silence before Clementine replied. 'Is Kerrison's still in business?'

Rufus followed her lead. 'It's probably not altered much since you left. What was it you wanted, Gyproc?'

'Mm, and Sugar Soap or Nitromors, so I can strip the skirting boards. Although if you'd rather I can just paint them white.' She shifted in her seat, moving as far away from him as space would allow, and continued talking for the sake of it. 'The Victorians would've laughed at our enthusiasm for stripped pine. They thought it was cheap and boring. It'd be perfectly authentic to paint all the woodwork if you'd rather, it's just that the drawing room's been stripped already—'

'Strip it,' said Rufus equably, surprising himself by not minding. 'I've already said you can do what you like, within reason. As long as it doesn't take too long.'

'Is there any reason why it all has to be finished within six months?'

Rufus shrugged. 'Only that I'll run out of money to pay you.' And I don't want it hanging over me any longer.

'But you're paying me less than if you'd employed a couple . . .?'

'I have to make allowances for your ambitious plans,' said Rufus drily.

'Oh.' Clementine settled back in her seat and frowned at him. 'If you don't want me to—?'

Rufus waved dismissively, a dangerous manoeuvre given their cramped surroundings, and shrugged again. 'I've already said, you can do what you like. But only with that one room. We'll see what it costs and how long it takes, and then I'll decide where we go from there.' He replaced his hand on the wheel, slowing down as they approached the main road. 'That doesn't mean I've given you carte blanche to do as you please with the rest of the house.'

He brought the van to a halt at the junction and turned to look at her. She was staring out of the window and he wondered if she had registered what he'd said.

'Okay? Clementine?'

It was the first time he had called her by her Christian name. It sounded curiously intimate in the confined space.

'Yes?'

'I . . .' Rufus's mind went blank. He sat with his hands resting on the steering wheel, racked his brains to think of something intelligent, or even something stupid, to say, then gave up, pulled out on to the main road and pushed his foot down on the accelerator. Clementine turned away to resume her perusal of the countryside, and the rest of the journey was conducted in uneasy silence.

Rufus parked in the square and they went their separate ways, Clementine striding across the cobbles to the hardware store, Rufus meandering in the other direction to the optician. As he sat in the dark, watching red and green lines and spots of light, listening to the clicks and clacks as the optician tried out different lenses and the *tut-tuts* as it became clear that his eyesight had deteriorated markedly in the four years since he had last remembered to have it tested, he allowed his imagination free rein and determined to find out more about his housekeeper. By the time he rose to leave, having carelessly chosen the first pair of spectacle frames he was offered and arranged to pick them up in a week's time, he was hungry. He could kill two birds with one stone, he decided, eat and interrogate Clementine Lee at the same time.

He took her to the Buck, on the other side of

Ashington, and got nowhere. She allowed him to buy her a half of bitter, but she refused to join him in the hot meals written up on the blackboard (the only ones, he realised, annoyed, that he could read), ordering ham sandwiches from the printed menu and paying for them on the spot. When Rufus, irritated by her determined independence, glowered at her, she affected not to notice, although she followed him obediently enough across the room to sit at his usual table in the corner.

'So, why did you come home?' he began without preamble.

'I was looking for a live-in job,' said Clementine, 'and you were the only person prepared to take me on without housekeeping experience.'

Not good enough. Rufus ploughed on. 'But why take a job as a housekeeper in the first place? It must pay a tenth of what you'd get as an interior designer. And why did you have to leave London to find work?'

'I didn't *have* to leave London. I—' Clementine took a gulp at her beer and changed the subject. 'Do you suppose Mary's all right?'

'Of course she is. Why wouldn't she be?' They had left the puppy stretched in front of the kitchen range, exhausted by a morning spent rushing up and down the stairs between them. 'But why did you decide after all this time—' He had worked it out from what Doris had told him. 'Sixteen years, isn't it? Why did you decide to come back now?'

Clementine prevaricated again. 'They're taking ages, aren't they? How long does it take to make a ham sandwich for heaven's sake?' Only when Rufus continued to stare at her, stubbornly demanding an answer, did she volunteer reluctantly, 'The lease on my flat ran out.'

'Yes, and?'

'And what?'

'That doesn't explain why you left your job.'

'Look—' She sounded belligerent now, clearly resented his questions. 'If you're not satisfied with my references you're welcome to check up on me. I'm sure Jonathan will verify my competence.'

'Who's Jonathan?' asked Rufus.

'Jonathan Harris, my last employer. He supplied my references, remember?'

'What have your references got to do with anything?'

'You just asked me—'

'Why you left your job.' Rufus scowled at the waitress, who had appeared with straw mats and cutlery wrapped in red paper napkins, leaned forward impatiently the moment she had finished laying their places. 'Well?'

'I . . .' Clementine rearranged her table mat, fiddled with the salt and pepper. '. . . staff cutbacks,' she said at last, as if she'd only just thought of it. 'I was made redundant.'

Seeing her increasing agitation Rufus felt his suspicions confirmed. She had been having an affair with her boss. He had beaten her up, she had left him, he had provided her with glowing references to salve his guilty conscience. And she had been forced to run all the way to Norfolk to escape him.

'Was it he who hit you?'

'What?'

'Mine!' growled Rufus at the waitress, as she reappeared with a plate of sandwiches and his steak and ale pie. 'Was it he who hit you?'

Clementine snatched at her plate and knocked over the sugar sifter. 'Oh Lord, I'm sorry,' she apologised, grimacing at her clumsiness.

'Leave it.' Rufus retrieved his knife and fork, wiped them on his napkin, then laid them down beside his plate. 'I should like to know, you see,' he continued, sweeping the mess into his hand and tipping it into the ashtray. 'Because whoever hit you shouldn't be allowed to get away with it—'

'Nobody hit me, I told you—'

'You told me you walked into a door. That's what people always say when they've been thumped.' Not true of course, people made up all sorts of excuses for deliberately inflicted injuries. 'But you don't get that sort of damage from a door, you get it from a fist.' That was true enough. He had known a girl at college whose boyfriend beat her up; her injuries had been identical with Clementine Lee's.

'It wasn't a fist, it was an elbow. And it wasn't deliberate, it was an accident.' Clementine stared fixedly at her plate. 'And if you don't mind, I'd rather not talk about it.'

Rufus opened his mouth to protest. If it was an accident, why had she lied about it in the first place? She hadn't answered any of his questions, hadn't told him any more about herself than he already knew. 'But—' he began.

'How did you come to buy Manor Hall?'

'Sorry?'

'That's all right,' said Clementine, graciously accepting an apology he had not been aware he was making, and she asked the question again, neatly turning the tables on him. Rufus picked up his knife and fork and attacked his pie. Fair enough, he reminded himself, she's as entitled to ask questions as you are. 'I met a man at an auction,' he said. 'At Thomas Lee and Son, to be exact . . .' He waited, hoping for a reaction, but she ignored the provocation. '. . . and we got talking. He'd put some furniture from a house he'd inherited in the sale, and he was waiting to see how much it would fetch.' He took a mouthful of pie, and munched in silence for a while.

'And?' prompted Clementine.

'And I happened to mention that I was a book dealer. He was short of money, he said, probate had taken longer than he'd expected and he'd borrowed heavily against his expectations. The bank was threatening to foreclose and sell the place for what they could get. He asked me if I would come and look his books over, tell him if there was anything worth flogging.' Rufus chuckled, unexpectedly amused by the recollection. 'I took an instant dislike to him, slimy little toad, but I never could resist a hoard of books, so I drove out with him right then, as soon as the auction was over. And of course, when I saw the place—'

'Manor Hall?'

'Manor Hall. The minute I saw it I wanted it. I made him a crazy offer on the spot, contents and all, far more than it was worth, didn't even look at the books, and then found I couldn't get a mortgage for love or money.'

Clementine leaned forward, sandwich in hand. 'So what did you do?'

'I sold part of my inheritance. My grandfather left me a large block of shares in the company he worked for, along with all his books.' Caught up in the enthusiasm he had felt at the time, Rufus forgot he was supposed to be interrogating her and continued. 'I sold the shares to buy the place and borrowed from the bank at a usurious rate of interest to do the major repairs, so I could qualify for a mortgage.'

'So why are you quitting now, without finishing it?'

Rufus balanced his knife and fork on his plate and picked up his beer. 'I've lost the incentive. I thought when I started it would help, having something to aim for, but it didn't.' He took deep draughts, quenching his thirst.

'Sorry, I don't understand, help what?' She was looking straight at him for once, and he was struck by the depth of brown in her eyes.

'I was married,' he said, not mentioning the boy because it was too painful. 'It wasn't working out. I thought Manor Hall would make things better but it made them worse.'

'Oh, I'm sorry.' She sounded genuinely contrite that she had upset him, and Rufus, disarmed, found himself for the first time in three years wanting to talk about it, about the boy. He put his beer down, opened his mouth, then shut it again. Don't, he told himself, you can't burden her with your tragedy – she already has one of her own.

Clementine, as if aware that he was struggling, changed the subject. 'So how did you get involved in selling books?'

The moment passed and Rufus moved on. 'The final parcel my grandfather sent before he died was *Phineas Finn*, by Anthony Trollope, published in 1869 by Virtue and Co. D'you know it? One of the characters is called Palliser – my namesake, Grandpa said – and his last letter set me a challenge, to find the rest of the Palliser novels.'

'Was it a first edition then?'

'Yes and no. Originally it was published as a serial, twenty issues of *Saint Paul's Magazine*, but it was the next best thing, the first hardback edition, bound in two volumes with illustrations by Millais—'

'The Pre-Raphaelite?'

'Mm. He illustrated four of Trollope's other books as well as the twenty drawings he did for *Phineas Finn*, eighty drawings altogether.' Rufus took another draught of beer. 'I found them all in the end, six novels in sixteen volumes, and they set me off on the rest of Trollope's work. I specialise in the nineteenth century now, Dickens, Conan Doyle, George Eliot, Galsworthy. Did you know Rider Haggard was the son of a Norfolk squire?'

'No. Are they the ones in the sitting room?' asked Clementine, remembering the neat rows of leatherbound volumes and astonished by the change in her employer's demeanour.

Rufus nodded. 'They're only in there temporarily, until I've organised the library. They need a constant temperature, you see. They'll go back as soon as it's sorted . . . except for the Palliser novels.' His enthusiasm faded visibly. 'I sold them last month, to a collector; he's coveted them for years.' He pulled a wry face, dismissing the heart-wrenching sacrifice he had had to make to get out of the pit he had dug for himself when he bought Manor Hall. 'I made an old man very happy.'

Clementine stared at him with her head on one side, like a puzzled, bright-eyed bird, he thought.

'Why?' she asked. 'Why spend all those years searching for them and then just let them go?'

Rufus finished his pie and laid his knife and fork together. 'Because it was the only way I could raise the cash to pay you, to do the house up and get out,' he said bluntly.

Clem was appalled. 'But couldn't you have sold something else, some other books?'

Rufus shrugged defensively. 'I could have, but I didn't.' It had been quite deliberate, the choice of his most treasured possessions, an attempt to walk away from the past and rebuild from scratch.

'I don't understand. Selling your most precious books so you can restore Manor Hall and then selling the house too; isn't that a bit like sacrificing your child to keep your home and then knocking it down anyway?'

She had put her foot in it again. 'You don't under-stand!' snarled Rufus angrily and she recoiled, flushed with embarrassment, then half-rose, anxious to escape. What on earth had she said this time?

Rufus rose with her, ashamed of his inability to con-trol his temper, then caught her by the wrist and pulled her roughly down to sit again.

'How do you bear it?' he demanded fiercely, desper-ate to know how she coped so he could use her secrets himself. 'How can you bear to come back here when you lost – when you lost—'

'Do you mean the accident?' She was staring at him in alarm.

Rufus breathed deep, started again. 'How,' he began, picking his words carefully, cursing his unsteady voice, 'how do you deal with the memories? Why don't you find it impossible, living a few hundred yards from the place where you grew up, seeing things every day to remind you of what you've lost?' He tightened his grip, leaned urgently across the table. 'What's the secret?'

'I don't know.' Clementine winced at the pressure being applied to her wrist. 'I'm not sure there is a secret. It took me sixteen years to pluck up the courage to come back, but when I did, I found it was easy.' She hesitated, unnerved by the turn of the conversation, continued reluctantly, 'I had the most wonderful childhood, sur-rounded by love, completely secure, and nobody can take that away, it will stay with me for life. Does that make sense?'

'But what if—' Rufus struggled with the words. 'What if . . .?' He faltered, stopped. You can't ask this, he thought, you can't load this on to her shoulders, you don't even know her. What if you were not entitled to mourn your loss, he wanted to say, how would you live with that?

'You're hurting,' she pleaded, twisting her hand.

'I'm sorry.' Rufus uncurled his fingers reluctantly, noticed for the first time how tightly he had been hanging on to her. 'Oh Lord, I'm sorry.' He frowned at the angry red imprint he had left on her skin, rubbed at the marks to make them disappear, then looked up in time to see her blush rosily at the intimate gesture. 'Should I kiss it better?' he asked, voicing the first thought that came into his head and making things worse.

'No, thank you.' For the second time, with his clumsy attempt to make things right, Rufus put Clementine in mind of a repentant, oversized schoolboy. Inappropriately amused at the thought of herself in the role of stern headmistress, she smiled, a proper, spontaneous smile that seeped right into Rufus's bones, suggested gently, 'I think we've embarrassed each other enough for one day, don't you?' then reached across to pick up his empty beer glass. 'My round, I think,' she said, and rose to push her way out into the crowd, leaving him sitting at the table alone.

Oh, *terrific*, Rufus congratulated himself, wonderful. You handled that absolutely superbly, you great big, stupid wally.

Chapter Fifteen

Clementine worked flat out for ten days, stopping only for brief tea breaks and snatched meals taken on the run. She wondered sometimes what she was trying to prove (and to whom she was trying to prove it) but she kept on, because now she had started she was beginning to enjoy herself and it took her mind off Jonathan and her uncertain future. Stripping paint or rubbing down walls, cooking, chatting to Dorrie, walking Mary the half mile to Hawe's Farm to sit in Jean's kitchen reminiscing, while the television wittered, Eddie cheeked his mother and Jean attended to her with half an ear, was so wonderfully uncomplicated, it lifted her spirits immeasurably. When she was not at Jean's she spent her evenings in her room, reading or listening to the radio: music, discussions, plays, A Book at Bedtime. She had made the right decision, she encouraged herself as September slipped away and autumn began in earnest, taking time out from the rat race to get herself back together.

This is just what I need, she thought as she let Mary out through the heavy oak door at the bottom of the walled garden and followed her along the towpath above the river towards the bridge, making for Lower Dinningham and a supper of sausage and mash, lots of peace and quiet and no pressure.

It was odd though, feeling like a stranger in her own home village.

Since his outburst in the pub she had hardly seen her employer. Most days he went out, visiting his shop in Norwich or attending auctions, even staying away overnight on a couple of occasions, and when he was not at work he seemed to spend most of his time in Ashington, asking her for lists, then heading off in his van and returning hours later, smelling of beer and weighed down with groceries, or packets of Polyfilla, screws and sandpaper, to go immediately to ground in his study.

She was quite happy with his absence – it allowed her to indulge in the illusion that she was renovating the house for herself – and with Mary to keep her company she was less lonely than she had expected to be. On the nights when Rufus was away Mary's warm, heavy-breathing weight on the end of her bed eased the trepidation she might have felt at being alone in such an enormous house, because when Mary took no notice of the creaks and sighs beneath the floorboards, the skitterings and scufflings in the attics above their heads, and the wind soughing past the ill-fitting window frames, she knew it was just the house breathing in unison with its occupants. Even the *cuckoo-cuckoo* of the clock on the landing was becoming reassuringly familiar.

Towards the end of the second week a letter arrived for her, forwarded by Mrs Green at the agency, and her peace was shattered.

'Here,' said Rufus as he dropped the envelope on the kitchen table. 'Your past has caught up with you.'

He poured his coffee, then took his mug and a plate piled high with toast and marmalade and made for the door. Having made a complete fool of himself the previous week he had been studiously avoiding his unsettling housekeeper ever since, in case he put his foot in it again. When Clementine's knock came he was sitting at his desk munching his toast and staring through the window at the pale sun slanting across the shrubbery, wondering where the summer had gone. She made him jump – so far she had kept well away from his study.

'Come in.'

Mary appeared first, squirming with pleasure, and Rufus reached down to stroke her. Funny, he thought, how you could get used to having a dog in the house, hadn't been such a bad idea after all. He raised his head, and the by-now-familiar but still disconcerting warmth began to spread. Much more easily than you could get used to having a woman in the house.

Clementine hovered awkwardly in the doorway.

'Yes?' said Rufus.

'Well, um, it's about my days off . . .'

Rufus sat bolt upright in his chair, horrified. 'My God, why didn't you say? You haven't had any days off since you got here!'

'It doesn't matter, it's only ten days or so, it's just that—'

'Doesn't matter? Of course it matters!' How appalling. How humiliating. How bloody *stupid*. 'Look, I'm a complete cretin. You should've reminded me. I just didn't think, I didn't—'

'I've told you, it's perfectly all right,' Clementine repeated. 'But I would be grateful if I could have this weekend off, if it's convenient.'

'Yes, yes of course. Whatever you like. Take three days, take four, I must owe you four at least!' Rufus's agitation increased as another thought occurred to him, 'Bloody hell, I haven't paid you either!' then manifested itself in a totally unjustifiable display of temper. 'What sort of housekeeper are you anyway, that you can't even remember to demand your wages on time?'

He looked so upset, so ludicrously outraged, that Clementine, already thoroughly shaken by the letter she had just read, began to giggle. Rufus, watching her mouth as usual, felt his irritation evaporate in a rush of pleasure. Is it possible, he wondered, suddenly confronted by a startling idea, that I am falling in love with my housekeeper?

It was like nothing he had ever experienced, this aching sensation beneath his ribs. There was none of the almost fatherly protectiveness he had felt towards Helen when they first met, and neither was he conscious of any particular desire to guide Clementine Lee, to take charge of her, as he had taken charge of Helen. She was too mature, too remote, and she was not at all like his ex-wife. Helen had never possessed a husky, richly infectious giggle either, her laugh was high-pitched, breathless, almost babyish. Clementine Lee's laughter was completely irresistible. Rufus grinned sheepishly at her, acknowledging his status as a fool worthy only of ridicule, then, because he couldn't help it, joined in her hilarity.

He set Clementine off again and Mary, excited by the noise, began to bark shrilly, leaping and pawing at each of them in turn and wagging her tail furiously. Dorrie heard them from the front door.

'Whatever is going on in here?'

Clementine wiped her eyes, clutched her stomach. 'Oh!' she begged Rufus. 'Oh, oh, will you please stop it! It hurts!'

'Sorry, sorry, I can't help it!' Rufus was bent double, roaring with merriment. Dorrie stared from one to the other.

'Just like a pair of four-year-olds,' she said, raising her

voice to make herself heard over the din. 'Having hysterics all over the place. Whatever is so funny?'

Clementine choked on her own laughter and hiccuped. 'It's him,' she accused Rufus. 'He started it, he said—'

'No, I didn't!' Rufus, sobering up a little, protested. 'If you hadn't started laughing I wouldn't have—'

'You said it was my fault you hadn't paid me!' Clementine collapsed again, clapping her hand in front of her face to stifle the whoops and gurgles of enjoyment.

'All right, so what?' Rufus grinned at her, revelling in the exquisite delight of a shared joke. 'I'm a complete idiot. But . . .' He rose from his chair and strode across the room to where Clementine stood, still hiccuping.

He wanted to. If Doris hadn't been there he would have; wrapped his arms round his housekeeper's waist, wherever her waist might be in those ridiculous dungarees, and kissed her hard. Instead he wagged his finger at her in mock disapproval and accused, 'Any housekeeper worth her salt would know to the last penny how much she was owed, and be prepared to demand her money with menaces. You're not a proper housekeeper at all, you're here under false pretences!'

It was meant as a joke, but it fell flat. Clementine went still and her eyes slid away from his. She couldn't help the hiccups, but the fun was clearly, as far as she was concerned, over. Mary, confused by the sudden change in atmosphere, sat back on her haunches and whined.

'So,' said Clementine stiffly, 'that'll be all right will it? If I have Saturday and Sunday off?'

She sobered Rufus up instantly. 'Yes, fine.' He nodded solemnly. 'Yes, of course, take however long you want.' He cast around for something neutral to say, a form of words to put her at her ease again. 'What will you do?'

'I . . . er . . . I thought I might take a trip to London, catch the train on Friday night, if that's okay?' She began to edge towards the door, anxious to get away before he could ask her any more questions. 'I'll make you a stew or something before I go—'

'I'm perfectly capable of fending for myself for two days, I've been doing it for the past two years, for Christ's sake!' Stop it, Rufus berated himself, hearing the snarl in his voice, what the hell is the matter with you? 'I'll give you a lift into Norwich.'

'No! I mean, that's very kind of you, but I can perfectly well get a taxi.'

'I wouldn't hear of it. Anyway, Sal's running low on stock for the shop and I've promised to take some books in. What train do you want to catch?'

Clementine hadn't even thought about it, had not yet made up her mind whether she would go at all. She bent down and clapped her hands, attracting Mary's attention, then scooped the puppy into her arms and buried her face in her soft shoulder. How comforting she smelled. Why couldn't Jonathan have left her in peace? Why did Rufus Palliser have to be so *big*? She straightened her back, determined not to let him intimidate her.

'I'll let you know. Thank you.'

'You're welcome.'

Just for a moment they reminded Dorrie, whose view of the world was permanently coloured by motherhood, of a pair of extra large kids, squaring up to each other in the playground, wanting to be friends but not knowing how to go about it. Rufus's fists were clenched by his sides, Clementine's mouth was set, and they glared at each other defiantly then both looked hurriedly away.

'I'll go and get on,' said Clementine.

'Right,' said Rufus, turning abruptly towards his desk.

'You'll let me know what time, then?'

'Yes, I will.' Clementine stood for a moment staring at his back, then made for the door, stumbling in her impatience to get away. Now what, wondered Dorrie, is going on here?

> *Clem darling,* the hastily scribbled note said, *where are you? Have been round to your place and it's empty. For Sale sign in the front garden and none of the neighbours know where you've gone. Went to the agency but the woman wouldn't tell me anything – not company policy, she said, to divulge clients' addresses, the cow. And it's a Domestic Agency! Clem, what are you doing? Are you out of your mind? I must see you – am contemplating doing something outrageous and gibbering with terror. I promise I won't try to change your mind about us, but please, Clem, at least give me a chance to explain. You don't need to phone me, or give away your hiding place – just send letter or telegram to above address to tell me you'll come. Will pick you up from anywhere in England, Europe, The World. Say you'll come. Please, say you'll come, Clem darling. I need you.*
>
> *Yours for ever, Jonathan   XXX*

Clementine, reading it again in the bedroom she was working on, was swept by a desolation worse than anything she had experienced since her retreat from London. She folded the letter and stuffed it in her pocket, then retrieved it and read the last line again, felt her eyes fill and blur. She didn't hear Rufus, became aware of his presence only when Mary skittered across the bare boards to the doorway to greet his arrival.

'I'm just off to Ashington,' he said. 'I'll get some cash to pay you and I'll do a standing order so I don't forget again. Anything else you need?'

He looked so big and soft, loitering in the doorway in his woollen shirt and ancient corduroy trousers, bending to pet the dog and smiling tentatively as if he was unsure of his welcome. Just for a moment he reminded Clementine of her father, of what it had felt like to be wrapped in the protection of a large male body. She ached to be held, comforted.

'No,' she said, 'nothing, thanks.' She turned her back and brushed at the tear which had chosen that moment to roll humiliatingly down her cheek, then shoved the letter back into her pocket, picked up the sandpaper and attacked the mantelpiece.

Rufus, alarmed by her distress, swooped on the piece of paper which had missed her dungarees and fallen to the floor. He flipped it open, found he could read the large, flamboyantly spiky handwriting, noted the 'darling' and the signature.

'Is he giving you a hard time?' he demanded of Clementine's back. They did that, didn't they, compulsive woman beaters? And they were always full of remorse afterwards but they still couldn't bear to let the object of their obsession go.

'Who?' She turned, saw the letter in his hand and snatched it away from him.

'Look, won't you let me help? You don't have to put up with—'

'Mr Palliser!' Clementine snarled at him, her face distorted, ugly with misery. 'Thank you for your concern, but my private life is none of your business! And if you don't mind, I'm busy!'

She took the sandpaper and swept the mantelpiece with all the force she could muster, then cursed under her breath and sucked her skinned knuckles.

Rufus wanted to put his arms round her, comfort her, but her stance said 'Don't touch, don't come near me.'

He shifted his feet uncomfortably, watched her shoulders hunch to ward him off, then turned and walked away. He was quite sure he had missed an opportunity, that if he had moved a moment earlier, phrased his words differently, she might have let him near, might have let him help.

'Blast,' he swore, as he made his way back down the stairs. 'Blast and bugger it.'

He met Dorrie coming up, carrying a pile of ironing destined for the airing cupboard. 'You all right?' she asked as she passed.

''Course I'm all bloody right!' he snapped. 'Why shouldn't I be?'

Upstairs in the bedroom the questions swirled around Clementine's head. What was Jonathan contemplating? Why did he need to see her? Why couldn't he have just left her alone?

She dropped the sandpaper, leaned her head on her arms and allowed the tears to come.

Chapter Sixteen

Jonathan stood in the Formica and laminated kitchen, with its fussy curtains, brightly patterned cushion-flooring and spotlights on stalks, half-listening to his client complaining about her predecessor's taste.

He had gone completely to pieces this week. It was four days since he had persuaded Mrs Green to forward his letter but he still hadn't heard from Clem. What if she just ignored his plea for help? It didn't bear contemplating.

'So what do you think? Should it be an Aga?'

The woman was anxious. Stripped pine was definitely still in at the moment, but she wasn't sure about Agas, practically *everyone* had one these days, and all these newfangled colours, weren't they terribly, well, *middle-class*? What did Jonathan think?

'Well, do you like cooking?' asked Jonathan, dragging his mind back with difficulty to the present.

'Me?' The woman was shrill with affronted hauteur. 'My dear Mr Harris, *I* don't cook! I have this marvellous little man, *Cordon Bleu* you know, trained under Escoffier or Mosimann or somebody. Now, what about the Aga?'

Jonathan pasted a noncommittal smile to his face and pretended to consider the options. What was the point of

having an Aga if you didn't cook? 'Why don't you discuss it with your chef?' he suggested, adding
maliciously, 'because they are rather expensive you
know, if you aren't really an enthusiast.' He left the
words hanging in the air, knowing which way she
would jump.

'An Aga,' she pronounced, as if she had been sure all
along. 'After all, they do give a kitchen such a *homely* air,
don't you think?'

'Oh, absolutely,' agreed Jonathan. Snobby cow, he
thought, you wouldn't know homely if it came up and
hit you with its hand-crocheted shopping bag. He
sighed. 'Shall we move on then?'

Driving back down the M40 towards London he tried
to picture Clem in some Post Office somewhere. Where
was she, Bermondsey? St John's Wood? Kent, Surrey, the
Scilly Isles? The woman at the agency had been deliberately obtuse when she rang to ask for a character
reference, had prevaricated when he asked what Clem
needed it for, changed the subject. He had obliged of
course, it being the very least he could do under the circumstances, but then, having left Clem for another
interminable week to cool down (foolishly hoping she
would miss him and thus make the task of changing her
mind easier), when he had set out in search of her he had
found her gone, vanished off the face of the earth as if
she had never been. And he *needed* her.

He had not worked out yet exactly how he was going
to plead his case; he changed his mind by the hour.
Sometimes he thought it would be best to gloss over
the personal side of his relationship with Sebastian and
push the money angle instead, play it for sympathy;
sometimes he longed to get it all off his chest, start at the
beginning and tell her everything. Late at night, when
he had eased his nerves with a drink or two, honesty

seemed like the best policy, especially with a woman like Clem, so straight herself, but in the cold light of day he knew she would never be able to accept the unvarnished truth, not if they were to have a future together. The state of abject terror in which he had been living for the past few weeks was rapidly being superseded by a new fear, that the plan he was about to set in train to break free of Sebastian was going to be a waste of time; Clem would ignore his letter and he would never see her again.

He had already told her too many lies, that was the trouble. He had fallen in love with Clementine Lee partly because she was so far removed from the louche existence he had been leading for the past eighteen years and if he told her the truth now, what chance would he have of persuading her to marry him? But then again, he thought, in the early hours of the morning when he was at his lowest ebb, if he didn't tell her, Sebastian almost certainly would.

During the four months of their almost Victorian courtship Clementine Lee had made him feel *clean* for the first time in years, and he simply couldn't bear the thought of losing her.

The bell over the Post Office door jangled loudly to announce Clementine's arrival. As she stepped into the cramped, overheated room and moved towards the stand of cards obstructing the central aisle, the animated conversation which had been going on between the three women at the counter stopped, and an awkward silence fell. As they all turned to stare at her the familiar Alice-in-Wonderland feeling, of being too big for her surroundings, washed over her. She stopped, bending down to make a pretence of examining the sickly homilies inside the old-fashioned cards.

There was a whispered consultation before Madge Dixon asked loudly, 'May I help you?'

Clementine kept her head down and muttered, irritated by the unwanted attention. 'No, I'll wait my turn, I'm not in a hurry.'

'It's all right, these ladies have already been served.'

Clementine risked a quick glance over the cards. Like her shop, Madge looked much the same as she had sixteen years ago; a little more worn, a touch more faded, but otherwise as Clem remembered her, a small woman with a thin, discontented mouth, a sharp nose, drab skin, and enormous, somewhat protuberant blue eyes. She carried a constant air of enquiry about her. When she conversed, Clementine recalled, she always leaned too close, as if she was storing up every word for future use.

'You're the new housekeeper at Manor Hall,' she accused triumphantly now, 'aren't you?'

Clementine pretended she hadn't heard.

'Palliser's place,' Madge explained for the benefit of the customer on her right, a pale moon-faced woman Clementine didn't recognise. 'You must've seen him, Deirdre, the one with the tatty van.' She turned to her left, adding for the benefit of the second woman, a darker, plumper version of the first, 'Actually it was me suggested he try *The Lady*, you know. You get a much better class of employee from those agencies, not like the local paper.' She leaned across the counter, resting her thin frame on her elbows, and raised her voice. 'So, how're you finding it then? I s'pose there must be an awful lot to do to the old place?' Failing once again to elicit a reaction, she turned back to her friends and dropped her voice to confide with relish, 'Of course, it was his wife leaving that started him on the road to ruin, poor man . . .'

She made Rufus sound, thought Clementine, her temper rising, like a drunken down-and-out. 'Excuse me,' she said sharply, 'Are you talking about my employer?'

'That's right, dear, Rufus Palliser.' Madge pursed her lips defensively, scenting disapproval. "Course, I don't expect you'd know much about him, being new.' She turned to Deirdre, justifying herself, as Clementine emerged from behind the cards and moved towards the counter. 'It was obvious from the start she hated the place. Told me so herself in this very shop, right where you're standing now, Deirdre, said she couldn't imagine what had possessed him to buy the *beastly wreck* as she called it, in the first place—'

'Well, I can see exactly why he bought it,' said Clementine tartly. 'But then I suppose not everyone has the imagination to be able to visualise how a project like that will turn out.' She reached the counter and added, in an effort to shame if not Madge, then at least her two fellow gossips, 'Besides, I think people's marital troubles should be private, don't you? It must make things so much worse if you have problems, knowing your neighbours are talking about you behind your back.'

'Oh!' The woman standing to Madge's left had the grace to blush, embarrassed by the unsubtle hint. 'Oh, I agree, absolutely—'

'Clementine Lee!'

Deirdre and her friend exchanged bemused glances – clearly the name meant nothing to either of them – and Clementine's temper slipped again. She fumbled in her coat pocket for some money. 'A first class stamp, please,' she said briskly. Damn Madge's retentive memory.

'You are though, aren't you? I *thought* you looked familiar!' Madge straightened triumphantly, folded her arms over her scrawny chest and dared Clementine to deny it. 'I never forget a face. So, what brings you back after all these years?'

'Earning my living, same as anyone else,' said Clementine, 'and if you don't mind I'm in a hurry.'

"Course you are, dear.' Madge flipped through her folder and produced a sheet of stamps. 'Just the one was it?'

'Yes . . . no.' If I buy enough, thought Clementine uncharitably, I won't have to come back. 'A dozen, and these.' She picked up a writing pad and a packet of envelopes from the counter.

'So . . .' Madge took the money and counted the change from one skinny hand to the other, taking her time. 'Why don't I introduce you? Deirdre Anderson, Susan Barker – Clementine Lee. Funny enough, Clementine, Deirdre was just saying when you came in that she wished she knew a bit more about the history of the village. Deirdre and Susan are in the new houses, where the old vicarage was – you remember, dear, where Jean Hawe used to live. One and Two Vicarage Fields they are now, vast improvement on that draughty old pile.' She beamed at her two acolytes, then passed the change across the counter. 'Clementine lived at Marshmeadow, didn't you dear, till that awful—'

Clem swept her purchases into her hand and turned away. 'Excuse me,' she mumbled as she passed Deirdre's startled face. 'In a hurry!' And she made for the door, escaping before she was forced to listen to Madge dissecting her past in minute detail for the benefit of two complete strangers.

'Of course,' Madge remarked as she reached the card rack, 'Palliser's had that many women in and out of the place you could practically hang a red light on the gate . . .' She waited for the door to close before adding confidingly, 'Not that Clementine Lee's in any danger, of course, far too plain, poor dear. Now, if it was money he was after, that would be another matter, came into oodles, she did, after the accident – did I tell you about the accident . . .?'

Crossing the green with her breath clouding ahead of her in the cold air, Clementine realised she was trembling with rage, and wondered anew if she had done the right thing coming home. She had forgotten Madge Dixon's malicious tongue.

Chapter Seventeen

By Thursday evening there was a pile of doors leaning against the wall in the kitchen corridor.

'It's cheating, I know,' Clementine explained as she handed Rufus a plate piled high with beef stew and mashed potato, 'but it's so much quicker to get them stripped professionally and I've found a place in Norwich that gives a discount if you take in more than six doors at a time.'

'Fine,' agreed Rufus, impressed by her ability to remove and carry downstairs seven heavy panelled doors and two pairs of window shutters without asking for assistance. 'We can take them in tomorrow when I run you to the station.'

'Oh, but there won't be room,' Clementine demurred, 'not by the time you've got all your books in the van.'

Rufus looked blank. 'Books?'

'The ones you're taking in for your shop. I thought you said—'

'Ah, yes. Er, no.' Rufus bent to fondle Mary, waiting patiently below the table in the hope of falling scraps. 'I thought I'd consult Sal first, find out exactly what she needs—'

'But surely you could do that on the phone and save yourself a trip?'

'Er, no, it's much easier to go through the shelves together. Anyway, Sal's expecting me. Have you decided what train you're catching?'

'I have to be at the station just before five, if that's all right?'

'Fine.' Rufus waved his fork at the stew. 'This is delicious. Aren't you having any?'

Clementine hesitated. She had been so busy, cooking for the two days she was going to be away, packing, trying to finish the rubbing down she was doing in the bedroom so she could start on the painting as soon as she returned, that she had not had time to eat before she served her employer as she usually did. She was extremely hungry.

'All right.' She brought a second plateful of stew to the table and sat down reluctantly, as far from him as politeness allowed.

'So, once the bedroom's finished, what will you attack next?' asked Rufus, rising unexpectedly just as she picked up her knife and fork.

'Whatever you like.' Clementine watched him suspiciously as he strode across to reach into the corner cupboard, frowned when he returned to the table with a bottle of red wine in one hand, two unmatched glasses and a corkscrew in the other.

'A bit chilly, I'm afraid,' he apologised. 'But near enough to be drinkable.'

He pulled the cork, poured, then pushed a glass across the table, challenging her to refuse it.

'Here's to a fine restoration,' he said, teasing her. He raised his glass and grinned, felt a buzz of elation when she reluctantly smiled back. 'The library, I think, don't you?'

Clementine, remembering Madge, eyed him warily.

*

They set off at four o'clock in driving rain, stopping on the way so Rufus could pick up his new spectacles. It was cold in the van, the heater didn't work, and the doors, jutting out over the rear sill, had had to be lashed in place with twine, leaving a gap nearly two feet wide through which damp, chilly air poured to swirl around the interior. To deflect awkward questions Rufus had grabbed a couple of dozen assorted books from the library and stowed them in the narrow gaps either side of the doors. Clementine sat huddled in the passenger seat with her coat collar turned up and her hands pushed deep into her pockets, feeling sick with apprehension.

Rufus was still smarting. The previous night his elusive housekeeper had politely refused the second glass of wine he offered her, finished her meal with almost indecent haste, then pleaded packing still to be done, which he had known was a lie because he had seen her soft weekend bag lying, already full, outside her bedroom door, and disappeared. Rebuffed, he had finished the bottle by himself and not being much used to wine these days, had started the day mildly hung over as well as offended.

'This is very kind of you,' said Clem, in an effort to break the uncomfortable silence.

Rufus peered stonily past the inefficient windscreen wipers at the rain.

'No problem.'

'Now, you do know where the doors have got to go, don't you? I've rung the man and he's expecting you.'

'Yes.'

'I really appreciate—'

'I've told you, it's no problem.'

Clementine gave up, pulled her collar closer round her face, and lapsed into silence again.

Rufus stopped beneath the portico outside Thorpe station, then leapt from his seat and strode round to open the passenger door with such swift energy that Clementine almost fell out on to the pavement. He obviously couldn't wait to get rid of her.

'Thank you,' she said, as he swung her bag out after her and dumped it by her feet.

Rufus succumbed to those soft brown eyes. 'What train will you be on on Sunday? I'll pick you up.'

'Oh no, really.' He was standing very close, right in front of her, and Clementine felt hemmed in, overpowered. 'I haven't a clue what time I'm coming back. I'll get a taxi.'

Rufus hunched his shoulders against the chilly wind spattering him with rain. 'Look,' he began, 'you don't have to do this.'

Clementine frowned at him. 'Do what?'

'This man, this what's-his-name, Jonathan. If he's putting pressure on you . . .'

'He's not putting pressure on me.'

She was wearing a long heavy coat of dark velour cloth, rather twenties in style, with a big shawl collar and wide cuffed sleeves. She looked pinched and cold; Rufus wanted to warm her up, raised his hands to tuck her revers further round her ears. She flinched. 'You should never give in to bullies,' he said, dropping his arms awkwardly to his sides. 'It only makes them worse.'

If only he knew, thought Clementine. He seemed to have formed a picture of Jonathan as a violent, woman-beating tyrant, when the opposite was true. Maybe if Jonathan wasn't so gentle, so easily led, she wouldn't be in the muddle she was in now.

Rufus was staring at her, waiting for a reply.

'I'll be fine,' she said firmly. 'Honestly, you've got it all wrong, it's not how you think at all.' How easy it would be, the idea drifted into her mind, to lean forward and bury her face in her employer's thick guernsey sweater, gain some badly needed courage from his bulk and physical strength. Alarmed by the unexpected direction of her thoughts, she stooped hurriedly to pick up her bag, said briskly, 'I'll see you on Sunday,' and stepped backwards, away from temptation.

'Yup.' Rufus wanted to take her in his arms so badly he could hardly bear it. He turned abruptly and strode back round the van, yanked open the door and lowered himself so hard into his seat that the entire vehicle bounced. Then he started the engine and pulled away without looking back.

He had to stop halfway along the Prince of Wales Road to recover. Of course he wasn't in love with his housekeeper, he told himself, shaken by the sense of loss he had felt with her departure, he was lonely, that was all. It was just primitive sexual attraction, nothing more. And even supposing (ludicrous idea) that he *might* be fool enough to fall for her, it was perfectly obvious from everything she said and did that Clementine Ambrosia Thomasina Lee wanted nothing whatever to do with him.

Clementine sat in a corner of the railway carriage, staring out of the window and wondering what she was doing, rushing back to Jonathan, when she had gone to such lengths to get away from him. She would tell him, she resolved as the train rattled southwards into the darkening evening, he must leave her alone. There was no future for them, and no point in pretending otherwise. She leaned back against the greasy headrest, closed her eyes and made a silent resolution.

She was never going to get involved with a man again as long as she lived.

Chapter Eighteen

Jonathan was waiting at the ticket barrier. He seemed taller than Clementine remembered, or perhaps she had shrunk since their last meeting. Perhaps, she thought, her mind set in melancholy, unhappiness diminished one. He was wearing an expensive-looking camelhair coat and his features were creased with anxiety.

'Clem, darling, you have no idea how glad I am to see you,' he greeted her, enveloping her in a bear hug that left her breathless and dishevelled. 'I thought you might not come!' Clementine, unprepared for his sweet face and his transparent delight at her arrival, felt all her resolution trickling away in a wash of affection, and wished she *hadn't* come.

Jonathan handed her into the leather-upholstered comfort of his BMW – a stark contrast to the spartan vehicle in which she had travelled into Norwich earlier – then tucked her coat solicitously around her, settled himself in the driver's seat and sighed heavily.

'Thank you,' he said. He felt for her hand, grasped it in both his, squeezed hard and added, 'You have no idea what this means to me, Clem.' Then he released her, started the engine and pulled out into the city traffic.

Clementine examined his profile, the curly hair, the boyish curve of cheek and chin, the slight bump on the bridge of his nose. Such a kind, open face, she thought, contrasting it with the grim, scowling visage she had left behind in Norwich. If only Sebastian Brown had never existed. If only she could forget what he had said. If only . . .

Jonathan lived in Chelsea, off the King's Road. Clementine had never been there before, all their assignations having taken place, at her insistence, in restaurants and pubs, at the theatre and the cinema. When she had answered his plea for help she had deliberately thought no further than meeting him at Liverpool Street station, knowing that if she did she was likely to change her mind and refuse to meet him at all. Her decision had had much to do with pity – he was in trouble and he needed her – but as they drew up outside his pretty terraced house, with its deep sash windows and bright yellow front door, the implications of what she was doing began to sink in. Maybe, she thought, licking her dry lips and swallowing the lump in her throat, it would have been more sensible to stay in hiding.

As she followed him up the front path she was assailed for the second time by that peculiar sensation; he had *grown*, she was sure of it, or she had shrunk. Or was she, she wondered, feeling an increasing sense of unreality, simply going mad?

She refused point-blank to cross the threshold until Jonathan promised her Sebastian Brown was nowhere in the vicinity. He could guarantee it, Jonathan assured her, Sebastian was not even in the country, he was taking a month's vacation at Cap d'Antibes. He, Jonathan, had refused to go, pleading pressure of work.

'Honestly, Clem,' he said. 'It's true I swear, and anyhow, we've never been, you know, *together* here, he has a flat in Knightsbridge and a place in Sussex and we always used to . . .' Watching him glow with embarrassment as he realised what he had said, Clementine felt immediately, helplessly, sorry for him again, allowed him at last to usher her in out of the rain. This weekend, she realised, alarmed by her inability to resist his charm, was going to be even more difficult than she had anticipated.

If the outside of the house was pretty, the interior was amazing. Jonathan, unencumbered by tiresome considerations of client preference, had gone to town on his own space, stamping his personality on his surroundings without inhibition. Downstairs the walls, painted terracotta, vivid cobalt blue or deep bottle green, were hung with wildly exuberant modern paintings. The sitting room sofa was draped with silky shawls and piled high with brightly coloured cushions; the dining area, in a gothic wrought-iron conservatory overlooking the darkened garden, made a lushly theatrical setting for rattan chairs and a bamboo table, already laid for dinner and lit by an exquisite Art Nouveau Tiffany lamp which perched among the jungle fronds on the back of a joky, hand-carved elephant. Even Jonathan's cat, a pale golden miniature lioness called Simba, might have been chosen, probably *had* been chosen, thought Clementine, specifically to blend with her exotic surroundings.

The kitchen, where they repaired so Jonathan could cook supper while they talked, was all rustic shelves, hand-thrown ethnic pots and shiny copper pans hanging from chrome-yellow walls with bunches of dried flowers and ropes of garlic. It occurred to Clementine, sitting at the green-stained kitchen table with a large gin and tonic, that if things had worked out differently, she might have been living here by now, she and Jonathan might have been lovers, even married. Watching him set about his task, she contrasted his elegant charm with Rufus Palliser's prickly, ramshackle moodiness and felt again an acute sense of loss.

There was no animosity; Jonathan was too openly pleased to see her for Clementine to bear grudges, but there was a distance, which she initiated, and maintained, despite all his efforts to get close. Losing his nerve, Jonathan admitted little more about his past than Clementine already knew, pleaded naïvety, fear of being alone and loss of his livelihood, and played for sympathy. He and Sebastian had never had a written agreement for their partnership, he explained, Sebastian had provided the capital to set the company up and he, Jonathan, had provided the talent – the only resource of which he had an abundance. They had barely broken even to begin with, and he still had no idea how much the company made in a year. Like the rest of his staff, he was paid a salary. 'A very generous salary actually.'

For what, wondered Clem, momentarily allowing bitterness to creep in, services rendered?

'I didn't know what I was doing, darling,' pleaded Jonathan. 'I've never had a clue about money, and when Sebastian explained how he'd set the finances up I didn't bother to pay attention. It never seemed important until now.'

Yes, he admitted, when Clementine repeated Sebastian's jibes about his 'flights of fancy', what Sebastian had told her about their relationship was true. 'But you have to understand Clem, the others didn't *mean* anything, not like you. He knew that. Once I started going out with you, I stopped sleeping with him, you see, and it was when I told him I wanted out of our relationship for good that he threatened to pull the plug on the business—'

Remembering Sebastian Brown's insistence that all the effort he had put into Jonathan gave him the right to dictate his partner's every move, and his contemptuous dismissal of Jonathan's previous lovers, Clementine was inclined to believe him. But it didn't help.

'Did they all know?' she asked.

'Know what? Who?'

'Everyone at work, Kathy, Sarah, Diane, Peter, Angela and the other secretaries, that new receptionist. Did they all know about you and Sebastian? Did they get together for a good laugh every time you and I left the office together?'

'No, of course they didn't!'

'Did they know about you and Sebastian?'

Jonathan turned back to his cooking, lifted lids, tasted, stirred, didn't answer.

'Why didn't anybody *tell* me? How many people work for the company? A couple of dozen at least. Why didn't someone warn me I was making such a monumental fool of myself?'

Jonathan moved about the room, collecting warm plates from the oven, straining rice, stirring sauces. 'Maybe they didn't like to approach you.' He picked up the loaded tray and made for the door. 'Come on, darling, it's time to eat.'

Clementine frowned at his back. 'What do you mean?' She followed him along the hall and through the sitting room. 'What do you mean, "didn't like to approach me"?'

'Clem—'

'Jonathan!'

Jonathan lowered his tray carefully to the table, unloaded the plates and steaming dishes, then pulled out a chair and invited her to sit. Clementine shook her head agitatedly. 'Well?'

'Well, it's just that . . .'

'Yes?'

What did he mean? And he *was* taller, she was *certain* of it.

He sat down, dispelling the illusion, and began to remove lids, distribute serving spoons. 'It's just this air of, er, aloofness you have, that's all. Some of the girls find you a little . . .'

'Yes?' Clementine's voice rose.

'Well, some of the girls used to find you a little . . . remote, that's all. Intimidating.'

'Oh!' Clementine sat heavily and stared at him.

'You probably don't realise you're doing it,' suggested Jonathan kindly. 'You know, discouraging people from getting too close. Actually, it was one of the qualities that attracted me to you.' He reached across and stroked her hand, softening the blow he had inadvertently delivered, then lifted a bottle of white wine from the cooler he had concealed behind a variegated *Ficus Benjamina* and poured. He raised his glass, smiled. 'I love that air of mystery about you, that distance you keep between you and the rest of the world. It's fascinating, a challenge.'

'Oh!' said Clementine, growing repetitive. Was she really so aloof? Did she really freeze people out, rebuff them? She picked up her glass, then put it down again, opened her mouth to protest – she wasn't like that at all, she was friendly, outgoing, extrovert – then shut it. How many mourners could she muster, she asked herself again, reminded of her journey back in time and a ramshackle old aeroplane with only a thousand rivets to hold it together. The one close friend she had was Jean, and it was Jean, not she, who had kept their friendship going, who had made the running ever since the accident. For over sixteen years, until a couple of weeks ago, it was Jean who had taken the initiative every time, Jean who had written, phoned regularly, visited. Clementine's contribution to their friendship had been one merely of passive acquiescence.

As for her relationships with men . . . but then, look what had happened when she *had* risked getting involved, when she *had* let her defences down, allowed herself to become fond of someone. At least if she was alone she had nothing, no one, to lose.

'Come on, eat up sweetie, it'll get cold.'

'Oh, sorry. It looks wonderful.' She picked up her knife and fork, no longer hungry. 'Why did you need to see me so urgently? You said you were contemplating doing something outrageous . .'

By the time they had eaten, Lemon Chicken, saffron rice and a delicate green salad, they were both exhausted, Clementine with the effort of keeping Jonathan at arm's length, Jonathan with frustration at his inability to make Clem see how much he needed her.

'But I don't see what difference I can make,' she protested. 'I can't sort your books out for you, and I can't help you break away from Sebastian.'

'I just—' Jonathan poured the last of the wine into the glasses and leaned across the table. 'I just need to hear you say you'll stand by me. Clem, darling, *please*—'

Outside the rain increased, hurling gusts of water-laden wind at the windows and pattering heavily on the conservatory roof.

'Tell me . . .' Clementine began, taking the coward's way out, changing the subject.

'Anything.'

'You'll think it's ridiculous.'

'Nothing you say ever sounds ridiculous.'

'Have you, er, *done* anything to yourself? You know,

changed your appearance . . .?' Said out loud it sounded perfectly preposterous.

'Ah.' Jonathan rose from the table and led the way to the sitting room. 'Promise you won't laugh?'

So she *wasn't* going mad. 'Yes, I promise, but only if you explain how you have managed, since the last time I saw you, to grow over an inch in height.'

Honesty is the best policy, Jonathan reminded himself. 'I'm wearing lifts,' he said, and flopped on to the sofa next to his elegantly snoozing cat, abstractedly stroking its golden fur and avoiding Clementine's eye.

Clem choked. 'I b-*beg* your pardon?'

'You promised you wouldn't laugh.' He sounded hurt, deflated. Clementine swallowed, took a deep breath and fought the giggles welling disobediently in the back of her throat.

'Sorry,' she said, when she was sufficiently under control to trust her voice. 'But *why*? It's not as if you're a midget, after all. You're actually quite tall compared to most people.' Rufus Palliser loomed briefly before her eyes.

'Because of you.'

'Me? But I never complained about your height! What on earth made you think—?'

'No, I mean – well, it *is* because of you, but only indirectly, if you get me.'

Clementine didn't.

'It's all about standing up to people—'

'Standing up to people? You mean—?'

'Sebastian. I'm deadly serious about all this, Clem, I wish you'd believe me. And I thought – well, I thought if I could look him straight in the eye, I might be able to, you know . . .'

Clementine opened her mouth to tell him not to be so ridiculous, then changed her mind. 'You're absolutely

right,' she said instead. 'Tall people can be very intimidating.'

Sal was just about to lock up when Rufus parked outside
the shop. She had already flipped the sign to 'Closed'
and she held the door for him with theatrical reluctance.

'What the hell are you doing here? Twenty-to-six on a
miserable Friday night and you've nothing better to do
than turn up on my doorstep?'

'I thought you might need some fresh stock.' Rufus
shuffled his cold feet. 'And I had some stuff to deliver, so
I thought while I was in town . .'

Sal sighed heavily. 'If we were running short of stock
don't you think I would have mentioned it?' She
switched the main light back on and examined his face,
then closed the door behind him and snapped the catch.
'I'll give you fifteen minutes, maximum. One cup of coffee and then you can bugger off, I've a heavy date
tonight and I need a bath.'

'You have a heavy date every night.' Rufus followed
her through to the office, the cloud of gloom that had
descended upon him with Clementine Lee's departure
lifting a little. 'Thanks, Sal.'

'So what's eating you?'

'Nothing, I told you—'

'Pull the other one, darling.' Sal stuck her head out of
the cubbyhole and regarded him with cynical amusement. 'This is me you're talking to, remember? What's
up, housekeeper walked out on you already?'

The guess was a little too close for comfort. 'No. Well,
yes, she's gone away for the weekend.'

'So?'

'So . . .' Rufus hesitated. 'Promise you won't laugh?'

'Yeah, yeah. For God's sake get on with it!'

'I'm worried about her.'

Sal flung her head back and roared. 'You're *worried* about her? You sound like that radio serial my mum used to listen to when I was a kid, what was it called . . .? *Mrs Dale's Diary*. "I'm worried about Jim," she used to say—'

'If you remember *Mrs Dale's Diary*,' Rufus retaliated, 'you've been lying about your age all these years—'

'Don't start,' warned Sal, thumping his coffee down in front of him and disappearing again to continue the conversation as a disembodied voice, 'or I'll throw you out into the rain. So you're worried about the housekeeper. What are we talking here?' She returned, munching on a chocolate digestive, to perch on the edge of the desk and shed crumbs all over her skirt. 'She's turned out to be a Russian spy and she wants to defect? She's developed a hopeless crush on you and gone into a terminal decline? You've just discovered she's escaped from a lunatic asylum and they want her back? What do you mean, you're *worried* about her?'

Rufus picked up his coffee and examined its murky depths. 'Well, she's got this boyfriend—'

'What boyfriend? Why should you be interested in your housekeeper's boyfriend?'

'Just belt up for ten seconds and I'll tell you.'

'Watch it, Buster,' threatened Sal. 'I don't have to stay here to be insulted, you know, nine to five-thirty I work and don't you forget it. She's got this boyfriend?'

'Well, I think he beats her up.'

'What do you mean, you *think* he beats her up? Either he does or he doesn't, surely?'

'Well . . .'

Until now, knowing Sal's propensity to tease unmercifully at the slightest excuse, Rufus had been careful not to give away too much information about his new housekeeper, supplying dribs of information here: 'She's younger than I expected, not much older than you actually . . .'; drabs of information there: 'I only took her on because she had a funny name, but she's turned out to be a bloody good worker . . .'; just enough information dropped casually into the conversation to stop Sal asking too many questions. Now, as he explained about their first meeting, about the bruises, Clementine's refusal to discuss her private life, the mysterious letter that had made her cry, Sal stared at him in amazement.

'But why are you getting so worked up about the situation?' she asked pointedly when he had finished. 'After all, you're only employing the woman on a temporary basis, aren't you? And she's gone off quite willingly to meet this chap, or so you say. Why would she do that if he'd been thumping her?'

'I don't know, I just have this hunch, that's all . . .'

He realised immediately that he had said too much. Sal examined him closely, then lowered her head to brush the crumbs from her skirt and pronounced accusingly, 'You're smitten, aren't you? You've gone soft on her!'

Rufus drained his coffee in half a dozen gulps and slapped his mug down on the desk. 'I have done no such thing, you ridiculous woman, I am merely concerned because she's my employee, that's all.'

Sal snorted disbelievingly. 'So, what are you going to do about it?'

'I don't know. Every time I bring the subject up she tells me to mind my own business.'

'Hm. Well . . .' Sal swept his mug into her hand, vanished to dispose of it, then returned to switch off the light with determined finality as she passed him on her way to the front of the shop, '. . . in that case, if you ask me there's only one thing you *can* do.'

'Yeah?' Rufus rose reluctantly and followed her,

obediently switching off more lights as he went. 'What's that?'

'Exactly what you've been told to do.' Sal stood back to let him past, then flipped the last switch and stepped out on to the wet pavement. She found the right key, inserted it in the lock, turned it, then shoved the jangling bunch back into her bag and zipped it shut. 'Mind your own business. And since you obviously have time on your hands, you can drop me off at my place on your way home.' Sal's place was on the other side of Norwich, at least five miles out of his way.

'Sieg Heil, mein Führer.' Rufus ushered her into the van with a bow, avoiding the kick she aimed at his shins as she passed. He felt better, miles better, for having unburdened himself. 'Close the shop early tomorrow,' he said, 'and come to lunch. I'll feed you roast beef and you can choose some books from the library.'

'You must have it bad.' Sal peered at his face in the half-light, frowning. 'The last time you closed up early was the day Helen left you.' She settled herself in her seat and straightened her skirt.

'This van is a disgrace. I'll bring a bottle, shall I, darling?'

Clementine had not realised until she stopped how hard she had been working over the past two weeks, what a toll the past month had taken on her energy. By ten o'clock the warm comfort of her surroundings had begun to take effect and her eyes were closing of their own accord. Stifling a yawn, she pleaded time to mull things over. Could they talk again in the morning, she begged Jonathan? She was too tired to think straight.

As they made their way slowly up the stairs he risked one last try, blocking her way to touch her cheek with a tentative hand.

'Clem, could we—?'

'No!' said Clementine, guessing what he was about to ask. 'We could not! I left my Dutch courage in Amsterdam and I don't think I'll ever get it back.'

So Jonathan showed her to the spare bedroom, an opulent, seductive Arab tent in shades of green, terracotta and cream, meekly kissed her cheek (a peculiar sensation, meeting his eyes without having to lower hers) and left her.

'Tomorrow,' he promised encouragingly, 'you'll see things differently tomorrow.' Clementine smiled sadly, shook her head, then shut the bedroom door, leaned against it and closed her eyes, too exhausted to confront the problem any more.

She woke with a start at around three o'clock, and lay back against the pillows, listening. She could hear the sound of a distant siren and the muted roar of London's traffic. She had opened the window slightly, needing air after the wine she had imbibed, and the room was filled with the yellow sodium glow of the streetlamp outside. The rain was still falling, splashing on the pavement and trickling in the gutters. The sound reminded her of Manor Hall, and earlier, of her bedroom at Marshmeadow where the river had formed a background music to her dreams since the day she was born. She strained her ears, wondering what she was listening for, then relaxed, let her mind go blank, and waited. When it came it took her by surprise – it was not the heavy, sonorous note of the Marshmeadow grandfather clock she had been missing, it was the Manor Hall cuckoo.

She began to drift in and out of sleep, wondered if Mary was all right, whether she would have managed to wheedle her way on to Rufus's bed or whether she would be stretched out along the kitchen range, chasing rabbits in her dreams. She sighed, turned over and burrowed into her pillow.

Tomorrow, she would tell Jonathan he must fight his battles on his own, and then she would go home.

Rufus took off his new glasses as the cuckoo struck three, then put down his book and lay back, listening. Even after only a couple of weeks it felt strange being alone again. He strained his ears but he could hear nothing except the rain pattering against the windows and the wind moaning beneath the doors and round the casements. On impulse he rose and padded naked across the room, out on to the landing and down the stairs, making for the kitchen.

Mary heard his bare feet slapping on the tiles in the long corridor and when he opened the door she was waiting for him, whimpering with delight.

'Missing her, are you?' asked Rufus. 'Come on then.' He turned and retraced his steps along the passageway, then made his way slowly up the stairs with Mary trotting obediently behind him.

When he reached his bedroom he dived back beneath the covers and patted the duvet encouragingly. Mary leapt, scrabbled, then settled down beside him, laid her head on her paws and sighed heavily. Rufus leaned across to stroke her ears.

'I miss her too,' he said as he turned out the light. 'Stupid, isn't it?'

Chapter Nineteen

For the first time since the previous winter Rufus had turned on the central heating. The house was creaking and cracking in protest, but when Sal arrived (in a taxi – why learn to drive, she always said, when there were so many men eager to ferry her wherever she wanted to go?), she was still not satisfied.

'You might have lit a fire in the drawing room,' she complained. 'No wonder your housekeeper did a bunk, she probably needed to thaw out!'

'I invited you for lunch.' Rufus was dishing up at the kitchen table, scowling. 'Not for a critique of my home-making skills. I'll light a fire after we've eaten. D'you want horseradish?'

'Mm, please. Shall I open the wine?'

'Yup. Corkscrew's in the dresser, left-hand drawer.'

While Sal wrestled with his primitive bottle opener, Rufus carved chunks of bloody beef, dropping occasional slivers of fat for the dog, and returned to the theme that was preying on his mind. 'I still think I ought to do something about it. She's probably too scared to stand up to him.'

The cork came away from the bottle with a loud *pop*. Sal stuck her pretty nose into the opening and breathed deep of the fumes. 'Mm, nice,' she said. 'I do love a good

Rioja. Shall I pour?' She crossed the room to the corner cupboard to ferret around for glasses, glancing sideways at Rufus's worried face. 'Look, darling, if she was really scared she would have stayed here, wouldn't she? But she didn't, she went bouncing back to London the minute he called. Now if it was me, and some chap had been duffing me up, I'd tell the bastard to get knotted—'

'But she's not you. She's different, she's . . .' Shy, reserved, wary. *Different*. But Sal wouldn't have a clue what he was talking about if he tried to explain his elusive housekeeper. With Sal, thought Rufus, what you saw was what you got, a brisk, no-nonsense, down-to-earth woman who happened to look like a sex siren. Subtlety was not Sal's strong suit – she was apt to miss the undercurrents of life, lived each day for what it brought, called a spade a bloody shovel and thought displays of emotion wet.

'You're right,' he acknowledged reluctantly as he bent to get the roast potatoes out of the bottom oven. 'I should mind my own business.'

By three o'clock they had finished lunch, Rufus had been bullied into lighting the fire in the drawing room, they had opened a second bottle of wine, and the kitchen table was littered with greasy plates, empty serving dishes and dirty cutlery.

'I'm taking my coffee,' said Sal, eyeing the mess with disfavour, 'to the drawing room.'

She led the way, carrying two mugs of thick black coffee, with Mary trotting behind her and Rufus bringing up the rear with the remains of the wine and the glasses. She was already at the drawing room door when Mary turned back, pricking her ears at the sound of tyres on gravel, and Rufus stopped abruptly in his tracks. When the front door swung open and a very tall, amply proportioned woman appeared in the doorway carrying a holdall, Sal guessed immediately who she was; turning swiftly to catch Rufus's reaction to his housekeeper's unexpected return, she felt her throat constrict with alarm.

He had never looked at Helen like that, or those other, more recent conquests, the ones who had figured so briefly in his life she could not even remember their names; she had never seen him look at *any* woman the way he was looking at Clementine Lee; the intensity of his feelings was etched vividly on his face, too strong to be disguised. Switching her eyes back to the housekeeper's undeniably plain face, Sal felt her stomach cramp as well as her throat. This one is different, she thought. My God, this one is *serious*.

'You're back!' Rufus took an eager step forward, then stopped, reminding himself that he mustn't crowd her. She was bundled up in the same coat, the collar turned up to frame her face, and the sight of her warmed him all through, as Sal, the wine, the central heating and a large roast lunch had signally failed to do. When she returned his greeting, her mouth stretching into a wide, genuine smile, he was seized by exultation, examined her face for signs of bruising and was swept by enormous relief that she appeared to have escaped unscathed from her meeting with the infamous Jonathan. When Mary launched herself across the hall to welcome her mistress home and Clementine dropped to her knees to greet her, Rufus felt as if the sun had gone in, and he blinked, jerked reluctantly back to reality.

'Aren't you going to introduce me, darling?'

'Sorry,' said Rufus, annoyed by the throwaway endearment he normally hardly noticed. 'Clementine, this is Sal Glover. Sal runs my bookshop for me. Sal – Clementine.' He forgot his irritation, lingered over her name, 'Clementine, Ambrosia, Thomasina Lee,' realised too late that he had given himself away. Whilst Clementine, busy with the dog, seemed not to notice, Sal shot him a swift, appraising look, as if to say, oh-ho, so *that's* how the wind blows, then swept her hair off her face and approached to take a closer look. Rufus could see her opinion written on her face as clearly as if she had actually spoken. 'Must be the ludicrous name you've fallen for, you silly sod, because she's not got a lot else going for her.' He should have known Sal wouldn't understand.

Clementine had been in this situation before, a hundred times. Faced with Sal Glover's stunning good looks she felt as she always did, like a plodding carthorse confronting a high-bred Arab mare, only this particular Arab mare was more delicately lovely than even a thoroughbred filly had any right to be, with her seductive curtain of shiny hair, her wide-set blue eyes and sultry mouth. Clementine took a step backwards and glanced uneasily towards the door.

'I hope you don't mind,' she began hesitantly, 'but I've brought someone with me—'

Rufus wiped the smile from his face and stiffened. As Jonathan emerged from behind her, Clementine watched her employer's jaw set and knew she'd done the wrong thing.

'Jonathan Harris, Rufus Palliser, um . . .'

'Sal Glover,' supplied Sal smoothly. 'Hi, Jonathan.' If this is the boyfriend, she thought, appraising Jonathan's appealing face, his elegant figure, Rufus has no chance. The knot in her stomach eased slightly.

'He did so want to see the house,' continued Clementine, babbling, 'and I didn't think you'd mind—' It was obvious from Rufus's expression that he did, violently. 'He's fascinated by old houses you see, being an interior designer . . .' A muscle began to jump in Rufus's cheek. '. . . And I thought, since he was kind enough to bring me all the way back from London, maybe I could show him – I mean, he could give us some useful ideas . . .' Silence. 'But I can see now is not the right moment.' Rufus clearly agreed with her.

This uncomfortable scene was not what Clementine had intended, or wanted. She had risen late that morning, then slipped out while Jonathan was in the kitchen making breakfast and walked up the King's Road towards Sloane Square, mustering her resources to tell him that she couldn't, *wouldn't* help him. She had wandered aimlessly round Peter Jones for a while, then returned to announce that she was leaving. There was no point in prolonging the agony, she told him, it would just make things more difficult for both of them. Jonathan had nodded, apparently accepting her decision, then insisted she at least allow him to run her back to Liverpool Street to catch her train. Once on the road he had simply kept going, pointing the car in the general direction of Norfolk because that was where Clementine had let slip she was working, and talking all the way, pleading, begging, wheedling, until, worn down by his persistence, she had promised to think again about her decision just to shut him up.

'But I'm contracted to this job for six months,' she had warned, stretching the truth to fob him off. 'I can't just walk out, even if I wanted to, he's relying on me.' Then she had weakly allowed Jonathan to drive her all the way back to Dinningham and, astonished by his dogged refusal to take no for an answer, had even more weakly allowed him to talk her into letting him see where she was working. Never before had any man pursued her with such single-minded determination.

Jonathan didn't notice the icy atmosphere to begin

with. As he advanced to shake Rufus Palliser by the hand, he was feeling more confident about the future than he had been for a month; Clem hadn't said no, hadn't finished with him, quite, she would come round in the end, he was sure of it. To his surprise, Rufus Palliser merely glowered thunderously at him. He stopped, disconcerted, and lowered his arm.

Rufus wanted to punch the man, to take him by the throat and hurt him as he had hurt Clementine. He could actually feel the blood pounding in his ears, was shaken by the strength of his fury. When Sal materialised by his side, laid her hand on his sleeve, and murmured, 'Cool it, darling,' he started and stared down at her in confusion; he had forgotten momentarily that she was there. Sal patted him reprovingly, as if she was dealing with an intemperate child, then raised her voice and attempted to retrieve the situation.

'Coffee, anyone? Rufus, fetch some more cups, would you? Jonathan, be an angel and open this door for me; I've got my hands full.'

She treated Jonathan to her most dazzling smile and tossed her head at the drawing room door, but he had no opportunity to do as she asked. Even as he began to move, Mary, who had been investigating his left trouser leg, suddenly let out a startled yelp, then bolted for the kitchen corridor with her tail clamped between her legs.

'Bloody cat!' snarled Rufus venting his spleen on Ginger, who had chosen that moment to stroll in through the open front door. 'Clear off!'

'It's only a cat,' suggested Jonathan mildly. The man was clearly not all there.

'Thank you!' Rufus's temper, fuelled by protective jealousy, boiled over completely. 'I am capable of recognising a cat when I see one!' He moved towards the door, putting some space between himself and Jonathan in case he hit him. 'Clear off!' he repeated. Ginger sat on the threshold, curled his tail round his paws and stared, unmoved.

Jonathan couldn't begin to imagine how Clem had managed to get herself involved with this enormous maniac, but the sooner he could get her out of the situation she had got herself into, the better he would be pleased. 'Oh, come on,' he protested. 'The poor thing isn't doing any harm—'

Rufus directed a vitriolic glance in his direction. 'And what would you know about it?'

'Well, I own a cat, actually, and this one's clearly been badly neglected—'

'I don't want him in the house. He sharpens his claws on the furniture.'

Jonathan, rapidly becoming as angry as Rufus, and wishing his lifts could make him half a foot taller, riposted sharply, 'Poor creature's obviously starving. Cats like their comfort—'

Rufus scaled new heights of scowling bad manners.

'It's a mangy bloody tomcat that's been living wild for years, not a pampered pet Persian! You'll be wanting me to put a bow in its hair next!'

'As you wish.' Intimidated, Jonathan reluctantly relinquished the argument. 'Clem, I'd better go.' He returned to Clementine's side, linked his arm through hers and asked loudly, 'See me to the car, darling?' It seemed important to stake his claim publicly, in case her neanderthal employer should be in any doubt as to his status.

Clementine, watching Rufus's hand tighten round his wine glasses, guided Jonathan hastily towards the door, anxious to remove him from the premises before he could make the situation any worse, and almost collided on the threshold with a plump, pretty woman in her early thirties, with cropped brown hair, a full, rather sulky mouth and a fresh complexion, leading a small child by the hand.

'Hi,' Jean addressed the assembled company brightly. 'Is this a private party, or can anyone join in?'

Ginger eyed Eddie with distaste, then rose and strolled out through the front door. Eddie sized up the company, then wriggled free of his mother's restraining hand, bounced up to tug at Jonathan's sleeve and examined him with alert interest, head on one side.

'You him?' he demanded.

'Who?'

'Him. Woofus.' Eddie inserted his index finger in his left nostril, wiggled it, extracted it, examined it, then wiped it on his shorts and smiled winningly. 'My Auntie Clemmie says you're peacoolier.'

'Ah. No.' Jonathan gestured over his shoulder. 'That's Woofus, over there.' He leaned closer, patted Eddie's shoulder. 'And your Auntie Clemmie's absolutely right.'

'Lovely boy,' he remarked as he passed Jean. 'And an excellent judge of character.' He wasn't about to argue with Clem's analysis of her employer; 'barking mad' would have been even better.

Rufus had missed the exchange; he had turned his back just as Jean arrived, and was staring fixedly at his feet, fighting to get his temper under control before he murdered somebody. Watching that muscle, still jumping in his jaw, Sal decided it was time to make herself scarce. She stood on tiptoe to peck his cheek. 'Thanks for lunch, darling. Look, I'll hitch a lift with Jonathan, shall I, save you running me home?' Rufus, as she was perfectly well aware, had never had any intention of running her home. She tapped the side of her nose, winked conspiratorially and dropped her voice to murmur, 'Just leave it with me, darling, I'll suss how the wind blows,' and then she went on her way, pausing only to present Jean with two mugs of rapidly cooling coffee and collect her coat from the chair by the door.

Sticking his fists into his trouser pockets, Eddie made determinedly for Rufus, planted his legs wide apart so he could get a good view of the biggest person he had ever seen, and demanded imperiously, 'So, *are* you pea-coolier then?'

Eddie was the last straw. '*What?*' snarled Rufus.

Eddie, undaunted, repeated his question, adding helpfully, 'Cause my Auntie Clemmie says you are.'

'No, I am *not* peculiar!'

Clementine, unexpectedly rescued by Sal's determined intervention from an emotional farewell scene with Jonathan, returned just in time to see Rufus, looking remarkably reminiscent of a bull elephant confronting a persistent mouse, step sharply backwards away from Eddie, and demand angrily of no one in particular, 'Where the bloody hell did *he* spring from?'

'Shouldn't say bloody,' Eddie reprimanded sternly. 'Mummy says it's swearwing.'

'*Eddie!*' Jean grimaced apologetically at Rufus and wished she had her hands free. 'Take no notice, he only does it to annoy.' Peculiar, she thought, didn't even begin to cover this menacing giant. 'Jean. Jean Hawe.'

'Who?' Rufus, badly shaken by Eddie's unexpected appearance, and still struggling with his temper, knew he ought to recognise the name but couldn't remember why.

'From Hawe's Farm, Lower Dinningham. You know, the other side of the river. Nice to meet you . . .' Jean was becoming annoyed. How could Clem just walk out like that, without even introducing her?

Rufus remembered; Clementine's friend, the one who had stayed in touch. He looked vaguely for somewhere to put his bottle, waved his arm awkwardly in lieu of shaking hands, slopping wine, then spotted Clementine over the top of Jean's head and silently begged her to come to his rescue.

'Jean, this is Rufus Palliser. Rufus, Jean's an old friend of mine . . .'

'And I's Eddie,' piped up Eddie. 'Auntie Clemmie, Woofus says he is *not* peacoolier.' He beamed up at Rufus, then added, kind but condescending, 'he dun't talk very nice though. He swored just now, bloody and everyfing—'

Rufus took a steadying breath. 'Sorry,' he said, amazed how normal his voice sounded. 'You startled me, that's all . . .'

'Thank you, Eddie, that will be enough!' Jean, looking for somewhere to put her restricting coffee mugs, made a note for when they got home, that she owed him one. 'Bit of a handful, I'm afraid. I hope you don't mind, but Clem and I have known each other since we were knee-high, so I thought I'd just pop round—'

And have a good old snoop, thought Clem, her cheeks still burning at Eddie's indiscretion. 'Rufus, I'll take Jean along to the kitchen, shall I, make sure Mary's all right—?'

'No.' It occurred to Rufus that he was making a complete mess of things. 'No, there's a fire in the drawing room. I'll go and make some coffee.'

'There seem to be two coffees here already.' Jean held up her mugs, still hoping to get rid of them.

'Ah. Right.' Rufus waved clumsily in the direction of the drawing room, sloshing wine again. 'Clementine, if you would show your friend—'

'Jean.'

'Jean. Yes. If you would show Jean into the drawing room I'll . . .' Rufus made a belated attempt to atone for his earlier appalling manners. 'I'll make you a cup of tea.'

Watching Clementine's flushed, embarrassed face, it hit him again. His emotions, dormant for so long, seemed to be spiralling out of control. He had never, not with Helen, not with any woman, had to endure the roller coaster he was riding now, from the blind fury Jonathan Harris's presence had aroused in him to the current leap of delight as Clementine smiled sweetly at him and said, 'Thank you, a cup of tea would be lovely.' Only with the boy had he experienced the heart-stopping thrill that was flooding him now, and that had been different, pure; this time the pleasure was all wrapped up with lust, with more sexual desire than he had felt for years. He wanted to touch her, to talk about it, tell her how he felt, take her in his arms and kiss her until she gave in and kissed him back, but his instincts told him if he did she would withdraw, maybe even flee back to London and the man who had just driven off with Sal, the man who had beaten her up. He was her sanctuary. He must give her space, steel himself to be patient, then maybe she would stick around, let him in.

He lowered his voice so Jean couldn't hear, asked anxiously, 'Are you all right?'

Clementine nodded. She looked tired, but not battered. 'Yes,' she said. 'Yes, I'm fine.' She didn't withdraw. Rather, she seemed touched by his concern. 'I missed the cuckoo,' she added, and smiled again.

Rufus's stomach lurched. He reached out to touch the thick fabric of her sleeve. 'I'm glad you're okay,' he said. 'I'll go and make that tea.'

Clementine, catching Jean's eager face over his shoulder, imagined the questions and lost her nerve. 'I'll just put my stuff away,' she said and grabbing her bag she made hurriedly for the stairs and the sanctuary of her room.

*

Eddie talked incessantly, clambered on the furniture, fiddled with Rufus's things, and stared at his host as if he was a newly discovered alien species. Rufus, unable to cope with Eddie as well as everything else, ignored him completely. Clementine, sitting silently on one sofa while Rufus made polite conversation with Jean on the other, was treated to a view of her employer she had never seen before, was surprised to discover, beneath the gruff, unpredictable exterior, a pleasant, friendly man with a gentle self-deprecating sense of humour. It was evident that Jean, not normally inclined to give incomers the benefit of the doubt, had forgiven his earlier display of bad manners and was falling for his charm.

Rufus felt as if, for once, he was getting it right. It might have been the wine, belatedly working on his system, or the large lunch he had eaten, it could have been the fire, filling the room with gentle heat and providing a softly crackling counterpoint to the talk, reminding him of the dreams he had had for Manor Hall when he had first bought it, or maybe it was having Clementine Lee sitting quietly opposite him as if she was a part of his life; whatever it was, for the time being at least, he managed to suppress the memories Eddie Hawe's presence invoked and found again the touch he had thought lost for good; Clementine's nosy friend succumbed to his efforts at playing the urbane host without noticing that he was stonewalling her every prying question.

Jean was enjoying herself so much it was after five by the time she finally looked at her watch and rose reluctantly from the sofa. 'Robert'll be wanting his tea,' she excused herself, and Rufus made no attempt to dissuade her; at last, he thought, he would have Clementine to himself.

His anticipation was shortlived. Jean insisted on tidying up first, piling the crockery on to the tray, then bearing it determinedly out into the hall and down the long corridor to the kitchen. When she saw the chaotic remains of lunch, still congealing on the table, she refused point-blank to leave until it was cleared.

'It's the least I can do,' she said, 'since you've put up with me and Eddie so patiently.'

Rufus met Clementine's eyes over the top of Jean's head, and shrugged; Clementine, grateful for his uncharacteristic patience, began to stack the dirty dishes on the draining board, then pushed her sleeves above her elbows and washed up, standing awkwardly at the sink with Mary, recovered from Ginger's visitation, lying heavily across her feet, and Jean prattling in her left ear, drying as she talked. Rufus put away and Eddie sat swinging his short legs on the edge of the table, picking at an interesting scab on his knee, then flicking the bits at his mother's back.

By the time Jean hung her sodden tea towel on the brass rail at the front of the range and announced that she really *must* be going, Rufus was ready to explode with impatience. When Clementine glanced up from wiping the draining board and said firmly, 'Bye, Eddie. See you soon, Jean,' making it clear she had no intention of seeing her friend off the premises, he offered to show her out himself, just to make sure she went.

'Thanks.' Jean glanced quizzically at Clem, then smacked Eddie smartly on the back of the legs. 'Come on, Ed, time to go.'

'But Mummee . . .!' Eddie was having a good time. He liked this gloomy, mysterious house, so different from the modern box, with its square rooms and metal windows, in which he had lived all his life; he was not going without a struggle.

As Clementine turned from the sink she was puzzled to see Rufus warily skirt the table, moving deliberately wide to avoid contact with Eddie, who was moodily kicking the nearest chair and glowering at his mother. Maybe he wasn't used to children. Then, unexpectedly, startlingly, as he passed Eddie's flailing legs his face twisted and she caught her breath, reminded of his strange outburst in the pub. But as swiftly as it had come it was gone, expunged as if it had never been, he strode briskly from the room, followed almost at a run by Jean towing the loudly protesting Eddie, and she wondered if she had imagined it.

She bent to ruffle Mary's head and shivered, momentarily chilly. 'A peacoolier man,' she informed the dog wryly. 'A *very* peacoolier man.'

When Rufus arrived back in the kitchen, the room was deserted and there was a note on the table.

> *Thank you for putting up with my friends. I'm sorry we wrecked your afternoon. Have taken Mary for a walk and will start work first thing tomorrow. Clementine.*

Not even 'Yours, Clementine'.

Rufus wandered across to the range and poured himself a cup of sludgy coffee. Then he pulled out a chair, sat down heavily at the table, and buried his head in his hands.

Chapter Twenty

Jonathan turned left at the end of the drive and drove the long way round the green, in two minds whether to go back and rescue Clementine, despite her insistence when they had said their all-too-brief goodbyes that she didn't need rescuing. They had been interrupted before he had had a chance to tell her half the things he wanted to, and now it was too late.

'Sorry,' he said, belatedly remembering his passenger. 'I didn't catch your name.'

Sal stretched languidly. 'Sal. Sal Glover. I run Rufus's bookshop.'

'Oh, I see.'

'Nice, isn't it?' Sal commented as they passed the schoolhouse.

'Mm.'

'Look at those arched windows. And that big room at the end – it must be spectacular inside.'

'Mm.'

'It'd make a splendid weekend cottage, don't you think?'

'Mm.' Jonathan's mind was not on houses. He was thinking about Clem, worrying about her manic employer.

'Of course, I've no imagination at all when it comes to things like that.'

'Sorry, what did you say?'

'I said, I've no imagination when it comes to doing up houses. My place is an absolute eyesore.'

Jonathan struggled to focus on the conversation. 'You could always get someone in.'

Sal eyed him speculatively. 'I wouldn't know where to start.'

'You need an interior designer then. Yellow Pages'd be your best bet.'

'And what do you do for a living, Jonathan?' asked Sal, all ingenuous interest.

'I'm an interior designer.' Jonathan glanced at the stunning girl sitting beside him, legs crossed, displaying yards of firm, slender flesh, then looked away again, concentrating on his driving.

'And how did you get into the business?'

Jonathan hesitated, opened his mouth to tell the usual lies, 'college . . . scholarship . . . family contacts', and found himself instead telling the truth. 'I was living in Tangier with Sebastian, and he was doing up his villa. I discovered I had a talent for decoration.'

Sal rearranged her lovely limbs, making herself more comfortable. 'Sebastian?'

'My boyfr – er, my – my partner.' What was the matter with him? Jonathan wondered. He must be in an even worse state than he'd realised; he seemed to have lost control of his mouth.

'I see.' Sal Glover's expression of polite interest didn't change. 'Rufus was under the impression you were Clementine's boyfriend.'

'I was – I am.'

'Ah.' Sal's face still gave nothing away. 'So she found out about the other . . . um, man, right? And told you to naff off?'

Jonathan swallowed. 'Look, Miss Glover—'

'Sal.' Sal examined him dispassionately, then tucked her hair behind her ears and began to pick at her neatly manicured fingernails. 'Pity,' she remarked. 'I was rather hoping you'd be able to help me out.'

'I beg your pardon?' Jonathan changed gear unnecessarily, losing track of the conversation altogether. 'Help you out of what?'

Sal returned to her previous theme. 'So, I don't suppose you'll be coming up to Norwich again if it's all off between you and Clementine?'

Jonathan sighed heavily. 'I don't know.'

'Don't know much, do you?' Sal sat in silence for a while, watching the countryside pass by her window, then asked calmly, 'How did she get this black eye Rufus is so worked up about? You don't strike me as the violent type—'

'I'm not!' Jonathan protested indignantly. 'I've never laid a finger on Clem! It wasn't me, it was Sebastian, and it was an accident!'

'Well, that's all right then. How did you break your nose?'

Jonathan couldn't keep up with her thought processes at all, it was like trying to avoid a steamroller. He gave up and told the truth again. 'I got in a fight with another rent boy over a client.'

'What a fascinating life you seem to have led,' commented Sal. 'Tell me, is there any sort of depravity you *haven't* indulged in?'

'Plenty!' Jonathan was indignant. 'Look Miss, er, it's not like it sounds at all—'

'Oh? How is it then?' Sal leaned across and treated him to a dazzling smile. '*Do* tell.'

There is something about being in a car. People divulge secrets in cars, swap intimacies that in different surroundings they would not dream of revealing.

Jonathan was in desperate need of an ear, and who better to confide in than a woman he was unlikely ever to meet again, a woman who appeared moreover to be completely unshockable . . .

Almost without realising he was doing it, Jonathan Harris found himself telling Sal Glover the story of his life, admitting to his impoverished family, boorish father, timid, downtrodden mother, two brothers, both in trouble with the law before they were in their teens, from whom he had cut himself off completely when he ran away from home shortly after his seventeenth birthday. He regaled her, as she sat serenely beside him in the opulent comfort of his BMW, with the story of his arrival at King's Cross station with no money and nowhere to go, to be picked up by a boy scarcely older but considerably more streetwise than he and taken to meet a 'friend' who would 'see him right', and after he had told her that there seemed to be nothing left to lose.

As he drove towards Norwich with the setting sun slanting across his right shoulder, it all poured out, his descent into the seedy London underworld of pimps and prostitutes, his rescue by Sebastian, who had picked him up in a Soho bar and taken him home, the subsequent trips to France, Italy, North Africa, learning new tricks and new pleasures along the way, seduced as much by beautiful things, beautiful places, as by the beautifully decadent lifestyle to which Sebastian had introduced him. He told her about the debt he owed his partner, which was not entirely financial, and how he longed nonetheless to escape, to be free so he could be with Clementine, and he explained that he was calling in an accountant to see if it was possible to break, if not the emotional ties, at least the financial chains in which Sebastian held him. By the time they reached the outskirts of Norwich he had confided to Sal Glover his most intimate hopes and fears, his desire for a family, his terror of exposure, of losing Clementine for good. Sal sat quietly, listening without comment, occasionally smoothing her skirt or tucking her hair behind her ears, offering neither censure nor advice.

'Mm . . .' was all she said when he had finished. 'And does the lady in question know all this?'

'No!' Jonathan braked too hard, causing the motorist behind them to swerve and hoot his horn. '*Please*. She knows I'm trying to break free of Sebastian, but she doesn't know about the rest of my past. If you tell her all the gory details I won't stand a chance.'

Sal leaned back in her seat and was quiet for a while.

'Jonathan,' she began as they drove past the Norfolk and Norwich Hospital and moved slowly with the evening traffic on to the Newmarket Road. 'You don't mind if I call you Jonathan, do you? What would you say to a bit of old-fashioned bartering?'

While the outside of Sal's home was pretty enough, the interior was dreadful, appallingly untidy, drearily furnished, conservatively decorated, staid, *beige*. 'I warned you, darling,' said Sal calmly. 'No imagination, you see. But I've just hit on a plan for transforming it from top to bottom, the whole bit, *Homes and Gardens*, *Country Life*, the works.'

'Can you afford it?' Jonathan was beginning to wonder if she was a bit simple; bookshop assistants were not, so far as he knew, generally overpaid. 'The materials alone, if you're thinking of doing it properly, could run into thousands, and then there's the labour, fees for the designer . . .'

'Ah,' Sal leaned across and patted his arm. 'But I'm not proposing to pay for the designer, that's the whole point . . . Oh, don't get me wrong, darling.' She poured herself a second cup of coffee and settled back on the couch with her legs tucked under her. 'I've a fair bit stashed away. Poor little rich girl, that's me. Daddy's a Baronet, pots and pots of loot swilling around, stately pile in Kent, servants; you know the sort of thing . . .' She paused, regarded Jonathan with her head on one side, amused. 'Come to think of it, I don't suppose you do, do you? Look, why don't I tell you the plan and you can decide whether you're willing to give it a go.'

'Let me get this straight.' Jonathan still wasn't sure he'd grasped what Sal was suggesting. 'You are asking me to redesign this place for nothing and in return for my professional services you will sort out my books, also for nothing. Is that right?'

Sal nodded. 'And while I'm in London extricating you from Sebastian, you will be in Norwich, rescuing Clementine from a life of domestic drudgery. Brilliant, don't you think?'

'But why? I mean, I do appreciate the offer and all that, but why go to so much trouble for a complete stranger?'

For the first time since Sal had climbed uninvited into his car, Jonathan caught her off guard. She unfolded her legs and rose from the couch, then walked across to the window and stared out into the dark street. 'It's Rufus,' she said. 'I'm crazy about the silly sod. I wandered into his shop just after it opened and saw him, sitting behind his desk with his brow all furrowed, trying to work out the cost of a pile of books someone had just bought, and I simply flipped, if you know what I mean.' She laughed, shrugged her shoulders. 'Not like me at all, frankly, until I met Rufus I was strictly a good-time girl.' She turned back to face the room, grimaced. 'Still am, come to that. I mean, sex is one thing, but love is quite another, don't you think?' She chuckled wryly. 'Someone, a chap actually, once told me I thought like a man, you know, being able to separate sex and love—'

'But surely . . .' Jonathan was completely mystified. 'You could have anyone you want, couldn't you? All you have to do is flutter your eyelashes and Palliser'll come running.'

Sal laughed ironically, then returned to the couch and began to rummage in her bag. 'Sorry,' she said, unexpectedly producing a packet of *Gitanes*, 'I don't as a rule, but I feel the need just now.' She found a lighter, flicked it, took a deep lungful of smoke, then offered the packet to Jonathan. He hesitated, then shrugged and took one. 'You too?' she asked.

'I gave it up,' explained Jonathan. 'When I started taking Clem out. It made her wheeze.'

They sat in silence for a while, blowing smoke, then Jonathan returned to the puzzle. 'I still don't understand why you don't just go for it. I mean, a girl who looks like you . . .'

Sal stubbed out her cigarette, lit another. 'More coffee?'

'No thanks, too strong for me.'

'Ah, that's the trouble.'

'What's the trouble? I don't understand.'

Sal exhaled through flared nostrils, touched the lid of the coffee pot. 'The coffee, the smoking, or rather the not smoking, all the other things. When I first met Rufus you see, he was married. Had a kid too, although that's another story altogether. Oh,' she added, as Jonathan glanced sideways at her, asking a silent question, 'that wouldn't have made any difference if I could have enticed him away from her. It was just that he didn't notice.'

'Didn't notice what?'

'Didn't notice *me*. My physical attractions made absolutely no impression on him at all.' She pulled a face, bit her lip. 'It was quite a shock, I can tell you – I'm not used to having my fatal charm ignored. Anyway, since my sex appeal had no effect, I thought I'd try a different tack, you know, kindred spirits and all that, creep up on him from an oblique angle. So I talked my way into working for him, learned to like his appalling coffee, lavished tender care on his beloved books, even stopped smoking in case I damaged them. And then when the kid died . . . when his marriage started to disintegrate, I thought I might be in with a chance.' She fell silent for a moment, contemplating the efforts she had wasted for almost six years, then crossed two fingers and leaned close. 'Like that, we are, Rufus and I. Except that the poor fool thinks I'm his little sister.' She settled back, fiddled with her hair. 'I'm resigned to it now, but I still can't bear the thought of him getting hurt.'

'What do you mean? Hurt by what?'

Sal examined the glowing tip of her cigarette. 'He just can't resist anything *different* you see, old books, crumbling mansions, oddball women . . .'

'What are you saying?'

'Do I have to spell it out? Didn't you notice the way he reacted to your arrival? My lovely Rufus is showing a definite, and possibly serious interest in your Clementine, and I don't think—'

'But he *can't* be! I mean, she's his *housekeeper* for God's sake, it's practically incest—'

'Don't be ridiculous.' Sal was dismissive. 'There's nothing in the rules that says a man can't fall for his housekeeper. After all, a housekeeper's only one step removed from an au pair, and au pairs are notorious for seducing their employers, even if they've got wives already.' Then, reminded of a distinctly dodgy episode in her own chequered past, 'Come to think of it, *specially* if they've got wives already.'

Jonathan was horrified. 'But surely you can nip it in the bud, can't you? I mean, Clem's not interested, you heard that frightened kid just now, she obviously thinks the man is soft in the head. If you just turned on the charm, he'd—'

Sal shook her head, took another drag at her cigarette. 'I don't want him like that,' she said, and Jonathan caught a quick, surprising glimpse of an altogether different woman hidden beneath the brisk, no-nonsense exterior. 'If he ever came to me, it would have to be because he needed me, because he couldn't live without me, not because I'd performed the dance of the seven veils or fed him an aphrodisiac over supper. He's the only man I've ever met who's seen past my physical attributes and liked me for myself, for my mind; that's the one comfort I have.' She took a last, deep drag on her cigarette, then ground it into the ashtray and brought the discussion back to the plan she had outlined. 'So, how about it? I'll sort out your books and get your partner off your back and, furnished with a bona fide reason for being in Norwich, you will attempt to entice your Clementine away from Rufus. Is it a deal?'

'You're quite sure he's keen on her?' Jonathan didn't want to believe it.

'Positive. I've never seen him look at any other woman the way he looked at your Clementine this afternoon. It's perfectly obvious that she's hopelessly wrong for him, but the pigheaded fool won't take advice, well, not my advice anyway. This is the only way.' The only way to stop Rufus making a terrible mistake. You have to be cruel to be kind, Sal told herself; the last thing Rufus needs is to get involved with someone who clearly has enough problems of her own.

She waited patiently while Jonathan mulled things over, nodded calmly when he begged for time to think, then gave him her telephone number, took his, and showed him out into the night.

'Let me know what you decide,' she said, 'and we'll take it from there. But don't leave it too long, the quicker we can get you and Clementine back together, the better, don't you think?'

Jonathan nodded vigorously, hesitated in the doorway. 'You won't, er, *tell* on me, will you?'

Sal snorted. 'Since I have swapped my darkest secrets for yours, I'm not in a position to blab about anything, am I?'

Jonathan took a step down the garden path, stopped. What had he got to lose? If this woman could provide him with an excuse to get close to Clementine, *and* help him escape from Sebastian, he should go for it. 'All right,' he said, and he turned back, offering his hand.

Sal took it, shook it. 'Good,' she said. 'I'll start the ball rolling on Monday.' She chuckled. 'Partners in crime, eh darling?' Then she blew him a smoke-filled kiss, and shut the door in his face.

Chapter Twenty-One

Rufus Palliser was only too aware of his own shortcomings, and patience was not a virtue he had ever possessed in great measure, except with the boy. Over the following days his self-control was stretched to the limit.

He saw Clementine only once on the Sunday. She failed to appear at breakfast, shutting herself away in the bedroom she was working on, with the radio turned up loud and Mary for company, and when he took her a plateful of sandwiches at lunchtime she thanked him politely and shut the door in his face. Sometime during the afternoon she slipped down to the kitchen to prepare him a cold beef salad for his supper and then she went to ground for the rest of the evening. It was like living with the Invisible Woman.

Early on Monday afternoon, having crept up the stairs to make sure she was safely at work, Rufus made for the kitchen and cobbled up a stew, using some sausages he found in the fridge and carrots left over from Saturday's roast lunch. By the time Sal rang at four o'clock, he had already spent an hour wondering how to entice Clementine downstairs to eat it; Sal solved his problem.

'Secret agent Glover reporting for duty,' she said

facetiously and was rewarded with an irritable grunt. 'I've done some detective work on your behalf and the man is clean.'

'What *are* you talking about?' asked Rufus shortly, his mind on stew and Clementine.

'Jonathan Harris.' Sal made a face at the phone; she didn't seem to be striking the right note. 'He's just a nice, ordinary chap who happens to be crazy about your Clementine.' Stretching the truth, the 'ordinary' bit, but near enough.

'She is not *my* Clementine.'

'Well, whatever, if someone did knock her about, it wasn't Jonathan Harris. The man wouldn't hurt a fly. He's a sweetie.' That at least was true. Jonathan, for all his murky past, had struck Sal as the original innocent abroad. And he *was* a sweetie. 'That's what you were worried about, wasn't it?'

'I suppose so.'

He sounded so disappointed, Sal's suspicions were confirmed.

'Is she still involved with him?'

Sal crossed her fingers to negate the lie. 'Oh, absolutely. They'd had a lovers' tiff or something but you saw them on Saturday, thick as thieves.' There was a chilly silence. 'She wouldn't have let him drive her all the way out from London otherwise, now would she, darling? So you can stop worrying about her, can't you?'

'Yeah. Thanks Sal.' He didn't sound very grateful. 'Was that all you rang for?'

'No, it wasn't actually. I need time off, have to go to London for a week.'

This time the reaction was more gratifying; Rufus sounded appalled. 'Now don't make a fuss, darling,' soothed Sal. 'It's not till next week, and you can run the shop perfectly well without me.'

Rufus, swallowing the fury that threatened to overwhelm him at the prospect of being taken away from Clementine for a whole week, sat down heavily at the shabby desk in his study and reminded himself that he had resolved to be patient, that he would see her every morning and evening, if he could catch her as she flitted past. A week in the shop would help him to keep himself in check, and it would give Clementine the space she so badly needed. He didn't believe a word of Sal's excuses of course; Jonathan Harris was clearly just a plausible liar with a smart line in oily charm and Sal had fallen for his patter because he was easy on the eye. Sal was a pushover for a pretty face.

'Hello? You still there, darling?'

'Fine,' he said, giving in without further argument. 'No problem, take as long as you want.'

Sal was offended and encouraged at the same time. Whilst his sudden volte-face made it painfully obvious that she was not indispensable, if Rufus was prepared to be so equable about minding the shop, he couldn't be too badly smitten, could he?

'And how will the lovely Miss Lee manage without you?' she asked, casually sarcastic.

'Don't take the piss,' came the snarled reply, and she wished she'd kept her mouth shut.

'Customers,' she said as the bell over the shop door went, glad of an excuse to escape the chilly silence on the other end of the line. 'Must go.'

'Right,' said Rufus, clearly still huffy, 'bye, then,' and he put the phone down.

Sal strode smartly back to her desk at the front of the shop. Of all the men in the world I could have fallen for, she thought wryly as she greeted a pair of A-level students in search of a cheap copy of *Lord of the Flies*, I had to pick a great soft stupid ox who wouldn't notice if I

took off all my clothes and lay down on his desk stark
naked. What the hell is the *point*?

Rufus waited until just after six, then took the stairs two
at a time to knock on the bedroom door. When
Clementine appeared, he resisted the temptation to wipe
away with his fingers the smear of paint decorating the
bridge of her nose, and stuck rigidly to the form of
words he had planned as he climbed the stairs.

'I have a problem with next week. Finish up whatever you're doing and we'll discuss it over supper. It'll
be on the table in ten minutes.' He gave her no chance to
think of an excuse, turning briskly on his heel to return
downstairs, and when Clementine appeared in the
kitchen ten minutes later, he congratulated himself; he
was beginning to get the hang of this business at last.

Clementine couldn't understand what the fuss was
about. 'It's no problem,' she reiterated as Rufus ladled
sausages and carroty gravy on to her plate. 'I'll be fine.
I've enough work to do upstairs to keep me busy for ten
days at least.'

'Good.' Rufus kept his expression carefully neutral.
'It's not until next week, and if there's anything you need
I can get it in Norwich during my lunch-hour. You have
only to phone—'

'Right.' Clementine picked up her knife and fork. 'You
didn't need to go to all this trouble, I would have done
the supper, you know.'

Rufus shrugged, demurred. 'You shouldn't have been
working at all today. You worked through Sunday, so I
still owe you a day off.' He took a couple of mouthfuls,
added casually, 'I wasn't sure whether you'd be eating at
your friend's tonight.'

Clementine shook her head. She felt better, miles better, than she had for ages. Rufus had been really kind on

Saturday, once he had recovered his temper, had not mentioned Jonathan or complained about her intrusion into what had obviously been a private lunch with his beautiful girlfriend.

'To tell you the truth,' she found herself confiding, 'I'm avoiding Jean at the moment. She likes to know what's going on, and I'm not sure I'm up to the Spanish Inquisition just now.'

'Ah.' Rufus poured water and counted to ten. 'So, where have you got to with the decorating?'

He could tell by her face he had got it right again, not asking about the boyfriend. For the rest of the meal she was more talkative than she had been at any time since her arrival, and when she had finished her supper she sat on with him, discussing the library and how they would tackle it once she had finished the bedroom.

'When do I get to see what you've done so far?' he asked, rising to clear the plates.

Clementine followed him across to the sink and ran hot water. 'Can you wait until it's finished, do you think? That way, if you approve it'll be a nice surprise, and if you hate it you'll get the shock over in one go.'

'Sure, whatever you like.' Rufus picked up a tea towel and began to dry the dishes. Watching her profile, seeing her mouth curve with pleasure at the surprise she was preparing for him, he felt his stomach tie itself in knots and his temperature rise. He picked up another plate, keeping a tight hold on himself.

'You're not going to bankrupt me, are you?'

She glanced at him in surprise. 'But you know exactly how much I've spent so far – you've paid for everything.'

'So I have.' He started on the cutlery, sweeping the cloth carelessly along the knives and forks then dropping them, still soapy, in a pile to put away later. 'Which reminds me, it's time you learned to handle the van. What if there was an emergency?'

'Like what?'

'I don't know.' Rufus flipped the tea cloth over his shoulder and picked up the plates, moving across to the dresser to put them away. 'I might get struck by lightning, fall down the stairs and break my leg, anything. If you could drive the van you could—'

'I could drag you all the way across the hall, carry you down the steps and pop you in the back, then drive at top speed for Cromer hospital. Of course. I see what you mean.' Clementine's voice was husky with laughter.

'Big strong girl like you,' complained Rufus. 'You could at least carry me across the hall instead of dragging me.'

The giggle came, that wonderful hiccuping gurgle in the back of her throat, and when she turned her head to look at him, her eyes were bright with mischief. 'Oh, no,' she said demurely. 'I don't think so. It's not in my contract, is it?'

How long, wondered Rufus, facing up at last to what he already knew, how long before I can tell you how I feel about you?

He stepped up his campaign the following day, ordering newspapers (cancelled in a fit of pique six months ago because even with his old glasses on he had been struggling to read them), *The Times* and the *Eastern Daily Press*. They were intended as a distraction, something to ease the atmosphere so Clementine wouldn't feel she had to make conversation over breakfast.

On the first morning she only glanced at the headlines as she moved to and fro making her tea and toast, then disappeared upstairs to work as usual. On the second day her eye was caught by an article in the *Eastern*

Daily Press about the conservation workshop being set up at Blackstock, a Heritage Trust property the other side of Ashington, and she sat down for a couple of minutes to read it while the kettle boiled, which gave Rufus the opportunity to make her a cup of tea. Then, of course, she had to stay and drink it; it would have been impolite to just leave when he had gone to so much trouble. On the third morning her tea was already poured and there was toast and honey laid in her place when she entered the kitchen – Rufus had been on stand-by for nearly half an hour, had already thrown away two rounds of soggy toast and a pot of stewed tea, and he was sitting at the table, invisible behind *The Times*.

When she thanked him for her breakfast he merely grunted; she didn't see the mile-wide grin he was wearing behind his paper shield. He had left his new glasses upstairs, so he couldn't actually see what he was supposed to be reading, but that didn't matter. The point was, the paper did away with the necessity to talk, gave her something to concentrate on so she didn't feel awkward about being with him.

His glasses turned out to be an unexpectedly useful weapon in his secret campaign. Rufus was careless of his appearance as a rule. The spectacles he had so casually approved at the optician's were old-fashioned, roundish, with thin tortoiseshell frames, and it was only as he sat up one night, ostensibly poring over his books but actually staring into space and fantasising about his unattainable housekeeper, that he happened to catch sight of himself in his study window.

Sal had always hated his old glasses, half-frames with thin gold rims, but she liked his new ones. 'You look like a vague college professor—' she said the first time she saw them, '—really sweet.' Certainly, he thought, examining his reflection in the glass, they softened the grim lines of his face, lessened the intimidating effect of his heavy black brows. Accordingly, when Clementine walked into the kitchen the following morning, her tea was made, her breakfast laid in her place, and Rufus, who had been up since six, was sitting at the table reading the paper with his glasses perched nonchalantly on his nose.

'Morning,' he said, glancing up briefly.

'Morning.'

He sensed her looking at him, wondered anxiously whether he had overdone it, made himself look like a fool. 'Sleep well?' he asked, hoping his voice didn't sound as unsteady as his stomach felt.

'Mm, fine.' She was still standing there, head slightly on one side, examining him, he could see her out of the corner of his eye. 'I didn't know you wore glasses.'

'I've worn them for years.' Rufus raised his head, realised he couldn't see her properly and pushed the glasses down so he could focus over the top of them. 'I only use them for reading.'

Clementine smiled, a lovely, breezy grin which sent Rufus's temperature soaring. 'They suit you,' she said. 'More coffee?'

The weather continued wet and chilly. Noticing the thick woollen jumpers Clementine wore all the time, Rufus, who did not often feel the cold and rarely found it necessary to light a fire even during the winter, guessed she might not be as hardy as he and set the central heating to come on first thing in the morning, so her bedroom and her bathroom would be warm. Then it occurred to him that if she was to be comfortable while she worked, he had better heat the rooms they were using during the day as well. Accordingly he added more hours to the timer, leaving it running until last thing at night. He was rewarded when she discarded the bulky jumpers in favour of a series of colourful shirts, reds and blues, checks and stripes, beneath her shapeless dungarees, and he discovered that her arms were as enticing as the rest of her, strong, big-boned with rounded elbows and pretty wrists. Lust-inducing wrists.

Her cheeks began to lose that pinched look too, although Rufus could not work out whether her improved demeanour was due to the rise in temperature or her growing confidence. That she *was* more confident was not in doubt. She smiled more often, laughed when he made stupid jokes instead of staring at him in alarm, volunteered remarks about the weather, about the task in which she was engaged. His elation grew daily.

The next step was to get her out of her bedroom in the evenings, but he was temporarily stumped for a solution to that one. In the meantime, at least he could make her feel that she was independent, that she need not rely on him for anything.

'Here,' he said on the Wednesday as they sat at breakfast, dropping his car keys on the table along with a list. 'The van's outside the front door. We're running low on provisions and I've some urgent paperwork to finish.'

'Oh.' Clementine stared dubiously at the keys, then at Rufus. He had pushed his spectacles up into his thick hair, and he looked nice, unthreatening, even attractive.

He fumbled about, then dropped his glasses back on to his nose and returned to the article he was reading as if what he was asking was of no particular moment. Clementine warmed her hands on her tea cup and surreptitiously examined his face. It *was* an attractive face, she decided, in its own way. His bone structure was good, well-defined cheekbones, a straight, rather patrician nose, a stubborn, no, a *firm* jaw, and fine eyes, dark blue/grey and fringed by thick black lashes. If he could only learn to look less grim, and get his hair cut, he would be quite a good-looking man . . .

When, unexpectedly, he raised his head, met her gaze over the top of his glasses and grinned, she was jolted to realise just how attractive he could be. Embarrassed by the unexpected direction of her thoughts, she snatched up the keys and the list, said briskly, 'Right, I'll get my coat,' and rose hastily from the table.

'Bugger!' muttered Rufus under his breath as she made for the door. He had overdone it.

Jonathan rang the following day.

'I don't think she's in,' Rufus prevaricated, curbing a strong desire to add, 'you bastard'.

'Well, would you go and check, please?'

Rufus took his time walking up the stairs, outraged by the man's nerve. There was a long delay before Clementine's voice came from the other side of the door.

'I'll be down in a minute.'

Did she sound upset, or was he imagining things? She didn't have to talk to the bloody man, he could tell him she wasn't in. He took the stairs two at a time then stopped in the hall, heard her steps on the landing and wondered if he was doing the right thing interfering. He gritted his teeth and returned to the study. 'She's on her way,' he growled and slammed the receiver down on the desk.

Clementine's face was pale and her mouth was set in a tight, anxious line. 'Thank you,' she said as she passed him, and she took the phone clumsily, almost dropping it. Rufus left her to it, but he had no compunction about eavesdropping and he heard every word she said. It cheered him, convinced him he'd done the right thing.

'Hello.'

'Clem, listen darling, I'm in Norwich for a few days next week, on business—'

Clementine was instantly suspicious. 'What business?'

'Mm? Oh, just someone I met, asked for a quote. Coincidence, isn't it?' Sal had warned Jonathan not to let on it was her he was working for. She didn't want Rufus blaming her when Clementine went back to London. She said 'when', not 'if'. Sal Glover, Jonathan was discovering, was a very positive person. 'She's asked me to do up her place in Norwich. Nice house, lots of potential, and she wants it completely refurbished from top to—'

'Isn't Norwich a bit far to come?'

'Not really.' Jonathan was on safer ground now and his confidence grew. 'What about that Georgian place we were working on when you first joined the company? That was west of Oxford. And I've just got a commission to decorate a medieval folly the other side of Chichester.' Subterfuge was easy if you could tell the truth at least some of the time.

'Oh.' Clementine couldn't think of anything to say. She leaned against Rufus's desk, picked up his glasses and peered through them at the blurry paperwork on his desk, calming herself down.

'Anyway, I'm coming up on Monday and I'll have a couple of hours free in the middle of the day, so I thought I'd take you out somewhere for lunch—'

'What? No!'

'Clem, *please*. I just need to talk. There are so many things I haven't had a chance to say—'

'No,' repeated Clementine. 'Jonathan, I don't want to see you anymore.'

'But Clem, you said—'

'I know what I said. I've changed my mind. I'm sorry, but no.' Clementine removed the phone from her ear, took a deep breath and replaced it firmly on its cradle. Then she stood for ages, staring at nothing and feeling terribly, terribly lonely.

When she left the study, the front door was open to the damp autumn morning and Rufus was standing on the step with his hands in his pockets, examining the shrubbery.

'I must do something about this garden,' he said, turning as he heard her footsteps. Her face was puckered, as if she was about to cry. 'Lunch?'

'What? Oh, no, thank you. I'm not very hungry.' She hesitated. 'Could I borrow the van again this afternoon, do you think?'

'Sure.' Rufus leaned against the doorjamb, feigning casual disinterest. He'd hardly seen her since her outing the previous day, and then only to say, 'All right?' when she'd handed back the keys. 'Yes, fine,' she had said briskly before scuttling up to her room, clutching two bulky parcels to her chest and leaving him to unload the rest of the shopping.

'How'd it go yesterday?' he asked now.

'Quite well.' She smiled, a half-smile that faded almost before it had begun. 'I'm better on my own, I don't feel such a fool when I miss the gears.'

'Good. Are you sure you won't have some lunch?'

'No, really, thanks.'

Their eyes met, held. 'Are you okay?' asked Rufus, stretching his self-imposed rules and longing to break them, wanting to comfort her.

To his surprise she gave him a direct answer, said in a small, shaky voice, 'No, not really.'

The ensuing silence lengthened and neither seemed able to look away. Rufus took a step nearer. 'Won't you let me help?' he asked.

Clementine was swept for the second time by a strong

desire to lean against Rufus Palliser's broad chest and weep.

'Thank you.' She dragged her eyes from his with difficulty, straightened her shoulders. 'If I could just borrow the van? It's only a headache, and the fresh air will sort me out . . .'

For the second time, Rufus had the feeling that he had asked the wrong question, or not quite asked the right one, had moved too close, or not close enough. She had slipped through his fingers again. 'I'll get you the keys.' He strode past her, making for his desk and the drawer where he kept them. Don't ask, he reminded himself. Just be there in case she needs you. *Jesus*, this is hard.

On Friday, over breakfast, he reminded her that the following day was Saturday.

'Yes,' she said, puzzled. 'I know.'

'Saturday is your day off.'

'Oh.' She looked taken aback, then bleak, as if she found the idea of taking time off uninviting, even distasteful. 'I've finished the first coat of paint,' she said. 'And I've started stripping the landing. I'll probably work through the weekend.'

'No you won't. Even domestic servants are entitled to time off.' How vulnerable she looked, thought Rufus, like a shy child facing the prospect of a room full of strangers. 'Why don't you go and see your friend?' he suggested. 'You haven't been over there at all this week.'

Clementine was feeling guilty about Jean. Not only had she not been to see her, but when Jean had rung while she was out she had not phoned her back either. She couldn't face the questions.

'You're probably right,' she acknowledged. 'I should have gone round days ago.'

Rufus chuckled. 'There's no need to sound so enthusiastic. I tell you what, you can have the van all day Sunday if you like. Take her out somewhere, visit old haunts. How would that be?'

His reward was a real smile, one that melted his bones and fired his loins. After she had left the kitchen he sat on at the table, waiting for the heat to subside. Then he rose and wandered out into the walled garden to clear his head.

Every day he became more deeply entangled and every day Clementine Lee seemed to slip further out of his reach.

Chapter Twenty-Two

'To what do I owe this honour?' asked Jean, glaring through the half-open door.

'I just came to say . . . er, well, hello, and I'm sorry I haven't been round this week. It's just that I've been so busy . . .'

Jean made no attempt to help her out, merely stared sullenly. Sometimes she looked remarkably like Eddie.

'Besides, I thought you'd be sick of the sight of my ugly mug by now—'

'Pull the other one,' said Jean dismissively. 'Better things to do, more like, what with all your glamorous friends—'

'What glamorous friends?'

Jean swung the door wider and moved grudgingly out of the way, curiosity getting the better of her resentment. 'I suppose you might as well come in. But don't think you can stay all evening, I'm making the Christmas cake and Robert's getting fish and chips as soon as he's finished outside.' Jean was always months ahead with her preparations.

Clementine hated Christmas. She had spent too many solitary Christmases, alone even when she was with other people, to associate the festive season with anything but isolation and misery. She followed Jean into the kitchen. There was a smell of cooking, a big pot simmered on the hob and Eddie was sitting at the table surrounded by cake-making ingredients. As they entered the room he snatched his hand away from the mixing bowl and adopted an expression of injured innocence.

'Aren't we quite the little angel?' said Jean sarcastically and smacked his fingers as she passed, just in case. She didn't offer Clem a cup of tea, or a drink. 'So where's the dog, then?'

'At home. I mean,' as Jean pulled a mocking face, 'at Manor Hall.'

'Well settled then, are you? Bully for you.'

Clementine's guilt was compounded by the growing realisation that this time Jean was not going to be so easy to placate. 'Jean, I've said I'm sorry. I honestly didn't mean to upset you—'

Jean snorted. 'You never do, do you? But the fact remains that over the God-knows-how-many years we've been friends, it's always been me that's put myself out – Eddie, will you get your grubby little hand out of that bowl!'

Eddie jumped guiltily and stuffed his index finger, laden with cake mixture, into his mouth. A heavy dollop fell on to the floor and he scrambled off his chair to sweep it up, along with a dusting of cat hairs and fluff, then shoved that in as well before it could be taken away. To Clementine's astonishment, Jean lost her temper completely.

'*Christ!*' she yelled, going scarlet in the face with rage, 'you are a disgusting little tyke! Get out of here, before I wallop the living daylights out of you, go on, get up to your room!' Then as Eddie dived for the door and the stairs she sat down at the kitchen table and burst into tears.

'Jean, are you all right?' asked Clem, patting her help-lessly on the back as if she was suffering from the hiccups rather than a gale of weeping. She had never seen her friend like this before. 'Jean, what on earth's the matter?'

She found kitchen towel, tore off strip after strip and handed them across while Jean mopped and sobbed, blew and sobbed again. Then she sat down beside her and put a clumsy arm round her shoulder. This was all her fault, a punishment for taking the best friend she had for granted. She didn't deserve her. 'I'm sorry,' she repeated. 'I know I'm a lousy apology for a friend. I don't mean to be. I . . .'

Her voice petered out into silence, and Jean's heaving shoulders drooped. She picked up the last piece of kitchen towel and blew her nose hard, then wiped her face, rose from the table and walked unsteadily across to the larder. 'I need a drink,' she said.

She returned to the table with a bottle of gin and two glasses, poured large measures, topped them up with lukewarm tonic, then handed one to Clementine and took a slurp at the other. 'Do you have any idea what it feels like,' she asked, staring morosely at the bubbles ris-ing in her glass, 'to discover that someone you thought you knew has a whole secret existence from which you are excluded—' Clementine opened her mouth to protest, but Jean waved a hand to silence her, '—from which you are excluded? I thought we were close, you and I. I'd always hoped you'd come home one day, imagined we'd revisit the old places, do some of the things we used to do when we were kids. And now you're here it's spoiled, because you're not who I thought you were at all.' Her voice trailed away into tears again, and she took another gulp of gin. 'I wish you'd never come back if you really want to know.'

'I'm sorry,' repeated Clem, like a mantra.

'You didn't even want to see me off the premises last Saturday. You didn't want me there at all. And you thought I was so fucking stupid I wouldn't notice.' Jean had always sworn when she was upset, even as a child, using the shock value of the words as a weapon. 'I'm not good enough for you any more, am I? Not now you've got a bloke with a BMW and a fancy line in chat.'

'No I haven't.'

'Yes you bloody well have, I'm not blind. Or deaf. He called you darling, I heard him as I walked in, and I passed his car in the drive.' Jean took another swig at her gin. 'I suppose I'll read about the engagement in the papers, will I, get to see the wedding photos if I'm lucky? Heaven forbid I should embarrass you by actually turning up for the nuptial feast—'

'He's not my boyfriend any more,' said Clementine. 'I thought he was going to marry me, but he turned out to already have a lover. Another man.'

'I beg your pardon?'

'Jonathan. He's bisexual. I'm not seeing him any more.'

Jean stared at her with her mouth open, then sniffed again, reached for the tonic and topped up her glass, clearly embarrassed. This was outside Jean's experience of life, too weird to take in. Clementine shrugged, attempting to belittle her calamity. Why had she come? Jean had wormed it out of her, as she had known she would and now her humiliation was complete.

'That gorgeous man?' said Jean at last. 'Bloody hell!' then, returning to her complaint, 'Why didn't you tell me?'

'Because—'

Jean cut her off. 'I'll tell you why, shall I? You didn't tell me because good old Jean, faithful friend that she is, is handy enough to keep you in touch with Mummy and Daddy, to remind you of your perfect childhood . . .' Clementine was shocked by the venom she put into the words, '. . . but she isn't grand enough to mix with your posh friends, is she? You're ashamed of me, aren't you?'

'How can you *possibly* say that?' Clementine was bewildered. 'Whenever you've been up to London, however short a time you were staying, I've taken you out, shown you the sights, made you welcome. Haven't I?' Even sometimes when she had been busy, when it had been less than convenient, she had gone out of her way. If she hadn't taken Jean to see where she worked, it was only because she had thought she wouldn't be interested. And often she had felt, when she booked tickets for a West End show, a table at a fashionable restaurant, or when she had arranged a surprise, a trip on the river, *Son et Lumière* at Hampton Court, that Jean was pitying her, that she went home and told Robert how sad it was, poor old Clem, such an empty life with no one to call her own, if it wasn't for her visits Clem would have nothing to look forward to at all.

'Didn't you enjoy *any* of it?' she asked.

Jean shrugged, dismissing the question. 'Of course I did.' She took another gulp at her gin. 'But you never introduced me to your friends, did you? You never took me out to dinner with your workmates, or your boyfriends?'

Clementine, shaken by Jean's continuing hostility, lowered her head and stared at the laminated table top, moving her glass round and round the wood-effect knotholes. 'I don't have friends,' she said simply. 'I have acquaintances, people I work with, people I know, but I don't have any close friends, apart from you.' She rose from the table and wandered across to the window. It was dark outside, and the light from the barn spilled out on to the yard, a big, yellow square on the concrete. 'I never took you out to dinner with my boyfriends because none of them lasted long enough to be worth introducing . . .'

Jean went to rummage in the larder for more tonic. 'Oh, *sod* it,' Clementine heard her say, and she emerged with a large bottle of coke. She brought it back to the table, then slumped in her seat again, and glared moodily into her gin while Clementine stared out into the dark at Robert's shadowy figure moving to and fro across the barn.

'I'm sorry,' repeated Clem at last. 'All the time, you know, when I was in hospital, then when I was learning to live on my own, when I started at college and I was scared stiff because I didn't know a soul, when I was so lonely I thought nobody would notice whether I lived or died, you were the only person who kept me going. I was so grateful. And I envied you . . .' She watched Robert emerge into the open to shoo the last chicken safely inside, scuff his boots against the yard broom and contemplate the sky, gauging what tomorrow's weather would bring. 'You had a family, someone to go home to, a place where you belonged, and all I had left was you.' She could hear Jean behind her, pouring more gin, then the hiss of the coke bottle and the fizz as it was added to the glass.

'Gawd,' said Jean, sipping experimentally. 'This tastes disgusting.' She rose and came to stand beside Clementine, reaching barely to her shoulder. 'How stupid,' she said. She sounded different, not angry now, just sad, and slightly slurred. 'I was jealous of *you*, have been for years, because you escaped.' She followed Clementine's gaze, watching Robert as he battened down the hatches, switching off the lights in the barn then moving around in the shadows, swinging the big doors shut and hefting the bar across to keep out marauding foxes before turning to make his way towards the kitchen and supper.

'He wasn't really getting fish and chips. I only said that to upset you.' Jean turned back to face the room and leaned against the windowsill. 'If you want to know, I used to come up to London, to your immaculate flat, and look at all your nice things and wish *I* had a place of my own, somewhere that no one could mess up, that I could decorate knowing Eddie wasn't going to smear chocolate sauce all over it, or that Robert wasn't going to say the minute I'd finished, why did you have to do that? I liked it the way it was.' She took another gulp of gin, grimacing at the taste. 'I used to feel, when I walked up your stairs, like I was approaching my own Secret Garden, a small pocket of civilisation in the midst of my chaotic life. I used to imagine running away, beginning all over again—'

'But you've got Robert, and Eddie. I thought—'

Jean snorted. 'You overestimate marriage,' she said. 'And motherhood, just like I did before I had them. There are times when I would cheerfully give Eddie away to the first person who walked through that door. Don't look so shocked. I love the little bastard to pieces, but sometimes I don't like him one tiny bit.' She made a face at her glass, then wandered back to the table and put it down. 'I can't drink any more of this, it tastes disgusting. You don't know, and I can't explain because you're not a mother – no, don't look like that, I'm not getting at you, it's just . . .' She leaned against the chair back. She sounded tired, defeated, not like her usual bouncy self at all. 'It's just that it's so *relentless*. Since Eddie was born, the only time I've felt like a real person, like I was *me*, instead of just somebody's wife, somebody's mother, somebody's daughter-in-law, everybody's bloody skivvy, was on those rare occasions when I left Eddie with Robert and came up to London to see you.' She sat down heavily, resting her elbows on her knees and her head in her hands. 'I shouldn't be drinking,' she said. 'I'm pregnant,' and the way she said it, it was the end of the world.

Clementine was shocked again. Being pregnant was good news, wasn't it? Just as having a husband and a child was good news, or so Jean had always led her to believe. You think you know someone, she mused, staring in perplexity at Jean's tragic face, and it turns out you don't know them at all.

She left the window and knelt by Jean's bent head, awkwardly stroking her short, springy hair. 'You'll love it when it comes,' she offered lamely, because that was all she could think of to say. Jean raised her head and managed a watery smile.

'I know,' she said. 'That's the trouble. You do. You love them to death, but sometimes you just wish you were without them. Does that sound dreadful?'

'. . . Mummy?'

Eddie appeared in the doorway, teetering flamingo-like, one leg wrapped round the other, his plump face screwed up with anxiety. 'I just – I mean – it's not my *fault*. It just done it, an' now it won't turn off—'

'*Did* it,' corrected Jean automatically. 'Did what? What won't turn off?' She wiped her eyes on her sleeve, and both women peered at him over the empty glasses, the coke and tonic bottles, the soggy pile of kitchen towel and the paraphernalia of cake making.

'The tap.' Eddie switched legs, scratched his bottom. 'In the barfwoom.' He glanced anxiously over his shoulder, listening for something. 'I was getting weddy for bed, see.' He paused, his finger hovering near his nose, thought better of it. 'It's stuck,' he added, elucidating, 'the tap. An' I can't get the plug out. It's not my *fault*.'

Robert appeared in the doorway behind him, a stocky, square-faced man with fair hair and the ruddy cheeks of a countryman. 'I'm starving,' he said. 'How do, Clem. Supper ready is it, Jeanie?'

Jean turned to Clementine and rolled her eyes. 'See what I mean?' she complained, and Robert, exchanging puzzled glances with his son, wondered why both women suddenly dissolved into whoops of hysterical laughter.

On Sunday morning they drove out to Blackstock. The great house and the formal gardens were shut for the winter but the park and the lake were still open to the public. They left the van on the edge of the estate then strolled, past shaggy Highland cattle, down to the water's edge, their scarves wrapped round their ears and their coats buttoned up against the cold. Then they followed the path towards the long ride of cypresses on the far side.

The branches met so close that virtually no light penetrated under the trees and it was almost like being in the forest at night. No birds roosted beneath the thick canopy and the quiet was absolute, almost religious. They had loved its secret gloom when they were young, considered it one of their most special places. Their feet made no sound and their voices fell dead in the silence.

'So when's the baby due?'

'Middle of May.' Jean glanced at her friend, striding beside her through a thick carpet of dead needles with Mary, intimidated by the enclosed space, trotting close by her side. 'You could be a godmother this time.' She had asked when Eddie was born, but Clem had said no, she couldn't face it.

'I'm sorry.' Clem felt as if she had spent the past

twenty-four hours apologising. 'I just wasn't ready then. To be honest, if it hadn't been for Amsterdam I wouldn't have come home at all.'

'Amsterdam?'

What better place to confess? Dropping her voice to suit the cathedral-like hush, Clementine told Jean about Amsterdam, about her interview with Sebastian in the hotel, the fog and the ramshackle aeroplane. She told her about her black eye, which made Jean laugh, and her nostalgic journey out to Dinningham, which made her angry that her friend had been so close and not come to see her. Then she explained how she had been ousted from her partnership, which turned Jean's ire against the iniquities of men in general and Jonathan and his lover in particular, and about Terry's decision to sell her flat, which caused Jean to lament again the loss her London bolt hole. Clementine promised there would be another. 'This job at Manor Hall is just temporary, until I get back on my feet again.' She left out only Rufus and the bunch of roses he had thrust into her arms at Norwich Airport, because she knew that if Jean thought there was romance in the air between her and her employer, she would latch on to it like a bloodhound on the scent and never let go. 'And I've decided,' she added, reminded of her resolution, 'that I'm never going to get involved with a man again as long as I live.'

They ate soup and sandwiches at the Buck, then took the back road home, stopping half a mile short of the village to give Mary a last run. They strolled slowly up Coppice Hill, all slights, all misunderstandings, forgiven at last, and sat on an uneven tree stump, all that remained of an ancient oak in whose branches they had played as children.

'Do you remember?' asked Clem, wallowing in

nostalgia, 'you carved J.S. loves R.H. on the trunk the first year you were going out with Robert.'

Jean laughed. 'And Pa was furious because I pinched his antique paper knife to do it and broke the blade. We had such fun, didn't we?'

From the brow of the hill they could see the whole of Dinningham spread out before them, the Hawes's modern brick slab in the foreground, then the thatched farmhouse in which Robert's parents still lived, the council houses, three pairs, pink-washed above, red-brick below, and Dorrie's row of tiny flint-faced cottages. On the far side of the river, beyond the bridge, the church tower rose grey and flinty above the bigger houses clustered round the green. It was a typical rural English scene, familiar, reassuring.

'Why isn't it enough?' Clementine picked out the white plume of smoke spiralling lazily into the sky from the drawing room chimney at Manor Hall. Had Rufus wanted her out of the house today so he could invite his girlfriend over again? And what did such a beautiful woman see in that vague, untidy, unpredictable man? Perhaps he had hidden depths . . .

'Why isn't what enough?'

'Mm?' Clementine dragged her wayward thoughts back to the subject in hand. 'Oh, you know, marriage, motherhood.'

Jean sighed heavily, her breath clouding in the chilly air. 'I don't know. I thought marriage was everything I wanted. It never occurred to me that I might need more. You know what my mum and dad are like – not a cross word in over forty years of marriage, all lovey-dovey and holding hands even now, at nearly seventy. Pa is Ma's reason for being. As far as she's concerned she was put on this earth to pander to his every whim and making him happy is what makes her happy.' She rubbed her cold hands together. 'It's only lately that I've noticed how much she's sublimated herself to him over the years, how much she's given up in her search for the perfect relationship.'

She glanced at Clem, sitting so tall and still beside her with her hand resting on Mary's shaggy head. 'Their marriage works because she gives in to everything Pa wants, and it's not just Pa. All her adult life she's been doing what other people want, friends, parishioners, her children. When I was growing up I thought she'd found the recipe for perfect contentment. I don't remember her ever raising her voice to any of us, not once. She made it seem so easy, bringing up three kids, running that damp, draughty old house, all the parish duties.' She sighed, hunching her shoulders against the cold. 'I was only fifteen when Robert and I started courting, and he was twenty-one. I was engaged at seventeen, still only eighteen when we got married, and he was a responsible old man of twenty-four. He never asked me where I wanted to go, or what I wanted to do, we just did whatever he'd decided.'

She stared across the washed-out landscape at her home, her prison. Robert would be pacing the kitchen, peering out of the window, waiting for her return. He loathed babysitting Eddie, couldn't wait to relinquish responsibility for his son so he could go and do something more interesting. Jean put a hand on her stomach, reminded of the second, as yet unborn being, who would be coming so soon to further constrict her life. 'I wanted a family right away, but Robert wanted to wait, have some freedom before we settled down to the responsibilities of parenthood, he said. But the freedom turned out to be all his, with his darts nights and his Young Farmers' do's, his shooting parties and his agricultural shows, and when I suggested getting a part-time job, just to keep me occupied, he said no, no wife of his would ever have to work for a living, as if he was doing me a favour. I thought the sun shone out of his eyes – I actually felt pleased he was so masterful; it took me ages to work out that he was just worried about whether his shirts were going to be ironed and his tea on the table. Then when his dad retired and he realised he was getting older, he started thinking about a son and heir, so we had Eddie.' Clementine was shocked again, by the resentment in Jean's voice. 'If I'd had my way, Eddie would be fourteen by now, practically off my hands. Robert wants a girl this time, to complete his family. Not *our* family, you notice, *his* family, as if he owns us. So here I am, pregnant again, and I've just noticed that my life is slipping away from me. I'm thirty-three years old. I've been nowhere, done nothing and now I'm never likely to.'

She went back to her reverie, staring out over her husband's land, hating it, hating him, but most of all, hating herself for allowing her life to be taken away without even putting up a fight.

The wind quickened, slicing across the open ground and biting at their cheeks. Clementine shivered and wrapped her scarf closer round her face. 'Think about what you're good at,' she suggested. 'What do you like doing best?'

'I don't know. Needlework, I suppose, sewing, knitting. You know me, I was never academic.' Jean rose and stretched, stiff from sitting. 'So?'

'So, how about doing something from home? Dressmaking, alterations, something like that? You've still got your sewing machine, haven't you? Or use your embroidery skills. Think of all those tapestry kneelers you made for the church, and those cushions you did for me.'

During the early years, Clementine had received

numerous examples of Jean's talent with needle and thread, exquisitely worked cushions or linen table napkins with intricate thread-work round the edges, a waistcoat embroidered with silk butterflies and a pretty beaded belt, all executed with consummate skill, all given and received with enormous mutual pleasure. Jean had made her own clothes too, when she was first married, knitted jumpers for friends and relatives, sewn the curtains for Clem's flat. Since Eddie, the creative urge seemed to have petered out. 'No time,' she'd say when asked or, 'Frankly I'm too tired these days. Kids are great, but they do take it out of you.'

'There's something you could do for me, if you like, for Manor Hall.'

'Oh, what's that?'

Clementine explained what she wanted. 'It would probably only take you a couple of days, but you know me, I'm hopeless with a needle. I've got the material already, and—' She must phrase it right, otherwise Jean would refuse to take any money. 'Rufus'll pay you,' she lied. 'He's given me some cash for the incidentals. And if you could find the time, you never know, it might lead to more work later on. What do you think?'

'I don't know,' Jean demurred. 'Robert probably wouldn't like it . . .' As she spoke a tiny figure burst at speed from the back door of Hawe's Farm, closely followed by a much bigger one. The smaller figure scampered across the yard, making a futile dash for freedom, but the other was in hot pursuit, and the little one barely made it to the lee of the barn. There was a brief struggle and the sound of a childish wail carried faintly on the air as Eddie, tucked under his father's arm like a bundle of rags, was manhandled back inside. The door was slammed, hard enough for the bang to carry.

'All right,' decided Jean. 'I'll do it. Bring the stuff

round tomorrow morning and I'll get on with it right away.' Her spirits lifted immediately but the euphoria was followed by an attack of guilt. 'We'd better get back now,' she said, 'Robert'll be wanting his tea.'

'She won't even talk to me.' Jonathan was stretched on the couch in Sal's dreary sitting room, on the telephone. 'She put the phone down on me. What am I going to do?'

Sal was lounging in a wicker chair in Jonathan's conservatory with a pencil tucked behind her left ear. The bamboo table was piled high with invoices, receipts, bank statements, tax returns, she was sipping a large Bloody Mary mixed from ingredients found in Jonathan's kitchen and she was stroking his cat, curled up contentedly beside her.

'Keep trying. There's nothing a woman likes more than a persistent lover. If she won't talk to you on the phone, go round. I'm going to need at least ten days on these books, so you'll be quite safe – Rufus'll be in Norwich minding the shop, that's the whole point of the exercise.' She took another sip at her drink, shook her head. The boy was a hopeless case. 'How're the ideas coming?'

'What ideas?'

'For the house, darling. I've done two years' worth of accounts so far. What've you done?'

'Oh. Sorry.' Jonathan lit another of Sal's cigarettes. 'Don't panic, I've done some work, it takes my mind off Clem . . . Do you really think if I turn up on her doorstep she'll—'

'You'll only find out if you try it, won't you? Listen, I can't talk now, I must feed the lovely Simba, who is pointedly sharpening her claws on my knee and then I'm going out.'

'Oh? Where?'

Sal chuckled. 'Thought I'd trawl the King's Road for talent. Know any decent pubs, darling?'

Clementine drove home slowly. It was only just after three and Rufus might still be entertaining.

He hailed her as she crossed the hall, 'How'd it go?' and Mary made eagerly for the drawing room, wagging her tail.

'Lovely. It was lovely, thank you.' Clementine fumbled in her coat pocket for the van keys and moved towards the inviting glow she could see through the open door. 'We walked round the park at Blackstock and had lunch at the Buck. Shall I leave the keys on your desk?'

'No, bring them in here, would you?'

She hesitated on the threshold, expecting to see Sal Glover and reluctant to intrude, but Rufus was alone, lounging on the sofa with a book in his lap, his spectacles swinging between thumb and finger and his legs stretched towards the fire. The coffee pot was sitting in the hearth and there was a half-finished mug of coffee on the table. He looked relaxed, comfy, and the room exuded a welcoming warmth, as Rufus had intended it should when he planned this encounter some two hours earlier.

He gave Mary a last caress and held out his hand for the keys. Clementine was flushed from the open air and the wind had whipped her hair into wisps and tendrils that curled untidily about her face. She looked glorious, a great buxom English wench, pink-cheeked, glowing, *comely*. Closing his hand too quickly round the keys, Rufus brushed her fingers, felt a fierce stab of lust. 'Sit down,' he said, rising too fast and tripping over Mary. 'The kettle's just boiled, I'll make you a cup of tea.'

'No. No, I'll—'

'I was just about to make more coffee anyway.' He swept the pot from the floor. 'And I want to talk to you about the library, I've thought of a better way of organising it.' He straightened up, avoiding her eye lest his lascivious thoughts show. 'Oh, and what's-his-name rang again. He said he'd call back tomorrow.' Risking a quick glance he thought he saw a shade of irritation cross her features. Good, he thought, the bastard's pushed his luck too far. 'Sit down,' he repeated. 'I shan't be long.'

It must have been the warm room after all the fresh air. She had taken her coat off and draped it over the back of the sofa, presumably so she could escape as quickly as possible when he returned, then sat down and fallen asleep. Rufus stationed himself across from her as the twilight crept into the room, drinking her in. Her head was tipped back, a little to one side, and she breathed lightly. He imagined her lying beside him after they had made love, her thick hair spread on his pillow, her mouth curving softly upwards, as it was now, and he made a resolution. If she ever came to him he would sell every book he possessed, somehow he would raise the money to stay here. They would restore the place together, fill it with children, and for the first time since the boy's death there would be some point to his life. His spirits rose. Patience. All he needed was patience.

When Clementine opened her eyes she was alone but for Mary, snoring and twitching at her feet, and the flickering firelight. She sat on in the darkened room, watching the flames make patterns on the ceiling and mulling over the problem of Jean, wondering whether a few sewing jobs and a little pin money were enough to pay her back for all the years of loyal friendship. She was astonished when she heard the cuckoo announce ten o'clock. She rose, placed the guard carefully in front of the fire and picked her way across the room towards the hall, to let Mary out for the last time. There was a line of light beneath the study door; Rufus must be working late. How kind of him, she thought, to let her sleep. He must have got his own supper. She took a last look at the drawing room, letting its silent peace wash over her. She felt calm, serene. She crossed the hall, hesitated outside the study. She thought she would put her head round the door and say thank you. She raised her hand to knock, then let it fall. Perhaps not.

Chapter Twenty-Three

Sal phoned to say she would be in London for at least ten days. Having gone to such lengths to get Clementine to eat breakfast with him Rufus lingered at the table and was late opening up every day.

It made little difference to his trade. His bread and butter, students, impecunious housewives, the unemployed, pensioners, were steady as always, but the more expensive end of his business began to pick up as October progressed. The genuine bibliophiles, those who knew the difference between an octavo and a duodecimo, between sprinkling and marbling, tree calf and morocco, came to buy their Christmas presents early or simply to indulge themselves, succumbing to the urge to spend. As well as the usual paperbacks, he sold leather-bound volumes of poetry, illustrated botanical works, heavy, gold-tooled folios, to enthusiasts looking for something special. He spent time advising, persuading; 'Yes, she loves Jane Austen, but I'm not sure that *Mansfield Park* is her favourite . . .' 'Oh, dear, I hadn't realised how many books John Buchan wrote. I can't make up my mind . . .' 'I don't suppose you have a copy of *The Golden Bough*, do you? It was my favourite as a girl, and I thought my granddaughter might appreciate it . . .' He sold a first edition of *The Posthumous Papers of the Pickwick Club* in blind-stamped purple cloth, to a collector who was so thrilled with his purchase that he left the shop almost in tears, and James Fenimore Cooper's *The Deer Slayer* to a woman buying for her father, who was the proud possessor of every volume in the series of *Leather-Stocking Tales* except that one, and would, she said, be ecstatic that she had tracked down the missing title at last.

Between customers he sat in his dilapidated office, making plans to catch his elusive Clementine instead of keeping up with the paperwork. Lounging in his moulting chair, he conducted long imaginary conversations with her, witty, erudite exchanges that brought them closer together, made her realise how much they had in common. Day by day he won her trust, and then her interest. He made love to her, exploring her curves and hollows, learning the smell of her skin, the feel of her hair, the taste of her mouth, and night after night, when he locked the shop and climbed into his chilly van for the journey home, he had to force himself to face reality. Clementine Lee, whilst as polite and conscientious as ever, was no nearer succumbing to his charm now than she had been on the first day she arrived. He had long since ceased to wonder what she might be doing to his poor, dilapidated home; the work for which he was employing her had become almost an irrelevance.

Impatient for her company, he threw his weight around. 'Supper together. If I'm going to be out every day, I'll need you to fill me in on any problems that may crop up.' He realised how odd he must sound, acting as if he had never left her alone in the house before, but she took him at his word, making sure there was a hot meal on the table every night, and sitting down to eat it with him. It was left to Rufus to make conversation though. Clementine, obeying the letter of his instructions but not the spirit, ate her meal in polite silence, then rose as soon as she had finished to tidy up the kitchen and decamp, either to her room or to Hawe's Farm, as she had since the day she arrived. Frustrated, Rufus tried another tack, lighting a fire in the drawing room every night to lure her into its welcoming warmth, only to watch her walk past the open door, call, 'goodnight,' and disappear, leaving him in solitary, ridiculous splendour. His compensation was the growing, and surprising, pleasure he was finding for himself in the room's quiet tranquillity, after so long spent avoiding it in favour of his spartan study.

'I've been told to bring you these,' announced Dorrie, appearing at the door with a plate of sandwiches in one hand and a glass of orange juice in the other. 'Rufus says otherwise you won't eat.'

'Oh! Thank you . . .'

Clementine was clearly not expecting her. She was not where she was supposed to be either, but Dorrie was getting used to that. On Tuesday, one of Dorrie's cleaning days, she had found her in the laundry room, stirring up a witch's brew in the copper with a length of muslin and gallons of blue dye; today she was in a dingy boxroom, flushed and dusty and surrounded by pictures of all shapes and sizes. She must be nearly finished, thought Dorrie, if she was choosing what to put on the walls. 'Rufus seen it yet?' she asked.

'No, it's supposed to be a surprise. What are you doing here on a Saturday?'

'He asked me to pop in,' explained Dorrie. 'Said it had just occurred to him you might be starving to death while he's not here. I don't mind, and he's paying me a bit extra. It's useful this time of year, for the little ones' stocking fillers. You going anywhere nice for Christmas?'

Clementine pushed an escaping lock of hair out of her eyes and took a bite at her sandwich. It was far too early to think about Christmas. 'Jean's I think. She's asked if I'd like to go over for the day.'

'Ah.' Dorrie examined her shrewdly. 'And you're not sure you want to?'

'No – I mean yes, of course I do—' The guilt was still there, the feeling that she did not, could not, give quite as much as Jean did to their friendship. 'But she'll have Robert's parents, and hers, both her brothers and their families. They'll be fourteen altogether, and I keep thinking I'll be in the way. What are you doing?'

'Going to Sandra's, bless her.' Dorrie beamed. 'She's had us the past five years. Lovely it is, not having to do it all.' She chuckled. 'Mind you, she has our Paul's lot over as well, plus this year she's got Mandy and her Vince coming and the others'll all be popping in and out during the day. I hope they'll muck in.' Paul was Dorrie's eldest, Mandy her youngest, only a year married to a local builder. 'D'you remember how Paul and Sandra used to carry on when they were kids? Always up to some practical joke, they were; we could be in for a terrible time of it.' She chuckled richly, enjoying the prospect. 'Families, eh, who'd have 'em?'

She realised as soon as the words left her mouth. 'Oh, Clem, dear,' she apologised, 'I'm so sorry.' She patted Clementine's sleeve, pink and flustered with remorse. 'I didn't mean—'

'Of course you didn't.' Clementine squeezed her fingers reassuringly. 'It's all right, Dorrie. It was a long time ago.' She wandered into the corridor and on towards the landing, heard the cuckoo whirr and clunk, announcing one o'clock. 'What about Rufus, does he have any family?'

'Not that I know of,' Dorrie followed with the orange

juice, her feet, still in their battered Scholl sandals even in October, clattering on the bare floorboards. 'Mind you, I don't suppose he'd tell me if he had. How d'you find him?'

'Rufus? Odd.' That seemed unfair, given how kind he had been lately, disloyal. 'All right, though,' Clementine amended. 'He never criticises, doesn't expect me to wait on him hand and foot.' He hadn't complained either, that she was taking far too long to finish the room she was working on. She took the last sandwich, then handed back her plate.

'How long have you been married, Dorrie?'

Dorrie was surprised by the question. 'Thirty-nine years, give or take a month or so. Why?'

'I just wondered. You seem so . . .' *Happy* was the word that sprang to mind, *contented*. 'And if you had your time again, would you still marry Frank?'

'Can't think of anyone else who'd have me,' said Dorrie, chuckling, then, seeing Clementine's face and realising the question was rather more serious than that, 'He's always made me laugh, see, dear, still does, even after nearly forty years. You can't ask for more than that.'

Clementine nodded solemnly. 'And what about the children? If you could go back and do it again, would you . . .?'

'Have so many kiddies? Oh, yes.' She sounded, thought Clementine, completely certain, as if she had never for one second harboured any doubts about her marriage, or the fact that she had spent most of her adult life going without, herself, in order to feed and clothe her large brood.

'So you would recommend it then?'

'What, marriage?'

'Mm, and children.'

Dorrie patted the newel post, drew herself up to her

full five foot three. 'My dear,' she said kindly, as if she was talking to one of her five-year-olds in the playground at Dinningham County Primary School, 'there is nothing more comforting in life than going home to a good man, and there is nothing in the world so worthwhile as bringing a child into the world and watching it grow. You'll see when it's your turn.' She smiled tenderly, as if Clementine was one of her own, then set off down the stairs. 'Time I got on. Frank'll be back for his dinner.' She paused to peer up shortsightedly at Clementine, still leaning against the balustrade above her. 'It's all about sharing, dear. Good or bad, either way it's better when it's shared.' She took another couple of steps, slowed again. 'The secret is to find the right man.' She chuckled fruitily. 'That's the only hard bit.'

Clementine waited until Dorrie's footsteps had receded across the hall, heard the front door open and close. Then she straightened up and went slowly back to work. The secret is to find the right man. That's the only impossible bit.

Jonathan rang an hour later. She cut him off, but she felt as if she was cutting off her last chance of experiencing all the things Dorrie seemed to think made life worthwhile, and it spoiled her pleasure in the work she was doing. The room was almost finished, just the final touches to do, the bits and pieces waiting at Jean's to be picked up, and then she would be ready to show Rufus. When the phone rang for the second time she was placing pictures, and she ran downstairs, cursing.

Jonathan started pleading the moment she answered, 'Please, Clem, can't we just talk?' and she slammed the receiver down, feeling a resentment out of all proportion to the interruption.

Chapter Twenty-Four

Rufus burst into the kitchen clutching a bottle of champagne and grinning hugely.

'Celebration!' He waved the bottle with one hand, greeted Mary with the other. 'I've made a killing!'

Clementine, hugging her surprise to herself, grinned back. 'Yes?' she prompted. 'What?'

Rufus shrugged his way out of his jacket and made for the corner cupboard, searching for the one proper champagne flute he possessed and talking over his shoulder. 'Those books, remember, the ones I took in when you went to London?' He didn't mention that he had forgotten to deliver them, had driven around for three days with them in the back of the van before he'd finally unloaded them. 'I was in a hurry when I picked them up, just grabbed a pile off one of the shelves without looking at them.' He found the glass, brought it back to the table along with a chipped tumbler and began to tear the gold foil off the champagne bottle. 'Anyway, a woman came in this afternoon and picked out *Seven Pillars of Wisdom*.' His face was transformed, alight with enthusiasm. 'It was only when she asked how much it was that I looked at it more closely—'

The cork came out of the bottle with a loud pop and

Clementine jumped. Rufus laughed, poured, waited for the bubbles to subside, poured again.

'I'd guessed it was a first edition, but that doesn't mean a great deal with that particular title—' He swept the glasses up and held the posh one out across the table. 'Here. It's not my period, of course, but even so, I don't know how I could have missed it.'

He looked like a giant *Just William*, tie askew, tousled hair, one shirtsleeve rolled higher than the other. 'Missed what?' asked Clementine, trying not to laugh. 'What *are* you talking about?'

'Sorry. Cheers!' Rufus raised his glass, drank, sighed gustily, drank again. Never mind the booze, he thought, listening to the husky giggle that had just escaped his housekeeper, I want to kiss you till you can't breathe. He took another deep draught of champagne instead, and topped up his glass. 'The first general edition was published in 1935, and there were so many printed you can pick up a copy even today for practically nothing. But there was a *private* edition, published in 1926, only about 170 copies. And that's the one I've got!' He took another gulp at his champagne. He could feel it fizzing in his brain; it felt wonderful, but not as wonderful as kissing Clementine Lee would be. 'A copy in mint condition will go for four figures, easily.'

'So did she buy it?'

His face split again, into that enormous grin. 'She couldn't afford it. But I just happen to know someone who can. I rang him before I left the shop.' He topped up his tumbler for the second time (or was it the third? He was losing count), and waved the bottle across the table. 'Come on, you're not drinking fast enough!'

'Sorry.' Clem giggled again, unable to help herself. She had never seen him like this before, so uninhibited, so . . . *frivolous*. Obediently, she held out her glass and he filled it to the brim. 'So, can you afford to pay off the mortgage now?'

'Not quite.' Rufus experienced again the ripple of delight he had felt in the shop, when he realised what he'd found. 'But it does mean I can afford to pay your wages for a bit longer than six months . . .' He leaned forward, suddenly intensely serious. 'If you'll stay, that is?' He put his glass down, ran his fingers through his untidy grey mane. 'You will, won't you, Clementine?'

His change of heart, when only a few weeks ago he had been so determined to merely patch the place up and sell it, was astonishing, but it was not the only shock. He used her name only rarely, but the way he said it now, the way he lingered over each syllable, seemed to Clementine to signal a new intimacy, a breaching of their formal relationship. She sat with her glass poised, the bubbles fizzing up her nose, and stared at him in startled silence.

Rufus knew immediately that he had overstepped the mark. 'I beg your pardon,' he apologised, attempting to retrieve the situation. 'What I meant was, I would be most grateful, Miss Lee, if you would consider the possibility of extending your contract of employment beyond the term originally agreed.' Then he ruined the effect by roaring with laughter at the absurdity of what he had just said.

He made her laugh with him, defused her alarm, and Rufus's buoyant mood increased; if he could only persuade her he had changed his mind about the restoration, promise her the opportunity to do it properly, she would stay, for sure. After all, she had no reason to go back to London now she had finished with her bloody boyfriend. The champagne was going straight to his head. 'Drink up,' he repeated, waving the bottle.

Clementine drank deep, excited by the thought of staying, by the surprise she had still to spring on him. She felt lightheaded, irresponsible. When Rufus leaned across the table to grab her hand he caught her off guard.

'Listen,' he began. 'I've decided . . .' He examined her fingers, running a large thumb across the calluses, noting the blue dye clinging to her fingernails.

'Decided?' Clementine's embarrassment was tinged unexpectedly with an edge of physical arousal.

'To do it properly. But only if you'll stay and help me.' He tightened his grip, raised his head and stared at her. 'Please?' She was looking, for once, straight at him, and she caught the message he was sending, blinked at him in surprise. Rufus hastily lowered his head.

Don't be ridiculous, thought Clementine, it's just an illusion, champagne on an empty stomach. 'I've something to show you,' she said, rising briskly from the table, and Rufus realised, as a charge like a thousand volts of electricity ran through him, leaving him weak with mingled lust and tenderness, just how serious, how complicated it was, this love that had come to him for the first time at forty-two years old, and how ill-equipped he was to deal with it.

They climbed the stairs side by side, as if, thought Rufus, every sense sharpened by his housekeeper's proximity, they were going to bed, and as Clementine led the way to the room she had been working on for almost three weeks, he had to force himself back to reality. It was too soon to push her – if he overstepped the mark now she would retreat and he might not get a second chance. She had not had enough champagne, not had enough time. *Patience*, he repeated silently over and over, holding his breath. He must have *patience*.

She made him shut his eyes before she opened the

door. Then she gave him a gentle push, propelling him a couple of feet into the room. Rufus planted his legs apart, unbalanced, dizzy, but not with champagne. When Clementine said, 'You can look now,' he caught the anxiety in her voice and for the first time it occurred to him – what if he hated it?

Clementine was not sure what she had expected – an exclamation? A smile? – *Something* at least, but Rufus just stood absolutely still, and her heart began to pound with apprehension. Then his hands began to move. They were big hands, with heavy wrists, powerful fingers and a broad span. Slowly, they curled into tight, bunched fists, until the skin was stretched across the knuckles and the bones stood out white. Clementine felt a painful stab of disappointment. He *hated* it. This was it, the first and last room he would let her loose on. She had tried so hard, guessing what he would like from the clues in the drawing room, making what she could from the jumble of furniture, paintings and odds and ends, and supplementing her official purchases of plaster, filler, sandpaper, paint, with extras bought from her own money. All for nothing . . .

Rufus absorbed it slowly, admiring the pale, polished skirtings and the handsome windows with their refitted shutters, no pelmets, blinds or curtains to spoil their uncluttered lines. To his left was a pretty inlaid chest of drawers and a tall ewer in a matching basin, white with blue flowers twining up its voluptuously curved sides; an elegant, if rather battered table, furnished with a writing pad, envelopes and a rush-seated chair, faced the window and Clementine had swapped the mahogany bed from her own room, unearthed a pewter lamp in the shape of a Greek maiden, swathed in a yellowing lace shade, to go beside it. The rug on the floor was worn in places, fraying slightly at the edges, but its colours were perfect and the cast-iron fireplace, with its newly blacked grate and Delft tiles, was decorated with a cracked white jug of dried flowers, blue monkshood and pink-and-white stocks, corn, barley and love-in-a-mist. A faded blue button-backed velvet chair sat beside the hearth with a small table next to it, ready for a glass of brandy or a cup of coffee before bed. The walls were deep, serene French blue, faintly marbled to give texture, and a length of perfectly matched muslin looped above the bed along an old brass curtain rod, then fell either side to settle in gentle folds on the polished pine floorboards. It looked quite wonderfully welcoming, right down to the sateen bedspread, vividly embroidered with birds and flowers and the perfect shade of blue . . .

Rufus wished he had had less to drink, or more, so he could either control his feelings or let them go. He wanted to turn and grab his housekeeper, his own personal interior designer, his *genius*, and hug her until she squeaked. He had wondered in the seconds before he opened his eyes whether, if not frilly pelmets – there were some hideous drapes stored away in one of the boxrooms – she might have gone in for fancy paint techniques, had reassured himself that at least on the amount of money he had given her she had had no opportunity to buy trendy wallpaper, prissy ornaments. He knew what interior designers did for a living; they tarted things up, fussed them around, look at the glossy magazines.

He examined the room again, savouring the small touches, the books on the bedside table, the plain oval mirror hung at just the right angle so it reflected the view through the window from the doorway, a dozen pale, delicate watercolours suspended from the picture rails on watered silk ribbon, all in keeping with the room, with its air of solid, respectable dignity. It was perfect.

No, not perfect, Rufus corrected himself, that was the wrong word, that implied a neatness, a primness, a lack of individuality. It was *complete*, as if the room were already in daily use and its occupant had just popped out for five minutes; it was comfortable, peaceful. You would look forward, he thought, to climbing the stairs to this tranquillity every night.

Jean had worked flat out. The bedspread was so badly moth-eaten it had taken her all week to repair it, bribing Eddie with chocolate biscuits and crisps to leave her in peace, and so engrossed in her work that she was late with Robert's supper three nights running. Robert, blaming 'that bloody Clem' for leading his wife astray, had sent her into defiant overdrive, blindstitching hems, darning holes and mending tears. 'Oh, Clem,' she had enthused as she reluctantly handed everything back, 'you have no idea how much I enjoyed doing that!' She had taken the money Clementine pressed into her hand with such a big beaming smile that Clem had declared the whole project worthwhile, just to see her cheerful again.

And now Rufus hated it .

'Well?' Clementine demanded, her patience deserting her.

Rufus turned at last, took a step towards her.

'You don't like it—'

She was taut with anxiety. Rufus managed a smile but his face felt stiff and his voice, when he found it, shook with emotion; the words that came out of his mouth seemed so inadequate they practically constituted an indictable offence.

'. . . You're a clever old stick.'

He laid his hand on the top of her head as he had once before, clumsily ruffled her hair. Then he brushed past her on to the landing and took off down the stairs.

Clementine stood in the doorway, staring after him. She heard his footsteps on the stairs, the front door slamming, then dropped to her knees, seeking solace in Mary's comforting presence.

'Well?' she demanded. 'Does he like it or not?'

She found him when she let Mary out, still in his shirt-sleeves, sitting on the stone step staring into the dark.

'Hi,' he said without looking up.

'Hi.' She sat down beside him, far enough away so she couldn't brush his arm by accident. 'I thought you must've left home in disgust.'

Mary pushed her way in between them, nudging Rufus with her nose in a bid for attention. He reached out absentmindedly and fondled her ears.

'Was it not what you expected?'

'No.' Rufus glanced at Clementine, sitting straight-backed beside him, looked away again. 'No, I thought it would be fancier, you know, fussier.'

'Is it too plain?'

'No.' His voice was unsteady again, and he had to pause before he could continue, getting himself together. 'It's absolutely . . . right. I would never have thought of painting it that colour, but it's *right*. And you left the windows.'

Mary turned her attention to Clementine, nudging her in turn, making sure she was not forgotten. Clem responded automatically, found herself stroking Rufus's fingers and tried to snatch her hand away. Rufus grabbed her and held on.

'You haven't answered my question.'

'Which question?'

'Will you stay?'

It was cold on the step. Clementine could feel the heat of Rufus's hand on hers. 'I thought you might change your mind about asking me now you've seen what I've done.'

'I haven't. Will you stay . . . please?'

Mary stirred restlessly. She was not used to them sitting so close together, or to being paid so little attention.

'If you're sure you want me to.'

Rufus turned his head again. Clementine was already looking at him, her eyes bright in the glow from the open front door. He gave her the only answer he was capable of, leaned across the top of Mary's head and kissed her full on her wide inviting mouth.

It barely qualified. It was no more than a brief touch of the lips, but its effect upon Rufus was out of all proportion to its duration and intensity. Clementine didn't pull away. Instead, to his delight and confusion she closed her eyes and met him halfway. He felt the lust he had expected to feel, and more, but there was another, even stronger sensation, for which he was unprepared, a sudden diminution of pain, as if an old wound, one he had grown so used to he no longer noticed it, had stopped hurting. He sighed, weakened by its absence.

'You're cold.'

Clementine shook her head. She was warm now, almost cosy, despite the damp night air. She rested her cheek on Rufus's shoulder. She couldn't remember when she had last felt so . . . *right*.

Mary was upset, squashed, squeezed and ignored. She squirmed, yelped, then snapped frantically at Rufus's face until he jerked backwards and gave her some room. Clementine, unexpectedly released, teetered on the edge of the step and overbalanced. Sprawling inelegantly, listening to Rufus's deep, infectious chuckle and feeling reciprocal laughter bubbling up from some-where deep in her stomach, she was reminded unexpectedly of Dorrie and her Frank.

'He's always made me laugh, see dear, and you can't ask for more than that . . .'

Chapter Twenty-Five

'So, have you been round there yet?'

Saturday night, a whole week gone, and Sal was getting impatient. What was the point of her staying in London if Jonathan wasn't going to make any effort to get back with Clementine?

'No, I've told you, she wouldn't speak to me—'

Sal changed the phone to her other hand. 'You've got to persevere. Get yourself round there, stick your foot in the door and don't move until she agrees to talk to you. Don't be so *spineless*, darling, or you'll lose her. Look, there's nothing you can do till Monday. Get yourself over here and we'll go through the books. I'm doing better than I expected and the news is good. All right?'

'All right.' Jonathan sighed heavily. 'I'll see you in a couple of hours then.'

'I'll start the supper.' Sal laughed suddenly. 'Romantic, eh darling? Pity we'd both rather be with someone else.'

'Will you *please* pay attention!' Sal was becoming increasingly irritated. Every time she went into even slightly technical detail, Jonathan's eyes glazed over. It was like trying to explain calculus to a five-year-old.

Jonathan grimaced at her. 'I can't help it. Can't you put it a bit more simply?'

'Accountancy for idiots, you mean? Right.' Sal rose from the sofa to replenish the drinks. 'Basically, the company is awash with cash. Sebastian appears to have been taking out on an annual basis almost as much as he originally invested, but there's still plenty left over. All you have to do is reorganise your business accounts so you have sole control of everything. He's made it ridiculously easy for you – they're all in joint names, either to sign.'

. Jonathan was aghast. 'But Sebastian's always dealt with that side of things. How will I know when to pay the staff? Who'll settle the bills?'

Sal refilled both their glasses, raised her eyebrows to heaven. 'They will be paid, as they have always been, by your accounts department, i.e. what's-his-name, Peter, who is a great deal more switched on, thank God, than you are. You seem to be under the delusion that your Sebastian is some sort of financial Rasputin, intricately involved in the day-to-day workings of your empire. The only input the man has is signing the odd cheque and helping to divvy up the profits at the end of the year.' She stretched her legs along the cushions, wiggling her stockinged toes against Jonathan's thigh. 'I was expecting him to have tied it all up so you couldn't get him out, but he simply hasn't bothered.' She chuckled condescendingly. 'Mind you, if I was him, I wouldn't have bothered either.'

Jonathan was beginning to wish he had never got mixed up with Sal Glover. She had cooked an indifferent supper and left the kitchen littered with dirty pans, pools of olive oil, onion skins and green pepper seeds; she had left indelible marks all over his kitchen table because she had spent the past week putting her coffee cups down wherever she fancied without bothering to find a mat, she had broken one of a pair of irreplaceable port glasses, and he was no nearer getting Clementine back than he had been when he started.

'So what next?'

'You face up to Sebastian and tell him thanks very much, it was fun while it lasted. You reorganise all the accounts before he gets back—'

'How do I do that?'

Sal told him, in minute detail. Jonathan looked bemused. 'We'll go in to the bank together first thing on Monday morning and I'll hold your hand. Okay?'

Jonathan contemplated the prospect of Sebastian's return. 'He'll tell Clementine. The minute he thinks he's losing me, he'll tell her everything.' He clutched at his hair, gazed despairingly at Sal's perfect face, begging her to *do* something, *help* him.

'Calm down, darling.' Sal dumped her glass carelessly on the carpet, then rose with sinuous grace from the sofa. How could someone so easy on the eye, wondered Jonathan, watching her miss the wine by an inch as she passed it, make such a God-Almighty mess wherever she went?

'Surely he doesn't know where she is?'

'But what if he goes looking for her? He can be very vindictive when he's crossed. I don't know why I let you talk me into this in the first place—'

'Stop being such a cissy. We just need a strategy that's all.' Sal paced the floor in silence for a while, then stopped abruptly. 'Got it, darling! When's he due back?'

'Next Wednesday. Why?'

'Well, on Wednesday, you sit him down and break the news that you want out. You explain that he has taken ten times his original investment from the company and you challenge him to deny it—'

'But he'll still—'

'I haven't finished yet. Then you invite him to meet your new girlfriend—'

'But I haven't got a new girlfriend—'

'Oh, yes you have.' Sal twirled theatrically, dropped a curtsy. 'You're looking at her, darling.'

'What?'

'Don't you see? Sebastian threatens to expose you. You say fine, how about dinner, meet the new love of my life. Call his bluff. You, me, Sebastian, an intimate little restaurant. I can see it now. We sit in silence while Sebastian hits me with the salacious details of your lurid past—'

'Hang on—'

'—the salacious details of your lurid past, then you turn to me and murmur humbly, "Sal, sweetie, can you ever forgive me?" I lower my eyes to the table, toy with my food. I lean across and squeeze your hand. "Darling," I say, "love conquers all." We gaze soupily into each others' eyes. Exit Sebastian, grizzling into his hanky.' Jonathan stared at her, awed by her capacity for deviousness. 'Well, what do you think?'

'I don't want to hurt his feelings . . .'

The man was completely exasperating. Sal retrieved her glass, then flounced about the room, waving her arms and sprinkling wine on the carpet. 'I've spent a week sweating over your bloody books, I've proved to you the man's been milking you dry for years, and I've come up with the perfect answer to any blackmail attempts he might make. You have a golden opportuntiy to break away from your past and start afresh. But you don't want to hurt the man's feelings. Fine, just fulfil your side of the bargain and we'll go our separate ways. Far be it from me to drag you away from your lover when you're obviously still crazy about him!'

'I'm not!' Jonathan was beginning to panic. What if she went straight round to Clementine and told her everything? 'You wouldn't, er . . .'

'What? Snitch on you to Clementine? What do you take me for?'

'I'm sorry.' Jonathan dropped his head into his hands and groaned. 'I'm *sorry*. But I just can't *bear* all this.'

Sal sighed. 'You're just a baby aren't you?' she said. 'You have no idea.' How had he managed to survive the life he had led? Had he got through it by simply not seeing it, like a child playing games of make-believe?

'Poor darling,' she soothed. 'It's all right, I'll look after you.'

Chapter Twenty-Six

Sunday morning. Rufus knew as soon as Clementine walked into the kitchen that she had withdrawn from him again. The previous night, just when he'd thought he was getting somewhere, she had suddenly upped and left him and now she was reluctant even to look him in the eye. She hardly touched her breakfast, making for the back door the moment she had done the washing up.

'Where're you going?' he demanded.

'To walk the dog.'

'Why?'

Clementine halted by the door. 'Well, because—'

'I wanted to start on the library this morning. Sal's still in London till Wednesday so if we don't get on with it today I won't get a chance until the end of the week.' Rufus's patience was fraying, unravelled by Clementine's inability to acknowledge the self-evident truth that they were made for each other. 'Why are you always in such a damn hurry?'

Clementine frowned. 'I'm sorry, I thought you said—'

'I know what I said. Even domestic servants are entitled to time off.' Rufus scowled at her. 'But not when I've got to be in the shop all week. Can't you take Monday and Tuesday off instead?'

Clementine was suffering from lack of sleep and a gaping hole in the pit of her stomach where someone had removed half her internal organs during the night. The sensation was at once invigorating and alarming, and she had experienced it only once before; she had already reminded herself a dozen times of what had happened with cousin Martin. You are not, she reiterated silently as she turned back to face her employer, going to get involved with a man ever again, remember? And *certainly* not with Rufus Palliser. But when she risked a glance he was looking straight at her and what was left of her stomach went into freefall; she turned away, catching her breath, panicking. 'Right,' she said, 'I'll go and make a start,' and she strode from the kitchen, making for the butler's pantry, where Rufus had decreed they would stack the books while the library was being redecorated.

Rufus called Mary in from the wet garden. 'What the hell do I have to do,' he complained, 'to make the blasted woman see sense?'

Don't be a fool, Clementine told herself as she marched to and fro with armfuls of books. Remember Martin. Just *remember Martin* . . .

As the week progressed, the atmosphere grew increasingly taut. It was clear to Rufus that he had overstepped the mark again, but he had tasted Clementine now, held her, if only for a moment, and it was ten times harder than before. It was no longer enough telling himself to be patient, he felt as he imagined an alcoholic might feel, having had one drink – he wanted more, and he wanted it *now*. When he came upon Clementine on the Wednesday morning, poring over the Situations Vacant column in the *Eastern Daily Press*, he lost his temper and accused her angrily of looking for another job.

'I'm not!' she protested, startled by his vehemence. 'Unless you want me to?'

'No, of course I don't bloody well want you to!' snarled Rufus. He rose from the table, slammed his plate down in the sink, then strode from the room before he could make things any worse.

Clementine cut out the advertisement she had found and stashed it safely in the pocket of her dungarees. Then she made her way along the hall to the library to continue painting the ceiling while Rufus slammed out of the front door to go to work, on time for once. Only when the sound of his van had faded into the distance did she heave a sigh of relief and allow her tense muscles to relax.

'I don't fancy him one bit,' she informed Mary with every brush stroke she made. 'Not one bit.'

'Clem, you're a genius!' Jean waved the advertisement in the air, grinning. 'It's *perfect*, and I hadn't even noticed it. I'll ring them this afternoon.'

She moved round the table, setting places for lunch. 'It's just occurred to me though . . .'

'Yes?'

Jean had been taking no chances with Eddie since his performance at Manor Hall. 'E-d-d-i-e,' she spelled above his head. 'He doesn't start s-c-h-o-o-l until January.' She lowered the handful of cutlery she was holding to the table, wilting. 'And then there're the holidays, and what about this?' She slapped her stomach, pulled a face. 'How can I w-o-r-k with a b-a-b-y round my neck?'

'Mummy, can I have a—?'

'No. Go and tell Daddy his dinner's on the table. He's in his office doing the VAT.' She waited until Eddie had disappeared, pulled a face. 'Which means he'll be in an absolutely foul mood. It's hopeless, Clem.'

Clementine leaned across the table, took the knives and forks and finished laying them herself.

'Look, why don't you worry about Robert and Eddie once you've got the job? You may not get it. There may be dozens of applicants, all better qualified than you. It's only three mornings a week. Maybe you could find a childminder, or persuade Robert's mum to look after—'

Jean snorted with alarm. 'For God's sake don't mention this to Robert's mum! First thing she'll do is tell Robert and then he'll forbid me to even try for it. It's hopeless. I don't know why I'm even thinking about it.' She ran a hand through her spiky hair and glowered at Eddie when he returned.

'Daddy says can you keep it warm 'cause he's in the middle of somefing.'

Jean stared at Eddie. Then she squared her shoulders and stuck her bottom lip out, just as Clementine remembered her doing during their childhood; her *Little Madam* face, Mrs Smith called it, because Jean always put it on when she was about to do something she wasn't supposed to do. 'You're right,' she said. 'I'll worry about the logistics after I've got the job.'

Clementine took her time walking home. She had spent three hours painting that morning, had worked right through Monday and Tuesday which should have been her days off. So she dawdled, turning right over the bridge to wander along the narrow path above the water while Mary rambled on ahead, nose to the ground and tail waving in the air.

The river was swollen with the recent rain, brown, fast moving and full of flotsam. Halfway through October now; soon the grass would be white with frost every morning and the trees would drop their leaves.

The ancient sloe hung low over the water; much more rain and its precarious grasp on the soft clay bank would be in doubt. Clementine had sat amongst its branches a hundred times, legs dangling, while her friends splashed and quarrelled in the shallows.

Mary scrabbled along the narrow shelf just above the waterline and when Clementine called her back she didn't want to come. Peering down from above Clem saw why; almost at the water's edge, half hidden amongst the sloe's roots, was a rabbit.

It was taking no notice of Mary. Even when she barked shrilly and pawed at it, it just flattened its ears and crouched lower in the wet grass. Leaning further over, Clementine saw the thick yellow pus oozing from eyes and nostrils, and recognised the last stages of myxomatosis. She hadn't seen a myxy rabbit for almost twenty years. Remembering the last time, she drew back sharply, then called Mary again, more urgently this time.

The dog was reluctant to come – Clementine had to go and get her, slithering down the precarious slope to drag her away from her find. Standing so close to the water, it looked as if the bank might give way at any moment. For the rabbit, she thought, averting her eyes, it would be a merciful release. She knew what she ought to do, what her father, the kindest, the gentlest of men, would have done, but she couldn't make herself do it.

She raised her eyes to the lowering sky and shivered. Then she shooed Mary back up the slippery trail and struck out for home. Her stomach churned all the way at the thought of the poor scrap she had left huddled in the grass, waiting to die.

She was finishing her lunch when the bell jangled in the servants' passageway. She left Mary in the kitchen and made for the hall, still eating the last of her sandwich.

'You have to listen!' began Jonathan before the door was even half open. 'I'm not leaving until you've heard me out!'

Clementine stared at him in astonishment. He was not supposed to be here. He was supposed to have given up, gone away, left her in peace. Outraged, she made to swing the door shut, but he anticipated her, shoving his foot in the way and refusing to budge. This wasn't like Jonathan at all.

'Can I come in?'

'No,' said Clementine decidedly.

Jonathan planted one foot either side of the threshold and tucked his hands in his trouser pockets, aiming for at least the appearance of confidence. 'Then I shall stay here all afternoon.'

'You can't. Rufus'll be back.'

'He'll have to get the police to move me,' said Jonathan bravely, remembering the man's size and thinking, some hope – Rufus Palliser could pick him up and dump him in the azaleas if he chose and there wouldn't be a damn thing he could do about it. '*Please*, Clem. All I'm asking you to do is *listen*. Surely you owe me that much at least?'

'I don't owe you anything!' Clementine glared.

'Yes you do.' Jonathan took a deep breath. Sal Glover would be proud of him. 'I meant every word I said about marriage and children. Clem, you can't blame me for wanting to protect my business. Sebastian was threatening to close me down if I went on seeing you – I *had* to play along with him, what else could I do? You'd have done the same under the same circumstances. I've never cheated on you, never been unfaithful—' I've just lied a little, that's all, stretched the truth, because all's fair in love and war . . . 'And as of tonight I'll be free of Sebastian for good!'

'How can you possibly—'

'Let me in and I'll tell you! I *swear*, Clem—'

'*Don't!*' begged Clementine, weakening. 'Don't swear anything! Five minutes.' Reluctantly she swung the door back and Jonathan moved into the hall. 'You can have five minutes and then I want you to go. Do you understand?'

Jonathan nodded, gestured towards the drawing room. 'Could we, er . . .'

'No,' said Clementine. 'We couldn't. You can say what you have to say right here.'

Jonathan had imagined sitting with her in some quaint country pub, putting things right, mapping out their rosy future while holding her hand across a rustic table and warming his feet at a roaring log fire. Standing in the gloomy hall of this gothic mausoleum, with the open front door behind him reminding him that he might be ordered to leave at any moment, made it much more difficult.

'Sebastian and I are finished.'

Clementine's face was eloquently disbelieving.

'I mean it. As of two days ago, Sebastian ceased to have a stake of any kind in the company.'

'Does he know?'

Jonathan's confidence slipped. 'No, not yet, I—'

'Ah,' said Clem. 'I see.'

'No you don't. He's still abroad. I'm picking him up from Heathrow at five o'clock and tonight I'll break the news that he no longer has any interest, financial or personal, in my company.'

The 'my' got to her, he could see. He took his hands from his pockets, advanced. Clementine stepped backwards. He stopped, began to plead again. 'Clem, I've done this for you, for us. If I'd thought it was over between us, I wouldn't have been able to go through with it. I've spent the worst week of my life cutting myself adrift from the man who has dictated my every move for the past eighteen years, and I've done it all for *us*, for our future together.' It was the plain truth; Jonathan could see that Clem believed him, that she was weakening. His confidence soared. 'We can get married as soon as you like. And you can come back to work as a partner, only you don't have to put any money in. I don't need your money, the company's more secure than I could have dreamed—'

'No . . .' she said again, but she sounded less angry this time, less vehement.

'*Please*, Clem. This is a chance to start afresh, to be together. It's all I want. I *need* you—'

'Jonathan, don't—'

The phone made them both jump.

'Excuse me,' said Clem as if the interruption was a relief, and she turned, disappeared into Rufus's study and shut the door. Jonathan took his hands out of his pockets and wiped them on his trousers.

'Hello?'

'It's me.'

'Oh,' said Clementine, her mind on Jonathan.

'Rufus.'

'Yes,' said Clementine. She could hear him breathing on the other end, had to make an enormous effort to collect her wits. 'Is everything okay?'

'Yup, fine.' Another long pause, more stentorian breathing. 'I'm sorry,' said Rufus gruffly.

'Sorry? What for?'

More breathing, a gusty sigh. Clementine was visited by a sudden vivid picture of Rufus Palliser standing somewhere scowling at the telephone, running his fingers through his untidy hair while he searched for words. Despite herself she smiled.

'I'm sorry I was so bad-tempered.' It had taken Rufus all morning to bring himself to the point of apology. He waited, knew when he heard her husky giggle that he'd done the right thing for a change. 'You're not, are you?' he asked.

Clem stared blankly at the phone. 'Not what?'

'Looking for another job. You're not, are you?'

It was there again, that pleading note in his voice, just like when he had asked her to stay. It warmed her, gave her strength.

'No,' she said. 'I'm not looking for another job. It was for Jean.'

'Oh.' Relief this time, pleasure, even delight. 'Good. *Great*. I'll see you tonight then.' There was a long, long, pause. Then he said, 'Bye, Clementine,' and put the phone down.

Clementine replaced the receiver and stood for a moment gazing out at the shrubbery, captivated, disarmed. Then she walked back to the hall to usher Jonathan out.

'I'm sorry,' she said, letting him down gently. 'But I'm not ready to come back to the rat race.'

Jonathan pounced on her choice of words, looking for some hope. 'Not ready. Does that mean . . .?'

Clementine was already closing the door. 'No,' she said. 'I'm sorry, Jonathan, the answer is no.'

Chapter Twenty-Seven

'It's no good nagging me, darling, I'm going as fast as I can.'

Sal, stunning in a simple black dress, was crouched over the bamboo table in Jonathan's conservatory, applying mascara with the help of a magnifying make-up mirror. Not bad, she thought, admiring Jonathan's Armani suit, the loose jacket unbuttoned to reveal a deep blue shirt and a narrow tie decorated with tiny, brightly coloured birds, not bad at all. Rather a handsome couple in fact.

She had known this evening was on since four-thirty, when Jonathan had phoned from Heathrow to say Sebastian's flight was on time; it was now twenty-five past seven and she still wasn't ready.

'It's essential that I make a good impression,' she reiterated for the tenth time. 'We have to make him believe this affair is for real, and we can't do that if I arrive looking like a wreck, can we? Just pass me those tissues would you, darling?'

Jonathan dropped the box of tissues beside her, then plunged his hands into his pockets and continued his pacing while she applied lipstick and blotted it. 'If there is one thing Sebastian hates,' he complained, 'it's unpunctuality. This is going to be quite difficult enough, without you making it any harder.'

By the time Sal pronounced herself ready he was shaking with nerves. When she remembered, just as he was ushering her out of the front door, a telephone call she absolutely *must* make, he gripped his head with his hands and moaned.

'Shan't be a tick, darling, honestly,' soothed Sal, patting him as she passed. 'But if I don't ring tonight Rufus won't know what's going on.'

Jonathan followed her back into the sitting room and slumped on to the sofa. 'Sebastian'll kill us both,' he muttered. 'I know he will.'

'Hi, darling,' purred Sal into the phone. 'How goes it?'

The reply was lengthy but inaudible. Sal bit her lip, twisted a lock of hair round her finger. 'Oh, well,' she said after a while. 'Look on the bright side, darling, that's why I'm ringing. I'm back tomorrow, catching the early train. I should be with you around ten o'clock . . . What? Well, yes, I suppose I can, if you insist . . . Yes, all right . . . see you then. Bye.'

'Well?' Jonathan rose from the sofa and crossed the room to peer anxiously into her face. 'What did he say? What's going on?'

'I'm not sure.' Sal's eyes were very bright. She blinked hard. 'He certainly didn't sound terribly pleased . . . actually, he sounded rather cheesed off, if you want to know. Apparently Clementine'd left some supper for him and gone out – that's a good sign, wouldn't you say? They can hardly be canoodling over the kitchen table if she's out. Anyway, the cat, um, Ginger – remember that moth-eaten old tom? – got into the kitchen and by the time Rufus found him he'd eaten half the grub.' She went over the conversation again. 'And he says he's fed up with being in the shop, wants me to open up for him tomorrow so he can stay at home.' She lifted her chin. 'But let's think positive, shall we? He's clearly getting nowhere with the lovely Miss Lee, and from what you said about your reception today you're still in with a chance—'

'Don't talk about her like that!' complained Jonathan, reminding Sal irritatingly of Rufus. 'Why do you always have to be so sarcastic?'

'Sorry.' Sal blinked again. 'I don't mean to, it's just that—' She swung her hair across her face and made for the door. 'Come on, darling,' she commanded over her shoulder. 'We'll be late.'

She was halfway to the car by the time he caught her up and during the drive to the restaurant she remained uncharacteristically silent. Jonathan's apprehension increased. The journey from Heathrow had been just as awkward as he had expected, the subsequent interview at Sebastian's flat even more difficult than he had anticipated. He had stood up for himself, looked his ex-lover straight (literally, thank heaven for the lifts) in the eye, and told him he wanted out. But Sebastian had simply laughed at the ludicrous suggestion that Jonathan might be able to manage without him, on a personal *or* a professional level. When informed that Jonathan was in the throes of a new, and serious, affair with the accountant who had won him his independence, Sebastian had, as Sal had predicted, demanded to meet his rival immediately, *today*. And they were late. Even Clem hadn't landed Jonathan in as much hot water as he seemed to be in now.

Sebastian was already there, sitting in a dimly lit corner of the fashionable French restaurant, chosen by Jonathan and booked by Sal for The Showdown. He had a Plymouth gin in front of him and he was drumming his bony fingers on the table. He registered, as they crossed the room arm in arm, what an extraordinarily handsome couple they made.

He greeted Jonathan with a curt nod and Sal with a long, stony stare. During the preliminaries, the deciding of places (Sebastian insisted on Sal sitting opposite him, with Jonathan, wilting like limp lettuce in a sandwich, between them), the distribution of menus and the ordering of aperitifs, the conversation was stunted by the palpable undercurrent of tension between Jonathan and his charismatic ex-lover.

Sebastian Brown undoubtedly *was* charismatic. Everything about him, from his crumpled linen suit to his red hair and pale eyes, the way he moved and spoke, proclaimed him to be both homosexual and eccentric in a way that Jonathan most decidedly was not. Despite herself, Sal was fascinated from the moment he ignored her outstretched hand and said in his refined voice, 'How very *naice* to meet you, Miss Glover,' as if she had just crawled from beneath a stone and he was looking forward to dissecting her under a microscope.

Sal was ready for him. She treated him to her most bewitching smile then, dipping her hair so he couldn't see, winked at Jonathan, reassuring him, there is no way this man is going to intimidate *me*.

Sebastian tried almost immediately, ordering, in impeccable French, for them all. Sal let him get away with choosing the starter because his choice happened to coincide with what she fancied, but she drew the line at the main course, calling the waiter back to inform him that, no, she would not be having the *Noisettes d'Agneau*, she would prefer *Truite à la Meunière*, 'if you don't mind, Mr Brown'.

Jonathan began nervously to tear his bread roll into tiny pieces. Poor boy, thought Sal, there was no way he could have managed this without her. She reached across to squeeze his knee beneath the table, making him jump perceptibly and Sebastian, tracking her every move, acknowledged the covert challenge with a cold smile.

'Forgive me, Miss Glover,' he offered drily. 'Sometimes I forget my manners.'

Sal turned the full power of her smile on him again. 'That's perfectly all right, Mr Brown,' she said sweetly. 'Sometimes, so do I.'

To her surprise, as the meal progressed it became easier rather than more difficult. Whilst Sebastian continued to analyse her every utterance and follow her every move, waiting to trip her up, the more she stood her ground the more he unbent, relaxed. By the time they reached the pudding she was beginning to think she was winning the game.

Sebastian began a tale of friends who had been staying along the Côte d'Azur while he was at Cap d'Antibes. His story was funny, acerbic, rude, and aimed exclusively at Jonathan. Sal, relegated to the role of onlooker, sat back and watched the show. Jonathan was clearly still in awe of his mentor, despite all the brave noises about it being over between them. He laughed in the right places, shook or nodded his head when required, listened intently as the older man told his catty tale, camping it up outrageously for his protégé's amusement and reminding Jonathan that they had eighteen shared years behind them, a history which must be sloughed off if he were to start again.

Sal was well aware of what Sebastian was doing – it was a ploy she had used successfully herself, cutting out a rival with intimate reminiscences, shared jokes, obscure references to events and people of which the interloper would understand nothing. But why, she wondered, had Sebastian Brown so far made no attempt to use his most powerful weapon, his intimate knowledge of Jonathan's sordid past? Not once had he come even close to spilling the beans about Jonathan's dubious passage to the top of his profession, and the part that he, Sebastian, had played in his ascent. What was he up to? Was he keeping his big guns in reserve, waiting for a moment of his own choosing to unleash them? As the pudding plates were being cleared she grew tired of the suspense and called his bluff.

'So,' she said, smiling sweetly across the table. '*Do* tell me. How did you and Jonathan meet?'

Both men stared at her. Sal heard Jonathan's sharp intake of breath and Sebastian reached into his inside pocket for a silver cigarette case, taking his time, checking his ammunition. Here it comes, thought Sal, at last . . .

'Excuse me!' Jonathan's voice was squeaky with nerves. He rose abruptly from the table, dropping his napkin and stumbling as he extricated himself from his chair. 'I must go to the loo!'

Sebastian seemed not to notice his departure. He tapped the end of his cigarette, lit it and returned the case to his pocket with slow deliberation. He was sweating though, Sal noticed, not quite as cool as he would like her to think.

'May I have one, please?'

'Of course.' Sebastian retrieved his case and flipped it open, held it out. Sal helped herself and leaned across to his lighter. The cigarette was Turkish, untipped, exotic, strong.

'Thank you,' She drew the smoke deep into her lungs. Sebastian said nothing, merely turned his head and raised a finger at a passing waiter. Apart from the sweating, his command was impressive; the waiter, a dark, pretty boy who clearly knew him well, changed direction instantly, begging in French to be apprised of Sebastian's wishes so he could fulfil them *immédiatement*.

'*Alain*,' said Sebastian. '*Armagnac, s'il te plait, mon cher, pour . . .?*' His accent was faultless and he used the intimate form of address.

'*Pour deux*,' said Sal, blasting the waiter with her smile, competing. Sebastian waved him away and blew blue smoke over the top of Sal's head.

'Now, you were saying, Miss Glover?'

Sal was puzzled. She had given him the perfect opening, a golden opportunity to hit her with all the gory details of Jonathan's past, so why hadn't he risen to the bait? She leaned back in her chair, enjoying the nicotine fix and wondering what he was playing at. Sebastian leaned back too, and returned her stare inscrutably. 'You were telling me how you and Jonathan met.'

'Ah. Yes.' Sebastian tapped out his ash with slow deliberation. 'What exactly would you like to know, Miss Glover?'

This was not what Sal had expected at all. She accepted her Armagnac from the waiter, waited while he removed the wine glasses, fussed around collecting the remaining cutlery, asked about coffee – '*Non*,' said Sebastian – and brushed the crumbs from the tablecloth. Then she exhaled at the man's departing back and said with innocent enthusiasm, 'I want you to tell me absolutely *everything* about Jonathan, Mr Brown.'

Instead of picking up the gauntlet she had thrown, Sebastian said calmly, 'I hardly think that is necessary, do you, Miss Glover?'

'Sorry?' Definitely *not* according to plan, this.

Sebastian placed his elbows on the table, wrapped his bony hands round his glass and lowered his nose to breathe in the fumes, staring past Sal's right shoulder at the other diners.

'My dear Miss Glover.' He was condescending, patient, dry as the Kalahari desert. 'I am not a stupid man. If Jonathan had thought for one moment that our meeting might put you off him, he would not have agreed to it. And whatever he may have told you, I have no Machiavellian plans to take my revenge upon you for stealing him from me. On the contrary, I have known for many years that sooner or later I was likely to lose Jonathan to . . .' He paused, considering his words carefully and drawing deeply on his cigarette, '. . . to a rather more *conventional* way of life.'

Sal was at a loss. This was not what she had expected at all. It was almost, she thought, as if the man knew that she knew.

'You have heard of Peter Pan, Miss Glover?'

'Peter Pan?' If he was trying to throw her off balance, he was succeeding.

'Peter Pan. The boy who never grew up. Jonathan is Peter Pan, Miss Glover, a charming, talented, affectionate, irresponsible child.' Sebastian stubbed out his half-finished cigarette, took another from his silver case, tapping, taking his time, choosing his words. 'Did you know, for instance, that in order to break the news to me this afternoon . . .' He paused, placed his cigarette, unlit, between the fingers of his left hand, and examined it with studious concentration, '. . . in order to break the news to me that I had been ousted from the company, Jonathan found it necessary to purchase a special pair of shoes.'

'Shoes?'

'Shoes, Miss Glover, long boat-shaped items, usually made of leather—'

'Yes! All right, I know what shoes are!' *Shoes?* Sal waited, completely confused.

'Jonathan is wearing lifts.'

'Lifts?'

'Miss Glover,' Sebastian sighed heavily, 'I would be deeply grateful if you could refrain from repeating the last word of every sentence I utter.'

'Sorry.' Sal suppressed a wild desire to burst out laughing. Was this the best he could come up with? A *shoe* fetish?

'Where was I?'

'Lifts,' said Sal helpfully. 'Shoes.'

'Lifts. Jonathan is approximately one and one half inches shorter than I—'

'That much? Wow!'

She raised both hands, palms out, apologising for the facetious attempt at a joke, and a wintry smile crossed Sebastian Brown's angular features.

'The point I am trying to make, Miss Glover—'

'—is that Jonathan found it necessary to boost his courage by making himself a bit taller, right?'

'Absolutely, Miss Glover. How very perceptive of you.'

Was this *really* the best he could come up with? Sal bared her beautifully white, even teeth and leaned across the table.

'Perfect, aren't they?' she said, waving a hand past her mouth. 'Almost all capped, you know.' She leaned back again, twisted in her chair and felt in her bag for her own cigarettes. 'The point *I'm* trying to make, Mr Brown, is that most people need a confidence booster of one sort or another to get through life. A *lift*, if you'll pardon the pun, to raise their self-esteem. It may be capped teeth, or high-heeled shoes, or colouring one's hair to disguise the grey—' She watched his pale eyes narrow and awarded herself an extra point for hitting his weak spot.

'And are your teeth your only imperfection, Miss Glover?' he asked, retaliating.

Sal laughed. 'Where would you like me to start? I'm bossy, rude, untidy—' She very nearly added, 'congenitally unfaithful', stopped herself just in time. Sebastian Brown didn't need to know that.

'And how long have you known Jonathan, Miss Glover?'

She had already rehearsed that one with Jonathan, getting the story straight. It had to be a whirlwind romance, given that less than two months ago he had been planning marriage to someone else, but it had to be believable too.

'Only a few weeks,' she said. 'We met at a party.' She took a sip of Armagnac. 'Jonathan was on his own.' She glanced at Sebastian from beneath her lashes to see whether he was buying it, but he wasn't looking at her, he was staring past her at the other tables, his cigarette still unlit in his hand. 'I was on my own, too, and a friend introduced us. Jonathan needed cheering up, he said, he'd just lost his girlfriend . . .'

Sebastian's eyes were on her now; she could feel them. 'It was love at first sight.' She swept her hair forward to hide her face and crossed her fingers under the table. 'Nothing like it had ever happened to me before.' It was not the sort of thing Sal Glover was in the habit of saying; anyone who knew her would hoot with laughter, she thought, if they could hear her. And yet, it *had* happened to her, once. She closed her eyes, conjuring up Rufus, and waited for the rush of emotion the thought of him always triggered. When she raised her head her eyes were awash with genuine tears.

Sebastian was taken aback, she could see; his face softened, and just briefly he seemed lost for words. But his self-control was admirable; he remembered his cigarette, searched for his lighter. Surely *now* he would hit her with the revelations. It would be the perfect moment – Jonathan would return soon so she could forgive him, gaze into his eyes, play the part she had set out to play . . .

Sebastian exhaled slowly. 'Miss Glover, you strike me as a very . . . *competent* young woman.'

At last. Sal sipped her Armagnac and waited.

'So I hope you will not take it amiss if I give you some advice.'

'Of course not.' Sal glanced at him again from beneath her lashes. He was perspiring freely now, mopping his forehead with a large handkerchief, and she suddenly felt rather sorry for him. 'After all,' she said, humouring him, 'you must know him better than anybody.'

'Indeed.' The silence stretched so long Sal wondered if he had forgotten her presence altogether, and when Sebastian finally spoke, what he had to say was not what she had expected at all. 'I assume that since by now you are intimately acquainted with the finances of Jonathan's company, you are also aware of his personal situation?'

'How do you mean?'

Sebastian stared past her again at the other diners. 'Let me give you a few examples. For instance, although I have, as you are no doubt aware, taken considerable sums of money from the company over the years, you may not be aware of how some of that money has been spent . . .' He paused, waiting for her to challenge him. 'Let us take Jonathan's house. Jonathan's house was bought, and paid for, by me. I am a solitary soul, Miss Glover, difficult to live with, and there are occasions when I need my privacy. It suited me to have separate establishments and it was good for Jonathan to have some independence.' He seemed to assume that she knew he and Jonathan had been lovers, but at the same time he talked about Jonathan as if he was a slightly exasperating child, as if setting him up in a place of his own was tantamount to a loving parent weaning an immature teenager from the family home.

'The deeds are in his name, but he has no mortgage, because if he had, he would not remember to pay the instalments. His bills, electricity, gas, rates, telephone, even his credit card accounts, are sent directly to Peter, who pays them on his behalf.' Sebastian leaned forward to emphasise his point. 'You see, Miss Glover, Jonathan has absolutely no interest in such mundane matters as paying bills. Organising one's finances is something other people do. Ostensibly, Peter is employed by Jonathan, but until now he has always deferred to me. Not, you understand, because he is disloyal to Jonathan, on the contrary, like all the staff, like almost everyone who comes into contact with Jonathan, Peter absolutely adores him. It is merely that he is aware of how unworldly Jonathan is. I trust Peter implicitly; that is why I chose him to oversee the company's finances. There is also a daily woman who deals with the practical details of Jonathan's home life and a secretary who ensures that he keeps his business appointments. Whilst I gather you told Mrs Ames she would not be needed during your stay, Angela, Jonathan's secretary, has been concerned because he has not been where he was supposed to be this past week.'

Sal remembered Angela, the woman had interrupted her at least twice a day while she was staying in Chelsea. Would Sal please ask Jonathan to phone the office when he got back? How long was he going to be away? Why hadn't he told her he was going to Norfolk? Had he remembered the appointments she had made for him? And so on and so on. Sal had taken the messages but not passed them on, not trusting Jonathan to concentrate on the business in hand if she did. For the second time, as Sebastian described the safety net he had set up around Jonathan, she caught a strong whiff of protective parent, checking on his favourite child, allowing him his head whilst ensuring he was safe from harm. Clearly someone had been keeping Sebastian Brown informed of Jonathan's bid for freedom.

'Jonathan lives in a very simple world, Miss Glover; it provides him with an extremely comfortable lifestyle and sufficient assistance to ensure that he never has to think about anything other than fulfilling his creative impulses.'

'Then don't you think you should have—'

'Taught him to fend for himself?' For the first time since they had started the conversation, Sebastian Brown laughed, a dry cough of amusement. 'Now *why*, Miss Glover, would I do that?'

Sal opened her mouth to make a tart rejoinder, then shut it again. It made, she had to admit, a great deal of sense. What better way to keep a young lover malleable than to make him wholly dependent, financially and organisationally, upon other people, people who had been put in place by, who were answerable to, Sebastian Brown?

'In other words,' she said, challenging him to deny it, 'if Jonathan tries to break away from you, you can, and presumably will, make his life so difficult he won't be able to survive.'

Sebastian leaned back in his chair and gazed past her again. 'I have no intention, Miss Glover, of doing any such thing.'

'Why not?' asked Sal incredulously.

'For one very good reason.' Sebastian placed his elbows on the table and joined his skeletal fingers at the tips. 'This time he seems to have found someone who is capable of looking after him.' He paused, analysing her as he had since the beginning of the evening. 'As you are no doubt aware, Miss Glover, I recently interfered in one of Jonathan's *affaires* . . .' He compressed his lips disdainfully, then abandoned his sentence and began again. 'I am, as I have already mentioned, Miss Glover, fond of solitude. I like to sit in a corner and observe my fellow man or woman, in all his or her ridiculous guises. I find there are in general two sorts of people – those who can give of themselves and those who cannot. When it comes to relationships, Jonathan's resources are, somewhat, ah . . . *limited*. Almost all his energy is expended on his work, it is the most important thing in his life. Do you see what I am driving at, Miss Glover?'

Sal nodded.

'However, conversely, he has a great need to be loved, to be surrounded by affection. Without this security he cannot function efficiently.' Sebastian drained the last of his Armagnac and placed his glass carefully on the table. 'Until now I have, with considerable help from those people I have mentioned, been Jonathan's main source of . . . how shall I put it? *Emotional succour*. His last . . .' he made a small *moue* of distaste, 'his last *romance*, the young woman he was involved with before you, struck me from the first moment I met her as being herself rather badly in need of affection. But she also struck me, Miss Glover, if this does not seem like a contradiction in terms, as a woman who had deliberately set herself apart, withdrawn from the normal interplay that exists between men and women. For what reason, I do not know. I have no particular interest, frankly, in what makes her what she is, except in so far as it is, *was*, likely to affect Jonathan.'

Sal lowered her head again, hiding behind her hair. So *that* was what Rufus had got himself mixed up with, the original Miss Frigidaire. It justified everything she, Sal, had done so far. If there was one thing Rufus needed it was the unconditional, unstinting love of a good woman (or even, she-should-be-so-lucky, a bad woman). Clearly, Clementine Lee was incapable of providing it.

'So I put a stop to it before he could make a dreadful mistake. This time is different. I have no need to interfere this time, because Jonathan has finally picked a partner who is . . . suitable.'

A compliment?

When Jonathan reappeared he brought with him a strong smell of brandy – he had obviously been boosting his courage at the bar – and as he slid into his seat he glanced nervously at Sal.

'It's all right, darling,' she said. 'Sebastian and I understand each other perfectly.'

Jonathan's smile was so innocently relieved, so sweetly grateful, that she felt immediately guilty, not a sensation Sal Glover experienced very often. What if she was abandoning the poor boy to sink or swim by himself, would he drown without help? What if he didn't manage to win Clementine Lee back, would his well-ordered life disintegrate? Suppose Sebastian was right, and Clementine was completely the wrong woman for Jonathan and here she was busily pushing them back into each others' arms? When Sebastian leaned across and fleetingly touched Jonathan's hand, she warmed towards him more than she had all evening and her discomfort increased.

'Miss Glover and I have agreed,' said Sebastian, as if he and Sal were allies, joined together by a determination to smooth Jonathan's worries away, 'that Peter should continue to look after your finances. That way there will be a minimum of disruption during the transition period.' *The transition period*? Sal took a long drag at her cigarette. Sebastian stared out again across the rapidly emptying room. 'I am satisfied that Miss Glover is more than capable of looking after . . .' He mopped his brow, wiped his hands on his handkerchief. 'But now, it is getting late . . .'

He was dismissing them. He didn't look up as Jonathan bent to say goodbye. 'You know where I am, dear boy,' he murmured, searching studiously in his pocket for his cigarette case, 'if you need me.'

Jonathan nodded. Sal could see he was close to tears. She linked her arm through his, then held out her free hand to Sebastian. He took it. His palm was warm and damp, but his grip was firm.

'Miss Glover—' he began.

'Sal,' said Sal.

'Sal. You will bear in mind . . .?'

'Yes.' Sal squeezed his clammy fingers between hers. She had to remind herself that this was just a game, because it seemed suddenly to have got rather serious. 'Yes, Sebastian, I will bear in mind everything you have said. It has been . . .'

What had it been? An unforgettable experience, certainly. Cynic though she usually was, Sal felt profoundly moved, sad for the old man, and oh, he did look so *old* at this moment. She wanted to promise him that it would work out, that Jonathan would end up happy, which seemed genuinely to be all he wanted. But she couldn't guarantee it. She had a gut feeling that his analysis of Clementine Lee was probably pretty accurate, that she simply wasn't capable of looking after Jonathan as he needed to be looked after. She had to remind herself that the alternative to getting them back together was to have her darling Rufus made miserable. After all, if the worst came to the worst, at least Jonathan could run back to Daddy.

It occurred to her as she was collecting her coat that they had left Sebastian to pick up the bill for the meal during which he had lost his lover; she hesitated, half-minded to go back and offer to pay her share. Jonathan, desperate to get away, took her arm and hustled her out into the night.

Life, thought Sal as she settled herself in the passenger seat of Jonathan's car and lit a last cigarette, life just isn't fair when you come right down to it. It isn't bloody well fair at all.

Chapter Twenty-Eight

She rang Rufus from the shop on the Thursday morning, just to hear his voice. 'Darling, you'll have to come in. I don't know what you've been up to but I can't make head or tail of the paperwork.'

'Tomorrow,' promised Rufus. 'I'll come in tomorrow, Sal. I'm up to my neck right now.'

Up to his neck in what? Sal bit her tongue, hard. 'Well, just make sure you do. I can't leave you on your own for ten minutes, can I, darling?'

'Sorry, Sal.' He sounded completely unrepentant. He sounded cheerful, too, more cheerful than he had been for ages. 'I don't know what I'd do without you. You're wonderful.'

'I know,' said Sal. 'See you tomorrow, darling.'

Rufus made his way along the corridor, whistling. Clementine had finished painting the library and today they would be together, sorting books.

It had been raining all week; it was dank outside and overcast, a good excuse to be indoors, but working side by side with Clementine in the confined space of the butler's pantry stretched Rufus's self-control to the limit. When their eyes met he found it hard to look away. When they bent together to retrieve a pile of paperbacks, or he found himself stacking books in the same spot as

Clementine, when his face was so close to hers he could taste her expelled breath, he would pause, half turn towards her, then move away in case he scared her off. The anticipation of each fleeting moment, each tiny touch, acted upon him as a powerful aphrodisiac, rendered him incapable of concentrating on anything else. Sometimes, when Clementine was not sure what to do with a particular book, she had to ask him two or three times before he managed to pull himself together sufficiently to give her a sensible answer.

He knew she was aware of him too, he could tell by the way she kept falling over her own feet, or Mary's, and when she met his eyes she stared for a moment, as caught as he, before looking hurriedly away. Her diffidence excited him, heightened his awareness of her every move; by lunchtime, taken on the run, he was ready to explode with frustration.

Only those books deemed worthy were to be returned to the library – the rest would remain where they were, stacked on shelves that had once held jars of pickled cabbage or bottles of vintage port, stove blacking or Cardinal Red, until space could be found for them at the shop. Rufus was no longer sure what he had inherited from the Misses Walker and what had come later, auction lots or attic clear-outs, boot-sale bargains or bric-a-brac stalls.

The sorting revealed an eclectic mix of old and new, heavy-duty literary works and lightweight popular fiction. They found piles of Leslie Charteris titles, *The Saint Goes West*, *The Holy Terror*, *Boodle*, going right back to *Meet the Tiger*, published in 1928, and a rare one, Rufus said, putting it carefully on one side. There was a 1933 first edition of *Introducing Inspector Maigret*, another rarity, a dozen D.H. Lawrence titles, one of which, *The White Peacock*, published in 1911, was worth more than all the others put together. Thank God, Rufus blessed his luck as he placed it with the other finds, the old ladies' nephew had been as ignorant as he was greedy, or he would have insisted upon a proper valuation, kept such delights for his own profit.

As the afternoon wore on, they worked their way through Henry Fielding and Elizabeth Goudge, Graham Greene and Emily Brontë, C.P. Snow and Alexandre Dumas. Rufus had to stop for a cup of strong coffee when he found a copy of Mervyn Peake's *Gormenghast*, published in 1950 and still in its original, Peake-illustrated dust wrapper, so he could pore over his reference books. When he reappeared in the library doorway, grinning, Clementine knew it must be something good, and when he set her searching for *Titus Groan* and *Titus Alone* she caught his enthusiasm, spent an hour lifting books, turning them over, laying them on one side, until at last she found *Titus Groan*, the dust wrapper, with its distinctive, brooding bird hunched over a stone crown and a broken chain, still intact.

'Got it!' she exclaimed, waving it triumphantly in the air, and was rewarded with 'Clementine, you're *brilliant*!' and a strange, awkward dance as Rufus went to embrace her in a bear hug, changed his mind at the last minute and instead patted her clumsily on the arm before taking the book into his hand and turning abruptly away to examine it. What would it be like, Clementine was startled to find herself wondering, to be taken in her employer's arms, and kissed properly? Her disappointment, when he moved off to renew his search for *Titus Alone* was surprisingly intense.

'Mary must need to go out by now,' she said, and calling the dog, she left the room, making for the kitchen and an escape from her own confusion.

*

It was late when the bell jangled in the passage. Whoever it was, decided Rufus as he strode across the hall, they could bugger off – all he wanted was a quiet supper with Clementine. He had found five books to excite him so far, had probably missed a couple when Clementine distracted him and, after the frustrations of the past week, it had been a terrific day. He didn't need anyone coming in and spoiling things.

'Yes?'

Jean was taken aback. There was no trace of the easy-going charmer she had sat with in that beautiful drawing room. Rufus Palliser was scowling as ferociously as he had been the first time she arrived on his doorstep. But she was cold, wet, and reluctant to go home and start the supper. She persevered.

'Is Clem in?'

Rufus swung the door back, curbing his impatience. 'Yup. I'll get her.'

Jean examined him dubiously. He really didn't seem at all pleased to see her. 'Actually, I have something to ask you, too.'

'Oh?' Rufus shifted impatiently.

'Well, can I come in then?'

'Er, yes. Right.' Rufus had the feeling if he once let her cross the threshold he would never get rid of her, but she was, after all, a friend of Clementine's. He ushered her into the hall, then led her along the corridor to the kitchen, where Clementine was starting the supper.

Clementine seemed pleased to see her. Rufus grudgingly unearthed glasses and a dusty bottle of red wine, which Jean promptly declined, patting her stomach mysteriously, then opting for coffee instead. She mustn't be long, she said, Robert was babysitting Eddie and she had promised she would only be ten minutes. She had come to ask a favour – would Rufus mind Clementine looking after Eddie for a couple of hours tomorrow morning, so she could go for a job interview?

'I'd ask Dorrie but she'll be here anyway, so I thought—'

Rufus settled down to peel the potatoes, curbing his temper. 'Sure,' he said. As long as he didn't have to have anything to do with the kid. 'I'll be in Norwich all morning.'

'Thanks.' Jean hung her dripping Barbour over a chair and sat down. 'The other thing is, I thought I ought to warn you. They're back.'

'Back? Who're back?' Clementine looked up from the chicken breasts she was chopping and absent-mindedly took the glass of wine Rufus offered her.

'The Davises.'

'Who?'

'The Davises. Marshmeadow, I told you about them, remember? They're back, for good this time.'

'Oh.' Marshmeadow unoccupied was one thing, Marshmeadow lived in by strangers another. Just the idea of it made Clementine feel peculiar.

'I thought you ought to know. I was in the Post Office just now, fending off nosy-parker Madge, when who should walk in but the famous Caroline.'

'The famous Caroline who?'

Jean had forgotten Rufus, still peeling potatoes at the other end of the table and glaring at her from beneath lowering brows. 'Caroline Davis, Marshmeadow. You must've seen her. Madam La-di-da.' She mimicked the posh accent, primped an imaginary hairdo. 'Anyway, we got into this stupid three-way conversation, Madge bootlicking and fawning and me muttering in the background and then, I can't remember how, she got on to the subject of decorating.'

'Who did?'

'Caroline Davis did. Seems the place hasn't been touched since they moved in, what with them being here so infrequently, and now that Charles is retired, she thinks it's time they did it up.'

'Oh.' Clementine concentrated on her chopping, trying not to think about Marshmeadow redecorated to somebody else's taste, and Rufus's temper frayed still further. All this talk about Marshmeadow was upsetting her, he could tell. The signs were obvious; her chopping was becoming increasingly clumsy, and she had that hunted look on her face he found so heartrending.

'So?' he asked rudely.

'So . . .' Jean was not to be hurried. 'She bought a jar of mustard, milled around while Madge paid out my child allowance, then asked me if I knew anyone who might advise her.' She glanced from one to the other, making sure they were both paying attention. 'I said no, I didn't, but she's asked me to ask you anyway, if you'd be prepared to pop over and have a look. She even suggested you take someone for moral support if you want to, in case being there upsets you—'

Clem was astonished. 'But why me, for heaven's sake? Why would an ambassador want a housekeeper to advise him on his decor?'

'He's not an ambassador, he's just a minor diplomat. And Caroline wants your advice because Madge told her all about you. She can't wait to pick your brains.' Switching her attention to Rufus, Jean was taken aback by the thunderous expression on his face and returned hastily to Clem. 'I knew you'd be upset – and I did *try* to shut Madge up, but you know what she's like, Clem, it's like trying to stop a runaway train—' There was an awkward silence; Jean shifted uneasily on her chair, then added defensively, 'I just thought I ought to warn you, that's all.'

'Thanks, Jean.' Clementine rose from the table and

carried the chopping board across to the range where the frying pan was overheating, blue smoke curling up towards the ceiling.

'Yeah. Thanks for letting us know.' Rufus lifted his saucepan and took it to the sink to add water. 'But if you don't mind, we've been working flat out all day and I'm starving.' He didn't even try to keep the irritation out of his voice.

'Oh. Right.' So that was his trouble. Robert was always bad-tempered when he was hungry. *Men*, thought Jean, *typical*. She rose and strode across to Clementine, now diligently stirring chicken pieces and onions. 'You're not too upset, are you, Clem?' she asked, twisting her neck to peer up into her friend's face. 'After all, it's only a house, when all's said and done, just a pile of bricks and mortar, isn't it?'

'No, I'm fine,' said Clementine, convincing herself as much as Jean. 'You're absolutely right, it's only a house. But now I *must* get on with the supper, or Rufus'll give me the sack.'

Jean turned to Rufus, trying an experimental tease. 'You wouldn't really fire your little treasure over one late meal would you, Rufus?'

Rufus shook his head, then added, not seeing the joke, 'But I might if she ever treated Manor Hall as if it was *only* a house.'

'Whoops.' Jean returned to the table to retrieve her coat, annoyed. 'Sensitive subject? I'd better be on my way before the starving Mr Palliser turns *really* nasty. I'll see myself out.' She made for the door. 'Thanks for looking after Eddie, Clem, I'll see you tomorrow, around ten. Bye, Rufus.'

'Bye.' Rufus poured more wine, waited until the door was shut, then picked up Clementine's glass and took it across to her. 'You okay?' he asked.

'Yes.' Clementine stirred distractedly at her pan. 'Yes, of course. Jean's right, it's only a pile of bricks and mortar.'

'Oh? And is that how you feel about this place?'

Clementine paused, her spatula hovering above the chicken, sighed. 'No, of course it isn't, I—' She met his eyes, shrugged. 'You know what I mean.'

Rufus nodded. He wanted to kiss her again, show her that he understood; he even leaned towards her, bent his head, then at the last second thought he'd better not and turned away. He didn't see her close her eyes, anticipating him, wasn't watching when she lost her balance and had to lean against the range, grabbing at the brass rail to steady herself; he missed the blush that swept her cheeks when the presaged kiss failed to materialise.

'We could go and see her together,' he said over his shoulder. 'If you want to.'

We. He made it sound as if they were a couple, and Clementine was reminded forcibly that he had a girlfriend, a very beautiful girlfriend. She felt foolish, then furious – he had no business kissing her when he already had a girlfriend – then deflated, because he *hadn't* kissed her. She lowered her head and began to concentrate on her cooking which was catching on the bottom of the pan.

'I'll go on my own,' she said, unaccountably annoyed, 'next time you're entertaining your girlfriend.'

'My what?'

'Your girlfriend.'

'What girlfriend?'

'Sal. I met her, remember? When I got back from London.' Perhaps Madge was right. Perhaps he had dozens of girlfriends.

'Sal?' Rufus turned back to face her, astonished. 'Whatever gave you the idea that Sal and I—?'

'Well, I assumed – you were entertaining her—'

'Sal's a friend. And my employee. She is not and never has been my—'

'Oh! Sorry.' Clementine began to scrub vigorously at the sticking food. Rufus ran his fingers distractedly through his hair and glared, frustrated, at her back. How was he supposed to woo the bloody woman if she kept getting the wrong end of the stick?

'Do you want the spuds on?'

'What? Oh, yes. Please.'

Rufus banged the saucepan past her on to the back-plate and tipped the lid to allow the steam to escape. Clementine looked flushed from the heat of the range. She looked soft, flustered, *delicious*.

'How long to supper?' he growled.

'I don't know, about half an hour?'

'I'll finish clearing up then.'

Clementine nodded, then moved away to find a casserole dish. She transferred the meat and onions, dripping juice clumsily on to the hotplate where it sizzled and spattered, added stock, then placed the dish in the middle oven. When she straightened up, Rufus had vanished, leaving the kitchen door open and a draught of cold air from the corridor behind him. She covered her pink cheeks with her hands and leaned against the range, feeling like a complete fool.

By the time Rufus returned to the kitchen half an hour later, she had taken her supper and escaped to her room to sit in her scruffy armchair by the blanked-off fireplace with Mary at her feet, pretending to eat while the rain pattered against the windows like a distant football rattle and the wind whined through the gaps in the casements, billowing the curtains and sneaking chilly fingers round the back of her neck.

When she went downstairs to let Mary out for the last

time the hall was in darkness. She stood on the step listening to the wind in the shrubbery. Rufus hadn't bothered to put the van away for the past few nights and it squatted below her, rusting away on the gravel with the rain pinging off its roof. She was reminded of the first time she had driven it, how Rufus had seemed to fill all the available space. Until now, she had almost forgotten what it was like, really fancying someone. For years she had turned off that part of her which had responded to Martin, deliberately curtailing every budding relationship the moment it started to get serious, avoiding future humiliation.

She folded her arms, rubbed her cold hands up and down her sleeves and recalled her slow gentle courtship with Jonathan. What had it actually felt like, kissing him? '*Nice*' was the word that seemed to suit, cosy, mildly arousing, nothing like the raw excitement she had felt with Martin. Jonathan, she had thought, would be able to handle her scars, physical attraction had played such a small part in their friendship to begin with that it had seemed unimportant, almost irrelevant, at least until the trip to Amsterdam, and by that time she had had so much confidence in him, he had seemed to have so much genuine feeling for her, she had hoped it might not matter. She had been grateful for the lack of pressure, content to settle for affection, quiet peaceful companionship. She had not imagined when it all went wrong that she would end up standing, cold, damp and confused, back home where she had thought she would never come again, as fired up as a lovelorn teenager because a man who had kissed her only once (and as chastely as a brother at that) had *almost* kissed her again. It had been so much less complicated when it was all turned off, when she could tell herself she didn't need anyone, that she *preferred* being alone . . .

Jonathan's fault, she thought, as Mary trotted back towards her out of the dark, building her hopes, then letting her down. Or was it Jean's pregnancy, triggering suppressed maternal instincts, telling her time was slipping away? Soon it would no longer be, 'I don't want children', but, 'I can't have children'. Was that what was causing this seething unrest?

She swung the front door shut behind Mary, shot the bolts and followed her across the hall, switching off lights as she went. As she climbed the stairs the cuckoo struck the half hour, eleven-thirty. Rufus had already retired – she could see the line of light under his door – and she snapped the last switch, then stood in the dark, imagining him lying in bed, in the only room in the house she hadn't seen. She was reminded suddenly, vividly, of that first time with Martin, not of the aftermath but of the sex itself. The sensation was so strong, so overwhelmingly pleasurable, it took her breath away.

Chapter Twenty-Nine

Mary, catching Clementine's restlessness, took a long time to settle, waltzing round and round on the eiderdown and flopping down, then rising to start the procedure all over again. Clementine burrowed down beneath the bedclothes, cold now the central heating had gone off, tucked her feet into the hem of her nightgown and listened to the rain beating on the window. Her mind was still on her employer, her body disobediently refusing to calm down. She heard the cuckoo strike one before she dozed off, to the sound of the wind wailing under the doors and round the casements.

She was roused out of a heavy sleep by Mary, whining and pawing at her arm. She sat up, only half awake, and switched on the bedside light. Just after five, said her watch, tipped on its side next to her book, but it couldn't have been the cuckoo that had wakened her, because the room was already filled with too much noise for her to have heard it – banshee howls, shrieks and bangs, interspersed with brief pauses during which she could hear a door slamming somewhere and the casements rattling.

There was a slipping, sliding rush high above her head and something came thundering down the attic roof, smashed against the parapet outside her window, then fell with a crunching thud to the ground far below. Mary began to panic, rushing to and fro between the bed and the door and whining desperately to be let out. Clementine swung her legs to the floor and stood up, shivering in the cold. She searched for a jumper to fling over her nightgown, found socks and knickers, and hopped across the room, pulling her boots on. A current of arctic air swirled past her face as she opened the door, lifting her hair from her shoulders, and she could hear the blanking plate on the stairs clattering madly against its stone surround like a giant sewing machine. She ducked as she passed it, half expecting it to crash down on her head.

The kitchen was warmer, and quieter, but Mary, still panicking, scrabbled frantically at the door. As Clementine drew back the bolts to let her out an ominous creaking began somewhere high above her head, and it grew to a roaring, crashing, smashing avalanche of noise. The door was snatched from her grasp and hurled back against the wall, the breath was whipped from her mouth by a gust of wind so strong it almost knocked her down, and debris began to rain from the sky, bouncing off the walls and plummeting to the ground below.

Mary was already gone by the time the first missile hit; she had bolted into the darkness the instant the door was opened.

The wind was playing havoc in the kitchen, lifting the pile of newspapers Rufus had left on the table and sending them flapping round the room, bowling a chair across the pamments to crash against the dresser and sending plates in all directions to add to the cacophonic orchestra playing outside. '*Mary!*' Clementine yelled into the void . . . and all the lights went out.

She felt her way round the table to the dresser, crunching china underfoot, to fumble in the drawer for the torch Rufus kept there. Then she staggered back to the door and shone the beam out into the maelstrom until she found Mary, battling towards the house with her ears and coat streaming. She was almost home when Ginger appeared, his fur sodden with water, his tail bristled to three times its usual size, making for the door at a run and yowling with outrage at the battering his lair in the cart lodge was taking. Mary, marginally less frightened of the storm than of Ginger, skidded to a halt, hesitated, then turned tail and bolted for the second time.

Clementine cursed, yelled again, then plunged out into a nightmare of flying tiles, freezing wind and driving rain to rescue her.

Rufus, having spent a fruitless evening staring into the drawing room fire, wondering if he was using the right tactics or whether it was time to start playing rough and sweep Clementine off her feet, had banked the fire up and gone to bed early, hoping to sleep the problem away, then spent four hours going round and round in circles getting nowhere and dropped off just after two, still stretched out, fully dressed, on the bed. Startled out of sleep by an almighty crash, he leapt from his bed and his room with his heart hammering against his ribs to race the length of the landing, convinced a bomb had landed on the house.

Clementine's door was swinging wildly on its hinges, smashing against the wall, then bouncing back to slam against the catch and bursting open again; with each arc it described, clouds of dust poured into the corridor. Rufus grabbed the handle as it swung towards him and forced his way in.

'*Christ*,' he murmured, skidding to a halt. The door banged shut behind him. '*Jesus Christ.*'

The lights went out, but the scene stayed with him. The bed, where Clementine should have been sleeping peacefully, was a tangle of bricks, tiles and plaster, splintered beams and bits of roof felting; through the gap where the ceiling had been, stars and racing clouds were visible. The wind roared through the hole, sending swirls of brick dust and lath-and-plaster pouring down into the room and filling his mouth with choking silt.

He fumbled his way across to the bed and began to tear at the mess, blindly heaving beams, dropping bricks and lumps of plaster on the floor, feeling the eiderdown to make sure Clementine's battered remains were not buried beneath the rubble. The bed was empty. He searched the floor, falling over masonry, tripping on the edge of the carpet, bumping into the furniture, calling her name, and Mary's, screwing up his eyes to see in the dark until he was completely exhausted and absolutely positive neither of them was there. The relief was so great he had to stop by the window and rest his head against the stone mullion to recover.

What to do next? 'Kitchen,' he decided, talking out loud because his brain was muddled by the noise and it helped to feel the words coming out of his mouth even if he couldn't hear them. 'They'll be in the kitchen.' Why hadn't she called for help? he wondered, feeling his way back across the room and out into the corridor, then along the landing and down the stairs. Why hadn't he realised she was in danger?

He lost his footing, miscounting the steps and landing with a jarring thud in the hall because his head was telling him there was still one more tread to go. He paused, suddenly stricken by the thought that she might be lying somewhere in the house, hurt, and he had missed her. The torch was in the dresser drawer; he would go through the place from top to bottom until he found her. But where was Mary? If Clementine was hurt why hadn't Mary come looking for him? What was the point, he wondered angrily as he felt his way towards the kitchen, of having a dog if, as soon as there was an emergency, she disappeared?

The kitchen, what he could see of it in the faint light from the window, appeared to be devoid of human beings or dogs. The back door was wide open and the room had been redecorated with sheets of newspaper; pressed against the wall, wrapped round the chairs, the fridge, the dresser, they flapped and rustled like a flock of giant birds. A page of *The Times* slapped him in the face as he stepped into the room, and as he made his way across to the dresser his shoes scrunched on broken china. The torch was missing.

'What the hell is going on?' he demanded, his voice drowned by flapping paper and howling wind, and when Ginger materialised, rubbing against his trouser leg, he swept him into his arms and yelled, 'Where are they? Is this your fault, you blasted troublemaker?'

Ginger felt thin and bony beneath the sodden fur. In the three-year war of attrition they had waged, it was the first time Rufus had ever picked him up. He went to put him out, but the cat was too old, too skinny. Ginger started to purr, nuzzling at his chest. Rufus carried him across to the range, opened the door of the bottom oven and placed him inside to thaw out. Where did he go from here?

When Clementine staggered across the threshold he was on the other side of the room, trying to light the oil lamp he had found in the wash house, the one Dorrie always kept primed and full of fuel because you never knew when you might need it. He had bashed his knee on the table in the dark and he was swearing. By the time he'd got the wick going she was sitting on the floor, where her frozen, uncooperative legs had unceremoniously dumped her.

She was sopping wet, as if she had been for a swim in the river, and her hair, falling loose to her shoulders, was tangled with leaves and bits of twig. She had one boot missing and she was liberally spattered with mud. When Rufus spoke to her she moved her mouth but no sound came out. When he touched her face it was ice-cold and when he leaned nearer and slapped her cheek, hoping to elicit some reaction, he saw that her lips were blue, her nostrils pinched and yellow-white.

For a moment Rufus panicked, didn't know what to do, but then common sense took over. It must be the cold. She was frozen, therefore he must warm her up. He went to shut the door.

He hesitated before he heaved it the last few inches; if Clementine had been out there, Mary must be out there too. But there was nothing he could do about it now – it was Clementine who counted, Clementine who needed him. He pushed hard, then shot the bolt to make sure the door couldn't burst open again. The sudden quiet was deafening.

He crossed to the range and opened the middle, hot oven, moving with exaggerated calm, his actions slow and his mind racing. Then he returned to Clementine, still sitting on the floor where he had left her, and slid his arm round her, feeling the wet soak through his sleeve.

'Up,' he said.

She nodded, folded her legs awkwardly, trying to make them work, clutched at his arm, flopped.

'Come on, *up*!' He heaved, felt her go with him a little. She weighed a *ton*. He left her and fetched one of the chairs, the carver because it had arms so she wouldn't topple off it. Bathed in the soft light of the oil lamp the room looked bizarre. The newspapers, deprived of the wind, had fallen askew on to everything, festooning floor, chairs, dresser, table, sink. The remains of half a dozen plates lay scattered across the pamments, along with all those odd bits and pieces which had accumulated on the dresser over the past three years until Rufus decided what he was going to do with them, old bills and circulars, reminders and receipts, used biros, bits of string. He swept last Thursday's sports page out of the way and placed the chair in front of the open oven, unhooked another catch to let more heat out. Then he went back to Clementine. He managed it this time, hauling her up until she rested on one knee, then pulling her forward so her own momentum brought her nearly upright. Then he half dragged, half carried her to the chair and lowered her carefully, already working out the next step.

'Don't go away,' he commanded unnecessarily.

She made a stab at a smile, but her mouth wasn't working properly and she grimaced horribly instead. He rummaged in the dresser for the pewter candle holder he knew was there, a Wee-Willie-Winkie one with a flat base and a metal loop-handle, found a stub of candle. He lit it, dripped wax into the holder, then pushed the candle down and waited for it to set before placing it on the range by Clementine's shoulder. Then he took the lamp and went foraging.

He came back with a huge white bath towel, a pair of his own socks and a clean nightgown from the airing cupboard – he knew what Clementine wore in bed now, ankle-length Victorian-style cotton with tucks and a demure high neck. He brought with him a swirl of icy air from the corridor and set the paper birds fluttering again, then with calm, matter-of-fact precision, he began to peel Clementine's clothes from her, taking no notice at all of her incoherent protests. When he had removed everything, jumper, nightgown, boot, socks, knickers, he wrapped her in the towel and rubbed her hard, until she gasped and yelped and her eyes filled with tears of pain, getting her circulation going, bringing some life back to her frozen limbs.

Clementine thought at first he hadn't noticed the scars, but when he pulled her back on to her feet so he could drop her clean nightgown over her head, guiding her arms into the sleeves as if she was a small child incapable of doing it by herself, his fingers stroked, too slowly for it to be an accident, across her left hip. She held her breath, waiting for him to recoil, but he just moved on when he was ready, rearranging her, then bent down to deal with her feet. She was so shocked, it wasn't until he had tucked her into the bliss of his enormous woollen socks and left her again, that she remembered Mary. Tears welled in her sore eyes.

He was away for longer this time, and when he returned, carrying an ancient tartan rug, she thought he ought to know. She gripped his arm and mouthed at him.

'Later,' he said. He reached across her to shut the oven doors, then wrapped the rug round her and led her out of the kitchen into the freezing corridor, holding the lamp aloft to light the way.

The change in temperature made her shake with a St Vitus's Dance of cold and her teeth chattered like castanets, but the fire in the drawing room was blazing and the room was blissfully warm.

Rufus had pushed the sofas together. He had laid blankets across the squabs, added more layers on top, then covered everything with the embroidered quilt from the Blue Room.

He placed the lamp on the table by the window. 'Bed,' he said. 'Now.'

Clementine needed help to negotiate the sofa arm, but once beneath the blankets she sank gratefully into the warmth, overcome by weariness.

'Clementine?' Rufus, seeing her eyes close, was afraid she would drop off too soon. 'What about Mary?'

She raised her head and opened her mouth to explain, then found she was too tired to go through it all again and shut it.

'Is there anything I can do?'

She shook her head, closed her eyes again.

'All right.' He stroked her tangled hair back from her face. 'We'll leave it till the morning.'

Dragging her eyelids up, she watched him moving about, settling the room down, banking up the fire and putting the guard across it, extinguishing the oil lamp. The first faint glimmerings of dawn were beginning at the window; in another hour the sun would be rising. She could still hear the shrubbery clashing disharmoniously outside but the wind had abated a little; too late for Mary.

'Better?' asked Rufus, returning to squat by her pillow.

Clementine found her voice at last. 'Yes.' It occurred to her that it must be freezing upstairs, and it was probably not safe. 'Where will you sleep?' she asked. 'Will you be all right?'

'I'll be fine,' said Rufus calmly. 'I'm sleeping with you.'

Chapter Thirty

Rufus lay still with his eyes closed, listening to the silence and going over it in minute detail.

Last night, in his sleep, he had got it spectacularly, sensationally right. Last night, in his sleep, he had made love to Clementine Lee.

He recalled it with peculiar clarity; the taste of her mouth, the shape of her breasts, the scars he had explored with such loving care. He went over it again, savouring the texture of her skin, the smell of mud clinging to her hair . . .

Scars? Mud? He opened his eyes, stared at the ceiling and wondered why it didn't look right, then turned his head slowly, holding his breath.

Beside him, her face tranquil in sleep, lay Clementine Lee, just as he had dreamed, but her hair, imagined so many times spread prettily across his pillows, was a tangled mess, and a streak of dirt ran from her left temple to her chin. He propped himself on one elbow and leaned close to feel the faint movement of her breath on his face; he felt enormous, heartstopping tenderness, murmured in her ear, 'I love you, Clementine.'

Her expression changed, as if he had disturbed her. She frowned, sighed, then slept again, but less easily now, and her mouth worked as she muttered to herself. She shifted her weight, stretched an arm outside the covers and bumped against Rufus's shoulder, then snatched her hand away and opened her eyes wide.

Clementine hadn't heard Rufus's confession. She was dreaming, grabbing at Mary as she slid away from her in a tangle of cascading earth and roots, then slipping and slithering into a wild cataract of water, snatching in the dark at branches barbed with needle-sharp teeth through air thick with flying leaves, reaching out to Mary and instead of rough animal coat finding the smooth texture of human skin.

For a moment all Rufus could read on her face was bewilderment. And then she remembered, he could tell. She smiled. Rufus held his breath, waiting for the embarrassment, the withdrawal, maybe even the polite grimace he disliked so much. The embarrassment came quickly enough, he could see it in her heightened colour, in the movement of her head and the way she hastily covered her bare arm with the quilt, but the smile stayed (pleasure outweighing discomfort?), stretched wider and wider until it was a big, beaming grin. Rufus grinned back, suffocating with delight.

'Hungry?' he asked, because it seemed important to say something, if only to make her feel the situation was natural, and the only other words in his head were, 'I love you', which even in her sleep had seemed to disturb her. There was plenty of time, now they had begun, for the next step and she hadn't frozen him out. It was a start. He tasted her again in his imagination. *Boy*, was it ever a start . . .

He reached across to pick a stray leaf out of her hair and dropped it over the arm of the sofa on to the floor. Her smile faded.

'What?' he asked, his optimism fading with it.

Clementine brushed a hand across her eyes. 'I just remembered Mary.'

She pushed herself up on the pillow, then clutched at the blanket as it fell away from her shoulders. Rufus slid his hand across and ran it, palm down, along her side, reminding her it was too late to be diffident. 'Tell me,' he said.

The small gesture had a profound effect upon Clementine. She would not have been surprised to find her scars gone, miraculously stroked away during the night. She rolled on to her back and held him against her, not wanting the sensation to stop.

'It was Ginger. He appeared from nowhere and he frightened her.'

'Were you in bed when the chimney came down?'

Clementine was puzzled. 'What chimney?'

'It's all over your bed. I thought when I saw it you must be dead, for sure.'

'Mary got me up, wanting to go out . . .'

'She saved your life then. Go on.' Rufus propped himself higher so he could see her face better.

'The door . . . the one at the bottom of the garden, it was open, blown off its hinges, and she went straight through—'

'Towards the river?'

'Mm. There's a sloe leans over the bank, near the bridge. D'you know the one I mean?'

Rufus nodded.

'She found a rabbit there, the other day.' Clementine pulled a face. 'I should have killed it when I had the chance—'

'What?'

'It was myxy, it had myxomatosis.'

She moved nearer, looking for comfort, and Rufus slid back beneath the covers, pulling her close.

'Go on.' He had to fix his face into a solemnity he could not feel, because everything, even the loss of Mary, paled into insignificance against the fact that Clementine Ambrosia Thomasina Lee was lying beside him with her bare thigh touching his and her breath warming his shoulder.

'Daddy found a myxy rabbit once. Have you ever seen one? It's a mystery to me how anyone could deliberately infect a dumb animal with a disease like that . . . We were out walking and he sent me on ahead with Dolly—'

'Dolly?'

'Our spaniel. He said his shoelace had come undone and he'd catch us up. When he didn't appear I went back to find him . . .' She tailed off into silence. Rufus tightened his grip and she dropped her head against his chest. The sheer *size* of him was comforting; how strange, she thought, that she should have found him so intimidating. 'He'd picked up a stone and he was hitting the poor thing over the head, putting it out of its misery . . .'

Rufus touched her cheek where the smear of dirt still clung to it. 'It was the kindest thing to do,' he said. 'I would have done the same.'

'But I didn't, you see. I couldn't bring myself to. I left it there, and when Mary got far enough along the path this morning she remembered it.' Her face began to work as she struggled not to cry.

'And she went to investigate?'

Clementine nodded. 'She got right in under the sloe, and by the time I caught her up . . . it was crumbling, collapsing, and I couldn't – she didn't stand a chance . . .'

'You've lost me. What was collapsing?'

'The bank. The river's higher than I've ever seen it . . . and then the sloe went, and she – I've lost your torch.'

'Never mind,' said Rufus gently. 'I'll find her.' It was the only solace he could think of. 'I'll bring her home and we'll bury her in the garden.'

'I'm sorry,' said Clementine, blaming herself. 'There was nothing I could do—'

'Shush.' Rufus wanted to make love to her again, but he didn't like to suggest it, too much pressure might make her retreat again. 'I'll make you a cup of tea,' he said prosaically instead. He felt her smile against his chest, was swamped by a tremendous wave of protective love.

'Don't go away,' he ordered, disguising passion with platitudes, and he clambered out of bed.

Clementine smiled again, cheered by the reminder of his earlier exhortation, when she had been unable to work her legs at all. When he leaned unexpectedly over the sofa to kiss her, she closed her eyes and sighed. Given the choice, she would rather have had more sex than a cup of tea.

Rufus retrieved his sweater from the hearthrug, talking about insurance and repairs, wondering aloud where he had put the documents so he could put in a claim for the roof as soon as possible, beginning a disorganised search for his jeans, dropped carelessly somewhere under the table.

Clementine lay back and watched him moving around the room. He was completely unselfconscious, as if it was a normal thing to do; unused to such casual nakedness she found the intimacy of it both shocking and exciting.

'What?' he asked as he emerged, even more tousled than usual, from the neck of his sweater. 'What are you smiling at?'

'Nothing.' Maybe, thought Clementine, enjoying the view, there was something in Mrs Rowenstall's theory about shoe size. She wiggled her toes inside Rufus's size thirteen socks and turned her head to the pillow, attacked by a sudden, inappropriate fit of the giggles.

Rufus, not noticing, struggled into the rest of his clothes, revived the fire, and went to make the tea.

Dorrie was late.

'Stop rushing about like a headless chicken,' complained Frank over the burbling radio. 'He won't expect you to be on time today.'

'That's not the point.' Dorrie was flustered. 'The phone's dead and I can't let him know. It's not as if you need me here—'

'Who's going to hold the ladder then, while I'm risking life and limb?'

Dorrie shrugged her arms into her big winter coat, chuckling. 'What, you mean you can't manage half a dozen slipped tiles by yourself? Poor old chap, must be past it.'

'Watch it,' warned Frank, grinning. 'Go on then, better make sure they haven't been blown clean away.' He wandered across to the television and pressed the switch. Nothing. He went back to the radio, twiddling the knob and bending the aerial backwards and forwards to improve the reception. The batteries were running low. 'Got it wrong, as usual,' he remarked over his shoulder.

'Who did?'

'Weathermen. That Michael Fish put his foot in it in a big way yesterday.'

'Oh, yes?' Dorrie was withering. 'Well, you didn't exactly hit the nail on the head, did you? Bit windy, was all you said when I asked if I should leave the washing out—'

'That's what I'm trying to tell you.' Frank moved across to straighten her collar, tucking her scarf in more neatly. 'Michael Fish was on the one o'clock news yesterday. Some woman'd rung in to ask if there was a hurricane on the way—'

'Hurricane? That's going a bit far, isn't it?'

'—and Michael Fish said not to worry, there wasn't.'

'What, a hurricane on the way?'

'Mm.' Frank had been up since four, helping Robert move the calves as the barn swayed and creaked and threatened to disintegrate in the wind. He had come home only for a change of clothes and something to eat, and as soon as he had seen Dorrie safely on her way he was off back to Hawe's Farm to help with the clearing up. 'You wait till you see it. It's like the Blitz out there.'

'Don't be daft.' Dorrie found her bag and made for the back door, patting the dog as she passed. The old girl had snored right through last night's storm. Must be getting deaf. 'I'll see you tea time.'

'Can't get out that way.' Frank shoved his hands in his pockets and jingled his change. 'You'll have to go out the front.'

'Don't be daft.'

'I mean it. Slept right through it, you did, must be getting deaf, poor old girl. You go and look if you don't believe me, just stick your head round the corner and you'll see.'

He laughed at her when she returned. She looked stunned.

'How long's that ash tree been standing?' she asked. 'And now it's gone, just like that.'

'Good job it wasn't a couple of feet nearer,' said Frank. 'Else it would've come right through our bedroom ceiling. I'll let you out.'

There were more nasty surprises outside the front door. The row of sprouts Frank had planted for Christmas lay flat across the path like felled soldiers and the rickety fence, for so long a bone of mild contention between the Medlers and their neighbours as to whose responsibility it was to maintain it, lay pole-axed in next door's garden. Further along the row, at number 3, the apple tree whose blossom had brightened spring days since the year Frank and Dorrie got married, had collapsed in ruin, smashing through a privet hedge and blocking the lane.

'Oh, my giddy aunt!' said Dorrie. Frank was right, it was like something out of the war.

It was worse the other side of the bridge. The ancient beeches, which had guarded the entrance to the village for as long as anyone could remember, were all down, bowled over like enormous skittles, and the road was blocked as far as the eye could see. The ornamental cherry in the garden of number 2 Vicarage Fields had snapped halfway up, forming a triangular arch over the petunias and marigolds, and the Old Ship, shorn of nearly a third of its *Cupressus* hedging, looked like a lady deprived in public of her skirt, embarrassingly exposed. One of the swings in the school playground lay drunkenly on its side with its legs in the air and Marshmeadow was almost invisible behind the tangle of leaves, branches and upended roots which yesterday had been a handsome lime tree.

Dorrie stopped to survey the landscape she had known all her life; with so many landmarks missing it was barely recognisable.

There were people everywhere: Madge Dixon, standing on the step of the post office with her arms folded across her skinny chest, gossiping with her two cronies from Vicarage Fields; the banker and his wife, renowned for keeping themselves to themselves, surveying the damage to the Old Ship's privacy and chatting animatedly with Dorrie's neighbour, Cora, as if they were old friends instead of virtual strangers. On the other side of the green a knot of gangling council-house youths, unexpectedly given a day off from the comprehensive, jostled and sniggered with the three pretty convent girls from Vicarage Fields, who would not normally have been seen dead talking to creatures from such an inferior rung on the evolutionary ladder. Half a dozen of the younger ones were roaring up and down, yelling and waving branches, across the thick carpet of leaves and twigs strewn about the green.

Caroline Davies was leaning on the gate outside her garden, surveying the damage. Her husband, coming out to join her, raised a hand to Dorrie and called, 'Hello, there! Frightful business! You all right down your end?'

Dorrie raised her hand in return, but she was taken aback by the familiarity of the greeting. Frank was right, it *was* like the Blitz.

As she turned right and hurried towards Manor Hall, she thought it looked as if it had escaped quite lightly. The shrubbery was rather battered, a bit threadbare round the edges, but the azaleas and rhododendrons were still standing, the tall gates and their supporting posts were no more askew than usual. It was when Dorrie looked higher that she thought something was wrong. She examined the roofline, frowning. It was as familiar as the school or the church, but craning her neck towards the twisted chimney stacks she was sure they looked different, nothing she could put her finger on, just *odd*. She stared for a moment, trying to work it out, then gave up, drew her coat tighter over her bosom and hurried on up the drive.

Rufus was crossing the hall with a pile of Clementine's clothes in his hands. 'You all right?' he asked, echoing Charles Davies. 'Everyone survived down your end?'

'Everybody's fine,' said Dorrie. 'Leastways, so far as I know. What about you?'

'Clementine and I are fine too. I didn't think we'd see you today.'

Clementine and I. Funny, the way he said it, so friendly, no, *cosy*, more like. That was how it had been when they'd bombed Norfolk in the war, of course, everyone suddenly all chummy, people who'd never met before greeting each other like brothers, lords mixing with labourers and dukes with dustmen. Be a good thing, thought Dorrie, Rufus and Clementine getting a bit more friendly. They were both lonely.

'Mary's missing though.'

'Oh, dear, I *am* sorry. But you mustn't give up hope, I'm sure she'll turn up.'

Dorrie's plump face registered sympathy, sorrow and encouragement, all at once. What a nice woman she was, thought Rufus, he must make more effort to be pleasant to her, tell her how much he appreciated her efforts on his behalf. He felt wonderfully benevolent this morning.

'Clementine doesn't think she could possibly have survived. She was out in the storm, you see.' He grabbed at Clementine's white cotton knickers, about to slide off the bundle he was holding, and gathered the pile more securely into his arms. 'She saved Clementine's life, got her up just in time before the chimney came crashing though her ceiling. Did you notice?'

'It never did!' Dorrie was aghast. So that was what had looked all wrong, a missing chimney; fancy her not spotting it! 'But Clementine's all right?'

'A bit bruised, and horribly grubby. I put her to bed in the drawing room.' Or to be more accurate – Rufus, allowing lust to creep up on him again, grinned – I *took* her to bed in the drawing room. 'She's only just up.'

'I'll pop in and say hello then, shall I?' Dorrie bustled across the hall and walked straight in.

Clementine was sitting in a tumbled nest of blankets and pillows, wrapped in a pretty quilt and leaning against the sofa back while she drained the last of a cup of tea. She looked, thought Dorrie, like one of those wanton women Robert Hawe liked to gawp at on page three of the *Sun*, the ones that made Jean so mad, all tantalising bits of bare skin and tousled hair. She should have knocked.

'Oh!' she blurted. 'Sorry dear, Rufus said . . .'

Clementine smiled at her over the rim of her tea cup. 'Hello, Dorrie,' she said. 'How are you?'

Rufus bent over the sofa and dropped Clementine's clothes in front of her. Dorrie's conviction that she was intruding on something rather private grew stronger. So much for getting a *bit* more friendly. If Rufus Palliser and Clementine Lee were still just friends she, Dorrie, was a monkey's uncle.

'I'll go and get on,' she said, backing towards the door. 'Anything in particular you'd like me to do today? Rufus?'

Rufus stared at her blankly, as if he had already forgotten her. 'Er . . .' he said. 'Yes, um . . .'

'I'll make a start on the kitchen then, shall I?' Dorrie struggled to keep her face straight.

'Yes, right. Thanks Doris.' Rufus smiled, but not at Dorrie. 'It's a mess in there, I'm afraid.'

'Have we got any electric?' asked Dorrie, and he dragged his eyes away from Clementine again.

'No, not yet.' He pulled himself together a little, concentrated on the problem. 'So there won't be a lot you can do, will there? Once you've sorted the kitchen you might as well get off home.'

Dorrie liked a bit of a romance, she was a right old soppy date, Frank always said, but she was a tiny bit doubtful about this one. Over the past couple of years Rufus had had so many little flings – she wouldn't want poor Clementine getting hurt. None of her business really, though. 'I'll go and get on, then,' she said again.

Clementine sat on the edge of the low table in front of the fire while Rufus untangled her hair. Even fully dressed she kept distracting him; the contours of her neck, the shape of her earlobe, the curve of her cheek, cleaned of its muddy streak with the aid of a large white handkerchief which Rufus held for her to lick, everything about her seemed new this morning, as if he had never really seen her properly until he had made love to her. He was fascinated by the way she held her head, by the nobbly bones of her spine beneath the red shirt he had found for her; he was even captivated by the way she breathed. So, this was the real thing at last; why had he taken so long to recognise it? Better late than never, he thought, settling back to survey his handiwork; if he hadn't decided to advertise for a housekeeper he might have missed her. The idea filled him with horror, then relief. He planted a kiss on her shoulder, pushing her collar aside to reach the bare skin beneath.

How could she possibly have thought she might marry Jonathan? wondered Clementine, shivering with pleasure. How could she have been willing to settle for what he was offering, when all the time Rufus Palliser had been here, in the place she loved best, waiting for her? She had found the real thing at last; how could she ever have thought anything less might do?

'Hi, Clem. Hi, Dorrie, you okay?'

Jean, holding Eddie firmly clamped by the wrist, filled the kitchen with her enthusiasm. 'Now Clem,' she warned, 'you'll have to keep an eye on him, he's dying to get out there and climb every fallen tree within a five-mile radius.'

Eddie squirmed like a fish on a hook. 'But Mummee,' he complained, 'I *pwomise* I won't—'

Jean snorted. 'We all know what your promises are

worth, young man. If you give your Auntie Clem any hassle, you know what I've said, don't you?'

Eddie pouted.

'I've told him there'll be no ice cream for a month—'

'You're surely not still intending to go for this interview, are you?' Clementine was incredulous. 'Apart from any other considerations, Dorrie says both roads out of the village are blocked.'

'I know.' Jean smirked triumphantly. 'Robert and Frank are out with the JCB, clearing trees up the north end. They'll be gone all morning, so I've pinched the Land Rover. I'm going across country—'

'But even supposing you can get through,' Clementine interrupted, 'they must be in as bad a state at Blackstock as everywhere else. Conducting interviews with potential conservators is going to be the last thing on their minds.'

'Ah.' Jean released Eddie, who made a beeline for the door and was headed off by Dorrie. 'That's where you're wrong. The chap who's doing the interviews happened to mention when I spoke to him yesterday that he was looking for someone who could work independently, and what better way to prove I can use my initiative than to turn up against all the odds and show him how keen I am?'

Under her elderly Barbour she was wearing a tailored suit, one Clementine hadn't seen before, and she had added a touch of lipstick and mascara to her usually scrubbed-clean face. She looked businesslike, determined.

'Well, shouldn't you at least phone to confirm you're coming?' Clem was still dubious.

'That was the first thing I thought of.' Jean was withering. 'All the lines are down. No, this is the best way.' She straightened her jacket, and her shoulders. 'Wish me luck?'

'Mummy's going to see a man about a horse,' piped up Eddie. 'An' Daddy dun't know—'

'Eddie!' Jean cut him off, impatient to be on her way across the fields. Her cheeks were flushed with excitement; she reminded Clem of the girl she had known all those years ago, constantly getting herself into scrapes, making adventures out of nothing. 'Wish me luck?' she asked again.

'Yes, of course I do.' Clementine, in a rush of affection, bent down to embrace her friend. 'I tell you what, why don't you take the quilt with you?'

'Quilt?'

'You know, the quilt you mended for me. I'm sure Rufus won't mind if you borrow it, and you could show this chap of yours just how good you are.'

Jean beamed at her. 'Clem, you're brilliant. Why didn't I think of that?'

'It's in the drawing room. I'll get it.'

Jean, following her, paused in the kitchen doorway. 'Dorrie, would you—?'

Dorrie chuckled. 'Go on. He'll be all right with me.' She shut the door firmly behind them, then turned back to Eddie. 'Now,' she said, 'where does your Auntie Clemmie keep the biscuit tin?'

'Whatever has been going on in here?' Jean was fascinated by the rumpled, makeshift bed, shocked when Clementine explained that she had had to move downstairs because her own bed was currently occupied by a ton and a half of bricks.

'God, what a lucky escape!' she said. 'And there was me thinking you and Rufus must've been up to something.' She giggled. 'It looks as if someone's been holding an orgy in here.'

Clementine, leaning over the sofa, froze with embarrassment. To her surprise, she was tempted to tell, to confess blithely, 'I slept with my employer last night, and I *loved* it.' It was only the habit of reticence that kept her bent over her task, made her avoid Jean's eye as they folded the bedspread. She would tell her later, when she had had time to get used to the idea herself . . .

Rufus was coming down the stairs as they crossed the hall. He greeted Jean amiably enough, but it was Clementine he smiled at. When Jean asked about the quilt he said, 'Sure, why not?' with perfect equanimity, but it was Clementine he looked at as he spoke. When Jean turned to go he said, 'Take it easy,' but it was Clementine to whom he moved close, Clementine whose arm he stroked. And Jean could have sworn, even in the uncertain light of the hall, that Clementine touched him right back.

When she wound the Land Rover's window down to wave she watched Clementine tilt her face up to his and she was sure – the makeshift bed in the drawing room had been shared. As she drove over the bridge and turned left on to the farm track beside the river, she made a mental note that she must have a word with Clem as soon as possible. The poor girl was so naïve when it came to men, if she wasn't careful she was liable to get herself into the most appalling mess. As the Land Rover bounced across the fields towards the main road she thought of all those years when she had envied her friend. Clem had always been so self-sufficient, so *in charge* of her life. Now just as she, Jean, had finally realised how suffocating men and relationships could be, Clem appeared to have let her defences down completely. It was *totally* out of character.

She slowed as she crossed the last meadow and approached the gap in the hedge leading to the main road, changing into second gear where the track narrowed. All right, so Rufus Palliser could be extremely charming when he chose, but she'd seen a less charming side of him twice now, and she didn't like it one bit. She knew his reputation too, everyone in the village did. How convenient for the bastard, she thought, working herself up at the thought of Clem being taken advantage of, an unlimited supply of nookie on the premises whenever he felt like it, all the hot meals he could eat and a professional painter and decorator, for nothing more than the cost of a live-in housekeeper. *Men*.

She peered up and down the road, empty but for scattered debris and a distant digger wrestling a fallen tree on to the grass verge – so far so good – then rolled the Land Rover carefully down the bank. A dangerous time for a woman, the thirties; you could be fooled into thinking you wanted to settle down just because your biological clock told you you were running out of options. Jean knew better. Jean knew there were worse fates than ending up on the shelf, and it was Clem who had made her see that she had a choice. What if Clem was mistaking a casual seduction for true love?

The Land Rover bounced and shuddered, then settled its front wheels on the tarmac and trundled forward. But how to warn her? Jean wondered as she accelerated away. How to give Clem the benefit of her inside knowledge without Clem thinking it was sour grapes? She wriggled her bottom on the seat and gripped the steering wheel, putting the problem aside. One thing at a time. Interview first, then Clem . . .

Rufus couldn't avoid Eddie; he was there when he walked into the kitchen, perched on the draining board next to the range, holding a cold sausage Dorrie had found in the fridge between two chubby fingers and blowing imaginary smoke rings. Ginger, taking advantage of the truce Rufus had called, was curled up at the back of the range, and every time the sausage passed he followed it with greedy, yellow-eyed concentration.

'Lo, Woofus,' Eddie waved his meaty cigar. 'See what Auntie Dowie gave me!'

'Very nice,' said Rufus stiffly. 'Clem, I'm going out to look for Mary.'

Clementine noticed the wide berth he gave Eddie but she said nothing. Later, she thought, she would ask him later, when they were alone. She could ask him anything now.

'So,' she lifted Eddie from the draining board and swung him high in the air. 'What are we going to do with you, young Ed?'

Rufus paused in the doorway, watching her. What if . . .? he wondered. He gripped the door handle, startled by the direction of his thoughts, then went in search of Mary.

He missed her to begin with, following the river for almost half a mile, looking for her drowned corpse, before retracing his steps to begin again. He heard her before he saw her.

The sloe had fallen across the water and snagged on the opposite bank, forming a precarious bridge. Its roots, obscenely stripped of earth, pointed to the sky, and its lower limbs had been crushed against the bank as it fell. Mary was trapped, hooked by her collar to a branch just above the waterline. She was wet, exhausted and terrified, but she was alive.

There was no way down to the water's edge, the bank had crumbled into the torrent, and Rufus had to clamber out to her along the sloe. It creaked and swayed alarmingly beneath his weight and he encountered inch-long thorns as he shuffled forward; they tore at his clothing as he reached down to pull her out by the scruff of her neck and as he edged backwards, holding her awkwardly against his ribs while she whined and shivered and writhed. When he put her down she toppled slowly over and lay on her side with one paw in the air, gazing up at him as if to say, how could you let this happen to me? Rufus ruffled her ears.

'All right,' he said, 'we'll do it the easy way, shall we?'

The light was on when he walked in, the fridge was humming to itself in the corner and Clementine was crouching under the kitchen table while Eddie roared round the room with a wooden spoon, assassinating her. When Clementine saw Mary's tail wagging feebly against Rufus's jacket, she shot out from between the chairs, delirious with delight.

'Oh! Oh, you found her! She's all right!'

'Not exactly.'

'Where's she hurt?'

'Don't know.' Rufus lowered Mary carefully to the floor next to the range where she collapsed again. She looked tiny, fragile. 'I can't find any damage, but she could have internal injuries.' He laid his hand on her ribs, trying to calm the spasms that still wracked her with the warmth of his palm.

'Would brandy help?' wondered Clementine. 'Maybe she's just cold.'

When Dorrie appeared from the wash house, where she had been loading the washing machine with muddy clothes and towels, they greeted her together, looking for reassurance, and she crouched down beside them to peer at Mary. Eddie, taking advantage of the sudden lack of attention, moved across to the table and dropped behind one of its legs to shoot, first Rufus, then Clementine, and Dorrie last, because of the sausage. Then he made his escape, like the man in the black and white film he had seen on the telly yesterday afternoon, darting towards the door on tiptoe, gun at the ready, just in case. He shot them again from the far side of the room, *pyow, pyow, pyow*, just to be on the safe side, but they didn't move.

Keeping his gun trained he turned the handle and eased the door open. Nobody turned round. Nobody said, 'Stop it Eddie,' or ordered, 'Come back this minute, Eddie.' Nobody threatened, 'Eddie Hawe, if you don't shut that door I'll smack your bottom so hard—' He pulled a face at them, hooking his little fingers into the sides of his mouth and waggling his tongue, then slid into the corridor, pulling the door carefully shut behind him so it wouldn't make a noise. Then he turned and began to edge along the wall, shooting at his shadow as he went . . .

It was Dorrie who found the gash running up the inside of Mary's left leg, almost invisible beneath the mud. They bathed the wound with Dettol and cleaned her up, but Dorrie still didn't like the look of it.

'I've an old dog basket at home.' She straightened up, her knees cracking loudly. 'I'll pop back and get it, shall I?'

'Oh, Dorrie, would you?' Clementine beamed at her. 'It's going to be hours before we can get her to a vet, but at least if she's comfortable while she's waiting . . .'

Dorrie heaved herself into her coat, wrapped her scarf round her neck twice to keep out the draughts, then peered across the kitchen. 'Now, where's young Eddie got to?'

'Oh, Lord!' Clementine swung round, expecting to see him still prowling with his spoon. How could he have disappeared so quickly?

'He can't have gone far,' said Rufus. 'Doris, if you'll go and get the basket we'll find Eddie.' An old, almost forgotten apprehension nibbled at him, the dread all parents feel when their child goes missing, but he pushed it away. It was three years since Rufus had had to worry about a child and he wasn't going to start now.

They trooped along the corridor to the hall and Dorrie went on her way, pausing to reassure Clementine as she opened the front door that Eddie must be in the house because he couldn't reach high enough to undo the latch. Then they split up, Rufus making for the door beneath the stairs and the servants' quarters, Clementine to search the drawing room, then race back to the kitchen in case Eddie had shut himself in the pantry or hidden in the wash house. As he opened doors and peered into cupboards Rufus began to ache all over, as if he had flu. He'll be all right, he told himself, trying not to think about the possibilities. He'll be fine, what could possibly happen to him? Something had happened to *his* boy though, in no time at all. He shook his head to get rid of the memory, but it stayed with him as he peered under tables and behind doors. His apprehension increased.

Eddie wasn't in the servants' quarters and Rufus made for the hall again. He could hear Clementine in the library, banging the lid on the window seat in case Eddie was hiding in the storage space beneath, calling his name.

'Upstairs,' he muttered to himself. 'Try upstairs.' Jesus, it occurred to him, what if—?

He heard him, *'Pyow, pyow, pyow!'* as he reached the landing, and he swore, then began to sprint, past the cuckoo clock and along the corridor, making for Clementine's room. Please, he prayed as he ran, *please* don't let anything happen to him.

Eddie was on Clementine's bed. When he saw Rufus he began to bounce. *'I'm the king of the castle,'* he sang, *'and you're the dirty wascal . . .'* It was hard keeping his balance, what with all the bricks and making sure his gun was aimed straight. Eddie grabbed at the beam, resting at an angle just by his left arm with one end on the bed and the other on the edge of the hole above. The beam creaked, shifted. Eddie glanced over his shoulder, alarmed. Everything seemed to be moving all of a sudden. '*Woofus* . . .!' he wailed, not liking it.

Rufus couldn't remember moving so fast in his life, ever.

Clementine found them on the landing. Eddie's arms were wrapped tightly round Rufus's neck and he was yelling fit to wake the dead. Rufus was leaning against the wall next to the cuckoo clock, holding him with one hand and stroking his hair with the other. 'Shh,' he was saying, 'shh, it's all right. It's all right. Shh.' Rufus's eyes were shut, his face ferocious; when Clementine touched his sleeve he started violently. 'Eddie's grazed his knee,' he said, and his eyes filled inexplicably with tears.

If only it could have been so simple with *his* boy. Rufus tightened his grip, feeling the small bones, the plump arms wrapped round his neck. It was three years since he had held a child in his arms; it felt like yesterday.

'Come on, Eddie.' Clementine could hear Dorrie downstairs and Rufus wouldn't want her to see him like this. 'We'll find you a plaster for your knee, shall we?'

Eddie didn't want to let go; Rufus had to prise him loose. 'Clementine . . .' he said, begging for help. His face was wet with tears and he couldn't see properly.

'I'll come straight back.' Clementine reached up to touch his cheek. 'Don't go away.'

Blinking to clear his vision, Rufus watched her carry Eddie, still hiccuping and snuffling, down the stairs to be looked after by Dorrie. Then he leaned against the wall and closed his eyes again. How had he become so dependent upon her so quickly?

When she returned he grabbed her and held on tight, breathing in her hair, and her skin, both still faintly scented with last night's mud. Even tainted she smelled wonderful, of fresh air and shampoo – apples? Peaches? She felt wonderful too, all luscious curves and soft, heavy flesh.

'Tell me,' she murmured into his sweater. 'It might make you feel better.'

He nodded, but he didn't speak because he didn't know where to start. It didn't seem to matter much; she made him feel better just by being there.

When Dorrie climbed the stairs to tell Clementine Jean was back, she found them standing in the shadows, very close. They were holding hands and Rufus was resting his forehead on Clementine's, as if he was tired. They weren't talking, they were just touching. Dorrie opened her mouth, then thought better of it. It seemed a shame to disturb them. She'd never seen Rufus look so . . . *soft*. Maybe this time it was serious. She was smiling when she reached the hall.

'Share the joke?' Jean was flushed with success.

'Oh, nothing much. Clem's a bit tied up just now.' Dorrie rubbed at Eddie's knee. 'We had a little accident, I'm afraid—'

Jean stooped to peer at the neat patch of pink plaster on Eddie's left leg. 'Can't leave the little sod for five minutes, can I?' she said cheerfully. 'Dorrie, I got the job!'

'What job?'

'Blackstock. They're setting up a conservation workshop in the stable block – you know, repairing antiques, renovating tapestries, stuff like that. They've taken me on three mornings a week, starting the beginning of

January. Only trouble is . . .' The doubts kept creeping in, despite her resolution not to let them. 'Only trouble is, I've got to find someone to look after Eddie.' She straightened up. 'Dorrie, I don't suppose you'd—?'

'No,' said Dorrie firmly. 'I'm too old.' She regarded Jean with her head on one side, just as she had twenty-three years ago, when she was a dinner lady and Jean Smith was an obstreperous ten-year-old causing havoc in the playground. 'Shouldn't you have thought about that before you went for this job?'

Jean pouted, just as she had twenty-three years ago when Dorrie told her off. 'If I'd thought about it beforehand I'd never have got up the nerve to try for the job in the first place.' She plucked distractedly at Eddie's jumper, all rucked up at the front, and pushed his hair off his face. 'I told the man I'd got a childminder.' She glanced up. 'Don't look at me in that tone of voice. You don't know what it's like to be stuck on your own in the house with a kid all day . . .'

Dorrie raised her eyebrows.

'Sorry.' Jean pulled a face. 'But you worked all the way through with yours, didn't you? You've always had something of your *own*. That's all I want, just the chance to do something of my *own*—'

Dorrie bent down and hauled on Eddie's socks, bunched up round his ankles.

'I'll ask about,' she said, then, as Jean went to thank her, 'but don't hold your breath. I'm not promising anything.'

'Thanks, Dorrie.' Jean looked at her watch. 'I must go. Robert'll be home for his dinner.' She took Eddie's hand and made for the door, hesitated. 'Dorrie—'

Dorrie waved her away. 'Get on with you. I've told you, I can't promise anything.'

'Thanks.' Jean grinned at her. 'And Dorrie—'

'I know – don't tell Robert. Get on with you.'

'Mummy,' Eddie wriggled within his mother's grasp. 'What mun't Auntie Dowie tell Daddy?'

'Nothing! For goodness' sake, get a move on!'

Jean hustled him out of the door. Dorrie could hear his penetrating voice as they crunched down the drive towards the road. 'Mummy, Auntie Clemmie says you're going to be a conservingnater. Mummy, what's a conservingnater? Mummy, what's a childminder? Mummy, if I don't tell Daddy where you've been, can I have a ice cream? Mummy . . . *Ow!*'

'Thank God I've got you!' Jonathan sounded frantic.

Sal was in a hurry. 'Look, I'm just leaving for work, assuming work hasn't been blown away during the night. What's the problem?'

'It's Clementine—' The line crackled, hissed, then cut out momentarily, '—been trying and trying. The operator says the lines are down. I heard—' Another hiss, another short-circuit, '—radio, and it sounds *terrible*. There've been people *killed*. Some man in Norwich—' Hiss, crackle, '—roof blown off! Sal, I'm *desperate*—'

'Calm down, darling!' Sal had been trying to reach Rufus all morning without success and she was quite worried enough, without Jonathan hassling her on the phone. 'What do you expect me to do, for God's sake, hire a helicopter? Send in the SAS? Get a grip. I've rung the police, and they've had no casualties reported, so they must be all right.'

'Of course,' the sergeant she had spoken to had added ominously, 'that road is still blocked, so we can't be sure until it's cleared . . .'

'Thank God.' Jonathan felt faint with relief. One thing about Sal Glover, nothing ever fazed her. 'Listen, I'm driving up. Where will you be?'

'Don't be ridiculous.' Sal was scathing. 'There's absolutely nothing you can do, and if they have got problems out there, the last thing they'll need is you milling about getting in the way.' She imagined Rufus opening the door to find Jonathan on the step. 'Rufus'll probably hit you.'

'I don't care, I—'

'Well, I do. Look, come up if you must, but only as far as my place. You've still got your key, haven't you? Rufus is supposed to be coming in to the shop today and as soon as he does I'll let you know. Okay?'

'Yes. Yes, I suppose so.'

Sal heard him sigh, pictured his worried face, smiled. Sebastian was right – it was like dealing with a ten-year-old.

'I'll phone you again on the way, in case there's any news.'

'If you must, darling. I'll be at the shop. Now I have to go, Rufus is probably sitting in the office right now, drumming his fingers on the desk. I'll see you later.' Of course Rufus was all right, why wouldn't he be? Please God.

It was past midday by the time she got through.

'Yes?' said Rufus briskly.

'Thank heaven. You all right, darling?'

'Yes, I'm fine. I was going to ring you.' There was an awkward pause, during which Rufus, always uncomfortable on the phone, searched for something to say and Sal faced the unwelcome realisation that he hadn't thought about her at all during the storm. 'Any damage your end?' he asked at last.

'Couple of slipped slates and a huge tree down on Tombland, everyone rushing around with chainsaws—'

'Good . . . Look, Sal, I must go, they've just cleared the

road and we have to take Mary to the vet.'

'Oh? What's the matter with Mary?'

'She got hurt, during the storm. Sal, did you want something urgent—?'

Sal curbed her temper with difficulty. 'I was worried about you. You were supposed to be coming in to the shop today, remember?'

She heard a door opening, then a female voice. *Clementine*. There was no justice. Why couldn't the woman have been neatly brained by a flying tile?

'I'll be right there,' said Rufus, muffled as if he was talking over his shoulder, then, louder, 'Look, Sal, there's no way I can make it in today, half the roads are blocked, one of the chimneys came down in the storm, and it's chaos out here. I'll give you a ring when I get the chance, okay?'

'I suppose so.' Sal couldn't resist a little dig. 'Your lovely Clementine not damaged, I hope?'

'My lovely Clementine . . .' Sal could actually *hear* him grinning, the bastard, '. . . is *perfect*.'

When Rufus walked into the kitchen he found Clementine in fits of laughter, Mary lying in her basket with her leg raised, and Ginger curled up beside her, licking her wound. Ginger was purring loudly; Mary clearly hadn't yet decided whether to die of fright or lie back and enjoy it.

Dorrie had left a note on the kitchen table. Her son-in-law, Vince, would look at the chimney, address and telephone number below, but Rufus had better contact him double quick or he would be snowed under. She could recommend him, he was straight, honest, and though she said it as shouldn't, a lovely lad. Rufus took Mary and Clementine into Ashington, dropped them at the vet's and drove straight round to leave a message asking Vince to call him as soon as possible.

It was a long, tiring day. Sometime during the storm the cart lodge had given up the struggle and collapsed into a pile of useless firewood (thank God, he had been too lazy to put the van away, said Rufus) and as many of its contents as possible had to be scavenged from the ruins. There was the door at the bottom of the garden to be repaired, the worst of the mess to be cleared from Clementine's bedroom without dislodging any more rubble, and the debris outside the back door to be dealt with.

Vince turned up shortly after three, a huge, jolly bear of a man with a ruddy complexion and curly brown hair barely confined beneath an ancient bobble hat, to clamber about on the roof with his assistant, Wayne. Between them they covered the hole in the roof with a tarpaulin, removed the remaining loose bricks from the shattered chimney, then disappeared into Clementine's bedroom to prop up the ceiling joists with rusty metal poles until they could get back to do the job properly.

It was going to be expensive, said Vince over a cup of coffee in the kitchen, shaking his head at the extent of the damage. Was Rufus insured? Yes, said Rufus with dignity, of course he was, if he could only find the policy documents and Vince let out a great booming roar of merriment at his inefficiency, setting Clementine giggling over the can of dog food she was opening. The two men, both well over six foot, and weighing more than thirty stone between them, filled the kitchen with their bulk and noise, made her feel feminine, even small. She found the sensation immensely pleasurable and was reluctant to leave them.

She phoned Jean from the study, to apologise. 'I'm sorry I missed you this morning. Is Eddie all right?'

'Where were you when I came to pick him up?'

'Er, upstairs . . .' Clementine hesitated and Jean pounced.

'Oh? At it with the boss, were you?'

'What? No, I was *not*—'

'Oh, come on, Clem.' Jean was impatient. 'I wasn't born yesterday. He was all over you when I left Eddie. Don't tell me there's nothing going on between you, because I won't believe you.'

Clementine took a deep breath and let it out very slowly. 'There was absolutely nothing *going on*, as you so elegantly put it, when you came to collect Eddie. I was just—'

'Dorrie told me what happened. Clem, I did warn you he needed watching, he's as slippery as an eel. He could have been killed—'

'Jean, do you think I don't know that?' Clementine's guilt, still fresh, was tinged with relief at the change of subject. 'You have no idea how awful I feel. Rufus found Mary, you see, and we were so busy worrying about her . . . I only took my eyes off Eddie for a few seconds, I swear. Up till then I'd stuck to him like glue—'

'No harm done,' said Jean, easily placated. 'Might even teach the little tyke a lesson, you never know. Now, about you and Rufus—'

'Aren't you going to tell me about this job?'

Jean hesitated, then succumbed. High on the adrenaline of success, she was longing to brag a little. By the time Clementine said, 'Jean, I must go and get on,' she had still not had her say about Rufus and the dangers Clem was exposing herself to.

'Look,' she suggested, 'I'll come round tomorrow. We *must* talk about this Rufus thing—' She raised her voice over Clem's protests. 'And in the meantime, don't do anything silly, will you? I mean, you're so naïve when it comes to men—' She broke off abruptly. Clementine could hear Eddie in the background, his high-pitched voice explaining something at length. 'Clem, I have to go,' said Jean. 'Eddie's just arrived in the kitchen with a dead rat. Now, *promise* me—'

'I promise I won't do anything silly, Jean,' chanted Clementine obediently. 'Can I go now?'

Jean giggled. 'I suppose so. Eddie – *Eddie*, get that bloody thing off the – oh, *blast*! Sorry, Clem,' she said. 'Got to go.' And she went.

By the time they had both had much-needed baths, at opposite ends, virtuously, of the house, it was after nine. Rufus became aware the instant he sat down to eat his supper that Clementine had retreated once again into her shell; she eyed him warily over her plate and replied to his attempts at conversation in brisk monosyllables. Something had to be done, and quickly.

'Can you clear up in here?' he asked, shoving his chair back and making for the door. 'I need to sort out a couple of things.'

Clementine began to wash the dishes, staring into space and wondering what to do. Jean was right; she *was* naïve about men. It didn't take much imagination to work out the possible consequences of starting an affair with her employer – look what had happened with Jonathan – and Madge's bitchy words niggled at her too. *'Of course, Palliser's had that many women . . .'* This morning had been the result of unique circumstances and even before her conversation with Jean she had realised there was no particular reason why Rufus should want to do it again.

Most women her age would be able to handle a situation like this with aplomb, she thought, would take a night of casual passion in their stride.

What did Rufus want from her? 'Not now,' he'd murmured as they stood together on the landing, holding hands. 'I can't talk now. I'll tell you later, when I'm ready.' Then he had kissed her lightly on the forehead and moved away. Had he made love to her to comfort her for the loss of Mary, or had he needed comfort himself, for whatever it was that was causing him so much grief? And what did it have to do with Eddie? Madge's words rattled round her head. Had he seduced her merely because she was there, and vulnerable?

She lifted the last plate from the soapy water and set it to drain, then reached for the tea towel. 'And what do I do about tonight?' she asked Mary, curled up in her basket by the range, nursing seven stitches in her leg. 'Do I wait to be invited into his bed?' She stretched across the hotplate to rub Ginger's battered ear. 'Or do I retire to the Blue Room and wait for him to come to me?' She sighed. 'Have you ever in your entire life come across anyone so pathetic?' She shook the tea towel and set about the drying up. 'Of course you haven't. Silly question; neither have I.'

Chapter Thirty-One

'I thought she'd be more comfortable in the drawing room. Will you bring the basket?'

Rufus carried Mary along the corridor, taking care not to knock the stitches the vet had put in her leg. He could hear Clementine following behind him and his own heart, thudding with anticipation.

'Could you open the door for me?' he asked, then waited while she juggled the basket to free her hand, held his breath as she turned the handle.

He had pushed the sofas together, made them up with clean sheets and his own duvet; he had placed candles on every available surface, a pair of branching candelabra, candlesticks of brass, pewter, tin, anything he could lay his hands on, so when Clementine swung the door wide a myriad points of light dipped in the current of air, flickered in the windowpanes and swayed in the mirror above the mantelpiece. She stopped, then smiled, entranced.

Rufus came to a halt beside her, holding Mary awkwardly against his chest. 'I thought . . .' It was more difficult than he'd expected. 'I thought we might want to . . .'

Clementine regarded him solemnly. 'Do it again?'

Rufus shifted from one foot to the other, shrugged offhandedly. 'Something like that.'

Clementine moved away from him across the room towards the hearth. 'Where would you like it?'

'I thought . . .' Rufus's voice was more than a little unsteady, '. . . on the bed would be nice.'

'I meant the basket.' Her mouth twitched.

'Oh.' It was going to be all right. Rufus began to enjoy himself. 'Just there will be fine.' He followed her across the room, waited while she placed the basket, then lowered Mary and tucked her in as if she were a baby. Mary sighed loudly.

Rufus straightened up, facing Clementine. He was seized by a desire to laugh, although he wasn't quite sure what was so funny. Sex and jokes – it was a new sensation; in Rufus's experience the two rarely went together. He hesitated, waited. Clementine stared at his chest.

'So,' he suggested at last, 'shall we . . .?' He waved vaguely at the duvet.

Clementine raised her head and examined him with serious attention.

'Er,' she began, 'would you mind awfully . . .?'

'Yes?'

'Well, er . . . I would rather like . . .' God, she was *hopeless* at this. She could feel the giggles starting too and that would never do. Clementine Lee, marks for sexual technique, nil. She started again. 'I mean, do you think you could . . .?'

'Ah.' Rufus got it. He moved closer, snapped the catch on Clementine's left shoulder, the one holding her dungarees up, then flipped the strap so it dangled down her back. 'That what you mean?'

'Mmm.'

'Right . . .' He snapped the other catch and let it go.

The dungarees slid, to land with a dull thud around Clementine's ankles. The giggle came.

'Stop it,' said Rufus. 'You're not taking this seriously.'

Clementine made a tremendous effort to pull herself together, lowered her eyes and concentrated on Rufus's fingers, moving efficiently down her shirt buttons, heard him choke and looked up.

'Will you *stop* it!' Rufus was grinning broadly. 'How can I seduce you when you keep laughing!' His voice cracked and Clementine giggled again.

'Sorry,' she said. She raised her hand to her mouth to stifle the hilarity, got in Rufus's way, giggled again. Rufus gave up, joined in.

He invited her to undress him, but she was so clumsy he had to do it himself in the end. She did everything wrong. She didn't know how to flick the button on a pair of Levis, struggling and muttering until he relieved her of the problem, she had to be pushed over the end of the sofa on to the duvet because when he tried to lift her she was too heavy. Even after he had extracted her ankles, with great difficulty, from her dungarees so he could get at the interesting bits, he kept finding arms and legs in all sorts of awkward places, and he was held up by her sudden last-minute refusal to let him remove her knickers until she was safely tucked beneath the covers. He had never, *ever* been so turned on by a woman.

He blew it in the end though. They had sobered up by then, begun to concentrate. He had been slow, gentle, taking more care than he had ever taken before, and he had held on, with rigid self- control, so they could come together, until it occurred to him that for the second time they had taken no precautions, that they might, at that very moment, be making a child. He lost it completely then, let go, dropped his head heavily against Clementine's cheek and groaned.

'Sorry.' He felt so soporific suddenly, so completely drained, that he formed the words only with the greatest difficulty. 'Couldn't wait.'

She turned her head against his cheek. 'What?'

'I couldn't wait . . .' Jesus, what a useless lover he had become.

'Oh,' she murmured, 'that's the nicest thing anyone's ever said to me.'

By the time they uncoupled he had recovered slightly. He slid his hand across to her damaged hip, pausing on her belly to wish his seed a silent *bon voyage*. Then he continued down into the warmth between her thighs, and began to rub.

'Oh,' murmured Clementine. Her breathing quickened. 'Oh . . . ohh . . . *ohhh* . . .'

Just before he succumbed to sleep, he told her again, because he wanted her to know. 'I love you, Clementine.'

She didn't answer. Her breathing had settled, and her head was heavy on his chest. Her eyes were shut and her lips were parted. She was asleep again.

'Time for bed, darling. I've got pins and needles in my arm.' Sal was stretched on the couch in her sitting room with Jonathan's head in her lap. 'You should have brought Simba,' she complained, sliding out from under him to make a half-hearted stab at tidying the mess of supper plates, ashtrays, bottles and glasses littering the coffee table. 'She'll be lonely all by herself.'

Jonathan pushed himself up on his elbows, then flopped back again against the cushions, resting his head on his clasped hands. 'She'll be fine. Mrs Ames is coming in first thing tomorrow to feed her. I've told Angela I'll be away till Wednesday.' He sighed heavily. 'Isn't there any way you can get Rufus into the shop tomorrow?'

Sal scowled at him. 'I've already told you, he's got a chimney down. The chances of him coming in before Monday are nil. What are you going to do about Clementine?'

'I don't know.' Jonathan swung his legs to the floor, resting his elbows on his knees and his chin in his hands. This whole thing was becoming a nightmare. He no longer had the comforting presence of Sebastian at his back and Clementine appeared to be irretrievably lost. The decorator he had booked to carry out Sal's renovations was due to begin on Tuesday, and for once he couldn't manage any enthusiasm even for his work. He had yet to find a local seamstress capable of making the complicated drapes he had gone for in the sitting room and Sal was impatient to see his sketches come to life. She had behaved from the beginning as if he was doing all this for a vast fee instead of for nothing, throwing her weight around, demanding to see swatches and paint samples, turning her pretty nose up at the colour scheme he had chosen for the spare bedroom and carping at the cost of the new carpets. None of his paying customers had ever treated him with such condescension. If he wasn't so tired, for two pins he would climb in his car and drive back to London, forget Sal, Clementine and the ghastly, windswept wastes of East Anglia, beg Sebastian's forgiveness and ask him if they could start again. It was all just too *much*.

'Stop sulking, darling,' said Sal. 'There's no sense crying over spilt milk, we'll just have to make the best of whatever opportunities come up.' She reached down and caught hold of his wrists, pulling him upright. 'You have to think positive. Your trouble is, you give up too easily. It's never over till the fat lady sings.' She felt around with her stockinged feet for her shoes. 'I've often wondered what that means. Who is this fat lady? What is she singing? Why is she singing it?' The faintest ghost of a smile crossed Jonathan's tragic face and she patted him. 'That's better, darling. There isn't any point in getting your knickers in a twist, you know. After all, if it comes to the worst you can always scuttle back to Sebastian with your tail between your legs—'

'I've already thought of that.' Jonathan's every syllable was redolent with gloom. 'But I don't want to go back to Sebastian. I want to marry Clem. I just don't see how—'

Sal clapped her hand over his mouth. 'Stop it!' she said. 'Stop feeling so sorry for yourself!'

She cupped his cheek in her palm, appraised him with her head on one side. 'I've just thought of a way of cheering you up,' she said. 'If you fancy the idea, of course . . .' She smiled, dazzlingly.

'What?' Jonathan's puzzlement turned to shock. 'You must be joking!'

'Why not?' Sal stroked his cheek, then his bottom, which was, she noted with satisfaction, round and taut. She smiled again. 'After all, it's not as if we're depriving anyone else. What d'you say, darling, purely for medicinal purposes?'

'I don't know how you can even contemplate the idea. I thought you were supposed to be in love with Rufus Palliser—'

Sal smacked his face smartly, leaving a neat row of pink marks, and flounced off, complaining as she went, 'Don't be such a prude, darling, it doesn't suit you.' She turned, looked him up and down. 'Anyway, given your chequered past, I shouldn't have thought one sexual adventure more or less would make much difference.' She curled her lip. 'Pity, you'd have enjoyed it too.' Then she retrieved her cigarettes from the mess on the table and sashayed across to the door, swinging her hips provocatively. 'If you change your mind, my room's the big one at the front.' She chuckled, her temper recovered already. 'But you know that, don't you darling?' Then she left him.

Jonathan stood for a moment, staring at the door, then sank down again on to the couch. What was he going to *do*?

When Sal reappeared fifteen minutes later she was wearing absolutely nothing except her own, spectacularly perfect skin. She had a pillow tucked under one arm, and she was dragging behind her a large, rather grubby pink blanket. Jonathan, brought up in a tiny back-to-back terrace in a grim Yorkshire mill town, found himself unexpectedly recalling the little girl next door, who had trailed with her everywhere an ancient comforter which her mother dipped every morning in a tin of golden syrup for her to suck. Sal Glover, it occurred to him, was just a grown-up, sexually explicit version of the kid next door with her security blanket. The thought cheered him no end.

'What's so funny?' Sal dropped the bedding on the end of the couch and stared contemptuously down at Jonathan's shaking shoulders.

'Darling,' she said at last, 'you are a complete waste of space.' Then she went, breasts and buttocks bouncing beautifully, to bed.

Jonathan lay on his back on the couch, wondering what fucking Sal Glover would be like. He had always enjoyed being told what to do, and there was no doubt that Sal was the sort of woman who liked to take charge. He had been without for six months now, ever since he had started going out with Clem. The strain must be catching up with him.

At two o'clock, unable to sleep, he rose, clad only in his black silk jockeys, and began to tidy up the coffee table, in need of something to take his mind off the disloyal and distinctly sleazy thoughts buzzing round his head.

Oh, my darlin' . . . The old song needled at him as he washed up plates and glasses, disposed of cigarette butts and empty bottles. . . . *oh, my darlin', oh my daarlin' Clementine; thou art lost and gone forever, dreadful sorry, Clementine.* The words seemed gloomily prophetic.

When the place was tidy he plumped up the pillow, wrapped himself in the blanket and settled down at last to sleep.

Chapter Thirty-Two

A detailed search failed to turn up the buildings insurance until the Tuesday afternoon, by which time Vince and Wayne were already hard at work on the roof. It was Dorrie who remembered seeing something from the insurance company amongst the papers blown about by the storm. Rufus found the reminder under the dresser and brought it out in triumph.

He had forgotten to pay the premium.

Clementine found him sitting in the kitchen with his head in his hands.

'How much is it going to cost?' she asked, sitting down opposite him.

'Thousands.' Rufus pulled a face. How could he have been so *stupid*? 'I'll have to borrow from the bank.' He glanced up at Clementine's anxious face and shrugged. 'Although whether they'll lend any more money to an idiot like me is doubtful.'

'I can lend you some.' It was perfectly simple. Rufus needed money, she had money, sitting in the bank doing nothing. It would be months before Uncle Harry checked up on her, and anyway he'd have to find her first. 'I've got some savings.'

Rufus shook his head. Clementine had brought

virtually nothing with her to Manor Hall; she couldn't have more than a few hundred quid. 'I don't want your savings. I'll sell some more books.'

'That's ridiculous when I have money sitting in the bank—'

Rufus rose from the table and crossed to the range, in need of coffee. 'Look, we're not even a third of the way through sorting the library yet. Let's wait and see what we can turn up, shall we?'

'All right.' *We* again. As in us, as in a pair, a partnership, a future. The thought made Clementine go warm all over. 'I'll leave the decorating for the moment and help, shall I?'

'Clementine . . .'

'Mm?'

'Thanks for the offer,' said Rufus. 'I love you.'

A glorious smile lit her face. 'That makes it all worthwhile,' she said.

So much for Madge's malicious tongue . . . or would she, wondered Clem, watching Rufus pour another mug of stewed coffee, wake up soon and find the whole thing had been a foolish fantasy, brought on by loneliness and a longing for someone to call her own? As she strode along the corridor on her way back to work, she pinched herself hard, making sure she was awake, then shook her head at her own whimsy and rubbed the sore patch she had made. She dug her hands into the pockets of her dungarees and performed a soft-shoe shuffle, her plimsolls squeaking on the tiled floor. 'He loves me,' she told the silent walls. 'He loves me!'

Jean visited, as she had threatened, bringing Eddie, who rushed straight up to Rufus, flung his arms round his leg and greeted him like a long lost uncle. Clementine, watching Rufus, saw him flinch as Eddie bellowed, 'Hi,

Woofus,' up at him, and noted the muscle jumping in his cheek. But he lifted Eddie and carried him along the corridor to the kitchen, jiggling him up and down so Eddie squealed with delight, and she couldn't tell from his face what he was thinking. Aware of Jean's growing suspicion of her employer, she found playing the detached housekeeper an enormous effort; it was a relief when Jean rose from the table and said she had better go.

'I'm trying to keep Robert sweet,' she explained, lowering her voice so Eddie, squatting over Mary's basket with Rufus, being shown how to move slowly so he didn't startle her, couldn't hear. 'He still doesn't know about the job.'

'What about a childminder?' asked Clem. 'Have you found anyone yet?'

'Not yet.' Jean seemed unperturbed. 'But Dorrie's asking around. She'll find me someone. Clem, when are you coming over?' She jerked her head towards Rufus and Eddie. 'So we can have a proper talk.'

Clem poured herself more tea. 'Soon, I promise. It's just that we've had so much clearing up to do, what with the storm and everything . . .'

'Clem—'

'Yes. All right. I'll come next week, honestly.'

'Promise?'

'Promise.'

'Good.' Jean was reluctant to leave it there. 'Just make sure you do. I *have* to talk to you.' She sounded almost threatening.

After they had gone Rufus slumped against the range, incapable of moving. He was feeling terribly tired, aching all over as if he had just run a marathon, carried a heavy load for miles. It was time he told her, he decided, maybe sharing the burden would make it lighter.

'I wanted to ask you . . .' he began.

'Yes?'

'In the pub.' He focused on her with difficulty, frowning with concentration. 'I wanted to ask you about . . .'

Clementine waited. She had been waiting weeks to find out what made Rufus Palliser tick; a little longer wouldn't matter.

'I had a—' he turned his back and began to clatter about, pouring himself a cup of coffee, was surprised to find when he picked up the pot that his hand was shaking. Dealing with Eddie had been harder than he had expected, more painful. 'It's a bit like having a tooth out,' he said. 'It hurts like hell at the time, but you feel better afterwards.' He carried his coffee to the table and sank heavily onto a chair. 'I think.'

What hurts like hell? You feel better after what? Clementine sat patiently, still waiting.

'It's Eddie. He reminds me – I had a boy of my own, you see. He died three years ago. He would have been six this year.'

A year older than Eddie. Caught by surprise, Clementine found herself bereft of comforting words, unable even to mouth the right platitudes.

'I looked after him from the very beginning, when he was tiny . . .' Rufus ran his fingers through his hair, rubbed his nose, cleared his throat. Even his mouth felt tired. 'I loved him to bits.' He stood again, so suddenly that his chair tipped over backwards and fell with a clatter on the floor. 'I'll show you,' he said, and grabbing Clementine's wrist, he pulled her up, out of the kitchen, along the corridor and across the hall to the drawing room.

'Sorry,' he said, releasing her. He had done it again, holding on to her so tightly he had left a red weal on her skin. He raised her wrist, kissing it better. 'I wanted to tell you then, ask you, but I didn't know you well enough.'

'Ask me what?' Clementine was trying to imagine what it must be like to lose a child. It must be even worse, she thought, than losing a parent. Children should outlive their parents – that's the way things are supposed to be.

Rufus began to rummage in the roll-top desk. 'You haven't though, have you?' he said.

'Haven't what?'

'Got all the answers. I thought maybe you had. I thought you might be able to tell me how to deal with it . . .' Give me a clue, pleaded Clementine silently, not understanding but reluctant to stop him now he'd started. '. . . With having someone you love die. What do they call it, these bloody psychologists, "coming to terms with your loss".'

Clementine sank on to the sofa and watched as he rifled agitatedly through the cubbyholes in the desk, reminded irrelevantly of Miss Emily, of pennies and sherbet dabs. 'Your son?'

'My wife's son.'

She could hear it in his voice, the begrudging acknowledgement of a superior claim.

'I thought you said he was your . . .'

'Wishful thinking. He was Helen's.'

He found the photograph at last, carefully hidden away in case he should come across it by accident, and he pulled it from its resting place; a trio of smiling faces, an ordinary English family standing on the Cob at Lyme Regis with the sea behind them.

'We were on holiday in Devon.' He closed his eyes but the image stayed. 'We'd been going through a rough patch, Helen and I, and we were trying to mend fences. Maybe if we'd been somewhere else . . .'

He couldn't stop now he'd started, it was like opening the sluice gate on a dam, it all came flooding out.

'. . . Although the doctor said he could have contracted it anywhere, at his playgroup, in the street . . . There was nothing we could have done, they said, we got him to the hospital as soon as possible, it's just that it's so quick, so lethal . . .'

When he looked up Clementine was sitting motionless, her hands folded in her lap and her eyes fixed on his face. He should have told her at the beginning. She would have understood. What a sweet mouth you have, he thought, momentarily distracted.

'It was meningitis. We had no warning . . . no, not true, he'd developed a temperature during the night, complained that his neck was stiff. He brought his breakfast straight back up the next morning, so we went for a drive. We thought some sea air might do the trick, so we parked the car and took him for a walk.' He glanced at the photograph, then away again, back at Clementine. 'There was a photographer, you know, the ones who take your picture and promise you a print within the hour? We thought he was improving because when the man said "smile", he smiled.' He left the desk, meandered slowly across to the sofa, then subsided heavily beside Clementine and held out the photograph. 'That's him in the middle,' he explained unnecessarily, 'the last time we played happy families. Ten minutes after it was taken he complained that the light was hurting his eyes and Helen noticed he'd developed a rash. She thought we ought to take him to a doctor, but no one seemed to know where the nearest one was, they were all tourists, like us. Then as we were walking back to the car he collapsed.'

Clementine examined the faces, Rufus, black-haired, young-looking in an open-necked shirt and jeans, grinning self-consciously for the camera, his wife, pretty, slight, in a cotton dress, bending down to embrace a miniature facsimile of herself in shorts and a gaily coloured T-shirt, a boy with straight brown hair, blue eyes screwed up against the sun, baring white, even milk teeth in an obedient grimace for the camera.

The relief was enormous. Rufus felt the weight lift as he talked, wondered if he had mistakenly been avoiding the cure all along, whether, if he had talked about it sooner, he might have got over it. He told Clementine everything, about the nightmare journey in his car, a flashy American Corvette in those days, described how the boy's legs knocked against his arm, dead weight as if he was already gone, about the terror, then the disbelief, then the aftermath, how he had left Helen and bolted from the hospital to conduct a desperate search for the seafront kiosk so he could retrieve the photograph, as if it might somehow bring the boy back to life.

He rambled on as the day faded outside, his words tumbling over each other, recalling as it grew dark how he and Helen had failed to comfort each other, how endless the paperwork had seemed, the arrangements for the funeral, the irrelevant tasks, obtaining the death certificate, registering the death, 'as if he couldn't be dead until we'd filled out their bloody forms in triplicate'. He told her how the registrar had been constantly interrupted by the telephone, how a man had come barging in with the details of his son's birth, bursting with pride at the new life he had brought into the world, while Rufus and Helen were ushering a life out of it. He relived the funeral, how Helen wouldn't let him near her, seemed to need to grieve on her own, how her mother had sought him out to tell him how lucky he was the boy wasn't his.

'It's not as if he was your own flesh and blood,' she

said, admonishing him for his manifest pain as if it were
somehow inappropriate, perhaps not even real. 'Never
having had a child, you cannot begin to imagine what it
feels like to lose one . . .'

'You should think yourself lucky,' she added as she
left, 'that you were not his real father.'

She was not the only one who twisted the knife. Even
Helen, plunged back into the dark depression of the
early days, accused him angrily when she found him
weeping over a toy car he had bought for the boy, 'What
the hell are *you* crying for? It's not as if he was *your* son.'
He had felt as if he had no business to be mourning, as if
his need for comfort was unreasonable, unjustifiable; he
had learned to hide his misery to avoid causing himself
more pain.

'I bought the cuckoo clock for him,' he said. 'It was the
last present I gave him, the only thing I kept; Helen
didn't want it, she thought it was a stupid thing to buy
for a three-year-old child.'

'What was his name?' asked Clementine.

Rufus had to rehearse it silently first, to make sure he
could do it. 'Michael. I . . . we called him Mikey.'

It was the first time he had said it for nearly three
years. Instantly Mikey was there, filling his senses. He
could feel him, delicate bones, child-chubby wrists,
stocky legs, smell him, the after-bath scent of soap and
baby skin, he could hear him, the sudden bursts of hilarity that would attack him for no apparent reason and
which always set Rufus off, chortling with his son until
the tears ran down his cheeks and Helen flounced off in
disgust, wondering aloud which of the two was the bigger baby. The sensation was so strong he collapsed
against the sofa, breathless with his loss. 'He was named
after his father, his real father. Clementine . . .'

Clem tilted her head, trying to make out his face, then,

unable to see in the dark, put out her hand to feel. Rufus turned his cheek into her palm.

'I'm hungry,' he said. 'Absolutely bloody starving. It must be time for supper.'

He rose, pulling her up with him, then leaned across to touch her mouth with his. 'You have no idea,' he said, 'how much I needed to tell you.'

'Yes I have.' Clementine slid her hand down his arm, found his fingers and laced hers through them. 'It took me two years to learn how to cry after the accident. I kept it all inside because I couldn't manage it, and all I did was make it worse.'

He changed his mind on the way to the kitchen, and took her upstairs instead, to the big mahogany bed in the Blue Room. Their lovemaking was more intense than anything he had experienced before, and afterwards he felt as if they had taken a step further, a step closer.

'I think you've kissed me better,' he murmured, spreading his fingers on Clementine's stomach and wondering if his child was growing inside her already.

'Snap,' said Clementine, and she moved his hand across, until it covered her scarred hip. 'Isn't sex *amazing*?' Her voice was full of childlike wonder, and she made Rufus laugh.

Clementine woke late, and slowly. When she reached out to touch, Rufus was missing, the only evidence that he had slept beside her a residual warmth and an indent in the pillow. He was sitting, fully dressed, at the writing desk in the window, one hand resting on Mary's head and the other cupping his chin, gazing out at the church. When he heard her moving he looked back at her and smiled, such a big, endearing smile it turned her stomach upside down.

'Happy New Year,' he said.

She reached for her dressing gown, shrugged her way into it, then slid out of bed and padded towards him. Rufus wondered how long it would take her to get used to him and wished fiercely that she could learn to face him naked, without inhibition. There was so *much* of her, so many rounds, curves, nooks and crannies, but she still wasn't ready to expose her scars in daylight.

'You're very good value,' he said, chuckling at her perplexed expression. 'Twice as much woman as a man has a right to expect.'

'Happy New Year?'

He twisted in his chair and reached out to pull her close. 'Because I feel as if I've started again, wiped the slate clean.' He tightened his grip, reeling her in until she was sitting on his knee, her demure cotton dressing gown with its pin tucks and gathers all askew and her hair falling over her face, looking like a naughty Victorian postcard. 'Not that I've forgotten, just that I woke up this morning and found it was bearable for the first time. Did that happen to you? Did you wake up one day and find you could bear it?'

Clementine stared past him at something in the distance. 'Yes,' she began, 'no . . . sort of. It was more gradual than that.' There had been days, weeks of pretending it hadn't happened, of hoping she would wake up and find it had all been a dream. Then after that, numbness, then pain, lots of it. Martin had helped with the pain to begin with, until they had slept together. After that he had become part of it. It was only when she had plucked up the courage to leave, as she had sat on the lumpy bed contemplating the dingy room she was renting in a bed-and-breakfast hotel, that the tears had come. That moment had been a catharsis, had given her the strength to carry on. The pleasure she had felt when she was headhunted by Jonathan had been for her parents as well as for herself, but analysing how she felt, now her career had come to nothing, it occurred to Clementine to wonder, so what if she had forfeited commercial success? She had replaced it with something far more valuable. She had rediscovered the sense of belonging she had lost at sixteen, found a level of private happiness she had never come remotely close to before.

Rufus was rearranging her dressing gown, parting it to stroke the well-upholstered thigh beneath. Clementine looked down. He was running his hand along her scars, feeling the ridges with his fingertips.

'Don't you mind?' she asked.

'Mind? Mind what?'

'This.' She lifted his hand away, slapped at her hip with her open palm, reminded of Martin. 'Don't you think it's *gross*?'

'No.' Rufus looked at her in astonishment. 'Why should I? They're just scars, that's all. I have one on my arm, where I fell off my bike when I was seven.' He unbuttoned his woollen shirt and rolled the sleeve up past his elbow, wriggling awkwardly so she could see. Clementine examined it minutely. 'There,' he repeated. 'It's just a scar. No big deal.'

'Really? No big deal? Oh . . .' Clementine stared at him for a moment, then at herself, as if what he had just said was a complete revelation. Then she rose from his knee and drifted round the table, brushing her bare leg against Mary, to lean on the stone mullion and gaze out of the window at the flint tower of the church.

'I think . . .' She began slowly, 'I have probably wasted the best years of my life.' She turned to face him, began to giggle. 'I think I have probably thrown away more opportunities than any other woman in England.'

'What sort of opportunities?'

The giggles increased. Clementine pushed herself away from the wall and twirled across the room, shedding her dressing gown as she went.

'*Bedding* opportunities.' She waltzed towards Rufus, then away again. Mary, intrigued by this peculiar form of morning exercise, joined in, nipping at her bare feet. Rufus began to laugh.

'How many?' he asked.

'How many what?'

'How many *bedding* opportunities have you missed?' He stood up, began to follow her round the room.

'Dozens. I thought—'

She had thought all men were like Martin. She had rejected more chat-up lines than she cared to remember, run away from more seduction scenes than she liked to think about. What a *waste*.

'It's never too late.'

Clementine stopped in mid-twirl. 'Really?' she said. 'So how do I make up for lost time?'

Rufus caught her up. 'Easy,' he said. 'We could make a start right now . . .'

Chapter Thirty-Three

'Ah.' Sal leaned away from the desk to see where Rufus had got to and pressed the phone closer to her ear. 'I'm glad I've caught you.'

'Well?' demanded Jonathan. 'What's going on?'

'That *book* you expressed an interest in . . .'

'Pardon?'

'I've managed to find you a copy, *sir*.'

'But I didn't—'

Sal fingered the book she had just taken from the shelf. 'That's right, *The Rival*. I can keep it for you until this afternoon.'

'He's there.'

'It is indeed,' said Sal drily. 'So if you would care to . . .?'

'I'm on my way.' Jonathan sounded flustered, panicky. 'How long have I got?'

'Hang on . . .' Sal tugged at Rufus's sleeve as he pushed past her. 'Darling,' she said, 'we really *must* go over the accounts. Can you stay late?'

Rufus was feeling generous, benign. 'Tell you what, we'll close up early. Then we can go through the books and still be away by five-thirty.' He reached across her for a reference book. 'That way you won't be late for your hot date, and I won't be late for supper. And it's *The Rivals*, plural. You should know that.'

He was beginning to get on her nerves, blundering about the shop, whistling. Sal took her hand away from the mouthpiece. 'We shall be here until five-thirty,' she said succinctly to Jonathan. 'Will that be sufficient time?'

Rufus wandered off, fumbling in his pocket for his glasses.

'It'll have to be, won't it?' said Jonathan, and put the phone down. This was his last chance.

Rufus had left Clementine a note, written with a stub of pencil he had found in the kitchen dresser on a ruled page torn from an exercise book, placed in a tatty white foolscap envelope. He had tucked it amongst the paint pots on the landing. *Marry me, Clementine*, it said, then, in a polite postscript, *Please*. He couldn't concentrate on anything else.

At five past twelve, as he was ushered into his bank manager's office, he was wondering whether Clementine had found his proposal yet. As his attention was being drawn to the size of his existing loan, he was picturing her on the landing, reading it, with a brush in her other hand and a smear of paint on her nose. While he was being lectured about the folly of taking on more than he could chew, he was considering the possibility that she might, by the time she had accepted her lunchtime sandwiches from Dorrie (would she talk to Dorrie about it, show her the note?), have made up her mind one way or the other.

When his interlocuter leaned forward in his chair, his buttocks squeaking against the leather seat, and demanded to know what suggestions Mr Palliser might have to improve the current situation, he was so far into his reverie that he jumped and said, 'Sorry, what situation are you talking about, exactly?' As he drove back to the shop he could see her, surrounded by dustsheets and paintbrushes, jars of turps and sheepskin rollers, discussing it with Mary – should she or shouldn't she, what did Mary think?

It was only when he walked into the office, as Sal greeted him with a cup of steaming coffee and a stern, 'Well?' that the seriousness of his financial situation hit him.

'Don't ask,' he said, slumping heavily into his chair. 'You don't want to know.'

Clementine was in the kitchen when he got home, laying the table for supper. 'How did it go?' she asked without looking up.

'How did what go?' Rufus bent to greet the dog, puzzled. Wasn't this the bit where Clementine was supposed to fling herself into his arms and make all his dreams come true?

'The bank.'

'Oh.' Rufus stared helplessly at the back of her head. 'I should have left well alone. Not only has he refused to lend me any more money, he said he was glad I'd come in today because he'd been meaning to talk to me about the overdraft I've already got. Then he made threatening noises about collateral, reminded me that the bank holds a second charge on Manor Hall, and informed me that they can put it up for sale to meet my obligations any time they like.'

'How much do you need?' Clementine continued to move around the table, keeping her back to him.

'Clementine —'

'Yes?'

Rufus lost his nerve. 'What's for supper?'

'Chicken. How much do you need?'

Rufus leaned past her and took the knives and forks away. 'I've told you,' he said, 'I don't want your money.

We're barely a quarter of the way through sorting the library. Something'll turn up.' He tried again. 'Clementine—'

Clementine straightened the table mats, laid serving spoons. 'Vince left the final estimate this afternoon. They've started on the roof joists. He says he'll have to take off some of the surrounding tiles so he can replace the felting, and he's found a crack in the other chimney.' She crossed to the dresser, picked out Vince's carefully itemised account, and handed it over the table.

Rufus forgot his other preoccupations for a moment, whistled. 'Jesus.'

'I've paid him,' said Clementine calmly.

'What?' Rufus didn't believe her. 'How could you possibly have paid all this?'

'I told you, I have some savings.'

'Yes, but—' Rufus was rooted to the spot with astonishment. 'I thought you meant you had a couple of hundred!'

Clementine took the cutlery back and waved it at the estimate Rufus was still holding in his hand. 'He's promised me faithfully it won't come to any more than that.'

A muddled mix of emotions hit Rufus: shame, that he couldn't solve his own problems; gratitude, for Clementine's generosity; relief, that the pressure was off, for the time being at least. He pulled out a chair and sat down. 'If I'd known you were a rich woman,' he said, essaying a joke to cover his embarrassment, 'I'd have seduced you earlier.'

Clementine laughed. There was hardly any reserve about her now. 'I'd have let you,' she said.

'Thanks,' he mumbled awkwardly, 'I'll pay you back, I swear.' Then he stood again, so abruptly he made

Clementine jump. 'Back in a minute,' he said, making for the door.

He took the stairs to the landing two at a time. Clementine had left the dustsheets on the floor and the paint pots neatly lined up beneath the cuckoo clock. The envelope containing his proposal was lying next to a jam jar full of turps and painty brushes.

He picked it up. Clementine's pencilled-in name was invisible in the dim light. When he turned the envelope over he discovered she had been using it as a palette to try out different colour mixes, had actually sealed the flap shut with thick daubs of paint. Deflated, he made his way slowly down the stairs. How could he show it to her now, when she had just paid his debts? It would look as if he was marrying her for her money. He dropped the envelope on the desk in his study, then closed the door on it and walked slowly back to the kitchen.

Clementine was dishing up. 'How was the rest of your day?' he asked, swallowing his disappointment.

'Difficult.' Clementine placed a pie, golden brown and slightly burnt at the edges, on the table between them, and began to cut the pastry. 'I had lunch with Jean. She's all fired up about her new career, and she thinks I'm running away from life.' She paused, the knife hovering above the plate. 'And Jonathan came round this morning.' Attending to the pie, she felt, rather than saw, Rufus's head jerk up. 'I sent him away,' she said. 'I told him—'

'Yes?' Rufus fixed her with intent grey eyes. 'You told him what?'

'I told him there was someone else.' Clementine balanced the knife carefully on the side of the dish. 'I told him to go back to London and get on with his life.' Unexpectedly, she giggled. 'And I gave him Jean's telephone number.'

'What? Why?'

'Well, he said he was looking for someone to make some particularly complicated curtains for him, and did I know anyone who would be up to the job—'

'Oh. Clementine—'

'Yes?'

'I *love* you,' said Rufus fiercely.

'Well, that's all right then,' said Clementine, and burst into peals of laughter.

Jonathan slumped dejectedly on the couch. Just pop along and sweep Clem off her feet – ha! Sal had the knack of making you think you could do anything, walk on water, heal the sick, raise the dead; the trouble was, the effect wore off once you were out of range. Bloody woman. All he'd done was push Clem into ending it, once and for all.

'So, what exactly did she say?' Sal stared into her whisky, trying hard to focus. She must slow down. She was already a glass ahead of Jonathan and she was rapidly getting drunk.

'Nothing.' Jonathan snorted with disgust. 'And everything. She told me she'd found someone else.' He drained his glass, then rose to fight his way across to the sideboard for another drink.

They were in Sal's dining room, marooned amidst a sea of sitting room furniture, the decorators having started work that morning. The mess made Jonathan's head hurt, offended his delicate sensibilities. He was getting rather drunk, but there didn't seem to be much else to do.

'Make sure you have an excuse for being there or she'll send you packing,' Sal had instructed him, so he'd blathered on about swags, pelmets, pleats, the difficulty of finding someone competent to make Sal's fucking curtains, without, of course, mentioning her by name. Clem had smiled sweetly, given him the address of that friend of hers, the one with the precocious kid, then told him politely to sod off. He poured himself a generous measure of whisky and took a large gulp. 'She said she was very sorry but it was all over and why didn't I go back to London and get on with my life.' He negotiated Sal's nasty teak dining table, squeezed past a pair of untidily stacked repro chairs, then clambered over the coffee table to flop down again on the couch.

'And what about Rufus, where does he fit into this jolly little scenario?'

Jonathan's gloom increased. 'Ah, Rufus . . .'

'Yes? Well?'

Jonathan gulped more whisky. 'I went round to see the curtain woman and she confirmed it. She says the last time she saw them they were all over each other and she reckons Rufus is going to break my poor darling Clementine's heart. *She* reckons—'

Sal bridled. 'Huh! Much more likely your blasted Clementine will break my poor darling Rufus's heart. I happen to know—'

Jonathan lost his temper. 'You happen to know bugger all, actually, so I'll thank you to keep your opinions to yourself, if you *don't* mind!'

'Why the hell should I? If it hadn't been for your frigid bloody girlfriend none of this would have happened in the first place and Rufus would still be available! So don't talk to me about—'

'How *dare* you!' Jonathan drained his whisky in one, then slammed the glass down on the cluttered coffee table. 'Clementine is *not* frigid! And who are you to pass judgement? Just because you'd sleep with your own brother—'

Sal's face grew pink with whisky and outrage. 'Talk

about the pot calling the kettle black!' she exclaimed and slapped him across the face with all the force she could muster. Then she staggered up, overbalanced, and sat down hard on the table.

They glared at each other. Then Sal tucked her hair behind her ears and picked up the glasses. 'Fancy another, darling?' she asked.

'Why not?' Jonathan lay back and watched her battling towards the sideboard. 'Let's face it, we've blown it. We might as well give up.' He rubbed his stinging cheek. 'You didn't have to hit me quite so hard, did you?'

Sal returned with a large whisky, held it out. 'Poor baby,' she soothed. 'Shall Mummy make it better?' Jonathan grimaced at her, but he was past getting worked up. The booze was taking over and he was feeling vague, comfortably miserable, disconnected.

Sal leaned across to stroke his glowing cheek. 'There, there, darling,' she soothed. 'Just close your eyes, lie back and think of England.' Her hand moved further afield and Jonathan closed his eyes obediently, groaned. 'There, there,' cooed Sal again. They were both in need of a little TLC. She ran her fingers across his flies, noted that he wasn't suffering from Brewer's Droop, yet. She took his whisky glass away.

She complimented him on the size of his equipment (so much, thought Jonathan in a brief moment of smug lucidity, for Mrs Rowenstall's theories), then produced a condom, 'because I don't know where you've been, darling', and took charge. 'Purely for medicinal purposes,' she reiterated. 'This won't hurt a bit.' When she had had her fun, she left him alone on the couch and went to bed.

'*Thou art lost and gone forever . . .*' keened Jonathan mournfully to the ceiling. '*Dreadful sorry, Clementine.*'

Chapter Thirty-Four

Over the ensuing weeks Rufus worked like a man possessed, attempting to sift through twice, three times as many books as he had in the shop, lifting, turning, examining, poring over auction records stretching back four decades, noting prices, dates, publishers, printers.

Seized by an enthusiasm he had not felt for over three years, he started early in the morning, stopped for lunch only because Clementine insisted, 'or else you'll go mad', then dived back to his task until he was stopped again for supper. His back began to ache with all the bending, his eyes to sting with the effort of concentration. He developed a permanent red mark on the bridge of his nose where his glasses rested. He found some perfect gems, the sort of beauties that under normal circumstances he would have kept for himself but could no longer afford to be sentimental about. He catalogued them, annotating the margins of his notes with the scribbled names of possible buyers, then placed them carefully on the shelves in the library, belatedly concerned for their welfare. But he didn't find 'The One', the apocryphal jewel all collectors dream of, the Legendary First which would solve all his problems at a stroke.

'Will you send them to auction?' asked Clementine, bringing him a cup of coffee as he sat at his roll-top desk in the drawing room surrounded by *Book Auction Records*, four editions of the *Dictionary of National Biography* piled high by his left elbow, a dog-eared copy of *English Collectors of Books and Manuscripts, 1530–1930*, and Joseph Connolly's *Modern First Editions*.

'Some.' He glanced up from his task, smiled at her over the top of his glasses. 'Maybe. Thing is, we need every penny we can get. If I send them to Christie's or Sotheby's they'll cream fifteen per cent off whatever they fetch, and then there's the buyer's premium, insurance. It adds up to over thirty per cent.'

Over the past fortnight he had entered his study only to collect reference books, because working at the roll-top desk in the drawing room he could be with Clementine. He had talked while he worked, easily, openly, relishing her company. He had explained how he met Helen, about their early days, how furious she had been when he bought Manor Hall without telling her.

They had been due to move a week after Mikey died, and he had insisted on sticking to the timetable because he couldn't bear to stay a day longer in the rented house off Earlham Road where Mikey was so vividly present and so painfully absent, while Helen had wanted to stay, clinging desperately to the last tenuous links with her child. She had been accepted as a mature student at the university, had even been given a grant and, secretly, she kept the town house on – he found out what she had done only months later – sleeping there one or two nights a week and telling him she was staying with friends.

Rufus didn't blame her for not wanting to be at Manor Hall; the place was a nightmare of noise, dust, mess; electricians, plumbers, plasterers, roofers, trailing mud, leaving doors wide open to the cold, demanding tea with two sugars, coffee with milk, coffee without, orange squash, 'Wot, no biscuits?' It was only months later, as they all began to leave, finishing off one by one then taking their pay and moving on to other projects, that he and Helen had noticed how empty their life together had become.

'It wasn't Helen's fault,' he told Clementine more than once. 'I expected too much of her, assumed she would feel about the place as I did.'

They had channelled their grief into different paths, moved in diametrically opposed directions, Rufus away from his beloved books into the obsessive renovation of his dilapidated white elephant, Helen into her university studies. Helen had made new friends and found comfort in their support; Rufus had cut himself off, closed himself in, opted out of life altogether.

It was only after Helen left him that he went home to his parents, for the first time in years, desperate for someone to understand. His father told him to pull himself together, make his marriage work or end it. 'Thank God,' said Celia briskly, as she passed him on her way out to a meeting, 'you had no children of your own. You can start again without any baggage.' He had not seen or spoken to either of them since.

Clementine neither criticised nor sympathised, she just listened. Relieved of his burden, Rufus felt better with every day that passed, lighter, more optimistic. If the worst came to the worst, he decided, rather than lose the house, he would sell every single book he possessed and start again from scratch.

'This desk.' Clementine, bringing Rufus yet another mug of coffee, leaned over his shoulder to look. 'It's just like the one Miss Emily had. There was a secret drawer in hers where she used to keep pennies to give us.'

Rufus dropped his glasses on the mess of papers in

front of him and rubbed the bridge of his nose. 'It's the same one,' he said. 'The roll-top's broken, otherwise I'm sure the nephew would've flogged it. Show me.'

Clementine reached past him to run her fingers along the edge of the central compartment. 'It was somewhere round here. She used to keep her back to me while she was doing it so I never saw exactly—'

Rufus vacated the chair so she could sit and she ran her fingers up and down the wood, feeling towards the back and trying to remember. It took her a few minutes to find it, a tiny metal catch, little more than a bump in the wood near the top, but when she depressed it there was a faint *click* and a narrow aperture appeared. 'Oh!' said Clem, and sat back in her chair, surprised by her success.

The long thin door squeaked on its hinges, and its bottom edge caught against the surround. Rufus leaned forward eagerly as Clementine reached tentatively inside to feel around. 'Oh, look!' she exclaimed, delighted. 'Look, they're still here!' She brought her hand out, full of pennies, ha'pennies, farthings, three-penny bits and sixpences, and began to turn them with her fingers, peering at dates and examining monarchs, Edward VII, both Georges, V and VI, Elizabeth. 'Do you suppose they're worth anything?'

Rufus was disappointed. There should have been something more exciting in a secret drawer, a cache of jewels maybe, or at least a bundle of love letters. 'Is that all?' he asked.

Clementine reached in again, and fumbled around, tugged. 'Only a tatty old book,' she said. 'Sorry.'

She held it out. *Beeton's Christmas Annual*, it proclaimed across the top then, in bold capital letters, *A STUDY IN SCARLET* and in smaller type, *By A. Conan Doyle*. There was an illustration, of a man sitting at a table, reaching from his chair to trim the wick on a hanging lamp. *Ward Lock & Co*, it said at the bottom, *London, New York and Melbourne.*

'What a shame,' began Clementine, making sure the narrow aperture held no more secrets. 'If this was a fairy story we'd have found a pot of gold—'

'I think we have.' Rufus carried her find across to the sofa and laid it gently down on the low table. Then he began, carefully, to turn the pages, noting the wood-engraved frontispiece, the advertisement leaves, the other engravings, after D.H. Friston and W.M.R. Quick. He examined the upper wrapper, still in almost perfect condition, felt a prickling at the back of his neck and a quickening of his heartbeat; it was a long time since he had been visited by such professional excitement. 'As a matter of fact,' he said, finding himself suddenly short of breath as the implications began to sink in, 'I think we've just found the Crown Jewels.'

He forgot his coffee, forgot everything except making sure what he had in his hands was what he thought it was. He collected piles of reference books and auction records going back thirty years, scoured them for confirmation. The last copy he could find offered for auction had been missing its wrappers and most of the advertisement leaves; the only other documented example had been displayed at the *Sherlock Holmes* exhibition in 1951, illustrated in Allen Eyles's *Sherlock Holmes: A Centenary Celebration*. Rufus remembered seeing it, too, years ago when he still owned a television, on a programme called *In Search of Sherlock Holmes*. It had stuck in his head; it was a Legendary First.

His initial thought was how tragic it was that he must sell it, his second, when he looked up and saw Clementine sitting straight-backed at his desk watching him, her mouth curving with pleasure at his enthusiasm, was that what he was holding in his hands was the key to the future. The realisation made him laugh out loud.

He was up early the following morning, ready to leave for work before Clem had finished breakfast.

'Won't you tell me what's going on?' she asked, as he collected his carefully wrapped parcel from the dresser.

Rufus grinned. 'Not yet. Not till I'm certain.' He looked ready to explode, *Just William* up to his neck in a world-beating adventure. He kissed her lingeringly, then made for the door. 'See you tonight,' he said over his shoulder, and was off, loping along the corridor in his eagerness to get to work.

'Now what,' Clementine asked Mary, waiting beneath the table in the hope of crusts, 'was *that* all about?' How could such an insignificant little book generate such enthusiasm? Where was the leather binding? Where were the gold-tooled titles, the sumptuous colour plates? It was so . . . *ordinary*.

Rufus stowed his find carefully in the safe, then spent the morning making telephone calls, checking and double-checking his facts, his exhilaration rising by the minute. He made a list of potential buyers, more calls. 'I'm damned if I'll let Sotheby's take thirty per cent of this one,' he told Sal when she asked why he wasn't putting it up for auction. 'This is our future.'

'Whose future?'

Rufus's attention had drifted back to his treasure. *Beeton's Christmas Annual, Price One Shilling,* published in 1887 and containing the original, the very *first* Sherlock Holmes story. With the proceeds of its sale stashed in his bank account, he could wipe out his overdraft, pay Clementine back . . .

'Whose future?' repeated Sal.

Rufus glanced up from his desk, grinned. 'Sorry Sal, I was miles away. Mine and Clementine's, of course.'

He didn't see Sal's eyes fill with tears, because she swung her hair across her face and turned hastily away to busy herself with something at the other end of the shop.

He made half a dozen appointments in London, two in Cambridge (one with Howard Carrick, his favourite customer and his best hope), persuaded Sal to type out a detailed description of what he was offering for sale and fax copies to all the likely buyers he could think of, in places as far apart as York, Brighton and Edinburgh, Amsterdam, San Francisco and Johannesburg. He had decided to go for postal bids, relying on his reputation as an acknowledged expert to generate interest. Yes, it was a peculiar way of doing things, he admitted when Sal queried what he was up to, but it would work, she'd see. And there'd be no buyer's premium, no fifteen per cent cut for the auctioneer; whatever he made would be pure profit.

Sal was oddly subdued, almost surly about the whole thing – boyfriend trouble, he guessed – but he didn't allow her to distract him, he had more important things on his mind. He would get a firm offer under his belt, he decided, before he asked Clementine to marry him. After all, there was no hurry now, now that he was going to be financially secure. He would do it right, too, go down on one knee or something, buy her a ring.

He had another piece of good news to celebrate, a call from Mr Tucker, the stained-glass specialist who was repairing the window on the stairs, to say the work was finished and when would Rufus like his men to come and fit it? Any time, said Rufus confidently – after all, he would shortly have the money to pay for it. He arranged for it to be done while he was away, hugging himself at the thought of the pleasure it would give Clementine to see it in all its renewed glory, then turned back to his desk, smiling. Only one more loose end to tie up.

He waited until Sal was busy with a customer and then he rang Helen.

His last meeting with his ex-wife had been to agree terms for the divorce – they had gone for a clean break and mutual consent, having lived apart for two years – and they had parted coolly, both still too raw to finish their marriage with dignity, too close to the pain to forgive. It was unfinished business and he needed to draw a line under that part of his life properly, mend fences.

'I'm glad you rang,' said Helen. 'When are you going to sign the final papers?'

'What final papers?' Rufus heard her sigh impatiently. A year ago, even a month ago, he would have resented it; now he didn't care.

'You're the Petitioner, remember? So you're the one who has to apply for the Decree Absolute.'

'But I dealt with all that weeks ago.' Rufus was positive he'd done it; it was before he got his new glasses and he'd had to get Sal to read it out because he couldn't see the print.

'That was the Decree *Nisi*. Rufus, you are *hopeless*—' Helen sounded irritated, exasperated. 'It's the Decree *Absolute* you haven't sent back.'

'Oh Christ, haven't I? Hang on.' Rufus tucked the phone under his chin and leaned across to the untidy pile of papers he risibly referred to as his out tray, grabbing his glasses as he leafed through it. 'Got it!' he bellowed triumphantly into the receiver. 'Look, Helen, I'm sorry, I didn't read it properly when it came, I've been having trouble with my glasses and I just assumed it was more legal gobbledegook..'

'Typical!'

Rufus could almost hear her shaking her head, pursing her lips as she had done so often during their last year together. He opened his mouth to make a sharp rejoinder, then curbed his tongue. The whole point of this conversation was to be friends again, to walk away without bearing grudges. 'I'm sorry,' he said meekly. 'I wasn't paying attention. I'll deal with it.'

'Good.' Helen was brisk, chilly, determined not to make it easy for him. 'When?'

'Today,' he promised. 'If I sign the form today and post it first class it should get there by Monday.'

'How will I know you've done it?' She sounded disinclined to take his word for it.

'Um . . .' Rufus shifted the papers around on his desk, glanced at the itinerary he had mapped out, Norwich – London – London – Cambridge, and had an idea. He could travel to Cambridge via Norwich, see Helen, then go on to his last two meetings.

'Look, I want to see you anyway. Can you meet me at Thorpe station on Thursday? I'll send the thing Recorded Delivery and bring the slip to prove I've done it.' Helen, softening at last, agreed and he arranged a time. It worked out well; he would have half an hour between trains, long enough to do what they had to do, but not so long they would start sniping at each other as they had done so often during the last year of their marriage. He found he was actually looking forward to seeing her and when he put the phone down he was grinning.

'Playing around already?' asked Sal sarcastically from the doorway. 'And does the lovely Clementine know you're seeing your wife again?'

Chapter Thirty-Five

Rufus was leaving Clementine the van; Mary's stitches had come out the previous week but she had a slight infection in the wound and the vet wanted to see her again on Tuesday, just to be on the safe side. So Clementine was dropping him at Thorpe station on Monday morning and, as he didn't know what time he would be finished, he was making his own way home on Friday. He didn't mention his meeting with Helen – until he had dealt with the paperwork he was not divorced and he didn't want Clementine to know what an inefficient fool he was.

It was only as he drove into Norwich, with Clementine gazing vacantly out of the window beside him, that Rufus noticed how distracted she was. Her contributions to the breakfast conversation had been perfunctory and monosyllabic and more than once he had had to repeat himself. He glanced sideways at her, wondering how long it would take to organise getting married, then considered, appalling thought, the possibility that she might turn him down. She couldn't, could she?

From the first time they had slept together, they had taken no precautions. Rufus was positive Clementine wasn't on the Pill, and since that first night the conviction had grown, despite Jonathan Harris, that he was, if not her first lover, then certainly the only lover she had had for a very long time. The women he had bedded in his student days and the nameless, faceless ones who had passed through since Helen's departure, had either been on the Pill or he had made his own arrangements, but with Clementine the subject of contraception had never even been discussed. On the other hand, she didn't seem to Rufus to be the sort of woman who would risk pregnancy for the sake of a casual affair, so she must care for him, mustn't she?

He glanced at her again, found her watching him and smiled. When she smiled back he felt that familiar spreading warmth and just knew it was going to work out. But where was she this morning? What was occupying her mind?

Their parting reminded him of the last occasion, when it was Clementine catching the train, only this time when he tucked her collar closer round her face she smiled instead of flinching, this time when he went to embrace her she leaned against him and hugged him in return. Rufus thought he would explode with the strength of his feelings.

'I'll be back on Friday,' he said, 'And Sal knows where I'll be if you need me.' Five days, a lifetime. What if she slipped away from him during those five days? She'd done it before, retreated unexpectedly just when he thought he had her. 'Clementine, you won't . . .?'

'Won't what?' Her brown eyes were fixed solemnly on his face.

He was being ridiculous. 'Nothing.' He tightened his grip, stretching his arms to accommodate her bulky coat and pulling her tight against him. 'I love you.' That glorious smile came and he was sure he was being paranoid. 'You'll be all right?' he asked, furrowing his brow at the prospect of five days without her.

'Yes,' she said. 'Of course I will. I've masses to keep me busy and I'm going to Jean's on Thursday for supper . . . Rufus—'

'Mm?'

'You'll miss your train,' she said, and stood back, letting him go.

What was it she had started to say? Had he missed the moment again? Rufus moved reluctantly away towards the ticket desk, crabbing sideways so he could keep her in sight. She paused in the station entrance, tall, stately, reminding him of the first time he had set eyes on her, raised her hand, then disappeared into the bright autumn morning, and Rufus stood still, staring at the spot where she had been, overwhelmed by emotion. It took him a whole minute to pull himself together sufficiently to go and buy his ticket, and he smiled wryly as he made his way across the concourse towards the trains. Twenty years ago he had watched his contemporaries falling in love and thought them fools to allow their hearts to overrule their heads. Now it was his turn, and who was the greater fool? Forty-two years old and he was as hopelessly besotted as any wet-behind-the-ears teenager.

Clementine sat for a while in the van, resting her hands on the steering wheel and recovering. Two months ago she and Rufus had been strangers. He had been away before and she had been glad of his absence; now she felt as if she had lost a part of herself. She had wanted to tell him just now, to say out loud what she was feeling, but the habit of reticence was hard to break and her tongue had stuck to the roof of her mouth. She wished she had said it, now it was too late. Pull yourself together, she scolded, then sat on, staring into space and remembering his face when he had said goodbye.

She made a detour into Ashington on the way home,

to buy provisions and call at the chemist. It was only over the past few days that she had realised how long it was since her last period, had begun to calculate dates and count weeks. It must have happened the very first time they made love; now she had worked it out, she ought to know for sure.

It was the most outrageous thing she had ever done, letting Rufus make love to her night after night without protection. Naïve she might be, but not so naïve she couldn't work out the possible outcome of unprotected sex. She had just wanted to do it. It had added an extra dimension to the loving, knowing that they might be making a baby, and she hadn't wanted to spoil it by talking about condoms or caps or pills. If she was honest, she wanted a child – Rufus's child – more than she had ever wanted anything in her whole life.

Vince and Wayne were hard at work on the roof when she got back, there was new scaffolding outside the back door, an untidy pile of broken bricks, shattered tiles and splintered timber in the walled garden and Wayne's radio was blaring out loud rock music. Mary, carefully shut in the kitchen before Clementine left, was quivering with nerves at the noise and the unfamiliar voices outside the back door, and delirious with relief at her return.

When Clementine entered the bathroom with her little box wrapped in its discreet paper bag, she found the view from the window obscured by a latticework of rusty green scaffolding poles, and Wayne ascending and descending a juddering ladder every minute with stacks of tiles, buckets of nails and rolls of bitumen felting. She could hear Vince lumbering about on the roof, whistling tunelessly and dropping unidentified objects at regular intervals, and the walls vibrated to the sound of drilling, sawing, hammering and Status Quo playing at maximum volume.

Clementine placed the packet on the bathroom shelf and left it there. No point in worrying about it now, she would do it later, when they'd gone home and it was quiet. She knew what the result would be anyway . . .

The stained-glass window came on Tuesday afternoon, on a lorry with a mobile crane attached, accompanied by Mr Tucker and the five men who would be needed to manhandle it into position. Clementine, returning with Mary from the vet to find the house in chaos, retreated to the kitchen with Dorrie and made coffee, Nescafé bought specially for the workmen, milk and sugar for Vince, just milk for Wayne and four white, two black and the sugar bowl for Mr Tucker and the window men because she couldn't remember who had asked for what.

'Not much point me stopping,' remarked Dorrie, settling herself comfortably at the table to enjoy the unexpected pleasure of sweet, milky instant. 'House full of men and dust everywhere.' She chuckled, reached across to the biscuit tin and picked out a digestive to dunk. 'So, where's Rufus escaped to?'

'London. Back on Friday.'

Clementine seemed preoccupied this afternoon, Dorrie thought, not quite all there. Must be the noise. 'So how's it going then? You two getting on all right these days?' As if she didn't know.

Clementine raised her head and smiled. 'Mm,' she said. 'Yes, we're . . .' She paused, coloured. 'Fine,' she finished lamely, clearly embarrassed. 'We're getting on fine.'

Good, noted Dorrie, splendid. 'So you'll be staying then?'

That one seemed to be harder to answer. Clementine rose from the table, taking a biscuit from the tin as she passed, and went to stare through the window at Wayne, making excruciating noises with an industrial tile cutter just outside the back door. 'Yes,' she said at last, raising her voice over the din. 'Yes, I think so.'

'Rufus changed his mind then?'

'Changed his mind?'

Dorrie sucked her biscuit and spoke with her mouth full. 'Well, he was going to tidy the place up and sell it in the spring, wasn't he?' She munched for a while, dunked again. 'That's what he told me, anyhow, before you came.'

Clementine shook her head decidedly. 'No, he's going to do it properly. He's asked me to stay on to help.' She continued to move restlessly around the kitchen, watched by Mary from her basket by the range. Dorrie waited, wondering what she was building up to.

'Dorrie . . .'

'Mm?'

'Did you—' Clementine stopped, started again. 'Did you know Rufus's wife?'

Dorrie shook her head. 'No, dear, I don't think anyone did really. She didn't seem to be here much even when she was living here, if you see what I mean. Why?'

'Oh.' Clementine picked up the dishcloth, began absent-mindedly to wipe the draining board. 'I just wondered. And what about his . . . er . . .'

Dorrie helped her out. 'Girlfriends? Must've been lonely, mustn't he? What with being all on his own in this great barn of a house?'

'Yes. Yes, I suppose he must.' Clementine extended her wiping to the range, disturbing Ginger, ensconced in his warm spot by the flue. 'Not that it's any of my business, of course—'

Dorrie chuckled. ''Course it is. Ask him if it worries you. I would.'

Clementine turned to face her, brown eyes wide. 'I couldn't,' she said. 'I couldn't possibly—'

'Come and sit down, dear.' Dorrie helped herself to another biscuit and patted the table with a plump hand. As Clementine advanced towards her she was reminded of the big, clumsy child, eight, nine years old, who had suffered so badly from the bullies but been too proud to ask for help. How do you persuade someone who's been keeping folk at arm's length for so long to let go, *trust* people?

Clementine sat down heavily opposite her, work-roughened hands locked together, fingers twisting.

'Don't you think, dear,' began Dorrie, 'it would be a good idea to *talk* to him? How will you ever learn to get on together if you can't ask him about the things that matter?'

Clementine shook her head. 'I don't know . . .' Her brow was furrowed with doubt.

Dorrie drained her coffee, licked the last drops from the rim of her mug and left it at that. 'I'll get off now,' she suggested gently. 'And I'll come in Thursday instead of Friday, shall I? Then the place'll be nice and tidy when Rufus gets back and I won't be under your feet if you want to . . . you know, have the place to yourselves.' She rose and bustled across to the sink, rinsed her mug and set it to drain. 'That do, dear?'

'Yes.' Clementine nodded slowly. 'Yes, that'll be fine.' She sat up straighter. 'You're right, Dorrie, I'll talk to him. Thanks.' She twisted in her chair and smiled; Dorrie was struck, as she so often was, by the transformation it wrought to that plain face.

As she made her way across the hall, dodging over-alled workmen, claw hammers and toolbags, she was looking forward to regaling Frank with it all.

'Soppy old date,' he'd say, teasing. 'You always were a sucker for a bit of a romance.'

*

Wednesday afternoon and problems with the window, swinging lazily from its crane while the driver attempted to winch it into position without destroying a rhododendron and two azaleas, and wondered aloud how they'd got it out in the first place. It would be getting dark soon and they were considering leaving it and coming back early the next morning. The hall was full of muscular men discussing the problem in loud voices and Clementine had to press the phone against her cheek to blot out the noise.

'Has Rufus rung you?' She could hear the blood pulsing in her ear, despite the din in the hall.

'No. Why should he have?' Sal Glover sounded brusque, unfriendly. 'Is there a problem?'

'No. No, I just thought . . .' Clementine bit her lip, started again. 'If you knew what train he was getting on Friday, I could save him a taxi.'

'I don't,' said Sal shortly. 'He's negotiating a sale and you can never tell with these chaps whether you'll be five minutes or four hours.'

'Oh,' said Clementine, taken aback by the woman's overt hostility. 'Sorry to have bothered you, then.'

There was an awkward pause before Sal replied. 'No trouble.' She sounded apologetic now, almost chummy. 'Look, if it's any help, he's passing through Norwich tomorrow on his way to Cambridge. You could try and catch him at Thorpe station. Hang on, I'll find out the time.'

Clementine heard the phone clatter, then the sound of rustling paper. 'Ten-fifteen,' said Sal. 'He's got half an hour between trains.'

'Thanks' said Clementine.

'Don't mention it,' said Sal. 'Glad to be of help,' and she cut her off.

Tomorrow. Clementine breathed deep, calming

herself down. Tomorrow wasn't so long to wait.

Sal sat on in Rufus's moulting chair, resting her elbows on the desk and her chin in her hands, then sighed, brushed the kapok from her skirt and wandered out into the shop. A late beam of sunshine had sneaked through the dusty skylight over the door and she leaned against a bookcase to watch the dust motes hanging in the air as the shame washed over her.

'Bitch,' she said out loud to the empty room. 'Sal Glover, you are a bloody, bloody bitch.'

'Hello, Sal?'

'Oh,' said Sal, slumping back into Rufus's chair and pulling a face at the phone, 'it's you. What can I do for you?'

'Well, you could sound a bit more pleased to hear from me, for a start.' Jonathan stirred Simba, basking on his sitting room carpet in front of the fire, with his foot. 'How's the decorating going?'

'What decorating?' Sal made an effort, pulled herself together. 'Oh, that decorating. Fine. They've finished the sitting room and started on the front bedroom, the carpet's going down tomorrow and it's starting to look really classy. I'm pleased with it. How are you?'

'Not so good.' Jonathan, feeling the lump building in his throat, swallowed hard. 'Actually, if you want to know, bloody awful. I'm *lonely*, Sal. I thought I'd drive up and see you—'

'No!'

'Why not?'

Sal picked at the peeling green leather on the edge of the desk. Today was turning into a complete bummer. 'Because I don't want you to. It's over, darling; we've lost. You know it and I know it.' Her eye caught Rufus's list, names, places, train times, and the shame washed over her again. She leaned across to hide it under an old Book Fair catalogue. 'Why don't you go back to Sebastian?'

'How can I?' Jonathan sounded bitter, resentful. 'You scotched that one nicely, didn't you? You and your brilliant ideas. You just made things worse. At least before you interfered I could have—'

'Oh, get real!' snapped Sal, losing her temper. 'It would never have worked with Clementine, and you know it. Why don't you just pick up the pieces and get *on* with your life?'

'That's exactly what Clem said.' Jonathan's voice cracked tragically. 'You've got to help me, Sal, I don't know what to *do*!'

Sal counted to five. 'All right, darling, calm down. Where are you?'

'At home. I can't work. I can't sleep. I can't *cope*—'

'Leave it with me. Pour yourself a drink and relax. I'll take care of it. Okay?'

'Sal, what are you going to—?'

'Trust me, darling.' She was brisk, her best Mummy-will-make-it-better voice, and she could hear Jonathan's relief when he said goodbye. His childlike confidence in her ability to fix things irritated her. Who was she making it better *for*? she wondered as she dialled Jonathan's office and asked to speak to Peter. Certainly not herself.

'Peter? Remember me?'

Peter sounded less than pleased to hear from her, was suspicious when she asked for Sebastian's number. But he gave it to her in the end, persuaded by her charm, which was potent even on the phone.

Before she rang Sebastian she took a cracked saucer from the cubbyhole where the kettle lived and lit a cigarette. She needed one.

'Sebastian?' She took a deep lungful of smoke and

blew it out slowly at the ceiling. 'Hi, it's Sal Glover. I'm ringing about Jonathan . . .'

The bell jangling over the shop door made her jump. The day had faded outside and it was almost dark in the office. She snapped on the light, dusted the kapok from her skirt for the second time and pasted a smile to her face.

'So,' she purred, sashaying towards the bug-eyed student hovering by the door. 'What can I do for you, darling . . .?'

When he had gone, clutching a pile of books and lighter by nearly £15, she sat down at her rickety table by the door and pulled a notepad towards her.

Rufus darling, she began, *after a great deal of thought, I have decided it's time to move on. Boredom is setting in and I'm long overdue for a change of scene . . .*

It was time she took her own advice.

Chapter Thirty-Six

Rufus packed his bag in a cheap bed-and-breakfast hotel near Liverpool Street station with clumsy impatience. Every night for the past three nights he had picked up the payphone on the landing and dialled Manor Hall. And every night, losing his nerve, he had depressed the button before it could connect. He was useless on the phone unless it was business, incapable of talking anything but facts and figures, details and dates.

He missed Clementine with such painful intensity it wrenched at his guts like a griping stomachache. Only forty-eight hours to go, he kept telling himself, only thirty-six, but the nearer he got the more intense the ache of anticipation grew.

So far, his business had gone well. The enthusiasm among his carefully chosen collectors was electric and already he had received two firm offers for his treasure. He swung his bag from the bed and dumped it on the floor, ready to go, then ran his eyes over the dressing table and the chest of drawers, making sure he had left nothing behind. *Helen*, he thought, glad of the distraction. Would she have changed since he had last seen her? Would they be able to mend fences, forgive? As he negotiated the narrow stairs down to the cabbage-smelling lobby to pay his bill, he realised he was genuinely looking forward to seeing her.

He sprinted from the train, dodging in and out of the thick stream of humanity making for the barrier, and he spotted Helen before he got there, standing a little to one side and craning her neck impatiently to see over the heads of the intervening crowd. Her hair was shorter than he remembered, bobbed to her chin in a shining brown cap, and it suited her. She looked sophisticated, grown up, very pretty, and he was visited unexpectedly by a wave of nostalgic affection, for the good times at the beginning, the shared moments with Mikey, the laughter. As he neared the barrier he thought, *only twenty-four hours to Clementine*, and grinned broadly; when he reached Helen he swept her into his arms, swung her round and planted a smacking kiss on her mouth, sharing his optimism. One by one, he thought, he was laying the ghosts, getting ready to go on instead of looking back.

He didn't see Clementine come to an abrupt halt only five paces from where he was standing, he was bending, draping his arm round Helen's shoulder and telling her how pleased he was to see her. He didn't see her back away either, then turn and run, making for the sanctuary of his scruffy van.

Escaping from the sight of Rufus embracing his pretty, blue-eyed, brown-haired, *small* wife, didn't help Clementine get away from the shock. It beat like a sledgehammer at her chest, weakened her legs and sucked the breath from her lungs.

As she drove away from the station she ransacked her imagination for explanations, excuses, reasons, a chance meeting, an innocent encounter into which she was reading too much, searching desperately for something to hang on to. She reviewed what she had seen, the embrace, the grin on Rufus's face as he greeted his ex-wife. 'It wasn't Helen's fault,' he had said more than once, defending Helen's departure, and, 'I expected too much of her.' He had blamed himself for the failure of his marriage. Yet he had told her, Clementine, that he loved her, in such a voice, and with such a look on his face, that she had believed his every word. Had it all been lies? Or had he genuinely meant the things he said in the heat of the moment? How could you be sure men were telling the truth when they said they loved you? And how could this be happening to her, for the second time in less than three months?

She spread a hand on her stomach, reminded of the news she had been so eager to share, and trying to calm her rising panic. She had wondered, to begin with, if Rufus thought she was on the Pill – he had never mentioned contraception, never suggested they should be careful – then later, as she grew more confident, she had become convinced the omission was deliberate, that he must be secretly as thrilled as she at the thought of making a child. Now the doubts began to flood in. Perhaps he *had* assumed she was on the Pill, perhaps he had been working on the premise that his latest casual fling would be, like all the others, without strings, without consequences . . . When she stopped just before the T-junction at the entrance to the village she wondered how she had got there, unable to recall the journey she had just completed.

There was nothing left of the stately beeches which had lined the road to Dinningham all her life, except a forlorn row of toothlike stumps, piles of sawdust and wood chippings. The fallen giants had been denuded of their branches, loaded on to lorries and secured with chains, then driven away to be turned into tables and stools, or to end up in the Blackstock souvenir shop as fruit bowls and salad servers.

Glancing across at the green, where a huge bonfire

had appeared since the storm, made of ruined garden sheds, the remains of a chicken coop, the still-green, sappy branches of number 3's apple tree, bits of fence and gate and joist, Clementine was reminded with a shock that today was November the Fifth. On Saturday a firework party was to be held, the village's newfound togetherness celebrated. *Life goes on.*

On the other side of the green, Marshmeadow's long, low outline looked different too, like a bearded man seen suddenly with a naked chin. The chainsaws had left behind a landscape Clementine no longer recognised. She had thought coming home would help her redis-cover lost certainties; instead she had found Rufus and Manor Hall and fallen in love and there didn't seem to be any certainties left any more. It occurred to her, now it was too late, that instead of running away she should have confronted Rufus, that any other woman would have marched up to him and demanded an explanation for this secret assignation with his wife.

She put the van clumsily into gear and drove slowly along the green, then turned in through the iron gates to squeeze between the window men's lorry, Mr Tucker's Fiesta and Vince's battered Toyota pick-up. Then she sat, frozen in her seat, until the window men unexpectedly poured out through the front door.

'Looks a treat in there,' said one of them as he passed, chucking his thumb over his shoulder. 'Lovely job, it is.'

They clambered over each other to fill the lorry, shout-ing cheerful goodbyes. Clementine pulled herself together, climbed out of the van at last, and walked on lead-filled legs up the stone steps.

Habit is one of the strongest instincts; the urge to make a cup of tea after a disaster, the use of the present tense when talking of a loved one no longer alive, the maintaining of a dignified front when the world is disintegrating around you. Over the years, Clementine had learned to hide hurt, loneliness, sadness, disappointment, behind a cool, aloof exterior; that was how she had got by. Whatever the turmoil she was feeling now, there was Dorrie somewhere in the house, dusting and polishing, Mary in the kitchen awaiting her return, Vince and Wayne to make coffee for, Mr Tucker to thank for the work his men had just completed. She took a deep breath, raised her chin and strode into the hall.

As if performing on cue, the sun came out, pouring through the newly installed window to cast dappling lights of green, gold and azure blue on the walls, the floor and the pretty fireplace opposite the stairs. It illuminated the age-spotted wallpaper and the patterned floor tiles, painted the pale stone fire-surround in glorious rainbow colours; despite her resolution, Clementine's eyes filled helplessly with tears.

Mr Tucker was on his way out. He had left his bill, he said, with Dorrie. What did Clementine think of his handiwork?

'Oh . . .' Clementine moved past him to the foot of the stairs, to gaze at translucent green-stemmed lilies, golden stamens and pale blue sky. 'It's wonderful, it's perfect, it's . . .' She shook her head, dazzled, and turned to stare blurrily at the patterns playing on the stone fireplace.

Omnia-something-something. She had noticed it that first day, as she stood in the hall listening to Rufus crashing plates in the kitchen. She had lost count of the number of times she had walked past it since, had grown so used to it she had ceased to wonder what the rest of the message might be. The light streaming in from the window behind her illuminated it for the first time, and she blinked to clear her vision. *Omnia Vincit Amor*, whatever that meant – two years of schoolgirl Latin had left Clementine untouched.

'*Omnia Vincit Amor*,' said Mr Tucker helpfully. 'Roughly translated, *Love conquers all*.'

He was halfway across the hall. 'What?' said Clementine, but the door was already closing behind him.

She ran shaky fingers over the inscription, fumbled in her pocket for a handkerchief and blew her nose, then stepped back and stared.

Love conquers all.

'Oh . . .' she said, and sat down hard on the stairs.

'Clem? It's Jonathan.' The phone had made her jump and Clementine was still shaking. 'I just phoned to tell you you're off the hook.' He sounded cold, stiff.

'Sorry?' What was he on about? 'What hook?'

'You will no doubt be relieved to hear that I shan't be bothering you again.' He sounded bitter too, nasty.

'Jonathan—' While she attempted to gather her scattered wits Jonathan surged on.

'I just want you to know that you've ruined my life. I hope you're satisfied—'

'Jonathan,' she didn't need this, not now, 'I'm sorry you're not happy about the way things turned out but—'

'And while we're on the subject, I've some advice for you . . .' Clementine heard the click of a lighter, the suck of air as he lit a cigarette. 'Because, frankly, I feel sorry for you.'

Clementine was bewildered. She had thought herself the injured party in their dealings but clearly Jonathan saw things in a different light.

'You never gave me a chance. From the moment you found out about Sebastian you cancelled me, wrote me off as if I was less than nothing. It's so *unfair*. Everyone has a past. Everyone comes with some baggage, except you, apparently. Little Miss Perfect, who can't tolerate anyone else's mistakes because she never makes any.' He sucked in another lungful of smoke and ploughed on. 'Of course, it's easy not to make mistakes if you never let anyone get close, because that way you never have to take any risks. But I tell you what, Clem, if you carry on the way you're going, you'll end up a very lonely old lady. Because unless you change your attitude you'll never be able to form a lasting relationship – not with Rufus Palliser, not with anyone.' He paused briefly, as if expecting a reply, but Clementine had lost the power of speech. 'Well, since we're unlikely to see each other again, I'll wish you all the best. To be honest, I think I've had a lucky escape. Bye, Clem.' And he put the phone down.

It took her a while to work it out; already badly jolted by the events of the morning, her brain was working only slowly.

Everything Jonathan had said was true, of course, she could see that now. Right from the beginning their relationship had been built on shifting sands. She had fooled herself into believing it was Jonathan she wanted, when in reality it was something else entirely she was searching for, and when it all fell apart she had turned her back, walked away, *because she didn't love him enough to stay*. It had been the idea of love itself she was in love with, a romantic illusion of marriage and children, hearts and flowers, roses round the door, growing old in sweet companionship, not the living, breathing, imperfect human being she had been planning to share her life with.

But Rufus was different. Sitting at his untidy desk, in his bleak, impersonal study, she knew without any doubt at all that this time it was the real thing she had found; it was Rufus, vague, difficult, damaged Rufus she wanted. And she was not going to give him up. 'Love conquers all,' she said out loud, and thumped her fist down hard on the desk.

Dorrie's Dr Scholls clattered loudly on the stairs, then faded towards the kitchen. Clementine was startled when she looked at her watch to find that it was nearly one o'clock; she had been sitting, staring out at the shrubbery, for over an hour. She waited until Dorrie had crossed the hall on her way home to get her Frank his dinner, then made for the kitchen and Mary's comforting, unjudgmentally enthusiastic greeting.

What was it Dorrie had said on Tuesday? '*Talk* to him. How will you ever learn to get on together if you can't ask him about the things that matter?' Jonathan, with his cruelly accurate analysis of her shortcomings, had merely reinforced the message. But Rufus was on his way to Cambridge.

She had twenty-four hours to sort herself out.

Jean answered the phone almost immediately.

'I'm sorry,' said Clementine, 'I can't make it for supper.'

Jean was annoyed. 'Oh, blast you, Clem! I specially needed you tonight. Dorrie's found me a childminder and I'm going to break the news about the job to Robert. I was relying on you for moral support. Why can't you come?'

'You don't need moral support.' Clementine fiddled with the untidy pile of papers on Rufus's desk. Her stomach was churning at the thought of what she had decided to do and she had no energy to spare for Jean's small problems. 'What you need is to sit down and *talk* to him—' She grimaced wryly at the phone. Hark at her, quoting Dorrie's advice second-hand, and to Jean of all people. 'Tell him you need a life of your own, reassure him that you've organised it so he won't suffer—'

'If he objects,' threatened Jean fiercely, 'I'll leave him!'

'No, you won't.' Clementine shook her head vehemently at the phone. It was so *simple*; why couldn't Jean see it? 'You'll persuade him to change his mind. Robert may not be perfect, but he's a good man. And he's a great deal better than being on your own.'

'Clem, you don't understand—'

'Yes, I *do*! Who is it, when Eddie's been driving you mad all day, who listens to your complaints, sympathises, takes Ed off your hands to give you half an hour's peace and quiet?'

'Well, Robert, but—'

'And who is it, when Eddie's done something outrageous, or when someone's upset you, or you've had a really bad day, who is it you take it out on, because you know he'll understand, forgive?'

'Well, Robert, I suppose.' Jean was grudging, sulky. 'But that's not the point. The point is—'

'The point is, you take Robert for granted; he's there all the time, a convenient shoulder to cry on, a sounding board when you want advice or a second opinion, someone to take it out on when you're frustrated or depressed. So maybe he puts his foot down too hard sometimes. Maybe you've let him get away with it too often. But he's never cheated on you, never let you go short or neglected you.' She paused for breath, then added, surprising herself with her own vehemence, 'You have no idea, until you've been there, what it's like to be lonely.'

'But I wouldn't be lonely, I'd still have Eddie, and the baby . . .' Jean paused, then added grudgingly, 'I'd probably strangle Eddie, wouldn't I, if I had to put up with him on my own all the time.' She sighed loudly. 'I just want Robert to be more—'

'So *tell* him!' Clementine began to shift papers, lining them up, straightening the edges, calming herself down. 'Tell him how you feel. Explain how frustrated you've been these past few years. You haven't, have you?'

'Haven't what?'

'You haven't told him what you want out of life.'

'No, I haven't; there's no point. He wouldn't understand—'

'Try him. How do you know he wouldn't understand if you don't try him?' Jean was so *obtuse* sometimes. 'Look, I must go. I have things to do.'

'Oh?' Jean seized on the change of subject with evident relief. 'What things?'

It was sheer force of habit that made Clementine say, 'Nothing important,' and Jean pounced triumphantly on the evasion.

'Honestly, Clem, you criticise me for not talking to Robert and as soon as I ask you a perfectly reasonable question you clam up! Talk about hypocritical!'

She was right, of course. So was Jonathan. So was Dorrie. Clementine took a steadying breath; go on, take your own advice, *talk* to her. 'All right; if you must know, I'm going to see Uncle Harry. I'm going to ask him to wind up my trust fund, to give me control of my own finances.'

'Oh?' Jean was fascinated. 'Why now, all of a sudden?'

She would fight for the best, Clementine had decided, sitting at the kitchen table sipping tea, with Mary resting a warm heavy head on her knee and Ginger rubbing round her ankles, purring, but she must plan for the worst. 'Because I'm thirty-two years old and perfectly capable of running my own affairs.' Because I'm going to

have a baby and if things don't work out with Rufus I
may have to bring it up on my own. 'I might need to
draw on some more of my capital.'

'Why? Are you going back to London?'

'No,' said Clementine adamantly. 'No, I'm staying in
Norfolk. As soon as I've sorted my finances out I'm
going to go and see Caroline Davis and persuade her to
let me redesign Marshmeadow.'

'Oh?' Jean digested this new information, then came
back with a more difficult question. 'So are you and
Rufus—?'

The sixty-four-thousand-dollar question. Were she
and Rufus—? 'I've decided,' said Clementine, postpon-
ing the problem, 'to take your advice. I'm going to set up
on my own as an interior decorator.' Whatever happened between her and Rufus, her child was going to be
brought up in the country. He was going to breathe clean
air, know the names of wild flowers; he was going to
climb trees and fish for sticklebacks. 'You can join me if
you like. How would that be? We'll set up shop in the
old schoolhouse and you can become curtain-maker to
the county set.'

'Wow!'

Jean was so stunned by the revelations she had
unleashed she was lost for words; she didn't even
protest when Clem said she had to go.

'Promise me you'll talk to Robert,' Clementine
repeated. 'Not shout at him, *talk* to him.'

'Yes, yes, I promise. Clem . . .'

'Mm?'

'When are you going to tell me about you and Rufus?'

'Soon,' said Clementine, and put the phone down
before Jean could ask any more awkward questions. She
wasn't ready yet to talk about Rufus.

*

She found it purely by accident. She was about to leave the study, and she knocked it as she stood up, so it fell from the desk to the floor. It seemed familiar when she picked it up; she realised when she turned it over and saw the heavy daubs of paint that it was the tatty old envelope she had found abandoned on the landing, the one she had used as a palette to test different paint shades. She might have to revise her colour scheme, she thought, now the window was back; it would change the light on the landing as well as in the hall. Then it occurred to her that if Rufus was reconciled with his wife she would never get to finish it, and she dropped the envelope back on the desk, clenching her fists. If Rufus had walked in at that moment she would have punched him on the nose, so fierce was the wave of anger that engulfed her at the thought of losing him.

It was ten minutes before she was sufficiently calm to ring Dorrie, to ask her to look after Mary while she was in Hertfordshire. She was doing the right thing, she reassured herself, recalling Rufus's face as he comforted Eddie, the way he had talked about Mikey. Whatever the future held, whether she and Rufus stayed together or not, she was going to make damn sure he was around to see his son grow up.

No, said Aunt April, Uncle Harry wouldn't be home until late, he was going to a business dinner. So Clementine packed an overnight bag before she set off in the van.

She made a detour into Norwich on the way, to buy herself a pair of shoes.

Chapter Thirty-Seven

Rufus paid off the taxi and waited while it manoeuvred carefully round his van, littered untidily in the middle of the drive with the offside door open. He allowed himself a smile at Clementine's automotive incompetence, then stood still for a moment, suffused with knee-weakening anticipation. He reprised his lines for the hundredth time, trying to decide exactly what he was going to say.

He had stayed in Cambridge overnight, as he always did when visiting Howard Carrick – the old boy lived alone, loved to entertain, talk books and ply him with fine wine – and he had enjoyed himself as he always did. But he had been on edge all evening, unable to relax. Howard had noticed his inattention, had enquired, chuckling drily, who was 'the lady in the case', and he had found himself blushing like a schoolboy.

The front door was open and when he stepped across the threshold he could tell by the quality of the light that the staircase window was back where it belonged. His smile widened. All this and Clementine too, if she'd have him. *Jesus*, he was lucky.

She was standing to one side of the stairs, behind the bannisters, leaning against the newel post with her chin on her hands, as if she was waiting for him. She was wearing her heavy velour coat and her soft overnight bag was lying on the floor in front of her. Rufus's stomach turned over. Christ, *she looked as if she was leaving*. What was it she'd said at the beginning? 'If it doesn't work I'll go immediately.'

'Clementine?' he demanded, forgetting the speech he had been rehearsing for the past five days. 'Where are you going?'

'Hello, Rufus.' She raised her head a little, but she didn't straighten up, just watched him as he moved across the hall towards her. 'How was the trip?'

'Terrific.' Rufus stopped, still staring, mesmerised, at her bag. 'It was terrific. Howard Carrick's made me the most stupendous offer . . .' He switched his gaze to her face. There was something odd about the way she was looking at him. She was standing in the shadows so it was hard to be sure, but she had an air about her of . . . what? Aggression? Hostility?

'Where are you going?' he demanded again.

She straightened up a little, but she stayed behind the protective barrier of the bannisters and she ignored his question. 'Did you see everyone you wanted to see?'

'Yeah.' Rufus was assailed by a sudden strong suspicion that the apparently innocent enquiry was loaded, that one wrong word, one inappropriate phrase, and all his precarious hopes would come crashing down around his ears. And he hadn't a clue what she wanted him to say. 'Clementine . . .' he begged, moving nearer so he could see her face more clearly.

'*Yes?*'

That '*Yes?*' sounded positively menacing. This was the moment Rufus had been waiting for for five days, the moment he had rehearsed over and over again. 'Please, Clementine will you . . .?' 'How do you feel about . . .?' Even, ludicrously, 'Would you do me the honour of . . .?' He had imagined wrapping his arms around her waist, bending his head so he could watch her wonderfully mobile mouth when she accepted his proposal, sealing the bargain with a kiss. Seized for the second time by the conviction that his entire future hung on whatever he said next, Rufus opened his mouth . . . and put his bloody great hoof in it.

'. . . I met Helen.' Why the *hell* did he say that? 'At Thorpe station, yesterday.' *Jesus*, what an idiot. 'I'd made a complete pig's ear of the divorce papers and she wasn't very happy . . .' He was in deep water now, way out of his depth, but he floundered on anyway because it was too late to swim for shore. 'I'm glad I did it. We've sorted things out at last, parted friends. Do you know, I was actually pleased to see her. It reminded me that it wasn't always bad between us – Clementine, where are you *going?*'

Clementine opened her mouth, then closed it again. She had been home for less than ten minutes, had spent the time before Rufus appeared in the hall leaning on the bannister, thumping the newel post and repeating determinedly, '*Love conquers all, love conquers all*', to boost her courage. In the process she had managed, against all her intentions, to work herself into a towering rage. How *dare* Rufus meet his wife behind her back? How *dare* he smile at her? How *dare* he kiss her? By the time she heard the taxi on the drive she was just about ready to commit murder. And now Rufus had snatched away the reason for her self-righteous anger. It was taking her a little time to adjust.

'*Clementine!*' bellowed Rufus, running out of patience. '*Where – are – you – going?*'

Clementine glanced down at her bag, still lying where she had dropped it. 'Oh,' she said vaguely, 'nowhere.' She pulled herself together, stood up straight. 'I've been to see Uncle Harry. He was out at a business dinner when I arrived, and it was so late by the time we'd sorted things out that I stayed the night. I've only just got back—'

The apprehension in the pit of Rufus's stomach eased a little. He hadn't a clue what Clementine was talking about, but whatever she had been so steamed up about, she seemed to be getting over it. He took a step nearer, then another. 'Yes?' he encouraged, trying to keep her talking. 'Go on.'

Clementine swallowed. She had spent the past twenty-four hours preparing herself for a fight and suddenly there didn't seem to be anything to fight about. Rufus looked like a big kid, all soft and worried and puzzled. *Talk to him*, Dorrie's advice nudged her, *tell him how you feel*.

'Er, um . . .' Somehow, this didn't seem like an appropriate moment to tell him she was going to have a baby. 'I—' Rufus moved a step nearer. 'I, er . . .' The habits of a lifetime are hard to break. Clementine began to waffle. 'Look, I'm not much good at this – no, actually I'm pretty awful at it, because I haven't had much practice – well, to be honest, I haven't had *any* practice . . .'

What the hell was she rabbiting on about now? Rufus had spent the past five days on tenterhooks, the past five minutes in a state of confusion and terror. All he wanted to do was take Clementine in his arms and ask her to marry him. And here she was, tucked away behind the bannisters talking nonsense.

'Look,' he interrupted rudely, 'I've been trying to ask you for weeks—'

Clementine, startled by his vehemence, lapsed into wide-eyed silence. Unaccountably, Rufus lost his nerve.

'Just stay there,' he commanded peremptorily. 'Don't move a muscle. Don't go *anywhere*,' and turning on his heel he made for his study.

He found it easily, lying on top of a pile of uncharacteristically tidy papers. He grabbed it and strode out into the hall again.

'Here!' He thrust the paint-stiffened envelope belligerently at her. Clementine took it, stared at it, frowned in puzzlement.

'Go on, open it!'

She turned it over obediently, slit it untidily with a ragged fingernail, fumbled.

'Oh, for God's sake!' Rufus snatched it away, reached inside, then thrust the scrap of ruled notepaper at her. 'Read it!'

Clementine screwed up her eyes to see, but the light under the stairs was too dim.

She moved out from behind the bannisters, into the sunlight pouring conveniently through the window. She read the message: *Marry me Clementine. Please*, smiled. Rufus, distracted by the sound of her feet tapping loudly on the tiled floor, glanced down and missed her reaction completely.

She was wearing shoes. Not her usual schoolgirl plimsolls, or the soft flat boots she sometimes wore, but a pair of plain, black court shoes. There was nothing particularly unusual about them – they were the sort of shoes most women wear when they want to look businesslike. Except that most women aren't six feet tall in their stockinged feet, and built like an Amazon warrior. Clementine's shoes, with their slender, spiky stiletto heels, added exactly four inches to her height. Which made her as tall as Rufus.

'Clementine,' began Rufus. He was beginning to think he had strayed into some particularly surreal dream. 'What have you got on your feet?'

Clementine glanced down, shrugged. 'I needed the extra inches,' she explained. 'So I could stand up to

Uncle Harry.' She waved the piece of paper at him. She had more important things to think about than her stupid shoes. 'Rufus, is this serious?'

'And did it work?' asked Rufus unsteadily.

'What? Oh, yes,' said Clementine. 'It worked beautifully. I terrified the wits out of him. He agreed to everything I asked. Rufus—'

Rufus fought the hilarity that was threatening to overwhelm him. 'Mm?'

'Is this serious?' She waved the paper again.

Rufus closed the gap between them, grabbed her by the waist, and pulled hard. 'Of course it is!' he bellowed. 'Idiot!'

Clementine bridled. 'I am *not* an idiot.' She wriggled her arms free, took hold of Rufus's lapels and tugged, until her mouth was an inch from his and she was staring menacingly straight into his eyes. 'And don't you *dare* call me one.'

Rufus sighed. This should have been the most significant moment of his life; it should have been dignified, romantic . . . and Clementine was *laughing* at him. 'Clementine,' he complained. '*Stop* it!'

He felt her give against him, and she turned her head so her cheek was resting against his. 'Sorry,' she murmured, then wrapped her arms around his neck and squeezed. 'Rufus,' she whispered into his left ear, 'I do *love* you.'

Rufus was filled with such delirious, triumphant delight, he thought there was a good chance it might actually kill him, unless of course Clementine squeezed him to death first.

The sun, illuminating the inscription on the stone fire surround, caught his eye over her shoulder. It was one of the features that had originally drawn him to Manor Hall, part of a longer passage, from Virgil. '*Omnia Vincit*

Amor,' he quoted out loud, '*et nos sedamus amori.*'

'What?' said Clementine, raising her head.

'Love overcomes all things,' translated Rufus, 'let us too yield to love.'

Turning his face so he could breathe Clementine's apple-scented hair, he felt her smile, heard that familiar giggle. He tightened his grip, and joined in.